D0818816

Twang

Twang is powerful and moving with profound insights into faith and forgiveness—of finding grace, mercy, and even beauty in the ugliest and most destructive of memories and events. *Twang* helps us realize that the shining of divine light on the secrets and buried bones of our past can actually set us free. A story that reads like a greased bullet, as if taken from a country song itself, is ultimately pleasing and redeeming.
—Walt Larimore, author of *Hazel Creek* and *Sugar Fork*

With an authentic Southern voice, Julie L. Cannon's *Twang* takes you into the heart of Nashville and the sometimes overlooked dark side of fame. But there's nothing dark about the characters in this delightful book. It had me tapping my toes to the music until the very last page. Bravo!
—Carla Stewart, award-winning author of *Chasing Lilacs* and *Stardust*

Unforgettable characters! And a beautiful story, beautifully told.
—Augusta Trobaugh, author of *Sophie and the Rising Sun* and *Music from Beyond the Moon*

Twang is a delightful journey through Nashville's Music Row. Protagonist Jennifer Clodfelter grabs your attention and sings her heart out, all the while immersing you in a story that will have you wondering if you are living your dream while fulfilling your God-given destiny or just treading water. It's a novel that validates the premise that forgiveness is a powerful force and faith really *can* move mountains. This book speaks to the heart and whispers to the soul. I'm so glad I read it.
—Jackie Lee Miles, author of *The Heavenly Heart* and *All That's True*

In her latest book, *Twang*, Julie Cannon once again brings characters to life with such accurate and picturesque detail and captures the cadences of Southern speech so perfectly that we feel as if each character has sprung to life as a neighbor or member of the family. Even more important, as we follow Jenny Cloud's struggle to move beyond the tribulations of her childhood, Cannon leads us inexorably to a conclusion in which we see the mysterious and transformative power of Grace and, in the process, makes us feel transformed ourselves.
—K. S. Schwind, author of *Vermilion Wanted to Go to the Movies*

Achingly honest and engrossing novel about a Taylor Swift hopeful who nearly loses herself when she finds fame. A must-read for fans of country music and anyone who's ever dreamed of becoming a star. I loved it!
—Karin Gillespie, author *Bottom Dollar Girl* series

In this heartwarming look into the pain and heartache that can lie behind stardom, Julie Cannon demonstrates that Thomas Wolfe was wrong: we not only can, we must go home again to forgive hurts we endured there before we can truly find peace in our lives.
—Patricia Sprinkle, author of *Friday's Daughter*

TWANG

Julie L. Cannon

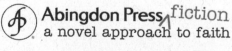

Abingdon Press fiction
a novel approach to faith

Nashville, Tennessee

Other books by Julie L. Cannon

Truelove & Homegrown Tomatoes
'Mater Biscuit
Those Pearly Gates
The Romance Readers' Book Club
I'll Be Home for Christmas

Twang

Copyright © 2012 by Julie L. Cannon

ISBN-13: 978-1-4267-1470-2

Published by Abingdon Press, P.O. Box 801, Nashville, TN 37202

www.abingdonpress.com

All rights reserved.

No part of this publication may be reproduced in any form,
stored in any retrieval system, posted on any website,
or transmitted in any form or by any means—digital, electronic,
scanning, photocopying, recording, or otherwise—without
written permission from the publisher, except for brief
quotations in printed reviews and articles.

The persons and events portrayed in this work of fiction
are the creations of the author, and any resemblance
to persons living or dead is purely coincidental.

Library of Congress Cataloging-in-Publication Data

Cannon, Julie, 1962–
  Twang / Julie L. Cannon.
    p. cm.
  ISBN 978-1-4267-1470-2 (trade pbk. : alk. paper) 1. Women country musicians—
Fiction. I. Title.
  PS3603.A55T93   2012
  813'.6—dc23

2012014935

Printed in the United States of America

1 2 3 4 5 6 7 8 9 10 / 17 16 15 14 13 12

When a flood swept through Nashville, Tennessee, in May 2010, people were killed and homes and property destroyed in fifty counties. President Obama declared it a disaster area. And although it was a true disaster in every sense of the word, the flood also brought out the good in this community.

Twang is dedicated to all those volunteers who selflessly worked to rescue other people and animals; who did the nitty-gritty work of recovering, clearing, rebuilding, and restoring; who provided emotional support for those whose lives were devastated. The compassionate spirit of volunteers helped Music City come out of this disaster stronger and more united than ever before.

Acknowledgments

Many thanks to Ramona Richards, my editor, and Sandra Bishop, my agent. They are stars in the industry, and it's no wonder. Ramona grabbed the bull by the horns and took me on a tour to show me all of Nashville, from the Grand Ole Opry to Music Row. She truly loves this city, and I couldn't have written this book without her guidance and support! I am fortunate to be published by Abingdon Press, where everyone does their job with great enthusiasm and extreme competence. Frances Merritt, Julie Dowd, Pamela Clements,

Lisa Huntley, Mark Yeh, Bryan Williams, and Susan Cornell—and many others who work to support and build the Abingdon fiction authors: thank you all!

I must also tip my Stetson to country music singers, past and present, whose songs echo in my soul.

This book wouldn't be the same and my acknowledgments wouldn't be complete without a mention of Kay Arthur and her devotional study called "Lord, Heal My Hurts." A neighbor dragged me to this remarkable study as I was in the middle of writing this story, and it gave me a terrifying, eye-opening window into tormented lives where the pain ran deep and memories were torture. I read stories of people delivered from personal hells, set free as they placed their tears and bitterness into God's hands, finding refuge and healing.

A special thanks to Tom, my husband, not only for being supportive and patient when we ate burritos almost every night through the writing of *Twang* but also for believing in me unequivocally since the very first novel. He put as much blood, sweat, and tears into this story as I did, and my gratitude to him is boundless.

Prologue

I thought the absence of a past meant freedom. I didn't exactly have a Norman Rockwell childhood, and when I set out for Nashville with my Washburn guitar, I was determined to leave my baggage buried deep in the red Georgia clay. That April evening in 2004 when I first glimpsed Music City from the interstate, the twin spires of the BellSouth building glittering against the sky made my heartbeat speed up. The little green Vega, windows rolled down, hit Broadway in the heart of downtown, and the music floating out on beery waves from inside the honky-tonks made my feet start dancing on the floorboard. Never in my life had I spent the night away from the pitch black of a rural countryside and it felt like a beautiful dream. *You're here, Jennifer. You're a strong, independent woman, and you're gonna be a star.*

Not that I was cocky or overconfident, but rather full up with the praise of a handful of encouragers. Looking back, I see I was also woefully ignorant about a lot of things. Time went on like it always does, and everyone I met in Nashville insisted that powerful country songs are the ones carved from the songwriter's own experience. Well, how could I argue?

From earliest memory, a transistor radio powered by a nine-volt battery was my life-support system. No matter how bad my day had been, no matter how bruised or lonely my soul, each night as I crawled into bed I tuned in to 103.9 FM out of Blue Ridge, closed my eyes and mashed the earplug into my ear, transfixed by the voices of country artists who sang of dusty roads and broken hearts. They painted auditory pictures of people so lonesome they could cry, of people looking for love in all the wrong places, of those whose soul mates were now on the far bank of the Jordan. I heard legends like Hank Williams, Porter Wagoner, Dolly Parton, Mother Maybelle Carter, and Tammy Wynette, and newer voices, like Sara Evans and Faith Hill. These artists became my friends, then my idols. They told me who I was and infused me with hope as they beckoned me to Nashville.

In the beginning, I absolutely adored making music. But then came the constant pressure to dig deeper, to stalk those painful memories that would be fodder for heart-rending, money-making songs. One place I sure didn't want the music to take me was home, and at the height of my career, I felt like I was wearing high-heeled pumps while trying to walk on ice. I never knew when I was fixing to slip and careen into some ugly memory.

Tonilynn, my hairstylist, was acting like a psychiatrist, saying I'd never move past certain issues in my life until I forced myself to dig them up and look them in the eye. She said, "Jennifer, I'm convinced your healing is through your music. Don't be afraid to use your pain 'cause pouring it into your art would be therapeutic. Plus, you'll touch other people, and ain't that what music's really about? Giving expression to experiences and emotions we all have? And if your music can help some girl through a rough spot, ain't that reason enough to brave the heartache?"

Although my journey's been fulfilling to me in a way words can't explain, although I can hardly ask for more than the feeling I get when I hear that something I wrote or a performance I gave touched somebody, there are still those shaky moments when part of me still asks, *Would I have been willing to allow the music to call me home if I had known the cost?*

FIRST VERSE:
MAKING IT BIG IN
MUSIC CITY

1

Those first days in Nashville were happy. Happier than any I could recall. It was no accident that I had Mac's cousin pull his sputtering Vega to the curb on the corner of Music Circle East and Division Street. The Best Western was in walking distance of Music Row.

All my belongings were stuffed into two huggable paper sacks, and when I marched down that strip of red carpeting into a marble-floored lobby with a chandelier, I knew it was a palace compared to that drafty cabin in Blue Ridge with peeling wallpaper and warped floorboards. Room 316 had pretty gold and maroon carpet, gold curtains at a window with an air conditioning unit beneath it, two queen beds, and two glossy wood tables—one in the corner with a lamp, an ice bucket, and a coffeemaker and the other between the beds with a phone, a clock, and a remote for the television. There was even a little bitty refrigerator, a microwave, an ironing board, and an iron. What else could a person need?

More curious about having my own indoor bathroom than a television, I tiptoed in there first. Nothing had prepared me for what met my eyes. Clean white tiles on the floor, a marbled sink, a blow-dryer, a stack of sweet-smelling towels, and fancy soap. The washrags were folded like fans, and there were free miniature bottles of shampoo and conditioner.

To say this felt like paradise would not be an exaggeration. Turning around and around until I got drunk with my good fortune, I collapsed and fell flat onto the closest bed, laughing like a maniac, some pathetic yokel finding out she'd won the lottery.

Although bone-tired on account of being so journey-proud that I hadn't been able to sleep a wink in forty-eight hours, I couldn't fathom closing my eyes. I hadn't eaten in as long either, except for some pork rinds and a Pepsi on the ride. But I was like someone possessed: hungry only for the feel of Nashville, thirsty only for the way she looked. I promised myself for the hundredth time I would not think about my mother and the fact I'd left no note. I told myself I'd eat some real food and get sleep later, after I'd explored my *new* mother. I took the elevator downstairs to find some maps.

At the front desk, a sign said the Best Western had free breakfast: sausage, biscuits and gravy, waffles, eggs, oatmeal, muffins, toast, bagels, yogurt, and fruit. The elation I felt at this was not small, and I couldn't help a happy little laugh.

A short, overweight man in a blue seersucker suit and bright orange tie bustled out of the room behind the front desk and said, "What can I do for you this evenin', missy?" He had a tall pink forehead like you'd expect on a bald man, but his hair—and I could tell it wasn't a toupee—was this lavish white cloud that put me in mind of an albino Elvis. I could see amusement in his startlingly blue eyes.

I didn't bother to mention I was twenty-two, hardly a missy, because he'd said it so kindly and I was used to being mistaken for a much younger girl. "I wanted to see if y'all had any maps and stuff about Nashville, please." I smiled back at him, noting the name engraved on his gold lapel bar: Roy Durden.

"We got maps coming out our ears! What other information you looking for?"

"Everything."

He nodded, turned, and stepped to a bookshelf along the back wall, squatting slowly, carefully, as I watched in utter fascination to see if he'd manage to get his enormous belly to fit down between his thighs. He unfastened the button on his suit coat and the hem brushed the sides of gigantic white buck shoes. Eventually, he rose with a loud grunt, carrying an armload of papers. "Alrighty," he said, spreading them on the counter like a card dealer in Vegas. "Let's see what we can do for you."

"Thanks." I reached for a glossy brochure that said *Tour the Ryman, Former Home of the Grand Ole Opry*. It was lavishly illustrated with pictures of artifacts from early Opry years and old-time country music stars like Minnie Pearl and Hank Williams. There was a headline that said you could cut your own CD at the Ryman's recording studio. Thanks to my high school music teacher Mr. Anglin, I had already accomplished that task.

"Snazzy, huh?" Roy was nodding. "Now, that there is one hallowed institution. Tennessee's sweet-sounding gift to the world. Place the tourists flock to." He was talking with his eyes closed and this rapturous expression on his face. "Up until '74, fans packed the pews of the Ryman every Friday and Saturday night. Folks loved that place so much that when the Opry moved to its current digs right near the Opryland Hotel, they cut out a six-foot circle from the stage and put it front and center at the new place. So the stars of the future can stand where the legends stood." Roy grew quiet for a worshipful moment.

"There's this one too," he said at last, pushing a slick brochure that read *The Country Music Hall of Fame & Museum* toward me.

Mac, my boss at McNair Orchards, used to say he could see my face in a display hanging in the Hall of Fame, right between Barbara Mandrell and Tammy Wynette. Mac got my head so full of stars, I could hardly think of much else except to get to Nashville to show the world my stuff. I stared at the photograph of a building that looked to be an architectural wonder in itself. One side was an RKO-style radio tower, while the main part had windows resembling a piano keyboard, and an end like a Cadillac tailfin. "That's nice," I offered.

"Yep, real nice," Roy said, his fingertips grazing more brochures reading Belle Meade Plantation, Margaritaville, General Jackson Showboat, Wildhorse Saloon, and The Parthenon. He lifted a map of Nashville. "Be helpful for you to know Second Avenue runs north, and Fourth Avenue runs south."

"I didn't bring a car."

"That a fact?" He looked hard at me. "Well, downtown and the Hall of Fame are in walking distance, but it's a ways to the Grand Ole Opry." Roy's index finger touched a spot on the map. "There's also a place called Riverfront Park you could walk to, but I got to warn you, missy, Nashville sits down in a bowl, between a couple lakes and rivers, so it feels like you're walking through hot soup in the summertime. Can be right intolerable." He swiped his florid face at the memory of heat as I flipped through the pages of a brochure, pausing every now and again to stare at a picture of a star singing on a stage, the crowd going wild. There was an energy in those photographs, a palpable current of voice and instrument and the sweet thunder of applause. For a long time I looked at a picture of Dolly Parton and Porter Wagoner, their faces suffused with a bright, joyous light.

"You like this one?" Roy asked, making me jump.

"Um, yeah."

"That was in '75, the night Dolly and Porter sang their last duet together. I was close enough to see Dolly's makeup." There were tears in Roy's eyes.

"Wow," I said.

"Wow is right."

"Can I have it? Can I have all these, please?" I tried not to look too eager, but every cell in my body wanted to scoop up the brochures, rush to my room to study them, to dream of climbing right into the beautiful photographs.

"Go ahead. You must be a first-time tourist."

I didn't think of myself as a tourist. I was there because of a promise I'd made, and the voices I'd heard over 103.9 FM back in Blue Ridge. Mountain Country Radio assured me that Nashville was the place for a person bitten by the singer/songwriter bug. "Um . . . I just like music."

"Wellllll, you come to the right place then. We got live music right here at the Best Western." Roy swept one arm out in a magnanimous gesture toward the other side of the lobby where I saw a doorway to what I'd figured was the dining area. A sign in the shape of a giant guitar pick said *Pick's*, and next to that was another that said *Great Drinks!*

"Y'all need anybody to sing at Pick's?"

"Naw. We got our bands booked a good ways in advance."

"Wonder where musicians who're looking for work hang out," I said in a casual voice, gathering the brochures.

"Nashville draws musicians like honey draws flies, and a body can't go ten yards without bumping into one of them looking for work. Tons of wannabes in here constantly, trying to make their way. Dreaming the dream."

From the tone of Roy's voice, I couldn't tell if he was trying to give me a warning or just stating facts. "Well, thank you," I said, turning to go.

"Wait. How long you plannin' to stay?"

Barring any unforeseen expenses, I knew about how far my much-fingered roll of $20 bills would go. The Manager's Special of $65 per night came out to two weeks for $910, leaving $90 for food and incidentals, and surely in that time I'd have some paid work singing. A recording contract if Mr. Anglin's prediction came true. Seeing his dear face in my mind's eye made a little guilty tremor race up my spine. I needed to get back to my room. "I paid for three nights up front," I said, turning to go again.

"Hey!" he called, spinning me on my heel to see those intense blue eyes looking at me. "You sing?"

I hesitated, then answered, "Yessir. Play *and* sing. Write all my own material."

"Well, well. What's your name, missy?"

"Jennifer Anne Clodfelter."

"Mighty big name for such a slip of a girl. Anybody ever tell you you're a dead ringer for Cher?"

I nodded. By twelve I was constantly compared to the dark, exotic celebrity when she was young, starring in the 1970's *Sonny & Cher Comedy Hour.* I was tall and willowy, and my straight blue-black hair fell to my waist. But, where Cher wasn't exactly well-endowed, I was ample in the bosom department. The other difference between me and Cher was that my eyes were green.

"So . . . what style of music do you do, Jennifer Anne Clodfelter?"

I borrowed some confidence from Mac's words when he handed me my last paycheck. "I'm the next Patsy Cline."

"Alrighty." Roy chuckled. "Then let me guess. You do traditional? Or maybe early country?"

"Huh?"

"You said you're Patsy Cline. But, there's tons of styles. Got your Nashville sound and your country rock. Then there's rockabilly, bluegrass, honky-tonk, outlaw, and Bakersfield sound. Cowboy Western and Western swing. Oh!" he clucked his tongue. "About forgot Texas country style, and the new traditionalist, and can't leave out the contemporary sound, and of course, alternative. Though I don't cotton to alternative."

My heart started racing for fear my ignorance would show. "I'm the old kind of country."

"I see. So, you want to be a star?"

I saw mischief in those blue eyes, and I didn't know how to answer this question either. At last, I nodded.

That's when he began regarding me with amused pity. "If that's the case, you'll really want to be here a little longer. Actually," he paused and drew a long breath, "you'll want to be here nine years."

"Huh?"

Roy cleared his throat, and it seemed he stood on tiptoes because he rose up at least two inches. "Nashville may be the creative center of the universe if you're a singer and a songwriter—got all kinds of resources here for learning the industry, lots of places you can sing—but folks don't call her the nine-year town for nothing. They say it takes nine years to break into the scene, to become an overnight success. I've lived here all my life and I love her, but if you're looking to break into the music business, she can chew you up and spit you out like nobody's business."

I must've looked sad or confused because Roy's face softened, his voice grew smooth as silk, "You got people here?"

"I'm on my own." Four simple words—the truth of it stunned me.

"I got an extra room at my house."

"Um . . . thanks. No offense, but I'm fine on my own."

"Ain't trying to rain on your parade, but I've seen plenty have to wait tables or worse. Randy Travis was a cook and a dishwasher at the Nashville Palace before he could make it on his music. Seen a good number turn around and head home, too, tail tucked between their legs. You might need a place if—"

"I said I'm fine."

Roy rolled his lips inward, considering. "Independent type, hmm? Well, good luck. But don't worry if you change your mind." He drew in a long breath. "If you change your mind, you just come right on back and see Roy. I'm here most evenings after seven. I just figured if you're new around town, trying to make your way in the country music scene, it'd be good if you had somebody to fall back on."

Back in my room, I sat on the bed, Roy's words hanging over me like a dark cloud. *Chew you up and spit you out,* and *Folks don't call her the nine-year town for nothing.* Just like that, a dark cloud moved over me. This spirit of despair was something I often felt, and it had a Siamese twin who drove me to do really rash and stupid things. That was how I'd made my worst mistake to date, acting on blind impulse. And now impulses to bolt from Music City were gathering forces. I knew despair was the worst thing, the killer that blinded you to possibilities, and so I clenched my teeth, closed my eyes, and forced myself to go back all those years to a little scene that happened on the stretch of linoleum between the music room and the gym.

"Really, Jennifer, you have a gift you need to share with this world." It was between classes, and Mr. Anglin whispered in this intense voice, his small mouth barely moving against my ear. "Promise me you'll get these demos to Nashville." I recalled that his hands clenched into fists, even after I gave him my word that I'd do it. Mr. Anglin often reminded me he'd heard thousands of singers in his job of music teacher at the high school and choir director at the church, but I was the only one who'd ever moved him to tears. My songs and the way I sang them pierced his heart.

Speaking of hearts, Mr. Anglin had been well-loved, and his memorial service in April of my junior year had been a large affair involving the entire staff and a good number of the nine hundred students from Fannin County High, as well as a huge flock of people from the church. The odd thing was that Mr. Anglin's burial, prior to the service, was private. Mr. Anglin was a bachelor and had been an only child with no living parents, so there was no family to have requested this.

No family I could confess to . . .

After the service, when everyone was in the fellowship hall drinking coffee and eating cakes brought by dozens of church ladies, I walked out to the cemetery to see his stone. I put my hand over my heart and said, "I'm sorry. I had no idea you'd take it so hard. Please forgive me." I walked around Mr. Anglin's new home. He loved flowers, and toward the fringes of the graveyard, there was soft purple wisteria dripping from tree limbs. There were flowers near the graves, too, and I'm not talking about artificial arrangements poked down into stone vases. There were daffodils and dandelions in pretty shades of yellow, and a line of white irises. When a jot of blue caught my eye, right at the edge of where the dirt had been disturbed for Mr. Anglin's casket, I let out a little, "Hah!" and bent to pluck the tiny stem of a forget-me-not. I turned to Mr. Anglin's headstone again, and with tears in my eyes I said, "I won't forget you, ever. I promise I'll take the demos to Nashville." But even with this graveside declaration, I'd continued on the path of that heedless decision that put him there in the first place.

Here it was six years later, and I was only just beginning to honor my promise. I felt the slick brochures from Roy Durden and looked down at the bold words: The Country Music Hall of Fame & Museum. "I might be in the Hall of Fame one day," I said out loud, picturing myself with all those legends and pressing my free hand over my heart to feel a trembling hopefulness deep inside that moved outward making all of me shake. Then it was like I had this knowing, this sense that what I was imagining I could actually achieve. I hopped up, splashed cold water on my face, and took the elevator downstairs again.

2

As I stepped outside, my eyes were drawn to the tallest building, the most familiar, what I would come to think of as my compass as I settled into my city. Later I'd hear the BellSouth building referred to as the "Batman Building" and would discover that no matter where you were in the downtown area or where you came into Nashville—interstates, Hillsboro Road, or any of the old Pikes that lead into downtown, almost every view showed this iconic building on the skyline. That night, to see the spires in a clear sky amid a bunch of twinkling stars made me feel bold.

I stood in the parking lot, a map in one hand and my guitar case in the other. Deep in the front pocket of my blue jeans was my hotel key card and a twenty, the rest of the cash hidden in a Tampax box in my room.

There was a steady stream of cars on Division Street, and I looked down at the map, imagining all the streets as arteries and veins leading to the heart of a city pulsing with excitement. As I was leaving, Roy reminded me to be careful, that any city was dangerous for a single girl. But oddly, I had no fear. I'd begun to feel as if—I don't know how to put it—I had some kind of immunity to danger, to anything that might thwart my destiny. Anyway, I fancied myself a strong person, and if there were risks that went along with achieving my dream, they were worth taking.

An impulse to go toward what was called Music Row kicked in and I took a left and started up a slight hill, going along beside a brick wall, passing several large buildings. There were no other pedestrians, and I realized this part of town was quiet in the way a business section is after dark, and I was just about to make a U-turn when up ahead I glimpsed what appeared to be a bunch of people dancing naked in the moonlight. I went closer and saw that it was nine bronze men and women, each more than twice life-sized, up on a piece of limestone in the middle of a traffic roundabout where Division Street meets Seventeenth Avenue. A female at the pinnacle held a tambourine aloft. I stood and stared, scarcely breathing. Was this the controversial sculpture called "Musica" I'd been hearing about? I thought it very tasteful, full of a deep creative energy that captured the spirit of inspiration perfectly.

At last, I turned my head and saw a little park to one side with another statue, this one of a man sitting at a piano. Curious, I made my way over to read the sign. Owen Bradley had been a record producer, architect of the "Nashville Sound," and a man who helped create Music Row. He'd produced songs for many great country music artists, from Patsy Cline to Ernest Tubb. I had that feeling of walking inside of a dream as I sat down beside Mr. Bradley's erect figure on the piano bench to drape my arm over his shoulder. I looked at his face. Depths of wisdom seemed to lie behind those eyes that stared out unblinkingly toward Music Square, that fertile field of record labels and recording studios.

"Anything you want to say to me?" I said in a playful voice before kissing his cheek, then hopping up. Something made me pause at one of the large stones around the edge of the brick courtyard. I bent over to read what it said by moonlight: "You've Never Been This Far Before"— Conway Twitty.

"You're darn right," I called to Mr. Bradley. "But here I am, and ain't nothing gonna stop me now."

This crazy dialogue made me remember where I actually needed to be: up on a stage. Since no record label or studio would be open for business on a Thursday night at 9:30, I looked at my map and decided to follow Demonbreun Street from the roundabout until I came to Fifth Avenue, which would take me to Broadway, to the honky-tonks. The nightlife.

Gradually the dark storefronts gave way to lit windows of restaurants and nightclubs. When I reached the corner of Fifth and Broadway, I paused, glancing in one direction at a humongous building that said Nashville Convention Center, and in the other direction to what looked like a gigantic street party. Six lanes wide, Broadway was full of people. Streams of folks were going in and out of doorways, clustering around storefronts, drinking, talking, eating, smoking, and laughing. Twinkling lights wound around tree branches put me in mind of Christmas, and from where I stood I could see a horse-drawn carriage and two statues of Elvis Presley.

Stars were in my eyes as I headed into the thick of it, passing various businesses: Cadillac Ranch, Whiskey Bent Saloon, Jimmy Buffet's Margaritaville, Wanna B's Karaoke, Rippy's Ribs, Big River Grille, Robert's Western World, and one I knew I'd have to visit: the Ernest Tubb Record Shop. Nothing had prepared me for the energy I saw and felt in every square foot. This place was worlds away from the life I knew of quiet hills, trees, and rivers. I'd come from a mountain town peopled with working folk whose idea of nightlife was a jug of whiskey and a poker game in a back room. Quickly, I reminded myself not to let the shadows cast by the past follow me to Music City. Music City . . . now I understood. A name so perfect for this place pulsing with melody and harmony and soul!

It was a pleasant temperature, and I wandered a while soaking it all in. Finally, I set my Washburn down to rest my arm, leaned back against a solid brick wall, and waited to see where I might go first, what called to me. After a good ten minutes, I walked a ways and stood at the doorway of a place, which judging from the crowd, was very popular. It was one of those rowdy honky-tonks you hear about in a million country songs—a line of folks at the bar holding foaming beers, crowds wearing cowboy hats and boots and moving to a band.

I remained just outside, feeling a bit uncertain of how to do what I'd come to do. Everybody looked so relaxed. Hipster girls with chic hair and lots of jewelry and fancy jeans, the guys with that confident swagger, that backslapping good-ol'-boy ease. I felt a little frumpy and out of it until I put my hand in my pocket to kind of huddle into myself and touched my guitar pick. And that was when I stood up tall, the siren call of the stage loud and clear. I needed to feel the love of the crowd inside. I needed to feel the music filling every cell as I sang.

I started to walk through the doorway, but a man held out his arm like a gate. "Hold on just a minute there. Gotta pay the cover charge."

I peered inside and didn't see any covers in the whole place. For a moment my mind went blank, then something I can only call my stage presence took over, and I said, "Well, covers or not, I'd really like to sing tonight."

He eyed me like I was out of my mind. "This ain't no karaoke lounge."

"Um, I know. Of course it's not. Who's that?" I nodded toward the stage.

"That's our house band."

"Can I sing when they take a break?"

He squinted his eyes at me. "I don't know what planet you come from, but like I said, we ain't no karaoke bar. There's some places around here, on certain nights, you might could sing, but you can't just wander in here and say, 'I'd like to sing.'" The last four words he said in a high voice that made me cringe.

"Please. I promise. Mr. Anglin said Nashville would *die* when they heard me, and I've got this song I wrote called—"

"What is it you don't understand? Do you know how many desperate gals come to Nashville thinking they're God's gift to country music? Think they got the voice that'll make them a star?" He guffawed and slapped his thigh. "I'll tell you what happens to most of 'em. Most of 'em end up dancing at the gentlemen's clubs. Yep, *they're* the reason there's a half-dozen of those bars down next to the interstate! All them females who didn't make it in country music still got to put food in their stomachs." Sizing me up, he smiled like a hungry wolf. "You look like you got the right equipment to make some good money dancing." He reached out toward me with his beefy hand.

"Don't touch me!" I backed away, tripping over my own feet. I can't say I was shocked at the disrespect in his eyes. I'd witnessed this in scenes from my former life, and as if to prove it, from the back room of my subconscious I heard a slight knocking sound. I clenched my teeth, terrified I was fixing to be the involuntary audience of some sleazy little documentary from my past. But something inside me snapped, and this surge of anger eclipsed the memory so that the film just beginning to roll in my head went mercifully blank.

When I got down the sidewalk a ways, I could feel tears of fury just under the surface, but I willed them away, thinking,

I will sing tonight! I'm here and no leering man with slimy paws is gonna stop me again.

Before I knew it, I was at the entrance to a place that said World Famous Tootsie's Orchid Lounge. I stood and let the beat of the drums and the bass guitar wash over me, restore me. Finally I craned my neck to peer into the main room. Like all the others, the place was packed. I noticed a picture of Willie Nelson with a paper beneath it that said he got his first songwriting job after singing at Tootsie's. A thrill raced through me! I fancied I could actually feel the presence of greatness, and I was glad to see there was a woman at the entrance. She was skinny, perched up on a stool with her legs crossed, wearing a red gingham blouse and hair much too black and shiny for her age. I pointed to the poster. "Do you know Willie?"

"Not personally." She smiled with yellow teeth. "Feel like I do, though, the way he sits there looking at me all the time."

"Does a person have to buy covers to come in here?"

She had a smoker's husky laugh. "Nope. Don't gotta buy covers to come into Tootsie's."

"Do y'all let regular folks sing here?"

"Sometimes, but not tonight."

She looked like one of those world-weary women who've seen it all, glittery blue eye shadow and black lines drawn in for her eyebrows. But she had a warm smile, and I decided to take my chances that she'd be kind. "Do you know anywhere I *can* sing tonight?"

"Hmm . . . let me think," she said, her silver chandelier earrings swinging as she tilted her head. "Believe it's open jam night at the Station Inn."

"At a hotel?"

"The Station Inn's a bar on Twelfth Avenue, darlin'." She made a gesture over one sharp shoulder. "That a way. In the Gulch."

"Can I walk there?"

"I reckon. Twelfth Avenue's right off Broadway."

I thanked her and left, quickly passing half a dozen more nightclubs, feeling drunk just listening to all that music streaming out of their doorways, some sounding sad, with sweet, plaintive fiddle notes, and some lively, with a beat you couldn't help moving some body part along with.

Twelfth Avenue was not a hop, skip, and a jump away, and I had to slow my pace after passing several huge, ornate churches, the courthouse, a high school, and a really big building that said Frist Center for the Visual Arts. As I walked on, I began to see a number of dark areas and hulking gray dumpsters, and I decided "gulch" sure fit the way things were looking. I went a while longer and decided that even if they did charge you for covers at this place, I was definitely going to pay.

I turned down Twelfth, panting hard, my legs getting really tired, until finally, past Demonbreun Street, I saw the Station Inn, an old nondescript concrete block building with a few windows.

Inside was a plain, low-ceilinged place with plywood floors. Red-and-white-checked tablecloths covered the tables, and church pews situated along the sides and the rear were full of folks holding bottles of beer. There was a stage with no one on it, and I got a rush just picturing myself there.

A big man in a big white cowboy hat was leaning near the door with his feet splayed out in sharp-toed boots. He smiled at me and said, "Evening, ma'am. Welcome to the Station Inn."

"Cover?" I asked, raising my eyebrows in a vague, world-wise manner, recalling the last man I'd spoken to with a flinch of anxiety.

"Ten tonight."

I held out the twenty and waited for my change before I asked. "Can regular folks sing here?"

"Absolutely. And every mandolin, banjo, or fiddle player who's anybody can play here." He smiled. "We *are* Bluegrass and Roots."

I wasn't sure what he meant by roots, but I shifted from leg to leg, thinking of endless late Saturday nights listening to *Bluegrass Time* on the radio; of Bill Monroe and his Blue Grass Boys, Lester Flatt with his acoustic guitar, and Earl Scruggs with his banjo. Lester and Earl had themselves a band called the Foggy Mountain Boys. Even Dolly Parton and Patty Loveless sang some bluegrass, and Alison Krauss sure could do that high, lonesome sound. My particular sound wasn't actually bluegrass, but it was acoustic, which is what bluegrass is all about, and it did tell a good story the way bluegrass songs generally do. I knew I could strum my Washburn and sing my song, "Walking the Wildwood," an octave above my usual. Everything inside me was jumping around and getting all excited as I smiled, lifted my guitar case, and said so clear and strong, "I'd like to sing a bluegrass tune I wrote called 'Walking the Wildwood.' It's a song that comes straight from my heart."

The man looked like maybe he could see how much this meant to me, and he must've known how much it was gonna crush me when he cocked his big head, gentled up his voice, and said, "Well, that sure sounds nice. You come back on Sunday, when we have our open jam."

My heart fell down to my feet.

He chuckled in a kind way and said, "Hey, hey, now. Chin up. Sunday'll be here 'fore you know it, and tonight we got Raul Malo. He's doing 'Crying Time,' and everybody loves him. Come on in and give a listen."

I could hardly believe I'd hit another brick wall! Part of me wanted to go back to the Best Western, turn on my radio, climb into a hot tub, and sulk. But the man's voice was so kind, and I'd already told myself I absolutely could not fall apart.

Crowds make me nervous unless I'm singing, so I walked in, ordered a Coke, and sat in an out-of-the-way corner to watch as Raul took the stage. People started whistling, calling out, and clapping while he tested the microphone and situated his guitar. There was no dance floor so when he began playing and singing, folks were moving their hips and shoulders right where they were, a sea of bodies rippling. Raul's music was alive, thumping against the walls, pulsing up through the floor. I sat on the edge of my seat through an entire set, thinking *Tomorrow. Tomorrow I'll go strut my stuff on Music Row. I'll be living the dream.*

Friday morning came, and I fixed strong coffee and carried a cup back to bed to sit cross-legged in a nest of covers with the Nashville phonebook on one side and my shoulder bag with the demos on the other. I scanned all the listings under Music Producers in the Yellow Pages, swallowing the last thick slug of coffee before I squeezed my eyes shut to rip out the page.

My retro country-music-star outfit was laid like a flat person on the other bed, and it looked like it could hop up and start singing all by itself. There was a white blouse with a half-circle of ruffles on the chest, and over that a red bolero jacket with a matching knee-length skirt that swished out like a bell when I twirled. Mac McNair had given me a castaway pair of fancy white pumps with ankle straps that were his wife's from the previous Easter. He assured me she wouldn't dare show up at church in the same pair of shoes two years in a row.

I put my outfit on and stood in front of the mirror. *Wow*, I thought, after I brushed my long hair to one shoulder and put on red lipstick, *that woman looks like she stepped out of a brochure about the Ryman!* Holding an imaginary microphone to my lips, I said, "Hello, I'm Jennifer Anne Clodfelter, and I'm gonna sing a song I wrote, a song that's in my heart and I know you're gonna love. Here's 'Walking the Wildwood' just for you." The shameless sales pitch didn't shock me because I'd practiced it ten zillion times. Also, whenever I played my music, stage or no stage, I became an entirely different person who did and said things that ordinarily scared me senseless.

Curious about the weather, I went to my window to slide the curtains over, smiling at clear blue skies, and down below, the hotel pool sparkling in sunlight. Beyond the pool was a grassy lot with several trees, and across the side street a big building that said BMI. Pressing my nose to the glass, I could see what appeared to be a residential neighborhood behind the Best Western.

Roy Durden was gone and the lobby was a busy place. A group of men in business suits were sitting on four sofas surrounding a coffee table, and two maids were wheeling a cart to what I guessed was the laundry room. The smell of sausage and warm biscuits was almost enough to lure me into the dining area, but I set my face like flint and stepped outside.

Nashville on a weekday morning seemed a good bit more subdued, and Mrs. McNair's pumps were stiff and unfamiliar, but I walked along with spirits soaring, my guitar case like an old friend. Broadway might be where the live music, the partying of my new town, happened, but legendary Music Row, Sixteenth and Seventeenth Avenues South, was the business side of country music. That was where record label offices, publishing houses, musical licensing firms, and recording studios sat literally hip to hip. I fingered the phone book page in the shallow pocket of my skirt as I walked along. My brain felt like a piñata had burst open inside, releasing swirling slips of paper with names of various companies: Bayou Recording, Center Row Recording Studios, Big Machine Records, Country Thunder Records, Elite Talent Agency, Sea Gayle, Big Yellow Dog, Masterfonics, Sixteen Ton Studio, Cherry Lane Music Publishing, Red Ridge Entertainment, Grand & Gee Music, and a zillion more. More than you can ever imagine. And every single one of them held promise, a wonderful opportunity just waiting.

I'd pictured a line of sterile, businesslike buildings, but as I started down Music Square East, I saw quaint brick and stone bungalows in Craftsman style, the occasional Victorian or Georgian, with columns and awnings and wrought-iron railings, set behind manicured lawns full of oak and magnolia trees. A nice feeling swept over me as I focused in on my first prospect.

I climbed four steps beneath a green awning, and with hardly a pause, pushed open the door to step inside. "Morning," I said in my most cheerful voice to a woman sitting behind a desk with a fern spilling over the corner. She looked up from what I recognized as a Krispy Kreme donut box, grabbed at a pair of glasses resting on her huge shelf of a bosom and set them on her nose. She cocked her head, squinted, then frowned with orangey lips underneath a pageboy haircut, which looked like it was on fire from the overhead lights.

"May I help you?" She looked me up and down.

"Yes, please. My name is Jennifer Anne Clodfelter, and I've got a song that's in my heart and on my lips I know y'all are gonna love. Here's 'Walking the Wildwood' just for you." I bent to unbuckle my guitar case.

"What?" she said in this shrill voice.

"I'm a singer." My heart was pounding as I looked up at her shocked face. "I wrote this really great song called 'Walking the Wildwood,' and I'm happy to do it bluegrass or pure country. What's your pleasure?"

"Well, aren't we all?"

"Excuse me?"

"You said you're a singer."

"Yes, ma'am. I've got over seventy original songs." I pulled my song notebook from beneath the Washburn and held it up.

"First of all, I'm just the administrative assistant here, and second of all, we don't accept unsolicited material." She nodded at a small poster on the wall with chunky black lettering; "We do not accept unsolicited materials. Due to the large volume of submissions we receive, we cannot always respond promptly."

"Well, of course," I said, more heartily than I felt. "May I please give you a demo?"

I heard her exasperated sigh. "Drop it over there on that tray on the counter. Mr. Clarke may get to it; he may not. He's a busy man. Now, if you'll excuse me, I have work to tend to." She rooted around in the Krispy Kreme box for a chocolate glazed donut.

I heard some men's voices coming from down the hall behind her. "Could I talk to Mr. Clarke? Real quick? I promise I won't even take five minutes of his time. I'll—"

"Leave your demo over there. If Mr. Clarke likes it, he'll call you to set up an appointment. Now, like I said, I have work—"

"Please. I've come all the way from Blue Ridge, Georgia, and I don't have a lot of time before my money runs out, and I promise you, ma'am, I've got this beautiful song, and I wrote the words and the music, and if you'll just give me a chance to sing it for Mr. Clarke, then I promise you I'll—"

The woman's nostrils widened. She half-stood behind her desk, and I watched shiny flakes of glaze glide off her lap. "Did you just climb out of the hills? You can't come barreling in here and demand Mr. Clarke's attention!" She shook her head in a rude way. "Do you know how many country music singer wannabes I get coming in here? Don't you know anything?"

I stared at the lipstick prints on her Styrofoam coffee cup and said nothing for a long time. I *had* just climbed out of the hills. "I'm sorry I disturbed you," I said, gathering my things together before I set a demo in the overflowing basket.

I stood on the sidewalk awhile, feeling shaky. *What if none of the labels would listen to a live singer off the street? What would I do? Throw in the towel and go back to Blue Ridge? Nope. That wasn't even a possibility.*

"That's just one music label," I said finally, the warm sun seeping into my skin through my cotton blouse. I closed my eyes, lifting my face for an infusion of its strength. For one fleeting moment I toyed with telling a lie when I walked into the next place, saying I was dying of cancer and my last wish was to sing a song to that particular record label. Everyone has compassion for a dying person, and I knew that once they heard me, I'd be forgiven the lie and welcomed with open arms. But just as quickly, I decided it might jinx me and I'd get cancer.

I readjusted my shoulder bag, which was bulging with demos, and marched to the next door down, which said Warner Music. Same story, and I left a demo, then crossed over Roy Acuff Place to see a building called Mike Curb College of Entertainment and Music Business. I had no money for college, so I passed it by, but I couldn't help wondering what it would be like to go to a place like that. It would be a dream, not one bit like school. I came to a big brick building that said EMI Music Publishing. I walked in, gave my same spiel, and was told to leave a demo. I crossed Chet Atkins Place, passed by an enormous, columned church called Belmont, and after that paused in front of a pretty red brick house. With a deep breath, I climbed ten steps up to enter Sixteen Ton Studio. The man sitting at a desk in the foyer stared at me with wide eyes and said nothing when I held up the Washburn and asked if I could sing; he only nodded at a shelf. I left a demo and dragged myself back outside to do pretty much the same at four more labels. After that, I knew without a doubt that folks in Nashville's Music Row didn't have the time to stop and listen to someone off the streets.

Still, every single refusal hurt like the first time, and it felt like I was leaving a part of my heart in the basket, or on the counter, or atop a shelf whenever I plunked a demo down. However, I knew that there was nothing to do but methodically step into the various labels and leave a demo until all twenty-five were gone. I worked hard not to picture Mr. Anglin's disappointed face by reminding myself that I was fulfilling my vow and that the demos he helped me make were full of original songs that made him weep.

Late in the afternoon, I trudged along, passing Music City Tattoo and the Rhinestone Wedding Chapel, also in Craftsman homes. Then I saw this unusual place that looked like a barn, with a colorful, oversized statue standing in the parking lot. It had a cheerful face that reminded me of the Big Boy that used to be outside of Shoney's restaurants. I was tired and hungry and I decided to let myself splurge.

After my eyes adjusted to the dimness inside Bobby's Idle Hour Tavern, I found a barstool and set my shoulder bag and my guitar on the floor. Bobby's was an unassuming place, with dollar bills taped to the posts and neon signs reading Rolling

Rock and Budweiser Select on the wall. A Washburn guitar hung behind the bar, and this seemed like a good omen. A couple other customers sat at the bar, laid-back older men, holding drinks, watching a television in one corner. The closest one tipped his head and said "Howdy, ma'am," in a voice that sounded like his words were smiling.

Another voice spoke to me from across the bar: a pretty, middle-aged woman with long brown hair pulled back. "You look tired, hon," she said kindly. "What can I get you?"

"Peanuts and a Coke?"

She nodded, and it wasn't sixty seconds until an icy Coke and a bowl of peanuts appeared in front of me. I wolfed them down, and they tasted so good I almost cried. Food in my stomach helped me feel a little better.

"You a singer?" asked the man who'd spoken to me earlier, his brown eyes measuring me and my guitar case resting on the floor.

"Sure am," I said.

"Sam Watkins," he said, holding out a hand.

Did I read anything but friendly in his words? No, I did not. Only a down-to-earth kindness and curiosity. "Jennifer Anne Clodfelter," I said, shaking his hand. "You sing?"

"Something like that." He smiled.

My heart soared to find someone with a mutual passion. "I write all my own songs and I've been delivering demos here at Music Row. Going to break into the Nashville scene."

There was a stretch of silence that seemed to go on forever and in which I wondered what was going on in Sam Watkins's head.

"Where'd you say you were from?" he asked finally.

"I'm a resident of Nashville."

He lifted his eyebrows, and there was another long pause while he rubbed his scruffy beard. I tried my best to wait for him to speak, but I couldn't help myself. "Music is who I am. I have lots of experience in the music business. Won tons of talent shows and my chorus teacher worked with me on studying stage presence, and he helped me make demos, and Mac, my boss at McNair Orchards says I'm the next Patsy Cline." I nodded down at my guitar case. "I've got over seventy completely original songs and I've been told *countless* times throughout my life that I absolutely need to be in Nashville, and that Nashville's gonna just *die* when they hear me." My thoughts and words were falling all over each other so fast I didn't even have time to be sad about Mr. Anglin.

Sam Watkins cocked his head. "Girl, I admire your spunk, but I'm not going to sugarcoat things. The music business is rough, even for a man like me who's been doing it twenty years now. You a member of NSAI and SGA?"

I shook my head. I didn't know what those letters even stood for.

"ASCAP, BMI, or SESAC?"

My heart sank as I shook my head again. I figured I must seem pretty pathetic, but I couldn't afford to be a member of anything. Sam Watkins broke into my thoughts gently. "If you're as good as you say, my best advice is to make sure you get some legal advice before you even open your mouth to sing. You need somebody you can trust to help you plan long-term. Too many sharks out there'll try to flatter you, tell you you're the next Loretta Lynn, and get you to sign as an exclusive writer. Then, later you find out you made the biggest mistake of your life."

The emotional roller coaster I was riding on dipped even lower as I absorbed all this information about the city's seemingly impenetrable music scene.

Sam lit a cigarette and blew a smoke ring above his head like a halo. He leaned forward into the warm circle of light that shone over the bar. "You're not really from here," he said, and I could tell he meant it kindly. "The place to start is to get involved with a group of other amateurs, local singers and songwriters. Meet some other creative-minded folks. There's a whole community of us here, you know, and if you want to make it in Nashville, you've got to learn the ropes."

I felt like I had to defend myself. "But I'm not some beginner! I've been writing songs and singing practically my whole life."

It got quiet. Sam had an expression on his face I couldn't read. I probably looked pathetic, my hands shaking on my knees, my shoulders drooped with exhaustion.

"Listen," he said at last, a softness in his voice. "Never got me nowhere, but some folks claim open mic nights are the backbone of the country music industry. There's a dozen or more places you ought to go try your wings at, play some of those original songs you're talking about. You ought to go sing at The French Quarter or the Douglas Corner Café or the Bluebird's open mic night. Get you some practice performing in front of a group."

I didn't need any more practice performing in front of a group, but he was so nice. "Thanks. Which of those is best, in your opinion?"

He stubbed his cigarette out in a black ashtray on the bar. "Well, I'd have to say it's the Bluebird on Monday nights. Every Monday they got a show goes, oh, two or three hours, where a dozen hopefuls get to strut their stuff. Great place to try out new material, work on your performing skills, meet other writers and singers, and just become a part of the songwriting community. Now I think about it, the Bluebird's where Kathy Mattea and Garth Brooks got their start."

"Really?" My heart sped up.

"Yep," he said, a grin on his leathery face. "If you're good as you say, you might catch the eye of a mover and shaker in the industry who's sitting out in the audience. It could be your big break."

"Oh, thank you, thank you, thank you!" I knew I sounded like a ninny, but fireworks were going off in my brain. I got to my feet, dug down into my pocket and set a five dollar bill down on the bar. "Bye, Sam." I wasn't quite out the door when he called after me. I turned.

"I'm going to give you some more advice."

"Yes?" I smiled.

"Lose the sweet-girl Sunday school outfit."

A hot flush rushed up my chest, and again I felt myself revisiting that time and place I'd buried so far in the red Georgia clay. Sam Watkins sure didn't seem to have the leering look in his eye. Hadn't my instincts assured me he was safe? I ran down the hot sidewalk, and my thoughts moved to Mr. Anglin. I'd never felt so safe as when I was perched on a chair in his classroom after class was over, him at his desk, his legs crossed at the knee, the picture of elegance and manners. I loved that he dressed like a gentleman: turtlenecks in the fall and winter, his slender wrists sticking out of flawless starched shirts with French cuffs in the spring. I never suspected he had anything in mind besides the rich enjoyment of music. You cannot fall apart now, I told myself, walking toward a large gray brick building that said Bench Mark Sound Music Publishing; you've got to honor your promise to him.

I put myself in this sort of trance where I was hardly aware of anything—not the passage of time, not rude folks. When I finished the recording companies on Music Square East, I headed to Seventeenth Avenue, to tackle Music Square West. Close to five p.m., my feet aching terribly and my arm exhausted from lugging my Washburn, I gave out my last demo and decided it was time to go home.

I was shocked to find that someone had made up the beds in room 316. There was also a fresh stack of towels, more coffee, and clean cups. I looked inside my Tampax box, and when I saw my money was still there, I hung up my blouse and skirt, put the pumps on the closet floor, and sat on the closed toilet lid to hold a wet washrag to the blisters on the backs of my heels.

3

Saturday morning I rode the elevator down and fixed a plateful of sausage, biscuits, and gravy. I didn't have a lot of experience being a woman in control of her own time, and when I finished I walked into the lobby feeling like I was waiting for something to seize me and shake me into consciousness over what to do with all the endless minutes stacked up against one another until Monday night. A picture of George Jones inspired me to go back upstairs and tune my Washburn.

After that, I worked on my pitch control so long my voice was as silky-smooth as Joan Baez's. Then I dug my turquoise blouse and blue jeans out of the bottom of one of my paper sacks, washed them in the sink with flowery shampoo and hung them over the shower rod to dry. Every now and again I'd feel a twinge of guilt over taking off from Blue Ridge without a word, but I squelched it quickly by saying to myself that I sure didn't have to take root some place just because I'd germinated there. Didn't birds swallow seeds only to fly miles and miles away to poop them out where they sprouted? How could nature be wrong? Speaking of nature, I'd been in downtown Nashville two days, and I'd begun to miss the wide-open outdoors a bit. But every time I thought about how I was actually in the place described as "a fertile womb for aspiring country musicians," how I was at the intersection of my dreams and real life, I smiled so hard my eyes almost disappeared. For the rest of Saturday, I sat on my bed, alternating listening to the radio with working on some songs as I ate Paydays and Lance Toastchee crackers from the motel vending machine. Sunday came. I'd never missed a Sunday of my life being in church, and all morning a certain guilty feeling hovered over me. I made coffee in my room and turned on the television to flip through a smattering of church services, listening briefly, yearning toward what? I wasn't sure. A bit after noon, when church would have been over anyway, I set out for another walk, as much to kill time as anything.

Every time I took a breath, whether I was rifling through tons of souvenirs and music at the Ernest Tubb Record Shop or checking out the menu of a meat and three taped to a window, I had one thought running through my head: *Bluebird, Bluebird, Bluebird.* As I walked the sidewalks of Broadway, I wandered into several old buildings with high ceilings where fans turned slowly. It seemed Mr. Roy Durden was right on when it came to fashion, at least on Sunday. Twirly sundresses and seersucker suits were staples of Southern ladies and gentlemen on their way from church to lunch downtown. What struck me was that Blue Ridge had a population of twelve hundred, and I'd read Nashville's was around six hundred thousand, but there was this graciousness about Nashville that made her feel vastly more welcoming.

At a place called J & J's Market, which looked like a convenience store but turned out to have a nice sitting area in the rear, I bought a Coke and sipped it as I tried to relax. Someone had left a colorful flier on my table. *Spend a warm afternoon at Riverfront Park, lounging on the grass overlooking the Cumberland River. Be sure to wave to the folks on the General Jackson Showboat!*

From childhood, I'd been drawn to the broad, slow curves of rivers snaking along through mossy banks, to gushing torrents gouging their way through sheer rock. The most peaceful moments of my past were those spent along the Toccoa and the Ocoee rivers. I finished my Coke and set out to walk the mile and a half down Broadway to Riverfront Park. As I turned onto First Avenue, I spied the famous Wildhorse Saloon and smelled the Cumberland River for the first time: a musty mix of dead worms and decaying plant matter. A wonderful smell. My heart was thumping like crazy as I crossed the street, leaving the asphalt and concrete to gallop past a lamppost with a sign reading "No Fishing or Swimming Permitted" and down a sloping bank of grass and clover striped by three terraces of cement steps.

Looking at pictures of the Cumberland had left me totally unprepared. She was majestic, a nice fat brown thread winding her way through the city. I sank down for an infusion of nature and the words to John Denver's "Annie's Song" rolled through my mind. My senses were literally overflowing as I watched a gray heron skimming along the water's surface, legs behind in a graceful curve while balmy breezes brushed my cheeks. I sat worshipfully still for a long spell, recalling what I'd just read about the Cumberland.

She went for 688 miles, beginning in southeastern Kentucky, flowing through northern Tennessee, and then curving back up into western Kentucky before draining into the Ohio River. The settlers who built the village that grew into Nashville were drawn to her wealth of natural resources, and historic Fort Nashborough there on the bank behind me was a New Deal reconstruction project to remind folks how Nashville began. Nearby, the remnants of Warehouse Row recorded a later phase in my city's history, a time when steamboats ferried goods along the waterway.

What awed me more than anything was thinking how this proud river had been here for centuries before any human eye had seen her grandeur. Native Americans made rivers into symbols of strength and nourishment for a reason, and the phrase "river of life" was perfect. I scrambled down some large boulders, pretending to be an Indian just discovering the Cumberland as I stretched my arm to trail my fingers in her waters, warm and cool as tears on cheeks, feeling the depth of her quiet strength.

Finally, I lifted my eyes to gaze across the waters. On the far bank several joggers bounced along, and there was a couple walking their dog, and beyond that a huge stadium said LP Field. Upriver I recognized the reclining forms of some homeless folks next to an old train depot. Turning to look over my shoulder toward the city I spied my landmark, the Batman Building, and what I figured was a radio station with the huge red letters WKDF.

Back at my spot on the bank, I basked in the soothing song of the Cumberland's waters, feeling more relaxed and complete than I had in a long time. It grew late and I realized I needed to find a bathroom. I rose reluctantly, wishing I could bottle up the beautiful sense of peace I had here and carry it with me. Then it hit me—I could come to the river anytime I wanted! Which seemed odd to me at first, reminding me that I hadn't yet fully comprehended being a woman in control of her own decisions, her own destiny. Part of me was still looking over my shoulder, making sure none of those things I'd left behind were trailing me.

As I trudged up the bank that Sunday afternoon, it occurred to me that the so-called God all those television preachers had been extolling, the one I'd heard about all my life, had let me down numerous times. In the past I'd asked God time and time again to keep me safe, protect me from a man who made the blood in my veins freeze just by thinking of him. But the rocks, the trees, and the rivers in my life—they'd never disappointed me! And now I had the Cumberland, and she knew what I needed. I could come and release all of my fears and tears into her depths, and her strength would carry them away. The fist clenched around my heart relaxed a bit, and I breathed in a mystic peace, a communion with this steady and constant river. My sanctuary.

—✺—

Roy Durden was at the front desk when I got home. I wasn't feeling social, only eager to get to my room and practice and think about tomorrow at The Bluebird. I thought he wasn't going to notice me, but when I was just past the mirrored column in the center of the lobby, steps away from the elevator, he called, "Jennifer Anne Clodfelter!" in this too eager voice.

I turned, made myself smile. "How are you?"

"More like, how are *you*? Nashville treating you okay?"

He was wearing a seersucker suit and a bright orange tie, had his Elvis pompadour going, a Solitaire card game up on a laptop sitting on the counter, but he seemed a bit deflated. Sad somehow. I'd overheard one of the maids saying Roy'd been a very successful musician in his younger days, a banjo player in a bluegrass group, but then had some falling out with the other band members.

"Treating me fine," I said, pushing the button for the elevator.

"Alrighty. Good. How'd you like to come set a spell and visit with an old man?"

"Um . . . " I hesitated, turned just enough to see the pleading look in his eyes, and then walked slowly over to the front desk. "Sure. Let me run use the ladies' room first."

"Sunday nights are slow around here," he said when I returned. "Thanks for humoring an old man."

"My pleasure," I said, and it became true as I was saying it, as I leaned my elbows on the counter across from Roy. "So, how's the solitaire?" I gave a nod at the computer.

"Solitary." He laughed. "Actually, not too bad tonight. Won four, lost two so far. Grab a seat, take a load off."

I looked in the direction he was nodding and there, several feet from his stool was a chair from the dining room. I sat down on the edge at first, then slowly slid my fanny back.

"Had supper yet?" Roy asked, his face lit up with eagerness.

"Nope," I said, suddenly realizing I was ravenous.

"Well, I'm fixing to call Big River Grille and order me a hickory bacon burger with smoked cheddar cheese and sweet magnolia barbecue sauce. Comes with a side of fries and creamy coleslaw that's just right. And I'm a fool for their tea. Can I make that two?"

My mouth was watering. "Sure," I said. "I'll go get some money from my room."

"Nope. Treat's on me. It'll give me pleasure." Roy dialed, ordered, then turned to face me with his arms crossed over his chest in an imperious way. "Best Western doing you right? You comfortable?"

I nodded, trying not to stare at his huge belly.

"Good, good. We want our guests to have a real nice experience. So, tell me, what you been doing in Nashville? I want to hear all about it. Every last detail."

My expected payment for the coming meal would be lively banter. I twirled a strand of hair around my finger awhile, not used to off-the-cuff conversation. "I um . . . on Thursday night I went to Broadway and looked around," I offered, and was grateful that Roy was perceptive enough to begin asking leading questions.

"You did? Well, that was a mighty fine idea. What did you think of beautiful Broadway?"

I omitted the part about the nasty-minded doorman, told him how I'd felt Willie Nelson's presence at Tootsie's, and how I ultimately wound up at the Station Inn. "I heard Raul Malo live," I said. "He was really good, and I stayed until they closed." I didn't tell Roy I'd spent the whole time pining to be up onstage, singing.

"I imagine old Raul really got that crowd going," Roy said, shaking his head in delighted wonder. "He was with the Mavericks for years, you know, but he left because they got so big they weren't leaving him any room for his spontaneity. Boy likes twanging his guitars like a madman." He pantomimed strumming an electric guitar.

"You do anything touristy?" Roy asked after a bit. "The Ryman, the Grand Ole Opry, or the Country Music Hall of Fame?"

I sat up straighter in my chair. I didn't want to sound poor or seem like I was hinting for charity. "Nah," I said. "Saturday I just hung around here, and today I spent at Riverfront Park. I'm more the outdoor type."

"Yep. I knew you were a tomboy the first time I laid eyes on you." He chuckled. "Let me warn you, though, there's some places around here a young gal ought not go alone. When you're going along the Gay Street Connector that runs right along the river, be sure you don't go beyond the Woodland Street Bridge. Plus, the Cumberland sure ain't no river to swim in. Got a fast top current, as you probably noticed, but there's also a strong, deep current you don't want to mess with. And I wouldn't even wade in it without getting a tetanus shot first."

I nodded, but inside I didn't take those warnings to heart. Being raised in the country had its advantages.

"What'd you do on Friday?"

"On Friday." I drew in a long breath. "I spent the entire day going up and down Music Row to all the record labels."

Roy pantomimed removing a hat. "You don't say! How'd it go?"

"Um, don't know yet. I left demos at a bunch of them. But I went to this place called Bobby's for a rest and met this really nice man, a musician, and he told me I ought to go to the Bluebird tomorrow evening for their open mic."

"Now, why didn't I think of that!" Roy slapped the counter with his palm.

"I don't know." I smiled at him.

"You don't by any chance need a ride to the Bluebird, do you?"

"Yeah, I guess I do. Thanks."

"My pleasure. Can't stay and give a listen as I've got to be somewhere by six and then back to my throne here by seven, but I'm tickled to get you there. Know what you're gonna sing?"

"I'm still trying to decide," I said. I'd been fairly certain I'd sing a song called "Spooky Moon" I wrote when I was nine, except I was beginning to feel queasy inside as I thought about it. Some part of me was afraid my subconscious would betray me and I'd end up with a soul-wrenching memory leaking out, the beginning of a crack in the dam holding back unmentionable times.

Roy nodded. "Yep. Sometimes it's hard to decide what you're gonna sing. But if I was you, I'd choose a song you could sing in your sleep. I remember back when I was still playing and singing, I always . . ." He trailed off and his body seemed to deflate a little.

"You okay, Mr. Durden?" I asked after a long, uncomfortable moment.

He nodded, ran a hand through his white cloud of hair. "Yeah, I'm okay. Forgive me. I promised myself I wasn't going to bring up my musical career."

"That's all right," I said, "I *want* to hear about it," and I did. For several reasons. Anything about a career in the music industry was fascinating to me, and also I felt that he *needed* to share this, and finally, not the least, I thought it would spare me from any more talk about my song choice for tomorrow night.

Roy shifted his position on the stool, stretched his fat, short arms overhead, situated his enormous belly, then rested his open palms on his thighs. "Twenty-one years ago this September," he began, and with that his shoulders slumped even lower, "I had me a gig in Arkansas with the Born Again Boys. Before I took off that morning, I kissed the kids; my boy, Carter—he was two—and Maygan—she wasn't but three months—then me and Angie knelt and prayed for traveling mercies, you know, on account of I would be on the road so long?"

I nodded.

"Well, the last words I said to Angie as I left out the door were, 'See you Sunday evening, Honey-bunch. Remember now, when we sing "God Gave Me You," it'll be you I'm thinking of.'"

There was a long moment of silence. Roy closed his eyes, and took in a deep breath. I sat there waiting, my heart knocking in my chest until he spoke again. "We didn't even get settled into the Holiday Inn good when news came that there'd been a car wreck back home. Thought I was literally gonna *die* when I learned all three of my people had died instantly."

I felt my throat tightening and my eyelids tingling. "I'm sorry," I said, so softly it was only a breath.

Roy turned to look over at me, his wet, pink lips trembling. "When you lose your people, Jennifer—the folks you love more than life itself—all kinds of things get shook up. You simply got to redefine yourself."

"Yeah, I bet."

"'Specially you got to redefine what it is you believe in," he said. "Gotta take a good, hard look at what you believe about us having this benevolent creator who cares about us down here on this planet."

I said nothing.

"I got to the point where I decided that if God's gonna do a person like he did me, he don't deserve to be worshiped, prayed to, served, whatever."

"Hmmm."

"I'll tell you when I'll listen to what he has to say."

"Okay."

"When he brings Angie and Carter and Maygan back."

I didn't know what to say. Finally I reached out to pat his wrist. "That must have been awful."

"Yep. Awful. I couldn't get out of bed, couldn't enjoy a single breath for over three solid months. I'd lived my whole life with this deep faith. You know, praying without ceasing and measuring everything by this heavenly yardstick. Tried my best to walk uprightly. Even singing and playing gospel music with the Born Again Boys was my way of trying to keep on the narrow path. I was living for God, and I thought he'd take care of me." Roy slapped his thigh. "What a load of crap!"

I was awed by such irreverence spoken aloud.

"Now, some folks *need* that kind of stuff, Jennifer," Roy continued. "They need themselves a crutch to lean on. And some just get indoctrinated as they grow up. Especially growing up down South, you know, in the Bible Belt. That was me. I was raised on 'The Lord loves you, and the Lord's got a plan for you.'" His gaze on mine was steady, intense. "In fact, Nashville's called the city of churches. There are more churches per capita here than in any other city. Southern Gospel and country music, they go together like a hand in a glove. You know?"

"Yeah," I breathed.

"But you know what?" Roy's voice was matter-of-fact. "I'm free now. I live life on my own terms. Way I wish I had from the very beginning." His blue eyes were intense.

"Really?"

"Really. I do what I want, when I want. I live without constantly thinking, 'Is this wrong? Shouldn't I be—?'"

A crowd of folks walked through the lobby, talking and laughing loud. Roy paused to take a swallow from his Dr Pepper. "I use to be, oh, what's that word I'm looking for? Repressed! I was repressed, or maybe oppressed is a better word. I didn't do a blasted thing without looking at it through this religious filter. I lived like there was this gigantic magnifying glass sticking out of the clouds, hovering right over me, and you know what? It cramped my style."

He smiled when he saw me looking so hard at him.

"God doesn't give a flying fig about us, Jennifer. If he did, why would he allow me to lose my family? Why doesn't he do anything about all the pain and evil in this world? Sometimes I even wonder if he doesn't get some sort of perverse pleasure out of watching us squirm down here."

I nodded, even though I was a little scared to think a thought like that. I'd been taught to believe in a being who, even if I had no warm fuzzy feelings toward or urge to pray to, was at least someone to be afraid of, to respect. But if what Roy was saying was true, it certainly would be freeing. I looked away, realizing that a moment like this was where my mother would operate on blind faith. She'd say something like, "Oh, the Lord has a purpose in it all. We'll see his purpose by and by." That was the moment I decided to hang my hat on the freedom of Roy's philosophy. I would be free and live life on my own terms. I felt like a baby bird cracking out of her shell, all wide-eyed and shaky, stretching her wings after tight confinement, right before the mother bird pushes her out to fall a ways before she soars up high, through lavender skies and golden afternoons.

I laughed then, just as the front doors opened and a skinny guy in a white apron zipped in holding two Styrofoam take-out boxes. Roy flipped up the lid on the one set before him. "My, my!" he said, looking up to beam at our server. "You outdid yourself again, Colin. This looks absolutely dee-licious!" He handed him two twenty dollar bills, waving a hand and saying, "Keep the change," as Colin bowed slightly and hustled back outside.

"Mmmm, this is to die for," Roy's voice cracked with emotion as he bit into his burger. I looked over at him as I took a bite, expecting to see tears streaming down his cheeks. But he was smiling around his mouthful, and so was I. I hadn't had a real, complete meal in more than a week.

Roy Durden was a serious eater. I watched his eyes literally roll back in his head as he scarfed down the burger, the fries, and the coleslaw. He slurped the last of his tea noisily, released a satisfied sigh, sat back, and focused on me. "Tell me about your music," he asked after a soft belch.

I literally jumped. I couldn't swallow my bite of burger until I told myself Roy had not asked about my childhood, nor my family. Just my music. "Well," I choked out after I'd finally swallowed, "music comes as naturally to me as breathing. Even when I was little I could sing other artists' songs after hearing them a couple of times. I started composing songs when I was around six. I'd be hanging out the wash, feeding the chickens, riding my bike, sitting in church, walking down the hallway at school, and it was like they just came through me, you know?"

He nodded.

"I'd be in the middle of something and I'd literally think up a bridge, or a hook, or a prechorus, and I'd have to stop to scribble it down. I practiced singing constantly."

"A natural," he mused. "What I really want to hear about is your first time."

"What?" My voice came out shrill because I thought for a split-second Roy was referring to sexual intercourse and I'd been going with my gut instinct that he wasn't the lecherous type.

"You know," he answered, chuckling, "the first time you sang for an audience. A real audience that wasn't family or friends."

Too much baggage, I thought, after mentally tiptoeing over a scene as carefully and quickly as if it were fiery coals. Finally, I squeezed my hands into fists and launched in. "Um, okay . . . I was six, and my mother and I were at church one night during revival week in the summer. There were lots of visitors there—folks who'd come to hear this new young preacher—and the woman who was supposed to sing a solo didn't show up."

"Really?" Roy encouraged. "Well, that's certainly interesting. She didn't show up. Did you get up there and fill in for her?"

"Um, yeah. . . the preacher asked if anyone in the congregation 'had a pretty voice they was willing to share,' because he'd been counting on Ms. Turlette to sing 'Love Lifted Me' to set the tone for his sermon. Normally I was hiding in my mother's skirts, but I shocked myself when I hopped up from the pew, ran to the microphone, and started belting out Dolly Parton's 'The Golden Streets of Glory.'"

The next part seemed a strange thing to share with Mr. Durden, but for some reason, I did. "I actually felt like Dolly was right there beside me that night, like her hand was on my shoulder and she was smiling at me while I sang.

"I mean, it amazes me even now how calm and confident I was with that sea of eyeballs zoomed in on me. Normally I was scared of my own shadow. But it was like I'd found my place in life, and I started strutting up and down in a little puddle of light from overhead, basking in those beaming smiles and nodding heads, singing pitch perfect. I could've stayed up there forever. The applause, the whistles, in *church*, made it feel like this out-of-body experience.

"In fact, that night was when the stage began her siren song for me. After that, I could never turn down a microphone, and anytime I'd sing—at church, at school, at local festivals and fairs—afterward people would flock up to me saying, 'That was incredible, Jennifer!' and 'You're truly amazing!' with these breathless voices, and I thought, *Okay, here's something I was born to do. I may get nervous in crowds, be tongue-tied in social situations, I may not be the brightest at math, but I can sing songs that make people smile.*"

"Six years old," Roy mused, "that's mighty young. How old are you now if you don't mind my asking?"

"Twenty-two," I answered.

"Sixteen years of experience, hmm?" The twinkle in Roy's eye let me know I was safe with him. "Bet you got a heck of a lot of songs, don't you, missy?"

I nodded. "After that night in church I wrote a song called 'Dolly, Hold My Hand,' and I kept it in a shoebox with other songs I'd write. This may sound weird, Roy, but I'd curl up in my bed at night, mash my face into the pillow, and practice saying stuff like, 'Ladies and gentleman, let's welcome Jennifer Anne Clodfelter to our stage tonight!'"

"That's not weird," he said. "That's beautiful."

After I finished my meal and Roy'd cleaned up the trash, he looked intently at me. "Sing for me, would you? Can you sing on a full stomach?"

I looked at his greasy lips curved into a smile. "What do you want me to sing?"

"Sing your favorite. You and Dolly."

I got to my feet, closed my eyes, and sang the first two verses and the chorus of "Spooky Moon."

When I finished, Roy hopped off his stool, stood not three feet away, staring at me for the longest time, then began clapping and nodding so hard his forelock came loose from the rest of his hair. I saw tears shimmering in those blue eyes. "You've got real, honest-to-goodness natural-born talent, Jennifer," he said, "and I'm gonna tell you something you can take to the bank. You're gonna do well here! Trust me. I've been in this town for a long, long time, and some things I know."

Warmth flooded my body. "Thank you."

"I'm the one should be saying thanks. That was what I call a holy experience." Roy lowered his voice to an excited whisper. "Care for some dessert?"

"Maybe," I whispered back.

"Don't let anybody around here hear me, but The Hermitage Hotel makes a milk chocolate crème brûlée I'd kill for. It's this perfect custard, topped with caramelized sugar and fresh strawberries . . ."

Roy's delight was so disarming, it was tempting to say yes, but something in me needed to give back. "Let me treat. Would you like half a package of Hostess Zingers out of the vending machine? They're my favorite."

"Certainly," Roy said, a twinkle in those blue eyes. "I love Zingers."

At last Monday dawned. I made coffee in my room, gulped it, splashed water on my face and went downstairs for breakfast. Sitting in the carpeted dining area with a cup of milk, a boiled egg, and two sausage patties, I looked at the stage across from the bar. I rested my elbows on the table, sunk my chin in my hands, willing the hours, the minutes to pass speedily.

Time passed the way it always did, and at five o-clock sharp I walked out to wait on the curb, guitar case in hand. Right on the dot this ancient white Cadillac pulled to a stop. It seemed just the sort of car Roy Durden would drive, and I didn't even check to see if it was him behind the wheel before opening the back door to slide the Washburn in, then climbing into the passenger seat.

"Afternoon, Madam. Where to?" Roy asked in a fake British voice, his nostrils widened on purpose.

I had to smile. "The Bluebird Cafe," I commanded in a snobbish voice. Trying to find a spot on the floorboard that wasn't littered with fast-food cartons and soda cans was almost impossible, but I nudged a Hardee's cup and a Dunkin' Donuts bag over and settled my feet. From the corner of my eye I could see the white swoop of Roy's pompadour, his big pink-knuckled fingers on the steering wheel, his enormous belly perched on his thighs.

"You ready?" Roy asked as we paused at the first stoplight.

"Mm-hm."

"Well, I've told you once, and I'll tell you again, I'm not going to fret about you one little bit, missy. You're going to do fine."

I nodded and we rode along in a comfortable silence, me thinking how great it was to have a friend who knew his way around Nashville. Roy seemed happy too. He fiddled with a radar detector on the dash, rustled around in a bag of potato chips on the seat between us, and slurped from a huge

Styrofoam cup between his legs. "Alrighty. Here we are," he said at last, nodding at a nondescript shopping center.

Heart thumping fast, I turned to look at a strip of businesses, and at last spied The Bluebird Café, next to a place called Helen's Children's Shop.

"Now wait just a minute here," Roy said when he'd pulled into the parking lot, idling not more than twenty feet from the Bluebird's door. He put a beefy hand on my arm and I didn't even flinch. "You knock 'em dead, okay, Jennifer?"

"I will, Roy," I said. "And thank you." He could not have known all that my 'Thank you' encompassed.

⎯⎯⎯⎯⎯ ❧ ⎯⎯⎯⎯⎯

There was no cover charge at The Bluebird Café, and I walked right in, surprised at how tiny the place was! I counted twenty small tables set so close together I wondered how waitresses could move between them. To the left was a bar beneath a Jack Daniels guitar-shaped clock, to the right a stage with spotlights. Christmas lights and a row of framed photos circling the walls made it feel cheerful.

It was 5:20 p.m., and there were a good number of folks there. Roy told me you signed up at 5:30 for a chance to perform, and then the Bluebird picked about twenty-four people per night. I had no doubt I'd be selected, and I wasn't surprised when a woman touched my arm. "You're here for open mic?"

"Yes ma'am. I'm Jennifer Anne Clodfelter."

"Barbara," she said. "Let's go ahead and put your name in the hat."

"Great." My fingers were crossed behind my back. I didn't want to go first, but I also didn't want to be last.

"Lineup's announced and show starts at six. If you're picked, you're allowed two original songs. We don't provide

58

an accompanist, and no tracks are permitted, but we do have a Kawai keyboard you're welcome to use."

"Thanks. But it's just me and my Washburn, and I'm only going to do one song."

Despite nothing since breakfast, I wasn't hungry, so I leaned against the wall, watching the clock over the bar, which ticked along annoyingly slowly. A little before six Barbara climbed onstage. "Welcome to open mic night here at the Bluebird, one of the world's preeminent listening rooms. Remember our policy." She held an index finger to her pursed lips and hissed out, "Shhhhhhh! Please keep your background conversation to a minimum. Our 'Shhhh' policy is designed to support a listening environment where the audience can concentrate on the song. Speaking of that, we've got a wonderful lineup for you tonight—"

Her voice faded to distant background noise as soon as I heard I got the number-four slot. I ran over the words to "Spooky Moon," vaguely aware of the first performer: a huge, hulking bear of a man in tight faded jeans and a sleeveless flannel shirt and with a long Charlie Daniels beard. He surprised me with a high-tenor voice accompanied by a saucy guitar line. He whined and wailed and twanged his way through a song called "Gimme Back My Catfish." There was a smattering of polite applause and a few soft whistles. Then up came a plump, peroxided blonde with a very low-cut spangled top that got some subdued catcalls before she even opened her mouth.

She introduced her song called "Mayhem Mama." She wiggled and jiggled around up there a while, strumming and singing way off-pitch on the very first line, but sounded okay in a hillbilly way once she got going. Seemed the audience was more focused on her chest than her music, however, and I was glad for my modest blouse with only the top snap left undone.

Next came a man in a white suit who reminded me of Colonel Sanders. He sang a song called "Walking the Railroad Blues" with a gravelly Johnny Cash sound. He got a good reception from the crowd.

When it was my turn, I climbed up onstage wrapped in that magical preperformance euphoria I always got. I leaned in to kiss the microphone, feeling the little electric buzz on my lips that I love. I adjusted the Washburn and moved my brain into that small-town dialect I'd sure heard enough of and that audiences loved, smiling at each face I could see.

"Good evenin'. My name's Jennifer Anne Clodfelter, and I'm gonna sing a song I wrote called 'Spooky Moon.' I wrote the chorus of this song one summer night when I was eight years old as I lay on my pallet out on the screen porch, which incidentally was my bedroom. I was watching the moon from underneath a little burrow I made out of my covers. Mainly, I wrote the chorus to calm myself down. You know, as a sort of good-luck charm, because my mother was constantly warning me not to sin, not to walk down that wide, easy road that leads to hell, and many a evening she'd grab my hand and look up at the sky and say this little poem that went, 'I see the moon, the moon sees me, please old moon, don't tell on me.' And of course, being a kid, the first thing I thought of when I did somethin' bad was that the moon was gonna tell on me." I paused as laughter rippled through the crowd.

"Well," I continued, "now I know the moon ain't gonna tell on me." I paused again, waited for the knowing smiles, the encouraging nods among the hundred or so people in the audience. "And so I wrote the rest of this song around that comforting chorus. A chorus I credit for getting me through many a long, scary night."

My guitar pick was like a part of my hand that found the right strings instinctively. My voice soared on the first note as I

strummed a mournful A minor on account of the song started
out sweet and melancholy:

> When I was a little, wide-eyed gal
> I hated for darkness to fall
> I hid in the covers and hugged myself
> Squinched up in a tight little ball
>
> Singin' 'Oh, spooky moon, you taken the
>   sunshine and you hid her away.
> But I guess it's your turn to shine.
> I know I done wrong, but if you'll keep your
>   mouth shut,
> I promise to be better next time.'

The melody moved into something more lively and playful,
and I switched to a D minor, and then after a few stanzas right
back to the tearful part, playing around with a sad bluesy line
about night falling way too quickly when you're little.

Everything felt smooth and natural, and when I reached
the chorus for the third time, I really poured my heart into the
lyrics, going back to the screen porch in Blue Ridge, Georgia,
where I did have lots and lots of fears, but not particularly
about the moon. I could sense that the crowd was totally with
me as I heard my own clear, high notes boomeranging off the
ceiling.

As I moved along to the final verse, I could see the people's
faces changing. I could feel every single person in that room
straining to hear what the adult me had discovered about
that scary moon, wanting me to overcome my terror. I saw
tears glistening in a few of the eyes on the front row when
I got to the part about how children believe whatever adults
say to them and how it affects them, for good or for bad. I
knew I was doing it right because I felt that surge of joy, a

velvety-petaled rose of knowing that bloomed inside me whenever I sang something the listeners connected to so strongly, when I literally felt myself merging with a song. Those final twanging notes rose and dipped and threaded themselves in and through the crowd, alive, by some miracle, lingering like a dream.

I finished, and there was a stunned silence of maybe three seconds, which felt like the calm before the storm, and then a thunderous burst of applause and boot stomps and whistles and "Yeah! Way to sing!" I knew without a doubt it was louder and longer and more heartfelt than the previous three performers put together. I bowed humbly from the waist, and said, "Thank you very much," just like Elvis, and then there was another sweet round of applause as people got up out of their seats and cheered with fists in the air.

Waves of love from the crowd rolled and crashed over me as I stepped off the stage, threading through the tables toward the back wall. I wasn't surprised by the lineup of hands patting my shoulder, my arm, touching my hair, or the voices saying more nice things to me. I wasn't surprised that I wanted to stop time and just revel in that moment a spell—like I always did after I sang. When the euphoria did pass, as the next performer was talking into the mike, I had such a letdown I felt trembly. But I kept a smile plastered on my face as I watched the skinny young girl in a Minnie Pearl getup warble a song about pickled okra, which was really funny and quite good. Before she finished, a man appeared at my elbow, tapping my forearm insistently, as though I should have been ready to acknowledge him. When my eyes met his, a feeling of awe washed through me, and I knew: *This man's a big shot, somebody I ought to know.* I held my breath, waiting for him to speak. "Mike Flint," he said, nodding without smiling, only he didn't look mean or grumpy as he held out a hand. I put mine in his and it was huge, warm and so solid.

"Jennifer Anne Clodfelter."

"I know," he said, "wonderful name, but I'm thinking we oughtta shorten it to Jenny Cloud." His voice was deep and very Southern, with a drawl that was soothing like a river can be.

I could only nod, staring at his face, which was attractive in a rugged way: a Roman nose and hazel eyes that had lots of smile crinkles, topped by intentionally disheveled sandy-colored hair in a Keith Urban style. He was tall, lanky, in his mid-forties I guessed, wearing khakis and a rumpled Oxford. For some reason I glanced down at his feet, and from what I knew from my forays into shops downtown, he wore very expensive cowboy boots.

"Looks like you created quite a stir," Mike Flint said, drawing my eyes to his. "How long you been singing?"

"I was born singing."

He didn't laugh. "It shows. You've got a gorgeous voice, and you were born to be onstage. What you did up there was amazing. You have the gift of truly connecting with an audience. They were captivated, and that's rare."

"Thank you, sir," I said, swallowing my pleasure, feeling it spread like soda bubbles through my body.

"You've got spunk too. I can tell you're a hard worker."

I nodded and didn't add the word *desperate*.

"Ever think about a career in the country music industry?"

"Maybe."

He didn't bother to ask if I wanted to leave, he just said, "We can talk better out in my truck," and started guiding me by the elbow toward the door. I had to twirl around to grab my shoulder bag and the Washburn.

My heedless trust that night amazed me later. The way I hung on and believed Mike's every word, never doubted his motives as I climbed into the cab of a huge red truck that smelled like chewing tobacco and cologne. Heart beating like crazy, I crossed my legs, clasped my hands in my lap, and waited as he sat quietly for a while.

"I don't think you know what you possess," he said finally.

Responding to this was tricky because I did know. I'd heard it so much I believed it. But if I answered yes, it made me sound like I thought I was really something, and I knew there were a lot of talented singers out there. I also knew humility was a very attractive character trait. "I've been told I've got a gift," I said.

Mike nodded. "You're phenomenal. Like I said, you had that audience eating out of your hand. I never saw anybody get a crowd into a song like that. And here's the amazing thing—you did it with *no* backup singers. Do you know how incredible that is?"

"Really?" More humility.

Mike nodded, leaned back and stared up at the ceiling. "You got any more original songs?"

I pulled my song notebook out of my bag and handed it to him. He turned the pages, leafing through them with his mouth open for at least ten solid minutes without a word. When he got to the end, he thumbed back through it and paused on the page with "Smoke Over the Hills" and began singing with his pointer finger tracing the lines. His pitch was way off, but he had the melody. He tapped his boot toe as he did the same thing with "River Time" and "Sitting and Rocking Is Good for Your Soul."

"There's enough here to make an album," he said after a loud breath, cradling my open notebook to his chest.

"Really?" I answered in my best amazed voice.

He rubbed his chin before he continued. "Listen, I've been retired from Rockin' Rooster Records for six months, but I've also been kicking around this idea that I might launch a new label. If I did, I wouldn't mind recording you if you can come up with another original tearjerker like 'Spooky Moon.' Something that tickles my fancy."

"Pardon?"

"I said, I'd like to record you if you can come up with another tune that works the audience the way the one you sang in there tonight did."

"You don't like any of these?" I retreated to the nervous gesture of twirling my hair around my pointer finger.

"They're good. *Real* good. But they all seem to be from a young girl's viewpoint. I want you to write a song from an older female's perspective, one that pulls the heartstrings. Maybe a woman in her twenties at least, chasing love or something like that? Romantic love gone bad? Wounds of the heart and all."

I swallowed hard, wondered if it mattered that I'd never had a boyfriend, much less a love gone bad. My warm fuzzy feeling was fast fading. Speaking of getting told on by the moon, I hoped that old lunar ball wasn't listening as I said, "Um, yeah, sure. Got lots of personal experience dealing with that kind of thing. With romantic love and all."

"Well, remember, what you want to do is tell a story here. Lyrics that convey a certain emotional arc, you know. Show some tension, some conflict, the way you did with 'Spooky Moon' but from an older, brokenhearted female's perspective."

"I know exactly what you mean," I said.

"Great. Just remember, give me some fresh imagery, some poignant stuff." Mike Flint stretched his left arm so his cuff rode up and he could see his wristwatch. "Okay now. You go home and write it and get in touch with me and maybe I'll take you on as a client." He rustled around in some papers on the dash, found a business card, and handed it to me.

I smiled as I slid it in my pocket. I felt like I'd won the lottery. I couldn't wait to get back to the Best Western and tell Roy and get going on my new song. I reached for my guitar and opened the truck's door.

"Hold on." Mike's voice stopped me. "You a member of NSAI?"

I shook my head.

"I'll cover your membership," he said. "We've got to protect our rights, you know? Also, before we plow on, I have to tell you it's my policy never to sign an artist unless I'm her manager, her agent, and the owner of her recording label. Kind of like a package deal. Understand?"

I didn't care if I understood or not. My big break was breathing down my neck. "Fine by me," I said. While he was in such a generous mood, I asked if he'd mind driving me back to the Best Western.

"My pleasure," he said, shifting the truck into reverse. "I can assure you you'll be glad to have a veteran like me taking care of you. Entertaining the crowd for one song at the Bluebird is one thing, but becoming what I think you have the potential to be is quite another. I don't think many folks know how hard it is to get to the top and stay there.

"It's a lot of work to reach the point I think you're capable of, Jenny, and even more difficult to stay there. The Nashville scene can be confusing, cutthroat, and now you've got someone with experience to guide you and help you build your career."

It felt odd to be called Jenny, but waves of pure delight rolled up and down me when he said that word *career*, and I managed to say, "Great."

My heart was beating like a girl waiting for her first kiss as Mike pulled beneath the awning leading to the Best Western's front door. I felt far, far away from life in Blue Ridge, Georgia, as I told myself: *This is the moment you've been waiting for. You made it! Your dreams have become reality.* I didn't yet know that Mike Flint was also handing me a shovel, and that very soon, like it says in that Randy Travis song, I'd start digging up bones.

4

Mike said he'd pay my hotel bill until I got on my feet. He wanted to be sure I concentrated on my music, and not on existing, and he gave me money for food as well. At the outset I was thrilled thinking of this arrangement: staying in my cozy room, listening to music, writing songs.

That very first night, lying in bed after I'd shared my good fortune with Roy, I closed my eyes and began brainstorming. But all I could think of was what Mike had said about a song on love gone bad, wounds of the heart and all, and my non-existent past in the romance department. The life I'd lived to that point held absolutely no inspiration. Sure, I'd had the schoolgirl's crush or two from sixth grade to my sophomore year of high school, but nothing had come of these, and since then I'd kept my heart sealed tight for reasons even I didn't want to see.

I tossed and turned. It was one thing to write songs about things you knew—honest experiences that birthed words and feelings. I'd never felt so absolutely empty. As someone gifted with writing songs, it had always come without a lot of effort. While I was picking apples or doing laundry or taking a bath or talking with someone, part of my mind was off on its own adventure, braiding melodies and words together. Meanings overlapped from what was going on in real time, to that song always half-exposed in my subconscious. Lyrics, a new melody, could strike at any time.

It was a crazy compulsion when I thought about it, my music constant as a mountain stream. That was why this lack of ideas was so frustrating. I wondered what I ought to do. I had no female friends, and I didn't dare mention a sensitive subject like romantic love to Roy. For three days I dragged myself around, haunted by that elusive song, by the knowledge that this was my chance, my shot at making it in Nashville.

"You okay?" Roy asked me as we shared a pepperoni pizza at the front desk.

I sighed. "Yeah. It's just that . . . I'm having trouble coming up with a song I think is good enough."

"All your songs are good."

"Thanks. But Mike wants one about a specific subject."

" 'Bout what?" Roy tilted his head back to take a humongous bite of pizza, chewing as he looked hard at me with those intense blue eyes beneath the white pompadour.

"Um, he wants a tear-in-your-ear kind of ballad," I replied, picturing Mike's straight, white teeth in the truck's dome light as he held the door open for me. "A guitar-drenched, slice-of-life snapshot. A song carved from my own experience."

Roy nodded. "Okay."

"About love," I added after a bit and felt a twinge of sadness for Roy and his loss. "Love gone bad—from a female's perspective," I amended quickly. "A girl in her twenties at least. He said to write lyrics that 'convey a certain emotional arc.' He wants tension and conflict."

"Smart man," Roy said around a mouthful.

"But I don't . . . " my voice trailed off. I reached down for my napkin to blot my lips. "I'm just not feeling it. It's like I've got writer's block or something." I heard myself using a whining tone I didn't like. "I've never had trouble writing a song before."

"Aw, come on," Roy said, lifting another floppy, greasy piece of pizza from the box. "This ought to be easy as pie."

"Really?"

"Sure," he said, nodding and chewing, "women love songs about men who done them wrong getting their comeuppance."

"How do you mean?"

"Well, in my experience, it's a powerful emotion when a woman gives her heart to a man and he stomps it flat, so to speak. You know, she's a virtuous woman, has eyes only for him, and he does her wrong by two-timing her with her best friend? Or by hooking up with some floozy in a bar?" Roy paused to tug another slice of pizza loose from the box. It was truly amazing how much food that man could throw down.

"Women eat that kind of thing up," he said, licking sauce from his fingers. "You need to put some vengeance in there too. Have the man meet with some misfortune. A barfly shoots him, or he gets hit by a train, or he crawls back to his woman, begging her forgiveness and she shuts the door in his face. That way it would, you know, empower the women."

I took a sip of my Coke, sat back in my chair chewing a bite of pizza crust, and pondered. *Surely it couldn't be that simple, could it? Some formula, some collective fantasy about revenge that got women enthused? Some 'Ha ha, you deserved it' kind of mentality?* All of a sudden, I felt a rush of knowing. My heart sped up as I realized the brilliance of what Roy had said. In my mind's eye, I could see my song forming. It would feel wonderful to let a virtuous, wounded heroine have her vengeance.

⸺⸺

At 2:23 that morning I sat cross-legged in a nest of covers on my bed, nibbling a Chick-O-Stick Roy gave me, my notebook open in front of me. It was not the slam-dunk I'd assumed. I kept scratching out lines that fell flat and lifeless words that led absolutely nowhere. Words like *He done me wrong, and my heart is breakin'*, and *I gave him my love, it was his for the takin', but he*—I had no earthly idea how to write about the heart of a woman done wrong, I felt no emotional connections to my wounded heroines. Everything sounded phony. I threw the pen, slammed my notebook shut and switched off the lamp. Sighing and flipping over onto my stomach, I forced my eyes closed. After a spell I began to drop off into that no man's land, that space between consciousness and sleep where mental blocks crumble. And that is when it came to me.

First, I heard the unmistakable roar of the V-8 engine in my father's Chevelle as it approached the cabin, felt my heart beating in my ears as I sat up on my pallet and peeked out the screen at the hazy gray of almost daybreak, the bliss of sleep evaporated. I remembered the sound of my mother's expectant feet running from their bedroom at one end of the house, through the kitchen, the words just flying out of her mouth, "Thank God, thank God, he's home; he's finally home," and then the front door opening and my mother saying, "Oh, no. No, you don't, Omer. You're not bringing another tra—" and him cutting her off saying, "Out of my way, woman!" real loud, laughing, drunk. I snuck to the door to look. My father had a strange woman hanging from his arm. She was glassy-eyed, a loose smile on too-red lips, her blouse hanging off one shoulder so low you could see her bosoms. Mother closed her eyes, said, "Lord, help me," then looked at my father and said, "Omer, you're nothing but an old tomcat, prowling around from one honky-tonk to the next, picking up trash and bringing it home." Then my father threw back his head, laughed, and said, "I'm a honky-tonk tomcat."

I lay motionless for several minutes, that final frame frozen in my head and sleep as elusive as snow in summertime. Then I snaked a trembling hand out of the covers to turn on the bedside lamp. Blinking, I sat up, reached for my notebook and scribbled down the title, two verses, the chorus, and some thoughts about a bridge:

HONKY-TONK TOMCAT

Mama begged Daddy to stay, with tears in her
  eyes,
He said, "Got work to do," but she knew it was
  lies,
'Cause he's a honky-tonk tomcat, prowlin'
  around.
Looking for women and paintin' the town.

She oughtta leave him, give him back his name,
Take back her heart and escape all the pain.
But she's a believer in vows, in miracles, and
  Grace,
So she just closes her eyes—and she prays.

He went cruisin' the bars, hunting ruffles and
  skirts,
Home drunk at daybreak, humming "Love
  hurts."
'Cause he's a honky-tonk tomcat, who follows
  the trail,
Of whiskey and perfume, a loud-calling smell.

She oughta leave him, give him back his name,
Take back her heart and escape all the pain.
But she's a believer in vows, in miracles, and
  Grace,

> She just closes her eyes—closes her eyes, and
> she prays.

> Possible Bridge: But she closes her eyes. She
> just closes her eyes.

I looked down at what I'd written, confused, like it had come from someone else's hand. But there were pink impressions on my fingers from holding that cheap Bic pen, and I knew I had the concept of a song with emotional impact, a compelling story. "Well, okay," I said in a flat, exhausted tone, "time to get some sleep."

❧

I woke at one in the afternoon, made coffee, showered, dressed, and rode the elevator down to buy Andy Capp's Hot Fries and a Coke out of the vending machines. There was something to be said for finally getting sleep. I didn't feel so frayed, like I was coming apart at the seams, and I decided to allow myself to look at the lyrics scribbled in my notebook.

Heart racing, I read through "Honky-Tonk Tomcat," wondering if I could summon up enough of a dispassionate disconnection to finish it. I honestly had no idea until I sat down at the desk in my room and crafted the remainder with a songwriter's discipline. I took Roy's advice and wrote a couple verses wherein I let my good-hearted heroine eventually grow deathly ill. The man realized what he had, repented of his tomcatting, but by then it was too late. She died—*she closes her eyes for the last time*. In the final verse, he's the one who's closing his eyes. Remorse and grief make him drink himself to death. The melody for my new song came effortlessly as I sat on the bed, strumming my Washburn.

I suppose if I had a moment of trepidation, of second-guessing the direction I was heading in my musical career, it was right then, as I paced in my room at the Best Western. Before I called Mike. I remember asking myself, *Is it worth looking back at whence you came in order to write "Honky-Tonk Tomcat"?* and also *Just how bad do you want this country-music-diva thing, Jennifer?* and then quickly reassuring myself that this song was the first and the last of that type. I firmly believed that looking back for inspiration to write "Honky-Tonk Tomcat" was a necessary evil to get my foot in the door of the music scene in Nashville, and I made a vow to myself that it was the absolute *last* time I'd allow any of my past to influence my music. There were things much worse back there, and after this, I'd move only in a forward direction.

It's funny, but as I ponder that day back then, I see clearly it was the crossroads for me, and I could have made the choice to go a very different direction from what I did in my journey toward fame. Of course, I didn't know then that "Honky-Tonk Tomcat" would set the course, the tone of my career as a wounded star. I couldn't see the future of choice A or choice B. None of us can. All I knew for sure was that I had exactly what Mike Flint wanted.

━━━ ❧ ━━━

One morning, weeks later, Mike found me standing in the closet of my room at the Best Western, wrapped up like a mummy in a terrycloth bathrobe still on its hanger, crying and shaking, and holding the sheet music to "Honky-Tonk Tomcat."

"What's wrong, babe?" Mike asked, his eyes bulging, his Herrera for Men cologne filling the closet. "The guy from the magazine is down in the lobby. You've got to get dressed. Fix your hair and stuff. Believe they want some photos too. Come on now, get yourself ready. Come on."

I could only shake my head. Anxious thoughts lay quivering like popcorn kernels in hot oil. I couldn't imagine spilling the dark, confusing stories of back home that inspired "Honky-Tonk Tomcat."

"For cryin' out loud, Jenny!" Mike urged, pulling my elbow to drag me out in front of the full-length mirror on the back of the bathroom door. "You're acting like a five-year-old. You ought to be thrilled. Your very first song is a runaway hit. Do you know how rare this is?"

I caught our reflection, Mike in his casually elegant Western-cut shirt and dark blue jeans, the big silver belt buckle, and his sandy-colored mop of hair—like a model in *Country Gentleman* magazine. Then beside him I saw this pathetic girl with long black tangled hair and a swollen face, who looked like she'd crawled out of a dumpster.

"Listen," Mike said, toning his voice down a notch. "You owe it to your fans. All those wonderful folks plunking down their hard-earned money for your music."

I knew what he was doing and I tried to resist the guilt, but couldn't help thinking of all those people paying for *my* song, listening, and maybe singing along to it. Suddenly, not knowing quite whether to laugh or cry, I pulled away from Mike and said, "Okay," turning on the faucet and splashing cold water on my face, again and again so that it shocked me into a numb state.

***

"You have a stunning voice. People are saying you remind them of Patsy Cline mixed with Tammy Wynette."

"Thank you," I said, sitting in the lobby and looking at the overweight, eager-faced writer from *Country Music Weekly*.

"In fact, I really *feel* that song. Especially the chorus." He closed his eyes and held an invisible microphone beneath his mouth and started crooning: *He's a honky-tonk tomcat who follows the scent of whiskey and perfume and women—*"

It felt like somebody stabbing me in the chest, so I bit my lip hard and tuned him out until he finished singing.

He scribbled something onto his legal pad. "Yep, that is some powerful stuff. A compelling story coupled with a memorable melody. Why don't you start with telling me where this particular song came from? The inspiration for your debut masterpiece."

They say flattery will get you anywhere, but after my meltdown in the closet, I wouldn't dare open up about where this song actually came from to anybody. I still could hardly believe I'd written what I did, though some part of me acknowledged that without the heinous memories there wouldn't be my very first hit song, an immediate smash at radio. "It was inspired by my best friend."

"Really. Tell me about it."

The rest of the lie came easily. "Well, my very best friend from childhood, from kindergarten on, had this father who used to run around on her mother. Right in her mother's face, as a matter of fact. My friend—her name was Lisa—didn't understand it. She hated her father coming home loaded, with all these various barflies. Sometimes Lisa didn't even hear him coming in, and she'd wake up and head to the kitchen in her nightgown, ready for some breakfast, you know? And she'd find her father and some trashy tramp on the sofa, tangled up together, half-dressed. You can imagine how upsetting that was to a little kid, can't you?"

"Oh, yes," he said, his full lips in an O. Then after a moment, "He sounds like a real scalawag."

"Yep," I said, feeling a little jab of fury. "Bad, bad man. I seem to remember he read a lot of X-rated magazines, and he had a really filthy mind. He would be so foul-mouthed, even when Lisa was around! He'd leer at other women right in front of his wife and his daughter. She didn't know what to think. Or do." I willed away the tears.

He shook his head.

A moment, and then the rest poured out. "But you know what's funny? Lisa's mother never would confront her father! Well, beyond her initial madness and a few words. She cried a lot of tears, I mean, that's what Lisa told me anyway, and I bet they were awful to listen to. But the next day, Lisa's mother would just say stuff like, 'Well, it's not his fault. It's that old Demon Alcohol, and I'm praying, and I just have to have faith that he'll see the light and change,' and . . . " Here was where my made-up storyline petered out.

"My, my!" The interviewer was scribbling stuff down furiously, shaking his head. "That is tragic. Really tragic." He looked up at me. "And then Lisa lost her mother. But at least her father did end up seeing the light, so to speak, realizing what he'd had."

I looked at him blankly, and he chuckled and added, "At least that's what the song says."

"Oh, yeah. Right, right. Well, actually, Lisa didn't know she lost her mother, because she ended up taking her own life before that part of the song happened." I felt the storyteller in me surging up. "As a matter of fact, I wrote this song in her memory. It's for Lisa, and every time I sing it, I think of Lisa, and I say a little prayer for her. God rest her soul."

He shook his head quickly, eyes shut, as if the "rest of the story" was almost more than he could bear. "I'll tell you something," he said at last, opening eyes shiny with unspilled tears. "You're a mighty fine person, Jenny Cloud. A person with a good Christian heart, and I can see why 'Honky-Tonk Tomcat' is taking the country music world by storm. You ought to be proud of yourself."

Back in my room I turned off the telephone's ringer, undressed, and shakily climbed into bed, curling into the fetal position with the covers over my head. I fell asleep almost instantly, a beautiful, numb escape from the continual waves of anxiety and self-loathing I'd been battling. Day turned into dusk, and still I slept, deeply and safely removed from reality, until finally my rumbling stomach betrayed me. I shrugged the covers off to blink at the red numbers of a digital clock. 8:17 p.m.

That meant Roy was at his post. Despite the butterflies still fluttering in my stomach, I hurriedly put on my blue jeans and a blouse, pulled my hair back into a messy ponytail and went downstairs in my bare feet. When I got to the front desk, I was glad to see Roy hadn't ordered supper yet. His collection of menus was spread out on the counter, and he looked up from them and smiled big. He was wearing his tan seersucker suit, which didn't bring out his eyes quite the way the blue one did, but he also wore a Panama hat atop his white swoop of hair, which made him seem somewhat like an old-time movie star. "Well, well," he said, pulling my usual chair from the wall to face his stool, then bowing ever so slightly, "if it isn't our own resident star. How you doin' this lovely evening, Miss Jennifer? You hungry?"

"I'm starved," I said, surprised to hear my own, normal voice.

"How you feel about Eye-talian tonight," he said in such a twangy voice I had to smile.

"Good."

"Alrighty. I don't believe we've had supper from Sole Mio yet, have we?"

"No."

78

"Sole Mio has handmade pasta and handmade sauces to *die* for. It's where the locals go to find the finest Italian cuisine in Nashville. I believe I'll order us two entrees of . . ." he squinted down at the menu in his hands, "Scaloppine di Vitello! That sound all right?"

"That sounds great," I said, sinking down into my chair. "Thank you, Roy."

"My pleasure. Now, I keep forgetting you're old enough to drink, and Sole Mio's got both Italian and Californian wines that complement their entrees like you wouldn't believe. What's your pleasure?" He raised his eyebrows.

I cleared my throat and said, "No thanks. I don't drink," bracing myself for the inevitable piercing question. But Roy just nodded, said with perfect sincerity, "Fine, because I do believe, now that I think about it, I'm more in the mood for some good old Southern sweet tea with lemon."

His florid face looked so happy as he ordered our food I had to laugh, and as I did I noticed this certain lightening inside of me, a little bitty internal sunrise in the dark recesses of my troubled soul.

"Time to eat!" Roy said a good fifteen minutes later, leaning back to make room for Sole Mio's deliveryman to place a tray on the counter—a Styrofoam basket of hot bread and butter in a small tub, two salads, also in Styrofoam, and two steaming platters of Scaloppine. When the lids were lifted, the scent of warm cheese mingled with rosemary, basil, garlic, and oregano.

"I hear 'Honky-Tonk Tomcat' is breaking all kinds of records," Roy said in a bit, busy with knife and fork.

"Yeah. That's what Mike says."

He paused and looked up at me with a huge smile stretched across his face. I wondered what he'd say if he knew that not only did I not have a best friend named Lisa but also that the story, besides the woman dying and the man repenting, was from my life. I wondered if Roy would understand that sometimes a person cannot tell the truth, even to her actual best friend, which he was now.

Roy blew on his scaloppine, then took a bite, closing his eyes in rapture. Eventually he paused from eating. "Well," he said, "I thought it was brilliant how you used religion to tug on folks' heartstrings. All that 'she prays, she's a believer in miracles and grace' stuff. That's what appeals to all those nuts out there who think God cares about them. Like I always say, ain't no more perfect place for that kind of stuff than in a country song."

I shrugged because I didn't know what to say.

"I mean it!" Roy waved his fork. "Whenever I'm listening to your new hit song, which incidentally comes on WSIX every other song, to those lines about praying, about believing in miracles and grace, I got to smile. It sounds so heartfelt, and 'course, I know you don't believe all that, but you ain't gotta believe it to use it, and you did a fine job, Jennifer. You sure know how to write 'em and sing 'em."

"Thanks." I tried to look happy, but I felt a little deflated.

After we finished our meal and Roy had cleaned everything up, he pulled open the bottom drawer of a filing cabinet. "You like coconut Neapolitans?" He looked hopefully over at me, holding up a Brach's bag bulging with pink, white, and brown striped candies.

"They're my favorite sweet," I said, thankful that this was the honest truth.

"Mine too! Guess that makes us birds of a feather. 'Cept, well, I'm also partial to Maple Nut Goodies and Orange Slices and Paydays and Moon Pies, the banana ones that is, and pecan pie, and Stuckey's Pecan Logs, and fresh-out-of-the-fat

Krispy Kreme donuts, and can't forget our own city's specialty, Goo-Goo Clusters, and . . ." his voice trailed off and his face looked wistful.

"What's the matter?" I touched his hand. "Roy, you all right?"

He frowned. "Well, last month I was having some chest pains, and . . . " I looked closely at him, hoping he wouldn't say what I knew he was going to. At last, he shook his head sadly. "Doctor Firth told me if I don't quit eating the way I do, I won't see my sixty-fourth birthday."

I felt my heart sink. "That's terrible. I hate that," I said, and I honestly did. If anybody loved their food, it was Roy Durden.

"But . . . " he said in a contemplative voice, "I don't want to live if it's going to be on oatmeal and steamed broccoli! What kind of existence would that be? I believe I'd be happy if I went out of here holding a piece of fried chicken in one hand and an eclair in the other."

I looked down into my tea.

"Uh-uh!" Roy said sternly as he noisily unwrapped a Neapolitan. "No long faces! None of us is gonna make it out of here alive! Better to have something to live for than worryin' about dyin'."

"Yeah, I know," I said, nodding as I felt the cloud above me scuttling away. I knew I'd die for my music the way Roy Durden would die for his food. He was right—we were all going to wind up dead sooner or later. So, no more feeling guilty about lying.

After Roy and I polished off the bag of Neapolitans, he cleared his throat and said, "Now, there's something else I need to say."

"Okay." I wondered what else was fixing to come out of his mouth.

"I'm all for you getting to be a country music superstar and getting rich. Believe me, Jennifer. Because I believe it's in the cards for you, and I don't think you'd be happy going down any other pathway. But I'm worried sick you're gonna get so famous you won't remember us little guys anymore. You're gonna leave the Best Western and get one of those big fancy mansions in Brentwood, and start hanging out with the stars and the important people."

I looked at Roy's worried pink face, shook my head, and said, "I won't! I could never forget you in a million years."

"Well . . . okay," he said. "Reckon I ain't got no choice but to believe you." He laughed to let me know he was kidding. "In between making albums, collecting Grammies, and signing autographs, Jennifer, I'd be honored if you'd stop by and see your old friend Roy and share a meal every now and then. Like old times."

"I will," I said, rising to go. "I promise. Thank you for the scaloppine and the Neapolitans. It was the best meal I've had in my whole entire life."

As I rode the elevator back upstairs, I noticed that the butterflies in my stomach were gone. The value of a quiet conscience, even temporarily, cannot be underestimated.

One month later, Mike Flint called to say that "Honky-Tonk Tomcat" was on its way to being the fastest-breaking single ever. It was the talk of country music circles, still number one on Billboard Country at week nine, remaining there since its debut following a record five-and-a-half weeks, dancing close to a crossover hit. I even had the promise of an album.

I don't know how to describe those early days, except to say that I was unaware of anything but my own delirious happiness. If I ever felt that old, familiar twist in the gut, one of those sharp thoughts that ambush a person, racing up their spine and culminating in a cold sweat, I just took a deep breath and reminded myself that I was moving on, living in the moment, living free like Roy Durden, and soon it was forgotten. With my past buried and my conscience silenced, life seemed magical, my future stretching out indescribably beautiful before me. I was certain luck would continue to shine on me.

Every day I walked to the Cumberland to spend a meditative, worshipful time as I gazed at the water, feeling one with her broad fearless currents. My favorite place to enjoy my shrine had become the Shelby Street pedestrian bridge, which stretched across the river near the train depot. You could enter by elevator, stairs, or walk up the ramp, and it was a quiet place. It had scattered foot-traffic, bicyclists, pigeons, and the occasional speedboat down on the water. I preferred perching on a bench looking out over the downstream side, where I had a birdseye view of the city skyline on one side and the stadium on the other. Occasionally I strolled over to LP Field where I would walk on the grassy patches, occasionally slipping off my shoes and walking down a cement boat ramp, wading out ankle-deep into the water.

I loved my home at the Best Western, taking long, hot baths while writing lyrics and composing melodies in my head, enjoying frequent suppers with Roy. I loved to set out on foot to downtown Nashville, buying food and drink at the various cafés, enjoying the local color and the street musicians.

But there was one particularly sweltering day in June when I had so much on my mind that I kept bumping into lampposts and fire hydrants. The day before, Mike told me he'd found the perfect place for me to live. Just as Roy'd predicted, it was in Brentwood—a gigantic home on five acres, way down some paved driveway with a gate that locked.

"I don't have the money to buy a house!" I'd said. I didn't want to leave Roy.

Mike didn't hesitate. "You will, Jenny. I have no doubt you're gonna make it big, real big, which means *we're* gonna make it big. So, I'll front you the money. Realtor's ready any second for me to make an offer."

It sounded like a fantasy, just one more unbelievable piece of good luck in an unceasing string. Still, I wasn't sure why a person living alone needed all that space, or a yard so big, and I mentioned this to Mike, but in his usual manner, he ignored my questions and steamrolled right along with his plan. "It's fifteen minutes from downtown Nashville," he'd said. "Convenient."

"You haven't even told me how much it costs."

"Place is listed at eight hundred seventy-nine, and we're going to offer eight forty-nine to see if he goes for it. I'm betting he'll say yes. But we need to jump on it if it's going to happen, Jenny girl. I can't say who, but there are some other stars considering it, and I promised Arnie I'd get back to him right away, let him know if you were interested." Mike's words came in such a flurry, were so full of assurance, that I just sat staring straight ahead, trying to wrap my mind around that enormous sum of money.

"Think about your neighbors," Mike added with a satisfied chuckle. "Trisha Yearwood, Kenny Chesney, Tim McGraw and Faith Hill, Dolly Parton, Little Jimmy Dickens, Alan Jackson, and Trace Adkins live in Brentwood, to name just a few."

I actually laughed aloud, imagining myself opening the door to receive a warm plate of brownies from Dolly, and her saying, "Howdy, neighbor!" in that famous voice.

On my last night at the Best Western, Roy threw me a party. We were gathered around the counter, dining on chicken wings, celery sticks with bleu cheese dip, and Ritz crackers with pimiento cheese slathered on top. The Ritz crackers were on a plastic tray, arranged in the shape of a smile, with CONGRATULATIONS! napkins fanned out beside it.

Roy didn't look very perky. He had bags beneath his eyes, a five-o'clock stubble on his chin, and his face was pinker than ever. There was a buffalo sauce stain in the shape of the state of Georgia on the lapel of his seersucker suit. After we finished eating, he cleared his throat until I looked his way, then he blotted his glistening forehead with a napkin, leaned over to the file drawer he kept his assortment of sugary treats in, and with a melodramatic widening of his blue eyes, lifted a clumsily wrapped gift. "For you," he said in this trembly voice.

From its size and shape, I expected to find a coffee-table book, so when I unwrapped a frame holding a copy of the article about my inspiration for writing "Honky-Tonk Tomcat" from *Country Music Weekly*, I couldn't speak. The wrinkled page looked like it had been ripped from the tabloid, and there were transparent smudges where greasy fingers had held it.

Looking at it made me feel sort of sick, and I could not utter a word. Thankfully, Roy didn't catch anything from me but stunned joy. "This is going to be real valuable one day, Jennifer. You're gonna look back and say, 'Wow. I remember when Roy Durden told me Nashville was the nine-year town, and I made it in nine weeks.'" He chuckled.

I closed my eyes, the picture heavy in my hands.

"What?! Don't I even get a hug?"

"Of course," I said, placing the picture face down on top of the counter, taking in a big breath and smiling brightly as I put my shaky arms around him. "I'm going to miss you so much," I sniffled into his shoulder.

"Me, too, but you got my blessing long as—"

I laughed. I knew what he was fixing to say, and I finished it for him, "You'll promise to come lavish some attention on an old feller every now and then."

"That's right," he said. "I'm gonna hold you to it."

All I could think was, *Then please don't die on me.*

I spent several hours packing up my things. I folded my clothes and tucked them neatly into a large wheeled suitcase with a pull-out handle Roy had let me dig out of the lost-and-found closet, gathered my shoes and toiletry articles, settling them into a row of doubled plastic grocery bags, then tucked my song notebook into my guitar case, and put everything in a pathetic, but neat line near the door. It was funny to think that this motley collection was the sole accumulation of the life I'd lived thus far.

That made me think of the humongous interior of my new home, Harmony Hill—room after room waiting to be filled. Mike said there were interior designers by the dozens who were eager and willing to help me decorate the place in any style I chose, whatever my personality called for. He'd brought me magazines full of ideas, and he kept saying, "What's your pleasure, Jenny?" and finally, after he'd heard, "I don't know," so many times, he stopped asking.

As I waited for him and his truck, I looked around my room trying to see it with a decorator's eye so I could tell them how I wanted the interior of Harmony Hill. It was comfortable, cozy and all the colors went together; the wood on the bed and the tables matched, the curtains complemented the bedspreads as well as the paint on the wall. But the main thing that I liked about it was that not one single thing was broken down. No worn out, broken-down furniture or threadbare linens. The carpet was plush and unstained. I remembered how I'd tiptoed around those first days, not used to the niceness of it all.

I felt a rush of melancholy as I envisioned myself walking around inside enormous, empty Harmony Hill, up the winding staircase and through the echoing hallways. I got into bed and pulled the bedspread around me tight. It wasn't too long when a bittersweet thought zipped in. How proud Mr. Anglin would have been to see my mansion! He'd often talked about his trips to Europe, where his greatest delight was seeing all the beautiful architecture. It was all I could do not to cry tears of joy because I'd "made it" in the country music scene just as Mr. Anglin had predicted but at the same time weep that he wasn't here to see it. Because of my foolishness.

⧉

Tall, stately trees and manicured lawns in Brentwood made a person think they were driving into some glossy two-page spread in *Southern Living* magazine. Harmony Hill was magnificent; a ten thousand-square-foot mansion worth more than half a million tiny cabins like the one I grew up in. More than I ever imagined owning. The first time Mike and his agent, Arnie, took me to see it, Arnie kept talking about how it was Scottish Georgian style because the architect had combined stucco and brick. "Miss Cloud," he said, in his high, breathless voice, "if you'll notice, the stucco is scored to look like stone blocks, and this makes a lovely contrast with the brick corner blocks. Don't you think the cut stone window lintels are absolutely beautiful?"

I nodded. I had no idea what a lintel was. What I saw was a pretty, perfectly symmetrical two-story house that wasn't made of wood. I walked around inside, Arnie following along at my elbow, chattering endlessly, saying "Now, this is what you call Southern grandeur, incorporating elegant iron railings and archways as artistic statements, and absolutely begging for furniture that looks as if it just arrived from a Parisian flea market." When we toured the two wings on either side of the central area, I discovered one was a state-of-the-art media room, and the other, as Arnie declared, was "a generous kitchen, suited for a five-star soiree."

I followed him through a laundry room, office, library, rec room, exercise room, butler's pantry, screened porch, sunroom, walk-in pantry, guest suite, loft, balcony, three-car garage, and five bedrooms. There were six bathrooms. I couldn't possibly need six bathrooms!

Overwhelmed, I was ready to tell Mike I'd changed my mind, that it just wasn't my style. Until I paused on the front steps, imagining myself wearing a voluminous hoop skirt, holding a Chinese paper fan in one hand and a sweating glass of lemonade in the other, while making coy faces at the Tarleton twins. Scarlett O'Hara was one of my favorite fictional characters. She was strong, a survivor, and if I owned my own Tara, I could be one too. This was not the home of a simpering, spineless female doormat. Owning Harmony Hill would somehow empower me to be who I needed to be.

⸎

At the beginning, I kept pinching myself as I walked across polished wooden floors, beneath vaulted ceilings, saying *I own this. I actually own this structure.* I took Arnie's advice and hired a designer who filled my new home with furniture that looked like it had just arrived from a Parisian flea market. But—and this was nonnegotiable—I told him that everything had to be brand-spanking new. No holes or rips, no broken legs, no disgusting stains, and no rump-sprung cushions. "Oh, yes, ma'am," he'd laughed. "It's all new. Some of it is distressed to *appear* old, but it's new."

Though I appreciated all my finery, it wasn't cozy like my room at the Best Western, and for an entire month I felt like a puff of dandelion the wind had blown aloft, swirling around over an endless field. I'd walked the property of Harmony Hill with Mike before signing contracts, but I hadn't really explored it. After the furniture trucks had come and gone, after the designer had finished his hanging of drapes and pictures, I stood at the back window with my arms crossed, looking out at my backyard. I'd always thrived on the *wildness* of the outdoors, on meandering creeks and undulating rivers and barbed-wire fences covered with honeysuckle, and the thought of such a manicured yard seemed silly. But I remembered my resolution to be strong like Scarlett, so I said, *Jennifer, bloom where you are planted,* and I went outside to explore my very own five acres.

The sun was warm, and there was a gentle breeze as I passed first the tennis courts, then a swimming pool surrounded by white pergolas, and a summerhouse with a brick terrace and built-in grill. I wandered the side yard, winding along between hedges in elegant shapes curled around bits of lawn and rock-bordered flowerbeds full of hollyhocks and snapdragons. Feeling this yearning, this ache for something I couldn't name, I sat down on a wrought-iron bench overlooking a fish pond outlined with large stones. Arnie had claimed the pond was "a delightful addition that will give you hours of pleasure." I stared at the orange bodies of a school of koi moving near the floating fountain in the center.

Finally I rose and went to dip my hand in the pond. That was when it hit me. What I grieved for, besides seeing Roy every day, was my daily trek to Riverfront Park. I missed grabbing my Best Western breakfast, then walking to the pedestrian bridge to be with the Cumberland River.

So, on Saturdays when I was not in the studio or on the road, I would lock the gate to Harmony Hill and drive my Lexus coupe (again, thanks to Mike Flint's urgings) to downtown Nashville. Parking at the Best Western, I walked to Riverfront Park, and sat on the pedestrian bridge to meditate. Mostly the Cumberland glided by serenely, a shimmering thread with a reflective, calm surface, but sometimes she seemed a bit restless, cutting through the banks and hastening along. But no matter what her mood, the curve of her was indescribably beautiful, my assurance that some things in life were constants.

People asked me later if I ever felt scared hanging out at the river alone. And to be frank, I hadn't. In the back of my mind were Roy's cautions, along with the stories I'd heard all my life about women who were vulnerable targets for criminals, drunks, and the desperate. But none of this seemed to apply to me, because after all, I was on the path of my destiny.

Finding a Sunday routine took a little longer. There were many restless Sunday mornings of wandering around outside over the dew-drenched acres of Harmony Hill, searching for what, I did not know. The memory of the habit of attending church all my growing-up years began to yawn and stretch, and finally it roused itself enough to demand something. So, I began climbing into the Lexus for a drive to kill time until noon had passed. I spent hours listening to Big D and Bubba on The Big 98 while rambling around Davidson and Williamson counties. I never stopped anywhere, just admired the scenery outside my windshield. Granny White Pike was a nice long stretch of road from Brentwood to downtown; lots of pristine green golf courses, stacked stone walls, grand entrances to estates, and stretches of pretty white fences with horses behind them. Roy informed me that these were "gentleman farmers" and that if I wanted to know the real farmers, with tractors and dirt under their nails, I should get out of the city, especially north and west, where they grew corn, tobacco, and soy. In fact, Roy went to great lengths to educate me about the social strata of various Nashville communities.

He told me that Franklin was Old Money, Old South, but that the truly rich lived in Belle Meade, and it was what you called Really Old Money. According to Roy, those people didn't like the country music industry at all. He maintained the folks in Green Hills were "Cliquish and married to their money."

One of my favorite stretches of road was along Franklin Pike, particularly the place where Tammy Wynette's former home sat behind a black iron fence. Back then, before the novelty of living in the same area as these idols of mine had worn off, I always slowed down there, rubbernecking as I tried to imagine their dazzling lives.

After I'd been at Harmony Hill for almost an entire year, I set out one particular Sunday for a drive along Old Hickory Boulevard. A road that once simply circled the city, it had become a complicated course interrupted by lakes and rerouted sections. I enjoyed the twists and turns, passing by what seemed to be an enormous church on every single corner. Roy called them "The land-baron churches." During worship services, a cop or two parked along the roadsides at every one of these mammoth churches, with blue lights flashing, waiting to direct traffic in and out. Something as foreign to my little church back in Blue Ridge as a paved parking lot. Back in Blue Ridge . . .

Sure don't want to go there, I thought, turning up the volume on the radio and mashing the accelerator. Near the Four Points Sheraton and the Waffle House, I spied a warmly lit Panera Bread and decided I sure could use a large espresso.

No one inside Panera recognized me, but I wasn't surprised because my face was not yet so familiar to the public, and plus, I wore no makeup and had my hair tucked up in a ratty denim baseball cap, pulled down over my eyebrows. My Sunday uniform consisted of a shapeless cotton shirt and slouchy Bermuda shorts and the raggediest high-top Converses you could imagine. I could have been the Queen of England and no one would have known.

I loved the fact that there were no waiters in Panera, and after I'd been nestled down with my espresso in a comfy chair in the tall-ceilinged front room for a while, the scent of warm cinnamon wafted out. I could not resist, and I followed it back to the counter where I discovered a mouth-watering array of carbohydrates behind clear glass: bear claws, giant cookies sprinkled with M&M's, good-looking muffins called cobblestones. I ordered a cinnamon crunch bagel and returned to my chair, sitting and happily watching the world go by outside the window.

I realized I'd found my safe place. Each and every Sunday after that, I drove to Panera, ordered an espresso and a cinnamon crunch bagel, and sunk myself into the same pillowy chair in the Great Room.

Panera had an assortment of magazines and tabloids scattered on the tables from *Strum* to *Country Music Weekly*, and as I sipped my coffee, I liked to pour over the latest news about country's hottest stars as well as music events around town. Whenever I came upon an article about Jenny Cloud, it was like reading a story about some stranger. I marveled at this chick and her growing, illustrious career in country music.

Funny, but even as a couple more years passed and my fame grew even more, I was never gawked at or accosted for an autograph inside the Brentwood Panera. Maybe the Panera staff just decided to let me have my solace, because once my career kicked into high gear, I could hardly go anywhere without people literally stampeding to me, begging for an autograph or a photo together.

When I was on the road doing concerts, what I missed most were my treks to the Cumberland and my visits to the Best Western to visit Roy. I craved the sight of his florid face, his dramatic swoop of white hair, and his belly, big and rounded, straining against his seersucker jacket as if he was pregnant with triplets.

But while I considered Roy a very dear friend, my best human friend, I could never reveal my heart to him the way something inside me needed to. Nothing is lonelier or more stressful than having to keep up a pretense, and I was probably suffering from generalized social anxiety coupled with depression. It was all an offshoot of my intense loneliness.

Holidays scared me. I rattled around in that huge, empty Harmony Hill, writing songs and avoiding invitations for Thanksgiving dinners with Mike's family. I never took Roy up on his offer of a Christmas Day together. I didn't want to rock the boat where our relationship was concerned.

What I craved, without being conscious of it, was the type of intimate friend you could pour your heart and soul out to, with unflinching honesty, without fear. I refuse to blame any holes in our friendship on Roy Durden. The problem lay with *me*. It was simply because of my own preconceived notions that I didn't expose my past to him. I wanted to make sure he kept me up on a pedestal.

I feel schizophrenic now when I say that at the same time I wanted to unburden myself to Roy, I adored the fact that he asked me no penetrating questions. He never once mentioned my faux friend, Lisa, the one I presumably wrote "Honky-Tonk Tomcat" about. And she'd become almost famous as journalists continued to pursue more details about the story I'd spun early in my career. He listened and gave me advice as I talked about writing "Never Change" and "Escape to a Place." I loved hearing about Roy's latest culinary experience or his brush with stars such as Faith Hill and Tim McGraw while eating breakfast at Bread & Company in Green Hills, or Keith Urban and Nicole Kidman while shopping at Whole Foods in Hill Center. I'd ask him were they friendly, and he'd say, "Yep. Nice enough. But didn't seem to want to chat." I just nodded, because I understood how hard it can be when a fan assaults you in public.

I read plenty of articles saying I was snobby. One even called me "stuck up." I've never been good at small talk, but I was even more standoffish and gave off the wrong impression at that point in my career because I didn't think people would like me if some things in my past came out.

Speaking of things in my past—and I know this may sound ungrateful—but looking back I don't really see Mike Flint as a friend. Then or now. I love Mike, I respect him, but one thing that hurts me is the fact that he never really listened to me, not even during those times I forced myself to spill a teeny bit of my guts to him. I tried to tell him I didn't want anymore autobiographical songs the first year, after "I'm Leavin' Only Footprints" was number one on the Country charts for months, then the next year when I went through agony to write "Blue Mountain Blues," and finally the next year when my album *Smoke Over the Hills* went platinum. After that, I figured it was useless.

When it came to accolades I had plenty. There was a doll designed in my likeness, a Jenny Cloud Country music star doll. People even wrote to tell me they'd named their horse or their boat or their airplane after me! For so long I thought being a star would solve all my problems, and when five years of megafame had come and gone and I realized it wouldn't, I was stupefied.

It took me those five long years full of pain and frustration to understand that with Mike, I would always be Jenny

Cloud, singer with a tortured past he wanted to exploit. He lived in a business world that didn't have time for emotional breakdowns, and it was always a devil dance between my artistic, emotional self and Mike's analytical world of bottom-lines. Yet I have to admit he was, is, a brilliant businessman. He's got this natural instinct for figuring out exactly what the country music market needs next, and he knows how to help me craft that certain song with an emotional arc. Also, the man's a brilliant salesman and marketer. I never doubt that I'm extremely lucky to have him. He just made my life a living hell there for a while.

Now I feel like a hypocrite, because it would be a lie to say I didn't love hearing all those reports about my number-one hits, the sales to retail outlets, the platinum-selling albums, record time on the Billboard 100 lists, and avalanches of new fans signing up for my Internet fan page.

Yep, to say that my life was all morose back then would be a lie. The parts I loved about my fairly quick rise to stardom, the parts I absolutely adored were those sublime moments of being on the stage and singing to an audience. I craved that microphone in my face like nothing else, and those times when the thrill of performing my music rushed up and down my spine were priceless. Day by day and song by song, the world of a country music diva unfurled before me, beautiful high points with me spinning deliriously, stunned and drunk with my successes.

But the low points were deep and dark and shoved me to the edge of despair. I worked hard at playing the mental game of rewriting, reframing my past, of trying to block certain images from the screen of my consciousness. Like Wynonna Judd sang in her hit, "No One Else on Earth," I put up my mental fences. But no matter what I did, there was one place where the bull always managed to bust through—that helpless, strange country between being awake and falling into dreamland, that state between consciousness and unconsciousness. Way too often I would find myself sitting bolt upright in bed, blinking in the dark, slightly hysterical about some evil memory that was trying to materialize. Many nights I paced around cavernous Harmony Hill, running from sleep, but at the same time knowing those objectionable little documentaries were where my hit songs germinated.

What I now call my "breaking point" came after five years, dozens of hit songs, two platinum albums, and one particularly ugly romantic relationship.

SECOND VERSE:
THE BREAKING POINT

5

At five o'clock on an overcast February afternoon in 2009 just outside Nashville, members of my entourage traipsed in and out, rocking the floor so it felt more like a boat bobbing around in the ocean than yet another trailer. I felt exhausted from pasting on smiles all day. My new hairdresser stood behind me with one pink cowboy boot up on the rung of my chair, painfully pulling out a set of hair extensions she'd put in for a photo shoot earlier.

"You're ruining your makeup, hon. The way you're sniveling and carrying on." Tomilynn's eyes met mine in the mirror.

"Who cares? I don't care," I said, shrugging at my image in the huge, brightly lit mirror, at black trails of mascara running down my cheeks.

She pursed her lips, raised her flawlessly applied eyebrows. "Well, I'm with you, hon, I never thought it was fair the way us women have to suffer so much for beauty. Men have it E-Z, while us gals are continually waxing, plucking, polishing, smoothing, firming, uplifting, dyeing, and enhancing. But," she paused with a dramatic sigh, "I reckon I ought not to complain about beauty, since it is how I make my living." She smiled as she yanked another strand of my hair.

I flinched and more tears came.

"Reckon you're just tender-headed," Tonilynn said around a bobby pin between her teeth.

I tried to ignore her, but I was offended at her insinuation that I was weak. "I'm not tender-headed!"

"What you crying about, then?" She fluttered around to the other side of me, leaving a trail of perfume that smelled like honeysuckle.

I focused on making my expression neutral. The words out of this woman's mouth were fire, and I was wood. A mental bucket of water I'd filled all those years ago and left near my vulnerable places stood by ready to douse any flames.

When the quietness between us grew too loud for Tonilynn, she used her free hand to squeeze my shoulder, then leaned down close to my ear to whisper, "If it's on account of all that ugly stuff they keep printing about you and Holt Cantrell bustin' up, I wouldn't give a fig. I'd say to myself, 'Sticks and stones will break my bones, but . . .'"

I ground my teeth together hard and totally disengaged from this meddling woman. Why did love have to be so difficult? And how dare she refer to personal things! Well, things the trashy tabloids printed were still personal. Whenever I happened on headlines or articles about Holt Cantrell and his accusations, it felt like someone was stabbing me in the chest with a sharp knife. All I wanted was for this day to be over. I longed with every cell in my body to hop back in the Lexus and drive home as fast as I could, get into my real clothes, and put on some Dolly Parton or Johnny Cash to drown out everything else, away from the people and the thoughts I'd dealt with all day long.

I had a quick little fantasy about firing this nosy beautician on the spot, but Mike said she was extremely good at what she did, and best of all, dependable, and I hated the idea of going through the hassle of hiring and breaking in yet another employee.

"Hey, hey, what's all this?" Tonilynn walked around and crouched down in front of me, examining the face I could feel crumpling. She took my hands and held them in hers, rubbing circles on my knuckles with her soft thumbs. "What's wrong, darlin'? You can tell Tonilynn, you know. Talk to Tonilynn. Some of my clients have told me I'm even better than their shrink."

Her regional twang made *I* sound like *ah*, but it was soothing, and her eyes were compassionate. It didn't bug me in the least the way she referred to herself in the third person. I did that, too, and I'd often wondered if it was something I ought to talk to a psychiatrist about—the way I thought of Jenny Cloud the country music star as if she were an entirely different person from Jennifer Anne Clodfelter of Blue Ridge, Georgia. A couple of times, I'd decided I would, but then Jenny Cloud talked Jennifer Clodfelter out of it.

"You're just one of them poor little rich girls, ain't you?" Tonilynn continued, her words so smooth they slid into one of the cracks in my soul. She couldn't know how right-on she was. I had a successful career where I made tons of money, beauty (according to all the articles I'd read about me), and enough fame that I had become a household name. I should've been the happiest woman in the world. But I was miserable.

I nodded, pulling out the favors and balloons for a full-blown pity party as more hot tears poured out of my eyes and snot began to trickle from my nostrils. Tonilynn made a noise like a dove's coo, bent forward, and wrapped her arms around me. Without thinking I snuggled my wet face into her shoulder, feeling her large bosoms so solid and comforting, inhaling her scent of hair chemicals mixed with honeysuckle.

She held me, talking a mile a minute about how she'd worked for Holt Cantrell once. "It was way, way back, when he first got to Nashville, and let me tell you, hon, I learned I couldn't trust that man as far as I could throw him. Some men are just snakes, believe me, and even if he is a star who makes millions of bucks for every hit song, he's still a two-bit scumbag slid down into sharkskin boots." She was shaking her head as she patted my back. "I can only imagine Holt's ego now that he's got to be so famous. But don't you worry about a thing because you're leaving him in your dust with the record sales. Right, darlin'? I believe I overheard Mike saying you're breaking all sorts of records."

I snuffled up a few tears through my nostrils. The title song of my latest album, *I'll Be Yours Until Forever*, was the one currently zooming up the playlists. It had been an immediate radio hit and was daily gaining support and visibility. Ironically, it had been written about my feelings for Holt Cantrell.

I managed a nod, but it didn't stop the tears. After a while Tonilynn pulled away and tugged a flattened tissue from the pocket of her blouse, patted my cheeks with it, cupped my chin in her soft hand, and looked directly into my eyes. "That ain't all that's bothering you, now, is it darling? You're carrying a mighty heavy load."

I gulped, blinked, nodded.

"Sometimes it helps to talk things out, you know. Tell your troubles to Tonilynn."

I opened my mouth, but no sound would come out. She was still looking into me with her eyes like chocolate pools I wanted to drown myself in. "I . . . I can't," I said after several false starts.

"Yes you can." Tonilynn threw out a lifeline. "If grass can grow in a sidewalk, you can tell Tonilynn your troubles. Trust me, everything's going to be A-OK. You're a strong woman.

You're a survivor. I say good riddance to that snake Holt Cantrell. Believe me, you're better off without him. I could tell you some stories, only I don't want to gossip on account of that's a sin. But like I said, good riddance.

"And listen, don't you worry 'bout the fallout from his ugly accusations affecting your career like the magazines are saying, 'cause you've got a voice that'll take you anywhere you want to go. I mean, you've hardly been here in Nashville, what? four, five years at the most? And you're already leaving lots of long-time stars in your dust." She wove a strand of my long hair between her fingers. "You hear me, hon? To zoom up to the top like you have in such a short time? You keep that chin up."

All of a sudden Tonilynn released my hair and stood straight as a two-by-four. She put her hands on her ample hips, snorted like a racehorse. "Hmphh! Makes me so mad I could spit! Those trashy rags have no right to run your name through the mud! All they're trying to do is make a dime off your misfortune; couldn't care less about the human part of a star!"

She searched my stunned face. "Don't that make you mad?"

"I . . . um . . . well, I . . . " My heart started racing, my palms got clammy, and my tongue froze. I still didn't know if I was to blame for what had happened with me and Holt or not.

Tonilynn laced her fingers together beneath her chin and tipped her head. "Oh, baby girl. You don't always have this much trouble expressing yourself, do you?"

I shrugged and sat there like a lump. But my silence didn't seem to faze Tonilynn. "Listen," she said softly, "I've been knowing for a while you're a woman who's toting some serious baggage around with her. Even before you and Holt Cantrell hooked up, before Mike called me about working for you, I'd see you on the television, singing and whatnot, and I'd say to Aunt Gomer, 'Now, there's a woman who's toting around a heavy load of something. I know in my heart somebody

103

took, no, they *stole* her dignity, and she's carrying around a load of shame so heavy there's times she can't hardly breathe. Somebody close to her wounded her.' I actually said that aloud to Aunt Gomer."

My skin drew up tight. "Who told you that?"

"Oh, let's just call it a little voice inside my head." Tonilynn reached over and got a container of hair clips from the counter, and began to rifle through them with her perfectly manicured fingers, finally closing the lid with a sharp snap.

Things were quiet for a while, then she said, "Now, I don't want to—how do the young folks say it?—freak you out, but the best way to describe it is to say I have these gut feelings, or intuitions. May sound like a magical power, but it's actually the spirit of revelation, one of the supernatural gifts of the Holy Ghost called the *word of knowledge*. Some folks call it *the spirit of knowing*. But either way, it's the Lord letting me see beyond a person's exterior. Many times smiling people are crying on the inside. Like I see your pretty stage smiles, but I know you're actually sad, sad, sad on the inside."

I looked at Tonilynn, at her flawless makeup, her perfectly coiffed hair, and suddenly a red flag flew up. Roy Durden appeared in my mind's eye and he was saying, "She sounds like one of those religious wackos who speaks in tongues and watches the *Ernest Angley Hour*." I cleared my throat, looked at my watch. "Gosh," I said. "Look how late it is! Time for supper."

Tonilynn reached over to pat my shoulder. "You don't need to be scared, hon. I don't know the particulars about your past." She paused dramatically. "But the Lord does."

I made a little sound in my nose, a snort, and said in my best cynical voice, "Is that so?"

There was a long silence. Tonilynn tilted her head to one side and pointed upward with an index finger. "Ain't you a believer?"

I shrugged. "Um, maybe. Not exactly. Used to be, but now . . . it's more like . . . more like I'm on to him. Like I realize God doesn't give a fig about us down here."

Tonilynn smoothed a rumpled towel. "Tell me why you gave up on the Lord."

I leaned my head back to stare at the ceiling. "Okay. When I was fifteen, it was late on a Friday night, and my father had all these drunks over to the house, and I . . ." I yanked my head back down and shook it so hard I thought my brain was rattling. Was I losing my mind?! I pressed the pads of my index fingers to the corners of my eyes to dam tears.

Tonilynn reached over to cup my chin. "That's all right. I'm sorry, hon. We don't have to go there if you're not ready. But let me tell you something you can take to the bank. You may've given up on the Lord, but he hasn't given up on you. He does too care about you! Every single little thing that concerns you concerns him! He ain't some distant creator who put you on this earth and then left you alone, saying, 'Good-bye, good luck. Hope you make it all right.'"

I pulled away. I'd broken out in a sweat without realizing it, and the cool air of the trailer made me feel dizzy. After a spell, Tonilynn cleared her throat. "Jennifer?" she said in a voice soft as dandelion down, "I don't want you to be scared of me. This sensitive ability I have, this super*natural* gift, which all that means is just 'more natural,' you know, *super* natural, is a divine impartation to perceive a person's need so I can minister to her, or him. You know, help out."

I could literally feel my eyes widening.

She laughed at my face. "Relax. I told you all that because I especially don't want you to confuse my gift with those psychic predictions of earthquakes and murders and the like. Those are Satanic prophecies, inspired by the enemy."

She was wacko, sure enough.

"Hey, speaking of the devil, there's something else I reckon I better let you in on if we're going to work together." Tonilynn smiled. "I have this habit that might seem strange if you're not used to it. I talk back, right out loud, to the devil. I'll be walking along, or doing something like fixing a client's hair, and I'll say, 'Get behind me, Satan!' and if I'm in earshot of anybody, they look at me like I've lost my mind!" She laughed and shook her head. "But I just remind myself it makes old slewfoot tremble. Gives him a colossal headache."

I stared at her in the mirror, wondering, *Is this real or am I dreaming?*

"It ain't no accident you and me got put together like this, you know," she continued, with a one-shouldered shrug. "Ain't no accident you're sitting in what I call the Hair Chair. The Hair Chair's a place where you can talk to Tonilynn. Let all the tears and the ugly stuff spill on out. Now, I'm not patting myself on the back. Believe me. This divine impartation I have is a gift, just like salvation."

I remained silent.

"Yep," she said, "Purely a gift, and I'm just trying to do the best I can with it." Tonilynn pulled the black cape from my shoulders, shook it out and began to sweep the floor. All the while her lips were moving, then she was smiling, nodding at things I couldn't hear. At last she cleared her throat, and in a trembly sort of voice asked, "Have you been born again? Are you saved, Jennifer?"

I didn't even have patience for my own tears much less hers, and I wouldn't answer. My nerves felt jangled and my stomach was starting to hurt. I realized I'd had nothing but quarts of black coffee since ten that morning. *Please*, I thought, *please just drop this uncomfortable subject. Talk about hair conditioners or waterproof mascara or foundations for photoshoots.*

Tonilynn had both her hands on the back of the Hair Chair now, and I could see her in the mirror as she leaned in toward me, her chin over my head. "Jennifer, hon, please answer me. Have you accepted Christ as your personal Lord and Savior?" I felt her words through my scalp when she rested her chin on my head to say, "Do you know where you're going to spend eternity?"

It seemed like time stopped. Tonilynn stood motionless, waiting, and I could not move a muscle, even to swallow. So much was buzzing around in my head. Evenings at all the summertime tent revivals of my childhood, where sweaty preachers warned of hellfire and the heart-booming fear of damnation had propelled me forward to accept Jesus on three different occasions. I remembered the pats of others in the audience after I left the altar each time, the gleam of the moon in their eyes as they said, "Welcome to the fold. You're born again." I remembered all that in a flash, and then, just as quickly, I remembered that in Blue Ridge I'd merely existed in a state of near death: fearful, isolated, and repressed. I didn't feel new life surging through me until I took control of my destiny and left for Music City, until I found my occasional moments of joy onstage, shreds of peace at the Cumberland River.

I wanted to use my snide voice to say to Tonilynn, *Yeah, I've been born again, and my second birth happened right here in Nashville. She's my mother now.* But as I gazed into her honest face, those tanning-parlor bronzed cheeks rouged with blush the color of pomegranates, a tuft of ash-blonde hair like cotton candy above doe-eyes ringed in black liner, my tongue just sort of shriveled. It felt like this woman really cared, like she had the kind of compassion that came from being knocked around by life a time or two.

And, even if she was one of those deluded, fanatical, over-the-top born-agains who needed religion as a crutch to lean on, even if she was only saying all this to make me feel better, it was still a kind thing to do. Had anyone else even bothered to ask me how I felt about Holt's accusations? About the so-called dirty laundry flapping out there for everyone to see? Mike hadn't. Seemed all he cared about was the money still flowing like a river, maybe even like a tidal wave since my big breakup. My mother hadn't, but then she didn't own a TV, read the paper, or take any magazines. She did have a telephone, however, but it had been six months since we'd even spoken, and I wouldn't dream of calling her up to chat about the drama involving a life she'd warned me about.

Plus, I could sure use a friend. Even a crazy one. What made my pain over Holt's ugly accusations even worse was that it was a Tuesday night, the day of the week I used to drop by the Best Western for supper with Roy. I still missed that man so much I could almost feel mad at him for dying of a massive heart attack the previous December, for leaving a huge gaping hole in my life. And so, in a moment of blind grief and exhaustion, when all my usual defenses were napping shamelessly, I decided to take the risk of opening up just a smidgen to Tonilynn. Even though this act of confession to a relative stranger made the rational me feel like I was sprinting out onto I-65 during rush hour.

"I . . . I didn't actually steal anything from Holt," I began, gently testing the waters. I saw Tonilynn nod as she bent to get a bottle of Windex from the cabinet underneath the sink. "But he's making it sound like I'm some kind of kleptomaniac, saying I've been stealing from him awhile now. Over Christmas, and yes, maybe on New Year's Eve, too, I admit it, I did pour some of his Jack Daniel's down the sink. But it was because he was getting kind of . . . I don't know how to call it, like he does sometimes, you know, nasty and all, and I . . . I was really scared. I didn't know if he might . . ."

The smile left Tonilynn's face as she spritzed the mirror, wiping it with a rag until it squeaked. She turned to look at me. "Was Holt drunk?"

"Yeah. Really drunk. I told him I was leaving him if he didn't stop doing certain things, if he didn't stop trying to make *me* do certain things he always does when he's . . . " I couldn't finish.

"He got furious. Right? Mean and violent?"

I nodded.

"Nobody refuses Holt Cantrell." Tonilynn's voice was filled with disgust. "And they're making you sound like some kind of off-balanced thief!" She literally growled as she jammed combs down into a tall jar of disinfectant. "That worm! Playing all this up and telling the media you're the evil one. He doesn't say what you 'stole' or the reason you poured his whiskey out."

"Yeah," I said, finding her indignant anger comforting.

"Pardon my French, but basically Holt's a slimy bas— uh, jerk. Sorry. Trying to stop cussing, but not having much luck with it, especially where men like Holt are concerned." Tonilynn closed her eyes and rubbed her temples with her fingertips. Then she blinked at me. "All I can say is he'll get his comeuppance. 'Vengeance is mine,' saith the Lord. Holt's a liar with a capital L."

I nodded, feeling like a hypocrite with a capital H because of my habit of putting pretty little ribbons and bows, which is a nice way to say "lies," on the ugly inspirations for my songs. "Whatever," I said quickly to change the subject. "I'm just glad to be rid of him." Yet another half-truth!

"I see," Tonilynn said, like she could see right through me.

For several minutes, I just sat there watching her as she dumped the filter and scrubbed the carafe from a Mr. Coffee in the kitchenette. It was 6:25 p.m., and the piece of sky I could see outside the window was black. The corners inside the trailer had grown dark. "I'm sorry I've taken up so much of your time," I said finally. "You probably want to get home to your family."

Tonilynn laughed. "No, definitely not."

I must have looked confused.

"Both Bobby Lee and Aunt Gomer were in the foulest moods when I left this morning." Tonilynn sighed loud, and I could see distress on her face. "I'm starting to wonder if Aunt Gomer doesn't have the old-timer's disease setting in, on account of she's been forgetful and real ornery, which they say are warning signs.

"But then, I remind myself she's a bear to live with every February because it's one of those wishy-washy times when it comes to gardening and she's chompin' at the bit for the weather to warm up so she can get outside and dig in her dirt." Tonilynn shook her head. "But what's sad is that this year she keeps forgetting it's too cold to garden yet, and I'll find her out there in twenty-degree weather, barefoot in her housedress, scratching around with the hoe. I'll say to her, 'Aunt Gomer, winter's not done yet. Tim the weatherman says we won't have the last killing frost until around April fifteenth. You absolutely cannot *force* something like gardening. Please come on back in the house.'" Tonilynn sighed. "I swan, Jennifer, sometimes it's like having two ornery young'uns I'm in charge of. Except one's eighty-six years old."

"Really?"

She nodded. "I don't know what's ailing Bobby Lee. Guess he wants the spring to get here, too, so he can get to fishing."

I detected a little bit of wistfulness in Tonilynn's voice and I glanced at her ring finger. There was no wedding band. "You don't mind driving in the dark? Mike told me you live pretty far away."

"Hon, I am what you call an in-dee-pen-dent woman. Had to be ever since I was sixteen. In fact, I realized last week when I turned forty-eight that I've been taking care of myself twice as long as I've had somebody lookin' out for me. Sixteen times three equals forty-eight, right?" She pushed up her sleeve to glance at her wristwatch and I could see several colorful tattoos peeking out—one that looked like a double bracelet of barbed-wire and the other the red, vulgar lips of the Rolling Stones logo.

"Anyway," she said, "it's only a couple hours drive from here to Cagle Mountain. You'll have to come up to the homeplace sometime."

Images of Blue Ridge, Georgia, came to me when she said the word *mountain*, and I broke out in an instant little sweat. I reached down for the floppy denim tote bag under my chair that held a spiral notebook of songs I was working on.

"Don't go hurrying off on account of me, darlin'," Tonilynn's eyes caught mine in the mirror and held me in my seat. "I'm enjoying getting to know you. Won't you please stay in my Hair Chair just a bit longer?" She gave my shoulder a squeeze.

I took a deep breath and settled back obediently.

"One story I just love hearing from all my famous clients is how they got started. You know, how their gift was cultivated by different folks along life's pathway? Maybe Mama encouraged them to take piano lessons or to sing in the church choir? Or Uncle Bill gave them a guitar when they were ten. Maybe daddy signed 'em up for music lessons when they were teeny, after he noticed that the voice coming out of his child was not your ordinary one? Sometimes they tell me they were singing duets with Cousin Sue out on the back porch when they weren't but five years old." Tonilynn paused for a breath and a swallow of a Diet Coke.

"I just find it so fascinating to hear the stories of stars as they were growing up, and I keep telling myself that someday I'm going to write a book and call it, *The Stars: Inspiration and Cultivation.* What do you think, hon?"

My initial reflex was to shut down. But Tonilynn's voice was soothing, in that way adults use with hurt children. Now her back was to me as she was rinsing out Diet Coke cans she'd gathered from all over the trailer, setting them upside down in the sink to drain. In addition to her hair being a big blonde work of art, she had what folks referred to as "a big back porch" encased in stretch denim. This was comforting to me in a way I couldn't explain. "Um," I ventured, "my family didn't really encourage, cultivate, whatever you want to call it, my singing or my songwriting."

Tonilynn turned to me, her mouth open. "Seriously?"

"Seriously."

"Well, I bet they're proud of you now."

I shifted my eyes to the mirror, startled at the contrast of our reflections. Tonilynn's hair spun like golden cotton candy and mine long and stick-straight, so dark it was almost navy. Good versus evil flashed through my mind. Immediately my finger took a notion of its own and grabbed a strand of hair at the base of my skull to twirl. Around and around it spun until it hurt and calmed me a tiny bit so I was able to contemplate my response. "Nope," I released the word finally, and the way it sounded made it seem like it was wearing boxing gloves, punching Tonilynn's last comment in the gut.

Her eyebrows flew up. "You're pulling my leg! Oh . . . wait a minute. I am so sorry, hon." Tears sprang to her eyes. "I bet your folks have passed away, haven't they?"

"They're alive."

Tonilynn breathed a sigh of relief. "Whew, that's good," she said in a bright voice, popping the pull-tab on another can of Diet Coke with her frosted pink fingernail. "Care for one?" She held it toward me.

I shook my head and for a moment I had the oddest feeling of disappointment when I thought she wasn't going to pursue the cultivation question. But after several sips, she looked over at me with a softness in her eyes. "So your family wasn't supportive. But you managed to get yourself here somehow, now didn't you?"

I shrugged.

"Talk to Tonilynn about the parent issue."

Was I dreaming? "What?!"

"That's what the Hair Chair's for. Talking through issues with Tonilynn. And speaking of the Hair Chair, what's said here, stays here. You have my word on it." Tonilynn leaned her backside against the wall, crossed her ankles. "You say mama and daddy ain't proud of their baby? Well, what do they say when you call up and say, 'I've got me another hit song!'"

"We don't have that kind of relationship," I said, shocked at the words spilling out of my mouth.

"You don't call your mama every time you get a new hit song?"

"Nope."

"Well, why not?"

It took a few seconds, but I said, "I only opened up to my mother one time about wanting to come to Nashville."

"Tell me, darlin'."

"All right. It was the summer I turned twelve, and we were in the kitchen canning tomatoes. I said, 'When I get bigger, I want to go to Nashville and be a country music star.'"

Tonilynn flexed one foot in its pink boot. "Did she say 'No, you can't go?'"

"She . . . didn't say anything for a long time. Then finally she looked at me and said, 'You do sing pretty. I could 'bout listen to you all day and all night.'"

"Oh! Now that was sweet!" Tonilynn chirped.

"Then she told me I was forbidden to mention my dream of being a country music star again, that I needed to accept who and where I was. She said, 'Chasing big dreams like that only leads to misery.'"

"No!" breathed Tonilynn, leaning forward to touch my hand. "Oh, hon, that hurts my heart. I bet she was just scared, trying to protect you in her own way. She didn't want her precious little girl to get hurt."

I shook my head. "She was scared all right. She was absolutely, 100 percent terrified. But it wasn't because she was trying to protect me."

"What on earth was she so scared of?" Tonilynn had grabbed a broom and was sweeping in little meaningless circles on the floor all around the Hair Chair.

"My father . . . " I could barely get those words out of my throat.

Tonilynn nodded. "And why was your mother so scared of your father?"

My mouth went dry. My heartrate accelerated. I wasn't ready for the mental land mines hiding beneath that question. "You . . . you really don't want to know. He's not a very nice man. He's pretty . . . " I blinked. *Sleazy* was the word I'd started to say. But I tossed my hair behind my shoulder, stood and smiled brightly. "I better be getting on home. The cat's probably starving." I wondered if Tonilynn's heavenly intuition could detect my lie.

She just smiled and said in the nicest way, "Sure don't want kitty to expire. We'll have lots of opportunities to get to know each other better. I'll tell you one thing: I am just itching to hear about what finally got you here to Nashville. I bet that's some story!" She plunged a cool flatiron into her wheeled suitcase bulging with cosmetics. "We'll see you next Tuesday, and remember about the Holt Cantrell thing: this too shall pass."

I knew I could never tell Tonilynn about that magical day with Mac at McNair Orchards without all the horrible, unmentionable stuff that led up to me working there. I also knew from looking at her face that she really believed what she said. Clearly the woman needed a dose of reality. Events do pass, yes, but they change a person before they do, and things you don't want to remember can exert tremendous power. They can metabolize themselves in the lyrics of a song.

6

The last Friday in March, I slept late and woke to a blissfully empty schedule. The weather was sunny, warm enough to go barefoot, and I stepped out the back door at Harmony Hill, still in my nightgown. I didn't get ten yards until I realized I had tender winter feet, but it felt so good to have nothing between me and the ground I walked along anyway, listening to the birds and admiring the scattered daffodils. I followed a winding trail to a bench and sat down to soak up sun for a while but then started feeling restless and got up to hike along randomly, picking a handful of daffodils. It hadn't rained in weeks and even with the Bermuda grass, dust coated my feet and ankles so it looked like I had brown slippers sticking out below my nightgown. When I felt my stomach growling, I carried my flowers into the house and put them in a glass of water before I poured a bowl of cereal.

Sitting on the couch, my breakfast balanced on my thighs, my knees went watery. A memory from when I was nine years old moved in. I was running fast, barefoot, along a rutted dirt road in my pajamas, my feet coated with dust. Images from a confusing scene at home circled in my head as I ran.

How could that day be coming back in such bold brushstrokes? I hopped up, sloshing milk onto the rug, determined to stop the memory in its tracks when the title zipped into my head like a bolt of lightning: "Dirt Roads and Sequin Gowns."

Somehow I found myself back on the couch with my Washburn, playing some changes to this rhythm going around in my head as I started spewing out the lyrics. The first line, "In the house where I was raised, teardrops fell like rain," was simply taking dictation, and the rest came together as easily, especially the chorus: "And I was running down those dirt roads, carrying some heavy loads and dreaming of sequin gowns. 'Cause I was dreaming of leaving, and I was believing, that nothing could keep me down."

The verses wrote themselves, and the structure of the song laid itself down perfectly. I did have to work a little bit to refine the verse melody, but the melody for the chorus came to me with hardly any effort. It was one of those songwriting experiences you long for. The kind tht makes you feel absolutely blessed.

Unless, of course, it's a memory you'd rather not visit. I stared down at those pages I'd written, now lying scattered on the floor beside the couch, feeling like a defenseless little girl and a furious grown woman, trapped in an endless tug-of-war.

I knew I could just ball it up, throw it away. But I didn't. I didn't seal myself up while I still had a snowball's chance. I was trembling as I called Mike and sang "Dirt Roads and Sequin Gowns" over the phone to him. He was so excited; he drove out to Harmony Hill right away.

⊗⊗⊗

Monday came and I trudged around the house, exhausted from two nights of short, fragmented sleep, an undertow of anxiety about my new song tugging at my thoughts. Not to mention that on Saturday, I'd overheard part of a celebrity gossip's show where the host talked about Holt Cantrell and his accusations. I started to worry that I really might be a neurotic, overreactive crazy woman who'd thrown away her only chance at love and happiness.

I guzzled a cup of strong coffee and went outside to lie on my back and look at the clouds in hopes it would get my mind off things. But as it happened, I'd hardly warmed up the patch of grass when I heard a car's engine. Lifting my head I saw Tonilynn's ancient Pontiac Grand Am. You couldn't miss her duotoned automobile if you tried—the white hood with orangish streaks of rust in sharp contrast to the pine-green body. It dawned on me that I'd totally forgotten my appointment in the Hair Chair. I flopped back into the grass, feeling like a selfish, inconsiderate heel.

Tonilynn spotted me right off, waved, and came striding across the stretch of lawn, waving a Panera Bread bag. She wore giant tortoiseshell sunglasses that made me think of movie stars from the 1970s.

"Howdy, hon," she said, peering down at me with an amused expression. "I bet you wish you'd never given me your gate code!"

When I didn't answer, Tonilynn pushed her glasses up on top of her confection of hair. "You okay, Jennifer?"

I didn't want to get weepy, so I made myself concentrate on Tonilynn's pink cowgirl boots, on the intricate curlicued pattern sewn with silver thread around the ankles. "I'm fine."

She wasn't fooled. "It's such a pretty day we can just sit out here in the grass and talk." Tonilynn plopped down on one hip, arranging her legs to the side, knee to knee like a movie star in an old photograph. "So what's going on?" she asked, handing me the Panera bag.

"Thanks," I said, unfolding the bag to sniff a cinnamon crunch bagel. "Sorry I forgot my appointment in the Hair Chair."

"You're welcome, hon. I had a feeling you were fighting the mulligrubs today."

She had no earthly idea. The emotional fallout from "Dirt Roads and Sequin Gowns" was staggering and what irritated me even more was that I was already working on my *next* song! I felt crazy—chasing after a career that bred insecurity even without a dysfunctional childhood. I'd come to the conclusion that I was more or less possessed. That music was in my DNA and there was no way I could stop pursuing those perfect lyrics, the song that would bring a tingle to my spine and a smile from my audience. Still, occasionally, I'd daydream about what I'd do with myself if I *could* manage the impossible. I had no other marketable skills except working at McNair Orchards, and I knew Mac would rehire me in an instant. But that was crazy thinking because even if I were able to quit, I would never, ever head back anywhere so close to the place I was running from. If I sold out, I'd invest what I had and go somewhere out of the country and simply lose myself. This was all small comfort because I knew it would be easier to escape my shadow than to get away from the urge to write songs.

"It's tough being in the public eye, isn't it, hon?" Tonilynn's voice pushed its way in. "I bet you feel like you need to just go crawl into a hole for a while sometimes."

"Yeah," I said.

"I understand. There have been times when I just wanted to yell, 'Stop the world! I want to get off!'"

That made me smile. "Sometimes I don't even want to write music or sing anymore, Tonilynn. I mean it! I am so, so weary of ripping pages out of my past and putting them to music."

Tonilynn reached for my hand, her big, brown eyes full of concern as she began quoting the liner notes from my recent album: "'Jenny Cloud grapples with memories of her Southern roots. Her world-weary sounds and lingering vocals touch her audiences' souls.'" She squeezed my hand. "You've got a gift, hon. A miraculous gift. Crafting a piece of art from nothing but words and notes the way you do? Touching folks? Surely you know the Lord gave you the ability to write certain things no one else can, and he wants you to use your gift for his glory."

I just laughed.

"Hon," Tonilynn said. "You've got to believe your music has a purpose. You've got to trust that the Lord was with you as you went through those hard places in your childhood, and that you're exactly where you're meant to be now."

I said nothing.

"My past used to torment me until I learned some things, and now I use it to my advantage. Well, to the Lord's advantage, I ought to say." Tonilynn smiled. "Helping folks in my little corner of the world. Know what I mean?"

I shrugged. She'd never shared with me the specifics of her past.

"I'm here to tell you there are songs only you can write, Jennifer. And in the great orchestra of life, you owe it to the Lord to play your instrument, your beautiful voice, the best you can. I'm telling you right now, hon, if you'll let him, he'll redeem your past and use it for the glory of his kingdom. Your music can have eternal value."

I glanced down at the ground. A voice in my head said, *She doesn't know what you've been through, Jennifer! She's making a lot of assumptions! Using a lot of weird terms. Just don't answer and maybe she'll hush.* But I looked up at Tonilynn, at those sincere eyes of hers, and I got a guilty feeling thick as molasses.

"Well," I said, "I appreciate your concern. Honestly. But I don't want to discuss religion. The fact is, I don't really even look most of my past in the eye. I make up stories to myself about it so I can handle it."

We sat for a while without saying anything. At last Tonilynn spoke in the gentlest voice, "Something I've been wondering, hon. Where do you run in times of trouble?"

"Huh?"

"What do you do when life gets stressful, throws you a curveball? When issues come up that you can't handle?" She used two perfect pink fingernails to pluck a clover from between blades of grass. "Where is it you go for relief from life's pain, in your hour of need? We've all got a refuge, an escape, and it doesn't seem to me that you're a drinker. Or into drugs."

I shook my head. I looked at Tonilynn's sparkly blue eye shadow catching bits of the sun. "The river," I said at last, "I go to Riverfront Park and sit on the bridge and watch the Cumberland. The water's soothing, peaceful."

Tonilynn thought for a while. "Yes, river water is nice," she said, "but I want you to know, Jesus Christ is the fountain of *living* waters. Where folks thirsty for things like love and beauty and joy and *peace in regard to their pasts* can come and drink."

"Well, that's nice." I was impatient to move on to other subjects.

"I promise, Jennifer, put your hand in his and Jesus will help you deal honestly with those painful pieces of your past. Then you can use them in your music to help folks."

That just about did me in. It was getting exhausting. "Let me get this right, I'm supposed to let myself get tortured and suffer just so other people can enjoy my music? Why would anybody in their right mind want to do that?!"

I watched Tonilynn's face droop, saw lines of her pancake makeup in the downturned corners of her mouth and the grooves between her eyebrows. "Listen, hon," she said finally. "It's not just something I got out of the Bible. I read about this fellow, he's dead now, but his name was Freud, and he was real famous for psychiatric stuff. He said that when a person locks things away in their unconscious mind, all it does is make things worse. He said it's important to dig things up and look them in the eye, release them because emotions are so powerful they'll backfire sooner or later if you don't."

I didn't know what to say. *Freud . . .* he wasn't exactly somebody I was familiar with. I'd heard of him but never studied him or anything he said about keeping stuff pushed back. Maybe it was real and maybe it was harmful, but it wouldn't do us any good to sit around talking about it. "I . . . I'm just really exhausted today, Tonilynn. I'll be just fine tomorrow." This came out thin and unconvincing.

Tonilynn took a deep breath. "If you'll allow the Lord, Jennifer, he'll use that awful stuff to bring you a blessing."

I sighed. It was useless to argue. Tonilynn had a stubborn streak a mile wide. I'd begun to grow so weary of her incessant talk about all the God stuff. I knew without a doubt, whatever Freud or God Almighty had to say to the contrary, that digging up the past was crazy. Part of me wondered if I could tolerate this fixation of Tonilynn's any longer. But just as quick I knew I would, because Tonilynn was my friend. My only friend and therefore, my best friend. I would just have to be more stubborn than her.

"Hey," she said softly after a bit, "you ready to tell me that one story?"

The hair on my arms stood up. "What?"

"You know, the one you promised to tell me about how you got to Nashville?"

First of all, I didn't remember promising, and second, it made me queasy to think of all the different events leading up to that day. I knew I couldn't tell one without the others. I took a huge bite of bagel so I wouldn't have to talk.

"Okeydoke, hon," Tonilynn said, getting to her feet. "Reckon we need to reschedule our Hair Chair appointment. I called Mike on the way here and told him he better call the photographer and move your appointment with him. How does tomorrow afternoon look? Say, three p.m.?"

"Okay." ·

"Great. Hey, why don't you just plan to come have supper up on Cagle Mountain after our session? I'll carry you up there in the Pontiac."

I was taken aback. I didn't want to sound mean or ungrateful, but I just couldn't imagine being couped up in Tonilynn's car while she was in this Jesus mood. I had to think up an excuse. "Um . . . I can't. I've got something going on tomorrow night."

She knew I was lying. "Aw, come on. You'll get a kick out of Aunt Gomer."

I looked at those pleading eyes and I said, "All right."

Later that evening, I ran myself a hot bath. With Alan Jackson blasting out of the radio on the top shelf of the towel closet and a full moon shining through the window, I lay back in the tub thinking, *How in the world did she get me to say yes to going up to Cagle Mountain?*

Bridge: Aunt Gomer

I was raised right here in the hills of Tennessee, with the sound of the mandolin, the banjo, and the fiddle as my lullabies. I may be eighty-six, but I'm still spry enough to dance a fine jig. 'Course I have to be careful my bloomers don't show if we got company comin' like we do tonight. Tonilynn's bringing that new country music star she fixes the hair and makeup for.

I'm excited because I love true country. Real country music has to have a twang to it, and I don't cotton to that so-called new, progressive country music I hear coming out of Tonilynn's radio.

Tonilynn says I'm stuck in the past and need to change with the times because Nashville and country music are both much more sophisticated than they used to be. Well, there's some things you just can't improve. I don't know why they think it's progress to ruin something perfect.

I told that to Tonilynn and she says if God was to allow Hank or Patsy to leave heaven and revisit this planet, they'd be the first to embrace the new country sound. She says it don't matter about the *style* of a country song as long as the *soul* of country is behind it. I disagree. My country music has to be 100 percent pure. The way this little gal, Jenny Cloud, does it.

A lot of these "contemporary country" songs are just rock 'n' roll if you ask me. I remember back in the sixties when rock 'n' roll got to be so big and caused the youth of our nation to go wild. In fact, it was rock 'n' roll what led Tonilynn astray. Music is powerful stuff. Satan was the minister of music up in heaven, you know, before the Fall, when he exalted himself and grew proud, which is why God kicked him right out of the heavenly choir loft. But old slewfoot's still in the music business today, down here on this earth, and rock 'n' roll is his specialty. I may sound old-fashion, be set in my ways, but I don't cotton to raunchy lyrics and a beat that makes young folks want to gyrate their bodies and lose their morals. It puts ideas into their heads and makes them desecrate their earthly temples. Just look at all the tattoos on Tonilynn. I asked her if she thought she could find herself a man who'd like all that stuff she has on her.

She said, "Aunt Gomer, I don't give a fig. You need to give up your dream of me finding a man. I work hard keeping the stars beautified, and when I get home, I don't have the energy to go off courtin'. Plus, I like spending time with my baby boy."

I told her, I said, "First off, Bobby Lee is thirty-two years old, and second of all, you could quit your job and spend time in the day with Bobby Lee, and in the evenings go find yourself a man. You don't need to worry about earning a living because I own this house and the land straight out, and we got the garden to feed us."

Thinking of Bobby Lee, I'm wondering if this Jenny Cloud person might be a good match for him. Tonilynn says she's twenty-seven, recently busted up with Holt Cantrell. Only thing is, I wonder does Bobby Lee's equipment still work? That's the one thing might be an issue and I may be bold of tongue as Tonilynn likes to say, but I don't dare ask Bobby Lee about his privates. That's why they're called privates. His legs don't work, but I don't know if all that stuff down there is connected. I do want him to look nice tonight, and I told him he was going to wind up like Absalom if he didn't cut that long hair of his. He just laughed.

Tonilynn says not to get fancy. Country music stars are no different from us—they got hopes and dreams and fears underneath all the fine clothes and fancy hairstyles. They talk about mortgages, shopping, and the weather same as we do. But in the very next breath, she tells me Jenny Cloud lives in a ten-thousand-square-foot mansion, which she owns outright, and that she has her a maid service and a lawn service and no telling what all else.

But the sad thing is, Tonilynn talks like Jenny Cloud doesn't have a soul on this earth. When Tonilynn asked me if she could invite her to supper, of course I said yes. I said we could be her adoptive family because Jesus wants us to care for the lonely.

⸻

You would think a star would enter a room and fill it up with her stage presence, her charisma and what not. But when Tonilynn showed up with Jenny Cloud, the girl was all but hiding behind her. When I introduced myself, she squeaked out, "Nice to meet you, ma'am. I'm Jennifer Anne Clodfelter," in the most pitiful little voice. Seemed uncomfortable in her own skin.

I'll give her credit, though. I respect folks who are kind to helpless animals, and once we got inside the house, she went right over, knelt down, and just buried her face in Erastus's stinky neck. 'Course, anybody who loves that hound is good in Bobby Lee's book, and he came wheeling in from the hallway. And I said, "Bobby Lee, this here's Jennifer Anne Clodfelter."

Then I turned to her and said, "This here's Bobby Lee Pardue, Tonilynn's son and the owner of this canine."

She got a real surprised look on her face, then said, "It's a pleasure to meet you, Mr. Pardue," and, "Your dog has the most beautiful, expressive eyes I've ever seen."

"I couldn't do without my Erastus," said Bobby Lee. "I'd be absolutely lost without this feller."

Jennifer asked was Erastus trained to help folks in wheelchairs, and Bobby Lee said, "Only thing he's trained in is chasing rabbits and scratching fleas." She started laughing and I was feeling real encouraged they were hitting it off so good.

We got seated around the table, and I said for everybody to bow their head while I asked the Lord's blessing: *Lord, bless this food to the nourishment of our bodies and our lives to your service. In Jesus' name, Amen,* and then I started helping myself to mashed potatoes and butterbeans and collard greens. I had hot pepper sauce and vinegar on the table, so I passed them to Jennifer, along with the biscuits and the platter of pork chops.

Bobby Lee helped himself to some sorghum syrup, and when he was done, I said to Jennifer, "You want some for your biscuit?"

"No, thanks," she said.

"You don't like sorghum on your biscuit?" I patted the side of the jar. "Ain't nothing better than a hot biscuit with butter and sorghum."

"Um . . . no, thank you. I really don't care for any."

"Just try it. Go ahead, you'll love it. I guarantee."

Tonilynn reached over and grabbed the sorghum right out of my hand and set it way over beside her plate and said, "What's on your head, Aunt Gomer?"

Well, she knew good and well what my garland was for, but I figured she was just trying to make conversation on account of Jennifer wasn't talking much. "It's my pennyroyal, to cure swimmy-headedness and headaches."

"Modern folks call that aromatherapy," Tonilynn said. "When a smell can help things."

"Well, whatever you call it, I believe the Lord gives us remedies in our natural world, and pennyroyal helps a lot of things. In addition to soothing human heads, it's a dandy natural insect repellant." I turned to Jennifer. "You like playing in the dirt?"

"What?" She looked at me like I was speaking a foreign language.

"She means gardening." Bobby Lee used his biscuit to sop up some pot likker.

"Oh, um . . . I guess." Jennifer forked up a single butterbean, looking hard at it before she put it into her mouth.

"Well, I'll have to take you out and show you my garden when we're done. I'm aiming to plant my melons and my zinnias tomorrow."

"Aunt Gomer," Tonilynn piped up, "we talked about this. You need to relax. It's not even April yet and the last average frost date is April fifteenth, and there's a reason the weatherman calls it a *killing* frost."

"I'll relax when I'm dead. I'm gonna get out there tomorrow and do my tilling." I turned to Jennifer. "Got to work our dirt hard on account of the clay and limestone. Tell you one thing, when the Lord starts sprinkling his yellow talcum power is how I know spring's here."

Bobby Lee shook his head. "The Lord's talcum powder," he said under his breath in a snide voice, but I got keen ears.

"Ain't a thing wrong with calling pollen the Lord's talcum powder!" I said.

Tonilynn didn't say word one to her sassy offspring. In fact, she was cutting up Bobby Lee's pork chop!

"You're ruining him," I said.

Tonilynn squinted her eyes at me. "How would you like it if you couldn't get up and walk or run around?"

"That boy, that *man*," I said, "is a lot more capable than you give him credit for. Bobby Lee could be somebody if you didn't smother him."

"Hush your mouth!" Tonilynn said, and her face got pink.

I did not. I said, "When it's something Bobby Lee *wants* to do—like fishing—he literally flies in that wheelchair! But when you come around, he turns into a helpless invalid."

Nobody said anything for a long spell. I saw Jennifer sliding her butter knife up under the side of her plate so the pot likker from the collard greens wouldn't run into anything. I had a mind to tell her that the pot likker was where all the good vitamins were, but I didn't want Tonilynn fussing anymore. So I turned to Jennifer and said, "I saw you on the television after that song of yours about the honky-tonk tomcat came out, and I told Bobby Lee your voice reminds me of Patsy Cline's, so pure and all. And you look like Cher, back when she was doing that show with Sonny Bono. Look just like an Indian with your long silky black hair and that pretty skin. You got any Indian blood?"

"I . . . I'm not sure," she said, her eyes darting this way and that.

I could not imagine not knowing what blood was in my family tree. "Well," I told her, "you ought to look into that whole Indian thing. That right there might be something that would benefit your career. Seems like if you got black or Indian blood in you, they roll out the red carpet."

Tonilynn gave me an evil look.

"Everything is real good, Miz Gomer," Jennifer said.

"Talk about a good cook," I said. "My mother made the best buttermilk biscuits in this world. She also made fried chicken, pound cake, apple cobbler, peach pickles, and fig preserves good enough to die for. She tried to teach all of us children soon as we could stand on a chair to reach the stove. 'Course, my first love was gardening and mostly I stayed outdoors, but I did manage to pick up a few tricks. It was Tonilynn's mother who was a real natural in the kitchen. Norma used to win ribbons at all the fairs."

"Really?" Jennifer turned to Tonilynn.

"That's what I'm told," Tonilynn said.

"Norma no longer walks this earth," I teased.

"What happened?" Jennifer set her biscuit down and looked at me.

"When she saw Tonilynn, she died." I knew as the words leapt out of my mouth, they was a tad on the mean side. That poor skinny thing grabbed hold of the table, and I noticed her fingernails were bit down past the quick. Tonilynn gave me one of those exasperated looks of hers before she turned to Jennifer and said in the softest voice, "She died in childbirth."

Jennifer's eyes got all sparkly the way they'll get when tears are fixing to spill, and I figured it was a good time to bring up the subject of marriage, so I said, "There's bound to be hard things on this earth, but I'm the type who chooses to look at the silver lining of every cloud."

I got quiet for a minute to let Jennifer's curiosity build. Tonilynn and Bobby Lee knew what I was fixing to tell because I'd told it umpteen times. "When I came of age, didn't no man come courtin' me. My three sisters had beaus coming out the woodwork, but at six-foot-two-inches tall, I towered over most of 'em. At first I didn't mind being alone. I didn't want to do anything anyhow but work in my garden. I was purely content.

"But then my sisters got married and moved off, and when I was thirty-five, Mama and Daddy went to their graves within six months of each other, and left me with only my hens clucking and fussing and hunting bugs in the yard.

"Well, I still had my garden, and gardening was the first job. Says so in Genesis. Says God formed man and then he planted a garden and there he put the man to till it. But what got me is what he said later, that it wasn't good for man to be alone, and I may not be one of those feminists, but I believe that includes females too.

"Of course I talked to the Lord about it, as he's the one said 'Ask and ye shall receive.' I told him I was still menstruating regular and that I was mighty lonely down here, and I didn't doubt in my heart he would answer me.

"Time galloped on and I stayed busy, kept my faith strong. I can still remember clear as anything the day I was out in the garden picking a mess of butterbeans and up drives Dr. Fred telling me Norma had died in childbirth. But what shocked me was when her husband ran off the day of the funeral. Left his infant daughter, Tonilynn Jasmine Pardue. Now I can't judge Dan. How could you blame an eighteen year-old boy?

"Tonilynn was the most precious thing. Little bright-eyed face with eyes like a hickory nut and hair like dandelion down. And smart as a whip. Knew how to read when she was four years old. But had her a wild streak.

"That's why I wasn't surprised when she got in the family way when she wasn't but fifteen, and her not married. I threw her out of the house because young folks need to learn their actions have consequences."

Just by the way all the color had drained out of Jennifer's pretty face, I knew she was most likely misjudging me, so I added, "Believe me, it wasn't no picnic. I missed my girl so much. I missed seeing that precious child she birthed. I didn't get to do all the cuddling a grandma wants to do." I paused to look hard at Tonilynn when I said the next part. "But I did what I had to, called 'tough love' when it hurts you *and* the other person.

"And you know what? After they came back up here to Cagle Mountain, I never did find out which one of those boys was Bobby Lee's daddy. But the years have passed and none of that matters. I couldn't love Tonilynn or Bobby Lee any more. In fact, they're both like my very own.

Jennifer stared at me with those unusual green eyes.

"Some things are just better the way they turn out to be than if we'd got what we asked for. All those years I pined for a family, and I finally got me one, and I can honestly say I couldn't have dreamed up anything better. That's the beautiful thing about a family. Doesn't have to be what's written in Webster's—male marries female, their sperm and egg meet, and they have children. No, families are built on love, and, honey, if you need yourself a family, we'd be proud to have you. Anytime you need a place to run to or just folks you can let your hair down with, you come on up here to Cagle Mountain."

"Well . . . thank you," that child squeaked in this tiny voice.

7

On the trip home, Tonilynn asked me to guess what Aunt Gomer's two greatest fears were. Feeling a little shell-shocked, I just said, "What?"

"Satan and having to go to a nursing home."

I didn't respond.

"Know what I say to her whenever she gets all worked up?" Tonilynn turned her liquid brown eyes from the road and looked at me like the answer was obvious. "I tell her, 'Aunt Gomer, first off, you don't have to be scared of the devil. The Lord's stronger than him and that's like saying you don't have faith.'

"And about the nursing home, I say, 'Aunt Gomer, *if*, and that's a big old *if* because 99 percent of the things we fear never happen, but *if* you have to go to a nursing home, you'll be so out of it you won't even know you're there!'" She laughed and slapped the stonewashed denim stretched over her thigh.

I don't think I even blinked. It was an eye-opening experience seeing from whence Tonilynn came. Her homestead was certainly what folks would call backwoods, maybe even *backwards*. That old tin-roofed farmhouse with tar-paper siding, hens pecking around a tractor tire on its side in the front yard, a lopsided well house with a communal drinking jar, and a hound dog whimpering at some dream as he slept beneath the kitchen table. I thought of how Aunt Gomer maintained that God answered her prayer with her sister's death, and that brought forth something I'd overheard one of the sound technicians at the studio saying about Tonilynn. He said, "She's just one of those wack-job born-agains who acts like Jesus is her best friend."

But wasn't it nice to feel like part of a family for a while? I sure didn't have to put on airs to hang out at Cagle Mountain. And even if Tonilynn was hopelessly wacko when it came to religion, she was unpretentious not to mention entertaining and easy to talk to. The same with Bobby Lee. What you first noticed about Tonilynn's son, after the wheelchair, was how ruggedly handsome the man was, with his sun-kissed skin and his long, unstyled chestnut hair. He favored his mother quite a bit, but where Tonilynn had deep brown eyes and a cute nose, Bobby Lee had hazel eyes and a classic Roman nose. Not bad to look at.

It was that very night, as soon as I decided to redirect my energy away from judging Tonilynn to just accepting her, that I opened up a space to create what I'd been yearning for—a true friendship. Where there'd been a cavernous, lonely ache inside of me, a tiny flame of hope flickered to life. The flame grew brighter with each thump of my heart as it dawned on me that I could reveal things to Tonilynn without fear of judgment. Not that I wanted to reveal everything. There were some things I'd *never* share.

<hr>

Generally I avoided the terrace at Harmony Hill, but the next evening a full moon lured me out onto the bricks. It had been more than three months since the ugly incident with Holt, and as I stood there looking up at the nighttime sky, a recollection moved in of the two of us during one of our good times. At one end of the terrace was an enclosed sitting porch, with candle chandeliers and a fireplace, and Holt and I were sitting on the sofa there, our legs entwined as we gazed out the big window, watching the stars make their appearance. Suddenly he jumped up, pulling me to my feet, and we danced to Josh Turner's deep, sexy voice singing, "Why Don't We Just Dance," and laughed at how we were acting it out.

The memory was so vivid I could smell Holt like he was right there in my arms again, that lingering scent of evergreen from his cologne mixed with the faint aroma of leather from his hatband you wouldn't notice if you weren't oh-so-close. I heard him whispering "Love you, babe," into that soft place behind my ear, making my breath catch in my throat. I felt his five-o'clock shadow tickly rough, making my insides melt as he whispered, "We're the next Faith Hill and Tim McGraw, you know."

For a while I was carried away, my body recalling all the delicious sensations of being held, adored by Holt Cantrell, with his bedroom eyes and that devilish grin he kept on his lips. Then all of a sudden, my breath caught in my throat and everything evaporated as I recalled a recent article in *Country Weekly*.

Maybe I *was* a thief and a psychotic mess! Maybe I *had* pushed and pushed until Holt finally reached his limit, having no choice but to twist my arm around my back until it almost snapped. I shouldn't have called the police because really, the whole episode wasn't Holt's fault! It was mine for pouring his Jack Daniel's down the sink. That was stealing, really, if I was going to be honest with myself.

I started to cry, and that's when I dug my cell phone out of the floppy pocket of my sweatpants. I needed to call Holt and apologize, set things straight. He was in Vancouver on tour, but he'd be home in three days, and when he got back to Nashville we could pick right back up where we'd left off.

But right before I pressed the button to call Holt, I remembered Tonilynn saying, "He's a snake, hon." It was hard, but I managed to stop myself with the thought that I'd wait and talk to Tonilynn some more about what led up to me pouring Holt's whiskey down the sink, about what he was watching on the screen of his laptop. Those things he said he wanted me to do!

—⧏⧐—

It was hard, going back and forth between pining for Holt and then remembering Tonilynn's warning. I had to make it through the two days until I was scheduled to be back in the Hair Chair, and there was nothing on my agenda except playing around with some songs in progress and an afternoon meeting with Mike about the liner notes for my upcoming album.

I wondered if I had it in me to talk to Mike this time. My stomach had started aching continually and I felt like I was walking across an emotional minefield anytime I'd sing or hear "Dirt Roads and Sequin Gowns." The spirit of the song was supposedly one about rags to riches and overcoming; this poor little girl lives in a shack on the side of a dirt road, and as she grows up, she sings to passersby, with her muddy knees and her dirty feet and wearing tattered dresses. She's dreaming of becoming a star, and then, years down the road, she's standing onstage at the Grand Ole Opry, in a sparkly dress, happy.

The final verse goes: *When she sings the song that plays in her heart, she's wearing a sequined gown. Sometimes it's red, sometimes it's blue, but it's never gonna be dirt brown. It's never gonna be dirt brown. When she sings the song that plays in her heart, she's wearing a sequined gown.*

She comes off sounding victorious, but I knew the story between the lines. I knew the soul-wrenching cost of fame.

⸎

Tomorrow came as it always did, and it was a rainy April day. Usually I loved rainy days for songwriting. I'd sit in a spot on the floor at one of the deep windows in the den with my coffee on the low sill and my notebook open between spread-eagled legs, looking out at what was blooming in my garden, and beyond that to the branches of trees reaching upward to the sky. It was calming and inspirational at the same time. But that day I felt a heavy weight pressing down on me as I contemplated the afternoon meeting with Mike. I penned the first words that flashed through my mind; *The dark side of a star.*

I held my notebook to my heart and almost wept from the truth. There was so much from my past I needed to keep buried, and I knew I could do it if I didn't have Mike constantly pushing, pushing, saying stuff like, "Being happy is awful for writing a country song, Jenny girl. Fans just want to hear about sad things, like leaving and heartbreak," and "You just need to put yourself in a dark place until you can come up with something good," and "You know as well as I do that as a songwriter, heartbreak's invaluable. It's good to have these terrible things you've gone through. Dig deep for that heart-rending song." He also loved quoting Conway Twitty: "A good country song takes a page out of somebody's life and puts it to music."

Just thinking of the superconfident way Mike said all these things made my skin draw up tight.

137

I dressed in my disguise and drove to Panera Bread for our two o'clock meeting. Even though my stomach had been sending out echoing rumbles, one bite of cinnamon crunch bagel and a third of a cup of espresso was all I could handle. I sat staring at the front door, hugging myself.

"Jenny Cloud! How ya doin', sweetheart?" Mike said loudly in that charismatic Southern drawl when he walked in, those fancy black cowboy boots of his making a grand entrance. I flinched, ducked down. It was a good thing the other chairs in the front room were empty at this hour.

"Fine," I said around a powerful whiff of Herrera for Men.

"Good, good. Lemme run grab a libation and we'll talk. 'Kay?"

"Sure."

Mike returned with coffee, sunk into a chair, and stretched his long khaki-clad legs out in front of him. "So," he said after a gulp, "you're absolutely gonna love what marketing came up with for our new album. No other word for it but genius." He pulled a folded sheet of paper from his shirt pocket and smoothed it out flat on his thigh. "Okeydoke. Listen at this: 'A country music star and the autobiographical songs that reflect the sorrows and pain, the disillusionment of her childhood.'" He looked up at me with those hazel eyes like bullets to my soul. "Nice, huh?"

I didn't answer.

"Or how 'bout this one? 'A Country Music Diva grapples with the drinkin', cheatin', lyin', and leavin' of her Southern roots'?" Without pausing for my response, he continued. "Here's another: 'When the music calls her home, a country music superstar must deal with the dark memories and the people who didn't keep their promises.'"

Mike grew even more excited, talking fast and gesturing with his free hand. "'Each of the songs on this album is the kind of a steel guitar-drenched, tear-in-your-ear ballad that Jenny Cloud can deliver like no one else. These are stories, songs carved from Cloud's own experience.'"

I finally managed to make a sound. I laughed, a humorless little snort.

Mike leaned forward and touched my wrist. "I knew you'd like them too. These are incredible, like I said." Smile crinkles radiated from the corners of his eyes. "Flint Recording is sure taking care of you, aren't they darlin'? We're gaining visibility in places where country music doesn't usually go. We are on a roll!"

I lifted my espresso for a drink and my hand was trembling so that some trickled from the corner of my mouth and dripped down onto my blouse.

"Key words here are *support* and *visibility*, Jenny," Mike continued, "which we're getting from radio and from the digital retailers. The goal here is to sell more albums, and speaking of that, we've got to make sure your CD's packaging will achieve that as well. I'm supposed to be getting design ideas for the cover tomorrow. You want me to e-mail them on to you, or do you trust me to choose?"

I dried my chin on my shoulder and looked at Mike, beseechingly, I thought.

"Okay," he said, switching directions seamlessly, "that's settled. I'll call on the cover. Now let's talk about what you're currently working on. What you got in the channel, darlin'?"

"I'm . . . a song called 'The Dark Side of a Star.'" This came out sounding like a question.

"Well, now, that's certainly a catchy title—'The Dark Side of a Star.' Can't wait to hear it." Mike's eyes were bright. He leaned back in his chair, laced his fingers across his big silver belt buckle. "Got Jerome playing around with the chords for 'True Love and Wild Blackberries,' and I believe he's really pleased with it. You'll have to come by the studio and give it a listen."

It felt like Mike had leaned forward and slapped me. I did not want to even *think* about that song. I'd written it, along with several other similar ones, while I was high on love for Holt Cantrell. I opened up my mouth, but the words of protest in my head wouldn't come out. I yelled internally; *Jennifer, you weakling! When are you ever going to learn to assert yourself! This is literally killing you!*

———⁂———

Loving music the way I did was a double-edged sword. It certainly seemed like I'd continue to sell myself out purely because I adored writing, singing, and performing. And, yes, I adored success, if I was going to be honest.

It was hard to fall asleep that night, and finally, as I closed my eyes sometime after two a.m., right as I fell into that no-man's land between awake and asleep, an unspeakable image from my past began playing on the screen of my mind. In that odd way of dreams, it was all tangled up with a vision of a business downtown on Demonbreun Street. Déjà Vu Showgirls was a nude club with a pulsing neon sign showcasing a woman's legs in a seductive pose. Every time I passed it, I felt heartbreaking, overwhelming pity for those young girls inside, the couch dancers. That night my pity mixed with a sharp, bright fury as I saw my own vulnerable self so long ago. The film rolled on and the darkness grew deeper, mixing with astonishment that he would use me like that, my own father!

Some vaguely conscious part of me was aware that the whole poisonous mix of guilt and the loss of my innocence would come crashing down, full force, if I didn't stop it. I struggled to sit upright, shaking in the dark, the breath-snatching shame like a hot cattle brand on my soul. I did not sleep one wink that night. My survival instinct kept me pacing through Harmony Hill, telling myself I'd keep awake forever, reassuring myself *I'll never let this one out. Not even for a perfect country song.*

Bridge: Aunt Gomer

It's been raining cats and dogs so many days I feel like I'm growing moldy. But like they say, April showers bring May flowers. I went out this afternoon when it slacked off a spell and cut two early irises for Bobby Lee to give Jennifer when she comes for supper.

Tonilynn said not to say word one about Holt Cantrell, especially don't mention his new hit "Livin' on Your Kisses" on account of that's a song he and Jennifer wrote together and he has claimed as entirely his. Tonilynn was like a broken record, saying, "Aunt Gomer, promise me, 'cause Jennifer's going through a lot of hard issues right now. Keep your lips sealed on anything about Holt Cantrell. Promise?" I almost told her, "Why don't you just write it down and fasten it to the Frigidaire?" Tonilynn ought to know I wouldn't hurt that nervous little gal for anything in this world.

When Bobby Lee wheeled out of the bathroom after lunch, I barely recognized him. He looked—I guess the word is *radiant*. Had his beard trimmed neat and his hair combed back into a nice, clean ponytail, and he was wearing a fairly clean T-shirt. I didn't like what it said, however—"You can smell our butts for miles. Slocumb's Barbecue."

But I ignored that because the most remarkable thing was the change in Bobby Lee's personality. His eyes were lit up, and he had this brightness about him. Generally, unless it's good fishing weather, he's a fairly hangdog kind of person. In fact, I used to wonder would there ever be anything besides fishing and hanging around with that smelly hound that would excite Bobby Lee after his accident. Well, not thirty minutes after Jennifer left the homestead that first visit, here he was with his laptop perched on his knees, his fingers going to town hunting up her website. Said it was just on account of his interest in music, but I knew the real reason he kept watching that video over and over. I'm more of a phonograph person myself, and I don't generally watch singers gyrating and crooning on what they call music videos. Of course, I couldn't help seeing Jennifer as Bobby Lee kept watching her singing a song called "Walking the Wildwood." It was real pretty, and I have to admit she wasn't dressed trashy or dancing suggestively. I could tell she was made for the stage. She did not act nervous like she does in the flesh.

Bobby Lee kept after me to carry him to Chattanooga, to the Best Buy to get the CD that song is on. He couldn't stand it until he had it in his hands, ripping the plastic off and reading the little booklet what came with it, and then listening to it on his CD player so many times *I* had it memorized.

I told Tonilynn she ought to look into getting him one of those special vans where he could drive himself using hand controls. I said, "It's a cryin' shame when a grown man has to beg me to carry him places. Bobby Lee's capable. He gets himself down to the lake lickety-split whenever those catfish are biting. Better'n most able-bodied men I know."

She was eating a bowl of Neapolitan ice cream and watching television, and she was not in a receptive mood. "Don't tell me what my child needs!"

"He's not your child. Well, he is *your* child, but he's not *a* child. That's where the problem is. If you love him, you'd—"

"He *can't* take care of himself! He's crippled!"

"He could if you'd ever give him a chance. Have you ever thought about what might happen if you and me both went on to Glory before him?"

"Don't go getting all gloomy on me."

"Speaking of gloomy, Bobby Lee'd be happier if you let him be independent."

"That is enough, Aunt Gomer! You want to know the truth? I believe the two of you are good for each other. You're so spry and able-bodied, and Bobby Lee is so . . . smart. Together, you two are like one perfect . . ." Tonilynn was sitting there, spoon in midair and hunting around for a nice way to say she thought my mind was going. My cheeks got warm and my heart started fluttering and it felt like the ground flew out from under me.

"Are you telling me you think I have the old-timer's? You think I'm losing it? Because I know I've flubbed up a thing or two lately, but I'll have you know, it wasn't on account of my mind going. It's because—"

"Please, Aunt Gomer! All I meant is Bobby Lee's so smart, and he can fix things, and you know, keep you from being alone up here. He can protect you! That's it. You need a man to protect you. Do you want me to fix you a bowl of ice cream?"

Well, I wasn't born yesterday. I knew if she didn't think he could live by himself, she sure wasn't thinking he would be my knight in shining armor. Anyway, I don't need a man to protect me. Never had one before. I've got my derringer in the drawer of my bedside table.

Rain or no rain, I had to walk straight outside into the garden to get my head together after that conversation. It took me a good half hour to turn all that over in my mind. I did not have any idea who else I could ask if they thought my mind was slipping. I decided I would think on that later.

⸺ ∞ ⸺

The menu is ham, lima beans, squash casserole, and some more of my biscuits that child seemed to think so much of. Made a pound cake for dessert. I hope Tonilynn's careful on the long drive off the main road. It's not paved and sometimes after rain like we've been having, you can slide into the ditch or clobber your head against the roof when you hit a pothole. I'm praying it's going to stop all this rain soon so I can finally get my garden in.

At five I decided I better make sure we had enough tea and clean glasses. It crossed my mind to ask Bobby Lee to do it and then comment about how independent he was over supper. "Bobby Lee!" I hollered.

He'd been in his bedroom, and he came wheeling out lickety-split. "Are they here?"

I smelled a cloud of that Axe spray we bought at the Walmart after we left Best Buy. "Not yet," I said, "I need to spruce up a bit before they get here, and I want you to see if we got enough tea and get out the glasses."

"Be happy to."

I almost fainted. Generally, Bobby Lee pitches a fit when I try to get him to do anything.

Well, I watched him as I swept the parlor and lo and behold, he was training Erastus to open the Frigidaire. Bobby Lee'd say, "Open, boy," and Erastus would pull on a dish towel hanging from the handle. Every time Erastus opened the door, Bobby Lee would give him a handful of Cap'n Crunch.

"Aunt Gomer!" Bobby Lee hollered after a bit. "Come'ere."

He was staring at the ham on the counter like it was a snake. "What's the matter?" I asked.

145

"She doesn't eat meat."

"Who?"

"Jennifer. I read how she's a vegetarian and doesn't eat anything with eyes or a mother."

I stood there listening to rain dripping off the roof and the wall clock ticking. In all my life I'd never known anybody that didn't eat meat, and I never dreamed I'd have to feed someone who didn't. It was crazy. "Oh, for crying out loud," I said finally. "Then she can eat beans, squash, and biscuits. And cake."

"Aunt Gomer," Bobby Lee said in his exasperated tone, "there's bacon fat in the butterbeans and the squash casserole, and the biscuits have lard in them. The only things truly vegetarian are the tea and the pound cake."

I looked hard at Bobby Lee. "Listen," I said, "I believe the good Lord meant for people to eat meat. That little thing *needs* her some protein. Might be why she's so tiny. Don't you say a word about the bacon fat or the lard. What she don't know won't hurt her."

<hr />

After Tonilynn asked the blessing, we started loading our plates. I passed the ham and the butterbeans around. The squash casserole was too hot, so I left it in the middle of the table. Jennifer helped herself to some butterbeans and a biscuit and a spoonful of squash, but her plate looked pathetic without a slice of ham on it, and so I said, just as innocently as you please, "Want some ham, dear? It's nice and tender."

"No thanks."

"You don't like ham?"

"I just don't care for any."

"Well, I declare. When I was growing up, ham was a real treat. Every Easter my mama fixed the prettiest ham, and she—"

"Eggs are good for Easter," Bobby Lee piped up, narrowing his eyes at me. "I think omelets . . . or a soufflé . . . no, maybe a crepe would be the perfect thing for you to serve for Easter."

"Aunt Gomer," Tonilynn touched my wrist, "I thought I told you Jennifer doesn't eat meat. We were talking about what y'all used to do when you were a child during the depression and there wasn't any meat? Remember?"

I tried to recall a conversation with Tonilynn about this, but I couldn't for the life of me. Nobody said anything for a while. Just the sound of forks and spoons clinking on plates. It flashed through my mind to slide a piece of ham between my second biscuit. "Now, who can tell me what's better than a ham biscuit," I said after a delicious bite.

"A tomato slice between a biscuit," Bobby Lee said, looking at Jennifer.

She didn't say anything, and hearing about tomatoes put me in mind of getting my warm season vegetables planted and so I rooted around in my brain and figured I'd make conversation about gardening. "Jennifer, did your mother have a garden?"

"Yes, ma'am."

"I bet she loved it same as I do."

"Nope. She didn't love it." Jennifer shook her head.

"Then why'd she do it?" Aunt Gomer asked.

"If we wanted to eat, she had to garden. Had to freeze and can and dry, too, because my father was one sorry slacker in the providing-for-your-family department."

"Bless her heart," I said. "Hard for me to fathom a person who doesn't like gardening, but I must commend a woman who does what she has to do to care for her family."

All of a sudden, that child dropped her head down into her hands real pathetic looking and mumbled, "Shoot. She didn't care for me any better than she cared for the garden."

"Well," I said, "the good Lord made us all different. Now, I'd be *happy* if I had to plant a garden and put by. I'm planting four types of beans on Good Friday—bush beans, snap beans, pole beans, and limas, and I'm also—"

"We don't need any more talk about gardening, Aunt Gomer!" Tonilynn glared at me, turned to Jennifer, and said, real soft, "It's all right, hon, you're gonna be all right. We love you."

There was a long silence. Didn't any of us hardly move a muscle. At last Jennifer lifted her head and drew in a deep breath. "My mother didn't take care of me. She lived in a state of denial. About a lot of things. She'd go around the house, sighing and saying, 'For better or for worse, that's what I promised in front of God and everyone.'"

I was going to say she sounded like a fine Christian woman, but Tonilynn was leaning over, petting her, saying, "I bet that was hard. Tell us about your growing up years."

Jennifer blinked. She looked like she was going back in her mind. "We lived in the foothills of the Blue Ridge Mountains, up this long curvy dirt road where Sugar Creek Road meets the Old State Route. Beautiful country, full of rivers, and creeks, and wild spaces to run if you needed to get your head together." Snot was running out of her nose and she blew a loud honk into her napkin. "It was perfect for me. I'd literally run for hours."

Bobby Lee about hopped out of his wheelchair. "'Walking the Wildwood!' I know that line 'bout you running so fast you'd forget to breathe and lying down next to the Noontootla. Is that a river?"

"That's a creek, runs into the Toccoa River."

Bobby Lee almost knocked his tea over. "I love the line that goes, 'He's gone, and I'm gonna run for miles and miles down red clay paths flanked with green mountain laurel, dipping my toes into blue streams clear as a violin's high note.'"

"Thank you." Jennifer blushed.

"Were you sad? About the man in that song being gone?" Bobby Lee was clutching the edge of the table.

"No. I was happy. I lived for those peaceful stretches, some going on months even, when my father didn't come around. I loved to run outside even when he wasn't home. When I was running, my feet on the ground, my eyes on the sky, or the trees, my mind was clear, and it was like I was more deeply connected to the world or something. It was a great way to . . . well, how can I put this? Think through some things I'd witnessed that nobody had to tell me weren't normal."

Now, I could certainly understand the healing power of being outside, dirt beneath and sky above. Outside was where I went when my mind got all a dither. Best thinking place I knew. But if it was too cold or stormy, I'd call one of my friends from church, Verna or Evelyn, and that was some good therapy too. I said to Jennifer, "Didn't it help to talk with your friends?"

"I didn't have any friends."

"What? You're teasing, aren't you, honey? Your mother didn't invite little friends over for you to play with?"

Jennifer sighed. "Mother had no lady friends, and I guess it just never occurred to her I'd be any different."

"You didn't have friends at school or church?"

"No. To be honest, I was scared to death of all those girls who danced through life worrying about what color polish to put on their fingernails or who was currently going with who. Probably didn't help that I didn't have the cute haircut or the nice clothes."

Tonilynn sighed. "Poor baby. Life's hard enough as it is without a friend to discuss your problems with."

"We all need friends," I said, reaching out for Bobby Lee's hand. "'Course, most men have friends where they work."

Tonilynn looked at me with those knife-eyes she makes, just itching to come back, but Jennifer piped up, and as they say, saved the day.

"Well, I didn't need a friend to tell me that what my father did—the kind of man he was, is—wasn't okay."

"What'd he do?" I asked, which just kind of naturally spouted out of my mouth. Tonilynn kicked me underneath the table, but Jennifer must not have thought it was all that awful of a thing to ask because she piped right up without hardly taking a breath.

"Basically, he's a drunk who has no respect for women."

"Is that right?" I asked.

"I used to beg Mother to take me with her and leave him. She'd say, 'Jennifer, I'm praying, and I know he'll change. In his heart, deep down, he's a good man.' She honestly believed that baloney."

Tears dribbled out of her eyes at that point, and I was touched when Bobby Lee took his napkin and passed it to her.

"Well, we all have hard things to bear, don't we?" I didn't really mean it as a question, but Jennifer started in again, and I was amazed at the vinegar came pouring out of that little gal.

"Like I said, she didn't *have* to bear it! For years, my daydreams, besides singing, were of me and mother leaving him. And when I finally realized she was never going to leave him, I prayed he'd die, maybe get drunk and fall down some stairs and break his neck or run off the road and hit a tree."

"Don't be silly," I said, "you don't mean that."

"Yes, I do. If you knew the things he did when he took drunk, or the things he said, you'd want him dead too. It wouldn't mean you weren't a good Christian."

Jennifer looked right at me and I could tell she was wanting me to agree with her. I've been going to church for eighty-six years now, read my Bible from cover to cover more times than I can count, but I was having a heap of trouble pulling up a nugget of wisdom to offer. Feeling flustered, I said, "Jennifer, you come on with me to church this Sunday for the Easter service. Just like you prayed for your father to die, you can pray for his redemption. God loves everybody, and God can save even the worst of us."

I could tell Tonilynn was put out with me, and I hadn't even mentioned Holt Cantrell. All of a sudden I remembered the pound cake. "Let me get our dessert."

Before I could even get to my feet, Bobby Lee shocked me by saying, "Keep your seat, Aunt Gomer, I'll get it."

8

Easter Sunday 2010 fell on April fourth, and I felt like a kid playing hooky as I drove down Old Hickory. Even though Mike's one of those obsessive-compulsive types of business-men, I was fairly certain he was spending the day with his wife and stepkids, so I wasn't letting myself think about the business end of anything. Easter's like Thanksgiving and Christmas and the Fourth of July. You're *supposed* to shut off thoughts about work.

The reason I felt guilty was that Aunt Gomer called me the day before. I was startled to hear her old voice coming out of my cell phone, but I guess she got my number from Tonilynn. "Good evening, child!" she said. "My offer to carry you to the Lord's house with me tomorrow to celebrate the Resurrection still stands. I'll come fetch you before the rooster crows and we'll hit the sunrise service at Bethel, followed by breakfast on the grounds. They do ham biscuits that are out of this world. Sound good?"

I told her I was sorry, that I already had plans. When I hung up, I felt a little shaky. My excuse wasn't an actual lie. My plan was a cinnamon crunch bagel and espresso so strong it would have me shaking.

The streets were still fairly empty at eight a.m., and I drove along, thinking about how bright and clean-washed everything looked outside. The sun shone in a cloudless sky and everywhere were shameless bursts of forsythia and all these silly, optimistic daffodils with trumpets that reminded me of the hoopskirts of Southern belles. Perfect weather for Easter.

Then I started thinking about the reason Aunt Gomer invited me to church with her. If I were honest with myself, thoughts of my father's demise still lived like bright glowing mushrooms in the dung of my dark fantasies. I viewed them from a sideways glance, like when Sarah Bean, a disabled girl, was sent to our regular classroom in middle school for something called "mainstreaming." You were *aware* of Sarah Bean at all times, even though you knew it was rude to stare at her.

Though the hate-filled words spewed out of my mouth easily up there on Cagle Mountain, I definitely didn't like to look at my death wishes for my father head-on. Even then I knew that they were not what nice little girls, good daughters, thought. Definitely, I did not have the "joy, joy, joy, joy, down in my heart" we used to sing about at vacation Bible school. But then again, I remembered thinking so long ago, being absolutely positive, that God would understand that it was precisely *because* of that absence of joy that I fantasized my father's demise.

I knew better than to stay on that train of thought, and so I summoned another image from Cagle Mountain: Bobby Lee going outside with me.

"Looks like it's finally clearing off?" Bobby Lee said just as we reached the Pontiac. "I bet Aunt Gomer's going to be out here dancing a jig."

I looked up. The moon was high and full and a luminous white, and when I looked back down I saw it reflected on the surface of a hundred little puddles of rainwater in the road and also in the chrome on Bobby Lee's wheelchair. I couldn't help noticing a Mason jar with two very tall purplish-white irises situated between his thighs. He saw me looking and nodded his head down and said, "These are for you." His long brown hair was pulled back into a ponytail, and when he bent his head I could see a jagged scar on his neck, running from behind his right earlobe and disappearing into the neck of his T-shirt. I was so surprised I didn't say anything for a minute. Then I said, "They're beautiful. Thank you."

He nodded, smiled, and patted Erastus's shoulder. "Thank *you*," he said. "Wanna know something? One of the things I admire most about you, Jennifer, is that you're famous but you don't go around with your nose stuck up in the air. You'll stoop to hang out with regular old folks like us."

I liked hearing him say that, but I didn't know what to answer, so for a while I just leaned against the door of the Pontiac, looking at the shape of the giant pecan tree to the side of the house, and then I leaned forward to scratch behind Erastus's soft, warm ears. "Thank you," I murmured. "That's so sweet."

"We're turning into the Mutual Thank-You Club, now aren't we?" Bobby Lee grinned as he wheeled forward and reached for the door handle to the backseat. He wedged the jar of irises between some shoes and boxes on the floorboard. "Speaking of thank-yous, after I got your *Blue Mountain Blues* CD, I must've listened to "Walking the Wildwood" a hundred times, and every single time, I fell into it. It's a beautiful experience. I know it hasn't been easy for you, judging from the story you told tonight, but there's no doubt you have an awesome gift of touching folks through your music. So, thank you."

Hearing that thrilled my soul. Being able to supply someone with joy, well, that was *almost* reason enough to keep pursuing the dream and braving the heartbreak of it all. Wasn't it? I rode along, hugging that memory of Bobby Lee beside me in the front yard on Cagle Mountain, the moon shining down and the smell of rain in the air.

Here was the dilemma: I knew music was my gift, and I loved knowing it brought happiness to people besides myself, but my whole goal in getting away from Blue Ridge was to forget everything, to NEVER resurrect it, no matter what, and the past was starting to blindside me even when I wasn't in that vulnerable place of falling asleep. It would hit at the craziest times. Just when I'd get to feeling fairly safe, something would prompt an earthquake that sliced that red Georgia clay wide open, and boy, was I a mess for a while. Thankfully, that episode between my sophomore and junior year was still safely in the grave.

All of a sudden, the idea of sitting in Panera with just my thoughts made me cringe. Wasn't Easter supposed to be about pretty baskets full of eggs, fluffy yellow chicks, bunnies, and little girls in frilly dresses? Having a childhood rocked by emotional ambushes certainly wasn't the proverbial "warm coat to wear when you're older."

I stomped on the brake, made a U-turn, and went speeding back toward Harmony Hill, telling myself the cops wouldn't ticket on Easter. Right before I reached my drive, I stomped the brake again, skidding to a stop on the side of the road. Inside my enormous house it would be as silent as the grave. Another U-turn and I felt like Mario Andretti, speeding toward Cagle Mountain.

I turned on the radio because whenever I felt myself drowning in fears, listening to music helped me kick back up to the surface where I could at least dog paddle for a while. Kenny Rogers was singing "Coward of the County," and then I was singing along to Dolly Parton's rollicking "9 to 5," and then really belting it out with George Jones on "He Stopped Loving Her Today." I was tempted to close my eyes as I sang along to "The Dance" with Garth Brooks, and also "Forever and Ever, Amen," with Randy Travis, but I managed to keep my eyes on the quiet roads.

When Willie Nelson's "Blue Eyes Crying in the Rain" finished, I figured I had to be about halfway to Tonilynn's, but then, wouldn't you know it, Tammy Wynette started singing "Stand by Your Man." I love Tammy, but those lyrics, particularly after my scene with Holt, were salt on a wound. For some dumb reason, I didn't turn it off, and the deejay came on when it finished, crowing something about how some singers do live out their songs. "Take Tammy Wynette and 'Stand By Your Man,'" he said. "This song was very successful, reaching the top spot on the Country charts in 1968, and then crossing over to the Top 20, peaking at No. 19 on the Billboard pop charts."

I drove along with the deejay's words echoing in my head, almost running off the road as the astonishing parallels of "Stand by Your Man" and "Honky-Tonk Tomcat" dawned on me. Both were about turning a blind eye to your man's faults and both had been number one on the Country charts and both had "crossed over" to pop. I didn't know if Tammy Wynette actually lived out her lyrics, but mine were 100 percent blood-bought.

When I burst into the kitchen on Cagle Mountain. Tonilynn was standing at the table, dyeing eggs in bowls of colored water, watching a little bitty television atop the refrigerator, where a preacher in a shiny black suit stood behind a row of Easter lilies. She looked over at me, surprised, and went to turn down the volume.

"Well, ain't this a nice surprise!" she said. "Aunt Gomer told me you had other plans, and she's gone to the sunrise service, followed by breakfast on the grounds."

I glanced up at the preacher banging his fist into his palm to bring home a point I couldn't hear. The camera panned the crowd and they were nodding, crying, and smiling. "I don't feel good," I said, an excuse that wasn't totally untrue.

Tonilynn held the back of her hand to my forehead. "You're not hot. What doesn't feel good? Want me to fix you some tea?"

"I just need some peace," the words tumbled out of my mouth. "I'd give anything for some peace. Is that too much to ask?" I dropped onto one of the oak chairs at the table.

"'Course not," Tonilynn knelt beside me, held my hand. "We all want personal peace. It's a . . . what do you call it? A universal desire!"

"Well, I can't even listen to the radio safely anymore, Tonilynn. I just heard a song that took me back to a bad place."

"Yeah," she sighed, "Certain songs are like a time machine for me, too. Whenever I hear Styx singing 'Lady,' I'm fourteen, and I'm at the high school dance, standing outside in the parking lot with Justin Predmore. I'm wearing this Pepto-Bismol–pink dress with a push-up bra, my heart going a mile a minute, and Justin's in this baby-blue tux, and we're smoking a joint and then . . . "

I was glad she trailed off. Though Tonilynn's confessionals about her former life were interesting in that way soap operas can be, I sure didn't want her expecting some give-and-take about our pasts. I glanced up at the congregation on television, eyes closed, faces lifted beatifically, and for one fleeting moment I felt a little bit jealous as I looked at those people communicating with some higher benevolent power. But just as quick, I returned to my usual fantasy about having a gigantic lever I could pull that would totally erase my past.

Tonilynn put her hand on my shoulder. "I'm praying the Lord will rip the veil off your eyes, Jennifer, and reveal to you just how much he loves you, how he wants to redeem those ugly things in your past and use them for your good and his glory."

I stomped my foot. "I don't *want* anybody to redeem those ugly things back there!"

She knelt beside my chair. "Are you still having issues about old Holt?" She asked after a spell.

I nodded.

"Time will shine the light on his evil ways," she said. "He likes to act like some refined country gentleman, but I don't even need my sacred gift to see what's inside of him! He'll get his comeuppance."

I liked hearing this. "Yeah."

"He's one of those 'bad boys' who's never gonna grow up." Tonilynn made a face like she smelled something nasty. "I remember, we were in Arkansas once, all the road crew was staying at this La Quinta Inn, and one night Holt came to hang out with us. Well, he got loaded and went down to the corner convenience store and bought himself some X-rated magazines. Then he came back and paid for one of those X-rated channels on the hotel television, and I'll tell you something I learned, hon, classical music does *not* make porn classy! It was vulgar! And *Holt* got so vulgar I had to give him a piece of my mind. Right there in front of God and everybody. Nothing but white trash!"

I stared at her. Suddenly I knew. *It's normal for a woman to react the way I did! I wasn't psycho or deluded!* At last, I exonerated myself for pouring out Holt's liquor. I also scrubbed the last shred of any feelings for the man right out of my heart. Part of that cloud following me disappeared, and I was actually hungry. I gobbled up the pecan spin and milk Tonilynn offered.

9

I got to Flint Recording early and walked up and down Seventeenth Avenue thinking about how this was the first time I was going to sing, "Daddy, Don't Come Home" in public. I felt panic like hungry little dogs nipping at my heels, and I started mentally screaming for Tonilynn to arrive. Finally I saw her crossing the street, wearing a sparkly aqua T-shirt and tight stonewashed jeans tucked into her pink cowboy boots.

I held the door for her, and she passed through wheeling the biggest, reddest Samsonite I'd ever seen, and cradled in her other arm, like a baby, an enormous load of flowers. "Brung you some hydrangeas for the road trip, hon," she said, her frosted pink lips stretching in a wide smile as she lifted the bouquet.

I was stunned. "Ohhhhh, thank you. Nobody ever gave me flowers before."

"Sure they did. I've personally seen dozens of bouquets lined up every time you have a concert or award ceremony."

"They all say 'To Jenny Cloud' on the little cards. Those people don't know me." I felt tears welling.

Tonilynn set the flowers on a table and took my hands in hers. "When we're all boarded, I'm going to sit down and write a little card, saying, 'To my dear friend, Jennifer Clodfelter, who is beautiful inside and out.'"

I blinked back the tears. Tonilynn loved me despite my flaws and it was a relief just having her with me. Maybe this tour wouldn't be the disaster I feared.

"Alrighty," Tonilynn said a bit later, "time to head to our home away from home."

We hit the sidewalk, striding along in the early morning air, walking the few blocks to the tour bus

"Thanks again for the flowers."

"Well, all I did was cut them. Aunt Gomer did the planting, the fertilizing, and the weeding. I swan, Jennifer, that woman may not know what she ate for lunch, but she recollects every little thing from her growing-up years! She started in telling me this long, convoluted story about how these hydrangeas are descended from ones on her great-aunt Myrt's homeplace, and you know how old people are, once she got going on the hydrangeas, that led to her having to tell about how she used to love to play marbles out on the packed dirt of their front yard, and then how on Saturdays, she and her passel of cousins would ride the train into the big city to watch a moving-picture show. She still calls them moving-picture shows! Ha! Then she got going on the gristmill. I don't hardly know what a gristmill is." Tonilynn laughed as she wrestled her luggage down a curb, turning the corner where the Eagle came into view.

"Ooooh weee!" Tonilynn stopped so abruptly I almost crashed into her standing there, her mouth open as she stared at the side of my forty-five-foot "Eagle Luxury Entertainment Coach," which Mike had recently commissioned to be painted with a huge color picture of me from the waist up, holding my Washburn, singing. Next to my giant head were the words JENNY CLOUD, LIVE! Milky-blue clouds airbrushed in the background gave the image an otherworldly look.

"That just beats all I ever saw," Tonilynn said after a spell. "A bona fide piece of moving art! The artist captured both your tomboy side and your sweet side. I love it. Don't you love it?"

"Sure," I said. But for the millionth time that day I felt really unsure. The stage had always ushered her siren call, offered me the promise of her transformative powers. I'd always anticipated her with full faith in a beautiful experience. But today, the fear was overwhelming. I still didn't know how Mike had convinced me to journey back to that place I had to go in order to write "Daddy, Don't Come Home." And though I'd rehearsed to a ridiculous degree what to say between numbers, working up a smooth transition from "Blue Mountain Blues" to "Daddy, Don't Come Home," trying my best to soften the bad feelings by coating them in vague words I didn't really want to call lies, still I had a sense of overpowering dread inside me. I was so nervous about tomorrow at the Toyota Center in Houston I could hardly swallow. *What if I lose it up there? What if I fall apart and embarrass myself in front of thousands of fans?*

Tonilynn hauled her luggage up onto the Eagle. "Soon as we put our things away, I'll make coffee and we can just sit and visit a spell."

We had a half hour before Mike and the band were scheduled to arrive, and I was glad to hang out with just Tonilynn and her chattering, get my bearings, and settle in for the week ahead.

Every time I boarded the Eagle for another round of concerts, a part of me was still astonished. To look at the Eagle from the outside, you wouldn't dream it could hold a kitchen, a lounge with a U-shaped leather sofa, a full bath, and a color satellite TV along with a complete sound system in all ten bunks. For sleeping, on one side of the bus was me, Tonilynn, Mike, my publicist, and the driver, and on the other, my five band members. The band and I shared a lot of mutual love and respect, but we didn't hang out together. I think they understood I'm the loner type. The rest of my entourage traveled separately.

After a bit I heard Tonilynn calling, "It's ready, hon!" and I met her in the lounge where she had two mugs waiting. She'd put my hydrangeas in a pitcher full of water.

"That looks pretty," I said.

"Well, I was gonna bring you some Queen Anne's lace, too, but I ran out of time because I made Bobby Lee pancakes and bacon."

"You're a good mom," I told her, cradling my warm mug in both palms.

"Lord help me, I try. Poor thing'll have to deal with Aunt Gomer by himself for a week. I just don't believe they're weeds, do you?"

"Huh?"

"The county agent said Queen Anne's lace is actually a weed, in the carrot family or something. But I think they're every bit as pretty as a rose. In their own way. I mean, who makes the scientists—or whoever it is that classifies stuff—the end-all-be-all as far as classifying something a flower or a weed?"

"You're right." I took a sip of my coffee.

"Hey!" Tonilynn laughed. "Maybe there's a song in that for you. About a weed being a beautiful flower fit for a queen? Guess I got something from Aunt Gomer, because I just love all kinds of plants, weeds or not."

"Me too." I was thinking of the ferns and mosses along the rivers from my childhood, the sycamores along the Cumberland.

"I take that back," Tonilynn said, a scowl crossing her face. "There's one plant, well two if you count Poison Ivy, I literally despise!" Her brown eyes narrowed. "I told Bobby Lee just this morning, 'I've a good mind to get the chainsaw and cut that nasty row of catalpa trees down. I don't know why on earth you have to obsess on those disgusting worms!'"

I figured she'd get around to explaining it all, and she did, in her roundabout way.

"I mean it, Jennifer. I told that boy I've seen artificial catalpa worms, which look exactly like the real ones he harvests from those nasty catalpa trees. I've seen them in the Walmart fishing tackle section. But he claims they got to be live for the catfish to go crazy."

I recalled Bobby Lee saying the large, juicy worms he harvested from his "worm trees" were like manna to catfish and bream.

"And, oh, my goodness," Tonilynn sighed, "it's that time of year when the boy's literally obsessing. Reckon why the Lord makes men love football and fishing so much?"

I didn't answer. An obsession with fishing or football was a walk in the park compared to one with drinking and chasing wild women.

"You can't tell Bobby Lee a thing when it's football or fishing season, either one," Tonilynn continued. "But I reckon I ought to call it *worm season*. Now that the catalpa eggs have hatched and it's caterpillar stage. And Aunt Gomer!" She blew out a blast of frustration that sounded like "Phwuh!" "That woman makes me spit nails!"

"Why?"

"She encourages him, says to me, 'Honey, Bobby Lee's just doing what he loves. He's not going to tumble into the lake. He's the best fisherman around here. Can outfish any so-called able-bodied man, blah, blah, blah.'" Tonilynn paused for a gulp of her coffee. "See why I get so put out with her? She needs to keep a better eye on my boy. He's out there at those catalpa trees day and night, determined to beat the wasps that love to eat the disgusting caterpillar worms. Our freezer's running over with them."

"He freezes them?" I was on the edge of my seat.

"Mm-hm. Now I admit that part's amazing. Bobby Lee explained it to me one day. He says it's something to do with a thing called cryogenics, and the worms are just suspended in the freezer, dormant. He says all he has to do is just tuck the jar near his backside, and before he even gets down to the water, they're wiggling around like new, absolutely frantic as they search for the leaves that keep 'em alive."

I could see it in my mind's eye, and I smiled. "I'd like to see one of those worms."

Tonilynn laughed. "I wouldn't touch those nasty things for nothing! Ooey gooey, pale-yellow wormy looking things, with a black spine and a horn on their rear. Bobby Lee says if you leave 'em be, they'll turn into some kind of sphinx moth. But moths are hardly better than worms or caterpillars, are they?"

I didn't answer. I liked moths.

"Anyway, back to the host trees for those buggers. Catalpas have got to be the messiest trees ever! Got big old ugly leaves, almost as big as tobacco leaves, and these enormous brown pods that look like cigars and drop off all over the place. The birds open them up for seeds and make a pure mess. I don't even like the flowers. They're these whitish-purple blooms that look cheap."

I was gripping my coffee cup's handle so tight my fingers were white, watching Tonilynn's furious face. I didn't think I'd ever seen her so riled up. "Aunt Gomer says to Bobby Lee, 'Go get 'em,' and 'You're amazing on those wheels,' and 'When you want to do something, there's nothing can stop you.'"

Something in me had the feeling that Tonilynn might be overreacting to Aunt Gomer and maybe just a little jealous of how happy those trees and caterpillars made Bobby Lee.

"Know what, Jennifer?" Tonilynn said after a spell. "I think Aunt Gomer has a mean streak in her she hasn't turned over to the Lord yet. Whenever I remind her Bobby Lee's handicapped, she says, 'Motorcycles don't crash themselves.'" She made her voice sound exactly like Aunt Gomer's, but despite the mocking, I noticed tears in her eyes.

"Know what I'm terrified of?" Tonilynn asked softly, leaning forward to whisper.

"What?" I whispered back.

"I'm absolutely terrified that Aunt Gomer's gonna get those nasty creatures out of the freezer and cook 'em up in one of her famous spaghetti casseroles."

"Ewww!"

"I thought she might have the old-timer's, but now I'm sure of it."

I felt the sides of my throat aching. Poor Aunt Gomer.

"I just know she's gonna get mixed up and cook those worms, and I'm going to be so exhausted from work, I won't even notice what I'm eating until it's too late."

"Surely she can see they're worms."

"I don't know. She's still spry and able-bodied for the most part, but I've noticed that in addition to her mind going, her vision's growing dim. I've seen her squinting at her gardening catalogs, and she's moved her rocker up not five feet away from the TV to watch her shows. I used to think Aunt Gomer and Bobby Lee were the perfect team."

Tonilynn blotted a tear from her cheek with a napkin. "Anyway, now I realize more than ever how much Aunt Gomer needs Bobby Lee, and here she is claiming I spoil him! That I'm squelching his happiness, and I ought to kick him out of the nest."

I watched Tonilynn twirling a little silver cross on her necklace, thinking how capable both Aunt Gomer and Bobby

Lee seemed to me. I was sure they'd each one do fine on their own. But I would never say this to Tonilynn.

"It just breaks my heart," Tonilynn's voice trembled. "If I ever did kick Bobby Lee out of the nest, he'd die of loneliness. None of his old friends come around anymore. Reckon most of 'em are married and got families to tend to, wives who want 'em home, but still, doesn't seem right to just totally abandon someone. Seems after they realized Bobby Lee wasn't gonna get the use of his legs back, they decided they didn't have no more use for him." She looked at me, eyes pleading. "I'm doing right by my boy, ain't I?"

I was thinking Tonilynn would be the one who'd die of loneliness if Bobby Lee moved out. I felt an urge to get up and hug her, but I was nervous because I'd never been the hugging type. Finally, I set my cup down and stood up to go settle on the sofa next to her, reaching my arms out to encircle her, saying, "Of course, you're doing the right thing."

Tonilynn smiled through her tears and whispered, "Thank you, hon," and for one brief moment my heart fluttered with joy.

I figured the joy came from knowing that I was not alone in my human frailty and that I did know how to connect with another human.

The Eagle was a smooth bird, cruising along I-40 and into Little Rock with hardly a lurch or a shimmy. Both Mike and my publicist hovered over their laptops. When we got onto I-440 West toward Texarkana, Tonilynn and I sat watching *Braveheart* on my laptop. I'd brought the movie to distract myself, to push my angst into one dark corner of my mind. Right before we merged onto I-30 West toward Hot Springs, we stopped to refuel the bus and grab some fountain drinks.

"Here's to knocking 'em dead in Houston!" Tonilynn said, lifting her Diet Coke toward me. "We'll be in Texas real soon. Yippee!"

"Yippee," I said, holding my Mountain Dew high, silently willing time to slow down, stop. I found myself short of breath, my heartbeat accelerating as I thought about performing "Daddy, Don't Come Home."

We climbed back on the bus and the driver tuned the radio to a local station. Taylor Swift sang "You Belong With Me," and then came "Lost You Anyway," by Toby Keith, followed by a surreal clip of me singing "Blue Mountain Blues," and an advertisement for tomorrow night's performance, the deejay saying it was sold-out.

"Listen!" Tonilynn reached over to grab my arm. "A total sellout! Old Holt's ugly mudslinging didn't hurt your career one teeny bit."

She turned to me when I didn't answer. "You hear me? Girl, your success has not faded one smidgen! You got your third consecutive album debuting at number one on Billboard 200 *and* Billboard Country!" Tonilynn gulped her drink, looked hard at me. "Seriously, Jennifer, sometimes I don't think you realize what you've accomplished. Nashville's like Hollywood—she chews up and spits out tons of wannabes every single new season."

Tonilynn was right. I wasn't grateful enough. Many singers and bands, even ones who got big radio play and had lots of money behind them, faded away fairly quickly. And she was right about Holt too. His accusations hadn't hurt my career as I'd feared. I guess it was hard to rejoice too much because Holt's career was in full upswing as well. If vengeance was the Lord's, like Tonilynn claimed, seemed his songs should be tanking. I mean, come on—a mean, drunk, porn addict? Happily, my feelings for Holt remained in the disgust category.

The few times we'd crossed paths, I totally ignored him. Recently I'd been sitting in one of the recording rooms of Flint Recording just staring at some pages in my song notebook, at lyrics about forever love and kisses to die for, and I began to wonder, *Why was I such a fool? How could I not have seen the truth about Holt? Could I really have been into a man who brought back ugly memories of someone else I knew?* Knowing I'd overcome this hurdle was empowering, but not enough.

"Jennifer, look at me."

I turned my eyes from the quarter moon I'd been watching out the bus's window.

"Talk to Tonilynn. Are you okay?"

I didn't know how to say what I was feeling. I wanted her to pull it out of me, use her supernatural gift. But then it struck me like a lightning bolt, that her asking me was I okay proved her so-called gift was a sham! I squeezed the padded armrests. *What was I going to do now?*

It was dark when the Eagle pulled onto US-59 toward Houston. Tonilynn was in her pink satin nightgown, a white mask of cold cream on her face. "I'm off to bed now, hon," she said a bit after eleven. "You get some good rest tonight, hear? Be ready to knock Houston off their feet."

I was so weary of fighting the memories, so tired of battling them alone. But how could I close my eyes when the concert was less than twenty-four hours away? The awful stage fright was proof I wasn't going to triumph after all.

"Know how you were saying you didn't have a friend in this world when you were growing up?" Tonilynn rummaged around in her beauty case for a palette of creamy foundations that don't melt under stage lights. "Well, it's put me in mind of that sweet hymn, 'What a Friend We Have in Jesus.' You know it, don't you?"

I didn't feel like talking. Besides being exhausted from a night spent tossing and turning, I had only three hours until I was up onstage, and before my concerts I liked to kind of draw inward, reflect on my song lineup, what I planned to say between numbers, and that sort of thing. Today this preparation was extra heavy on my mind and even heavier on my heart. I shrugged one shoulder, but Tonilynn didn't take the hint.

"Well," she said, leaning in and squinting to dab concealer beneath my right eye, "I like to picture this image of Jesus holding my hand like a best friend. In my mind's eye, you know? I do that whenever I get to feeling scared or down or just plain-out lonely. And let me tell you, he's got the gentlest hands. Sometimes I can even feel where the nail scars are. I want you to have that too—the assurance that if you put your hand in his, you can walk through fire."

Tonilynn raised an eyebrow and leaned in closer when I didn't respond. "Jennifer, I'm feeling a lot of anxiety in you. I want to make sure you have peace. Every single one of us goes through hard trials, you know? We all fall into the pit from time to time. But if you got Jesus holding your hand, you know everything'll be all right in the end. You know all those ugly things have a purpose." She squeezed my shoulder. "'Course, before I was saved, I couldn't see how any of the messes in my past would ever work out to make me stronger."

Tonilynn seemed sure that someone somewhere orchestrated everything to her advantage, the good and the bad. I had to admit it would be nice if some benign higher power could wave a wand over my past and make it all okay. But there were things in my life I *knew* had no redeeming aspects whatsoever. You could dig them up, analyze them from every angle, and never find a way to use them for good. What a simple soul Tonilynn was! This realization made me feel tender and mad toward her at the same time. It also hit me then, like a knife in the heart, that I'd never have Tonilynn's peace. I would go on my whole life just like this, running and hurting.

"Hey, hey, what's this about?" Tonilynn moved to the end of my kneecaps. She set the foundation palette down and took my hands in hers. "Don't cry. If you got ugly things back there, just commit them to the Lord, and I promise he'll use them for your good. It may not be right now, or even in the next couple of years, but someday he'll *use* them."

All I could do was shake my head, swallow my tears. Tonilynn let my hands go so she could wrap me in her arms. She pressed my tense body to her, and I buried my face in her shoulder. It felt good to be held as I breathed in her honeysuckle smell, and she murmured comforting words, telling me it would all be fine, that I was a sweet little lamb, and I'd never have to walk through life alone. After a while she pulled away, lifted my chin with her pointer finger, looked at me with pleading eyes. "I think it's time to tell you a little story about bad things working out good in the end.

I nodded, and she hooked a lacquered fingernail into the collar of her blouse, pulled it away to expose a tattoo inked over her left breast. It was a red and blue heart, like a medical drawing in a textbook, with black wings spreading out on either side and a banner scrolled across the top, stretching to the tips of the wings that said: "Robert Lee Gooch."

"Janis Joplin was my idol. I thought she was so cool." Tonilynn let her blouse fall back. "I was fourteen, running around with a bunch of wild kids. We'd skip school, get drunk, and go for rides all over the county. Thought we were invincible. Didn't give a fig about nothing or nobody." She shook her head. "If I needed money for beer or cigarettes or dope, I just took whatever I needed, including every last dime from Aunt Gomer's handbag or the jar of change she saved for the missionaries. At times us kids would be so high we didn't hardly remember plowing down somebody's mailbox, trenching their lawn, or worse.

"But we were living for the minute. I got to hanging out so much with one particular group of brothers, three of the Gooch boys, and by and by I fell for Robert. I'd just turned fifteen, thought I knew everything. He was a good bit older, a bad boy, pure wild, and when he started flirting around with me, I thought I was Miss Everything. One day he said 'Let's drop out of school and go traveling across country on my motorcycle.'

"I thought that sounded like the best thing in this world. Getting away from a Holy Roller to run with a Rock 'n' Roller." Tonilynn chuckled. "Me and Robert took off, free as birds and partying like there was no tomorrow. Well, I got knee-walking drunk one night when we were in Louisiana, and woke up with the tattoo I just showed you."

She paused to pop the tab on a Diet Coke. "But I wasn't mature enough to realize actions have consequences, and pretty soon I found out I needed more'n a boy's idea of love. When I told Robert I was pregnant, you never saw a change in nobody so fast in all your life. Robert claimed he'd never really loved me. Claimed it wasn't his. Left me in a back alley in Shreveport.

"Sometimes, I look back and shake my head. It was kind of like history repeating itself, you know? How my own father took off?"

I managed a nod.

"Well, anyway, I called Aunt Gomer and she quoted Proverbs 11:22 to me: 'As a jewel of gold in a swine's snout, so is a fair woman without discretion.' Made me so mad. I cussed and yelled at her, and at God, or my idea of him anyway, until my voice gave out. It just made me determined to be even wilder, and I fell in with an even worse crowd." Tonilynn paused to tuck a wisp of hair back up into place.

"I got into the big H, you know? Heroin felt like the answer to squashing the awful pain inside me. For a while anyway. I didn't care if it hurt me, but I probably wouldn't have done it if somebody told me it could hurt the baby. I'm always thanking God that my Bobby Lee has no side effects from all my stupidness. That's pure mercy. Thankfully, I got busted for possession, and when I got probation, I managed to kick my habit, got a job at a dry cleaners because by that time I did have a baby to support. But my soul still hurt me, you know? So eventually I started up all over again with cocaine. Getting high as often as I could afford it, which wasn't too often and which made me start stealing things.

"I was pretty talented, you know? But one day I got busted for shoplifting some jewelry, and sitting in jail the only person I could think of to call was Aunt Gomer. I sure didn't want to, and part of me, a big part, figured she'd do me like she had before. But she was my last chance. She was my baby's last chance too. I'd never been a religious person, but I got down on my knees on that cement floor and I said to God that if he could perform a miracle and make Aunt Gomer happy to come get me, then I'd know without a doubt he existed and I would straighten myself out and . . ."

Tonilynn trailed off, gazing into the distance, smiling nostalgically.

"What happened?"

"Man, oh man," she breathed in an awestruck voice, still staring. "I vomited all over the floor, and then I called Aunt Gomer, and when she said, sweetly, 'Let me get my handbag and I'll be there directly,' I thought I was having a dream, and then, when I realized it was real, I felt this million-pound weight lifting off me and I started screaming, 'Thank you, Jesus!' over and over so loud the guards had to restrain me.

"I knew then God was real, and I knew he was powerful when Aunt Gomer didn't fuss a lick that whole long car ride home. When we got back to Cagle Mountain and I'd gotten myself cleaned up, I found a part-time job at The Beauty Nook, and learned I was a pure natural when it came to both hair and makeup. I felt like the Lord had a plan for me, you know?"

"Hm."

"I asked him to do a makeover on me. He swept away all the pain and the guilt, and day by day, I found peace with him, also with myself and other people. Now heaven knows I ain't no saint," she laughed at her rhyme, "and I still may not be exactly what I should be 100 percent of the time, but I sure ain't what I used to be."

She waited for me to respond. When I didn't, she said, "See? I wanted to wring Aunt Gomer's neck that first time, when she wouldn't come rescue me. But looking back, I see it was all part of the Lord's plan, his timing. I *needed* to go through all that ugly stuff, to experience pain, so when I finally *did* get saved I'd be able to use what I learned to help folks. It helps me understand what certain folks are experiencing. I truly believe my purpose here on earth is to beautify not only people's outsides but also their insides. I love leading them to Jesus so he can wash all their ugly stains away."

I wouldn't look at Tonilynn. Did she think her story meant anything to me? I couldn't help feeling mad about her acting like her faith was this magic wand she could wave to smooth over the bumps and valleys in her past. Though I now felt blameless in the blowup with Holt Cantrell, another ugly stain was my part in Mr. Anglin's death. Plus, there were plenty of others, most originating with my father. As I started thinking of him, I felt the root of bitterness nestling down farther into the rich soil of a hidden place in the depths of me. "Save your breath," I told Tonilynn in a cool voice. "I've asked God for help more times than I can count, and you know what? My father's still breathing."

"Jennifer, Jennifer. This hate you have inside isn't healthy. When you fantasize evil, you're giving the enemy ground, and if you don't get rid of that bitterness it'll end up destroying *you*."

My heart was pounding. I swore under my breath.

"You love your mother, don't you?" Tonilynn asked softly. "I remember you saying you send her money."

"It's really nothing for me to write a check," I said. "I thought if I sent her enough she wouldn't be afraid of being homeless or penniless and she'd leave my father. But the fact of the matter is, she didn't stand up to him when I was growing up, and she doesn't now."

"What did you want her to stand up to him about?"

"I don't care!" I spit the words. "It doesn't matter anymore!"

"You're angry at your mother too."

"Yeah, I am! I don't understand how she can live like she does. My mother's choice is spineless acceptance, trudging along, swiping her forehead with the back of her hand and sighing 'Ahh, well, this is my lot in life and I will endure.' Problem was, I was forced to endure right along with her." I looked at Tonilynn, shook my head. "Even as a kid, I realized people could choose their destiny to some extent, that they could transcend what life gave them, and I despised her meekness. I used to tell myself that when I made it big, I'd send her so much money that she'd grow a backbone and see she could reach for better things too. She'd feel brave enough to leave him."

"Poor baby. You didn't have it easy."

I felt tears welling. "I wished my father dead, I hoped and prayed we'd leave him, and then, later . . . I just wanted my mother to lift her head out of the sand and admit what he did to me that night when . . ." Suddenly, every cell in my body shrunk back. I began trembling so hard my teeth chattered.

Tonilynn dropped to her knees on the floor at my feet. There was such radiant love in her eyes, I thought I might feel some presence, a glimpse into another world. But it wasn't enough for me to reveal the worst.

"Oh, darlin'," she cooed. "It hurts when a mother doesn't support your dream, doesn't it?"

"She didn't encourage my singing, that's true," I said in a tight voice. "But I could let that go, if she'd just . . . I mean, I've tried to talk to her about some other things. Some things that are very painful to . . . but . . . she just denies . . . " I felt like an angry child, and I liked it. I reached down deep and yelled, "A mother is supposed to be that one person in the world who loves you, who protects you! And she didn't protect me!"

Tonilynn jumped and rocked back with wide eyes. At last, she cleared her throat, "Let's just ask the Lord to help you dig up all that ugly stuff. Okay?"

"What if I don't *want* to dig some of it up?"

"If you don't look at it eye-to-eye, then you sure can't forgive it and be free of it."

What a stupid comment! I knew there'd *never* be a day I could forgive my father! Didn't Tonilynn know that to forgive him would be the same as saying it didn't matter?

I took a long, deep breath, gathered all my courage and walked out onstage to smile at that sea of faces, to absorb their energy and anticipation for a nice long minute before strumming a rich G-chord, leaning into the microphone, and saying, "Good evening, Houston." Wild hoots, whistles, and cheers began to erupt, to crest, and at last to wind down, giving me plenty of time to study my crowd. There were the usual swaying Stetson hats and glinting belt buckles, the various colorful bandannas being waved or fastened jauntily around necks, lots of plaid Western shirts with blue jeans, and short flirty skirts paired with cowgirl boots.

Glancing beyond, I could see the sun hunkered low in the west, the sky streaked with purple and pink at the horizon. Bright stage lights above me and to my back and sides lit me up in a warm, familiar way. My stage manager motioned my cue from the wings to begin and my voice surprised me as it vaulted out, "All right! Thank you very much! Thank you from the bottom of my heart for that nice, big, warm welcome. You always hear about Texas being the state with the big heart, and I know it's true!" More whistles and cheers. "And now it's time for us to take a trip together. A trip to the Georgia mountains!"

Behind me a drum, a rhythm guitar, and a piano bloomed into the beginnings of "Blue Mountain Blues." I knew the song like the back of my hand, and it was good to have a slow, easy ballad that I could sing in a high tenor to lead off.

When I was a young girl, no more than eleven, I found a place to wind my summer days away, place like heaven. Rocky rills, and soaring hills, creekbeds flowing through trees. But I'm far away now and visit you only in my dreams.

Blue Mountain Blues, I'm missin' you.

Blue Mountain Blues, it's true.

When I reached the chorus, I was carried away on the wings of the music. I actually felt the soft moss on the banks of the creek beneath my feet, the water licking my ankles.

The audience began swaying as I sang the chorus three times to end the song, growing softer and softer. Some fans had eyes closed, lips moving along to the words.

I segued into "Gimme Some Sugar, Sugar," and I could feel it working its way into the crowd, lighting them up with this warm, golden buzz. Thrilled, I leaned out and threw double-kisses. I was alive up onstage, like no other place.

I kicked off into "I'm Leavin' Only Footprints" and "Walking the Wildwood," then "River Time," "Spooky Moon," and "Smoke Over the Hills," a soft, mournful waltz with a fiddle that sounded like tears floating in the air. And finally, a silly tune with a rocking beat called "Old Spice and Vitalis," about an elderly Romeo I met when I sang at a nursing home.

Everyone was smiling by the end of that song. Finally it was time. "Now I'm gonna do a brand-new song for you," I said, feeling the electric buzz of the microphone on my lips in a surreal way. "Never sung it in public before. About a time when I was still in high school. You all know that time in our lives is hard enough as it is. Right?" I paused and saw a sea of heads nodding, heard random "Amens" and "Sure enoughs."

"Yes, we're all exceptionally vulnerable then, and I wanted a song that would say to you young people, 'Don't let anybody kill your dreams. Don't let anybody tell you that you can't do something if it's in your heart to do it.'" My fingers trembled as I strummed up and down the fret for my usual pause before each song. All of a sudden my pick wasn't feeling like an extension of my fingers anymore. My eyelids and my throat began to ache from holding back tears, and I was so exhausted from my performance, I didn't have much reserve left to fight the crippling cocktail of emotions—the anger and the hatred, sure, but also shame and despair. I stood up there on that stage disappointed with myself for *feeling* those things when I'd vowed to suck it up. If I fell apart in front of everybody, if my fans knew the truth—how pathetic and broken I really was—then it was all going to be over.

I could see the anticipation on everyone's face, and I began strumming the wistful, melancholy opening bars of "Daddy, Don't Come Home." There was nothing to do but suck it up and dive in.

> I come in from school, and Mama says 'He's home'
> I don't know what's waiting for me yet
> But my heart feels like a stone.
> Mama says, 'He loves you, you're his daughter,'
> But I know the man sure don't walk on water.
> I sung him my song, and it didn't take long,
> 'Til he'd stomped on my dream,
> Him and his friend, Jim Beam.
> My tears wet the night,
> and I knew it wasn't right,
> I wanted to say, I wanted to say,
> 'Daddy, don't come home.
> I'd rather be alone
> Just walk out that door, 'cause I can't take it no more.'

I sang on through the high, lonesome sound of the chorus, falling helplessly into the second verse. The faces I could see were totally into it, empathizing with the pain of this young girl, and I gripped my guitar even tighter, stomped my boot, worked hard to sing like it was somebody else's song, steeling myself to stay in control. But the feelings I'd recently unearthed to write the song were too fresh, and before I knew it I was right back there in that awful time, my dreams newly crushed like a muscadine on the highway.

A young woman in the front row wearing a strapless top and tight jeans was crying so hard her eyeliner ran down into her lips. I wondered if she had a father like mine, and I fought my impulse to pull her up onstage and give her a big hug. Then the floodgates really opened, and my voice got a really tearful twang as I poured out my soul in a vibrato born from pain. Things got even worse as the emotion crescendoed through another stanza. I wanted to run offstage and hide.

Miraculously, just as I thought I was on the vergeof dying, I managed to switch myself to the tough, resilient Jenny Cloud, and I belted out the chorus one more time, adding a rollicking guitar lick between it and the final verse. Swiveling my hips, I tapped out the rhythm with the toe of one boot in a kind of hillbilly stomp, and bringing the song around to its last rousing chorus—*I'd rather be alone. Just walk out that door, 'cause I can't take it no more.*

Taking a bow, I leaned into the microphone and said, "Good night, Houston. I love you all!" I pressed both palms to my lips and blew kisses to the crowd. A tidal wave of applause from twenty thousand fans splashed my face with spray before engulfing me.

Aboard the Eagle, Tonilynn sat in the kitchen in her satin nightgown, cold cream slathered on her face. "You were sensational, hon! Care for a little girl talk before bed?" She smiled and gestured at a Diet Coke on the table. I shook my head and walked past her to my bunk, climbed up on my mattress and lay there. I wanted more than anything to fall down into the sweet abyss of sleep, drift in a deep blackness of no thoughts. But it was not to be. I watched a mental replay of my performance, especially the face of the girl on the front row as I sang "Daddy, Don't Come Home." Her connection to my pain had been real.

─────⊗⊗⊗─────

"Pizza, the breakfast of superstars." Tonilynn smiled as she shook the plastic cup of thousand island salad dressing she'd requested on-the-side all over her salad. "Mike says the buzz is fantastic about last night's performance." She tore off a chunk of crusty French bread and slathered it with butter.

At 11:40 in the morning, Frank's Pizza was fairly crowded. I sat there, my old baseball cap pulled low, a piece of untouched pepperoni pizza on my plate. I sure didn't feel like a superstar. I felt like a pathetic, divided, and tortured soul who adored her career and hated it at the same time. Music was my gift, but it was also my curse, a huge, itchy mosquito bite between my shoulder blades I couldn't ever seem to get scratched to satisfaction.

And fame? Fame could be tough in country music circles, where the legitimacy of a new star was scrutinized like a newborn baby's face. Folks were saying I didn't deserve to shine so quickly and so brightly because I hadn't "served my time" by spending a decade singing in bars. It irked me to hear things like, "Jenny Cloud had it handed to her on a silver platter" and "That girl was just in the right place at the right time. She got lucky."

The ability to write songs and a good voice were gifts, yes, but if my critics only knew the compost heap they sprouted in! I sat there, trying to think what it was I needed. I needed peace. I needed sky and water. I needed the Cumberland River.

"Hon? You okay? Please answer me, Jennifer. Oh, Jesus, help this child . . . "

It took me a minute to realize Tonilynn's soft voice was calling to me. I blinked, sat up straight. "Sorry. Listen, I'm not feeling too good. I'm going back to the Eagle and lie down."

I stood, but Tonilynn grabbed my wrist. "Don't go."

I sat back down.

"What's the matter, hon?"

"I'm just . . . I hate my life."

"Silly!" Tonilynn laughed, threw a napkin at me. "You're just exhausted. We'll get you tucked into your bunk nice and early tonight and you'll be fine. Now eat."

"I'm not hungry, but I'll wait until you're done."

Tonilynn dipped a crouton in dressing and ate it. "Remember what we were talking about day before yesterday? Folks would kill to be where you are."

I played with the sweetener packets while her words rattled in my head like marbles in a cigar box. At last, I got a great big gulp of air down into my lungs. "I know, Tonilynn. I'm truly grateful for all that Mike and the folks at Flint have done for me. And I love the music, the singing, and my fans. But I never realized how hard it was going to be." My hands were shaking and I twined them together in my lap. "When I sang 'Daddy, Don't Come Home' last night, I lost it up onstage. That's never happened to me before, Tonilynn." I felt my heart accelerating. "I can't sing about my dysfunctional childhood anymore."

"I know it takes guts to sing about that stuff you've shared with me."

I just shook my head. There was so much Tonilynn didn't know about what lay beneath and between the lines. I thought about what the writers at Flint Studios worked up for my upcoming CD cover; "The music calls Jenny Cloud home. She gives us an intimate peek into the dark corners, the heartache she witnessed in childhood."

My career had been spawned on lyrics about fear and tears, on dysfunction, and Mike's goal was still to sell me as a wounded artist. But I wasn't a totally unwilling participant, was I? The stuff my management team came up with was not just media hype they made up to sell records.

Tonilynn pushed her empty plate back. She dug in her purse, applied fresh lipstick, then reached across for my hand. "Hon, I know I sound like a broken record, but what you need to do is just ask Jesus to help you dig up all those hurts, that bad stuff, once and for all, and deal with it."

It made me queasy thinking we were going to get into this discussion yet again, and I pulled my hand away. "I know I sound like a broken record, too, but I don't *want* to dig it up. I'm not going to."

"It's the only way to healing, Jennifer." Tonilynn's brown eyes went soft with concern. "Having a father like you did, do, you probably can't relate to a loving heavenly Father, but believe me, God cares and he understands our hurt. He used my hurts as a way of ministering to others when I finally looked them in the eye, and he can use yours. Pull up whatever it is that's still buried and use it to write a song."

I thought, fleetingly, of that girl on the front row with black mascara running into her mouth as I sang "Daddy, Don't Come Home." There was definitely a connection, and maybe my lyrics had empowered her to make some change. That was good. But what about me? Without peace, what was anything else worth?

"Well, I don't care," I said. "I don't care if I ever sing again."

"You're fibbing." Tonilynn shook her head, smiling. "I see you when you come off that stage, hon, and you've got a glow like Moses when he came down the mountain. He was so full of the glory he had to wear a veil over it so folks wouldn't get blinded."

I shrugged, but Tonilynn wouldn't let it go. "You brought down the house last night! Mike says they're playing 'Daddy, Don't Come Home' all over the place. Speaking of that one, I don't believe I've heard you talk about the story behind it."

My stomach lurched. "No more stories about the stories behind the songs. They're too real."

"But it's got to be real for an audience to feel it! Surely you know that by now. Nobody gets to be a multiplatinum recording artist just by singing pretty. Your songs were hard won, Jennifer, and they're your gifts to this broken world. Your beautiful gifts."

"Well," I said, getting to my feet again, "it doesn't feel beautiful to me. Feels like a black hole sucking my soul in, and I'm quitting."

"You can't." Tonilynn reached across to grab my hand and pulled me back into my seat. "I know some things may be hard, but what would we do without Jenny Cloud? You're *touching* people! The world would be so much poorer without your songs. You've got to understand, hon, in God's economy, nothing we experience in this earthly life is wasted! Please let him pour his love out on hurting, vulnerable people through you. He can make something beautiful and good come out of your ugliest experiences, if you'll just let him! I'm begging you, just ask him to help you dig it all up! You have a message and a mission with your music."

It bothered me when Tonilynn started going on and on about this religious stuff like I agreed with her, like we were some little private God-club. I took the first bite of my pizza, but it was sawdust in my mouth.

"I didn't even finish high school, Jennifer." Tonilynn shook her head. "But the Lord helped me get my beauty degree, and while I'm beautifying the outsides of my clients, I share my journey and let him take care of their insides. I'm like one of those full-service gas stations we used to have."

Tonilynn paused, and when I didn't respond it didn't dampen her zeal.

"Sometimes I think about having my tattoos removed, but then I think, no, these are my battle scars. They're a road map of my testimony. See? People can *use* their pain, Jennifer Anne Clodfelter, and your songs about what you've been through are powerful. Combine that with your incredible voice and your looks and the way you can hold an audience in the palm of your hand, and there ain't nobody who can't say you don't have all the perfect ingredients for what I like to call a *divinely appointed mission!*

"I'm constantly praying for you, and I know you can triumph if you'll just reach out and grab hold of his hand."

I sat there, blocking out Tonilynn's voice. When you started listening to someone like her, so persuasive in her simple way, you forgot what it cost. You forgot you were trading pieces of yourself for friendship. I needed some thinking time before I did something I'd regret.

THIRD VERSE:
THE NEW, IMPROVED
JENNY CLOUD

10

When the Eagle returned me to Nashville three weeks later, I drove straight to Harmony Hill and climbed into bed without unpacking and without undressing any more than slipping my boots off. I didn't listen to the radio. I didn't watch television. I didn't want anything that reminded me of being human. I just lay in bed, looking at the ceiling, the thought of continuing to live like this intolerable.

I decided to ignore my phone after a flurry of calls from Mike and Tonilynn. They wanted too much, were sucking even more of the life out of me with their chatter and questions. Mike's words amounted to reports of what a hit our Texas tour had been, that like "Honky-Tonk Tomcat," "Daddy, Don't Come Home" was getting tons of drive-time play on radio stations across the country, and had made the Billboard Hot 100. Tonilynn kept offering to come pick me up and carry me out to celebrate. She wanted to take me to the Douglas Corner Café just a short drive from downtown, or to Bobbie's Dairy Dip on Charlotte Pike, or to Sambuca, a swanky place with lobster enchiladas and live music. I lied and told her I had a lot of work in the studio to tend to.

"I'll miss you, hon," she chirped. "You've got my number if you want to talk."

Toward the end of the second day of my hibernation, my head began to ache so bad I could hardly keep my eyes open. I got even more irritable. All I wanted was to leave the past in the past, and, boy, did that seem to be a losing battle. I told myself if Tonilynn truly cared, she'd stop saying, "Ask Jesus to help you dig it all up." Why would anyone in their right mind invite their world to crash down like that?

If Jesus truly wanted to help me, well, he could take the shovel and whack my father upside the head with it. Put us all out of our misery.

"Religious nut!" I fussed out loud. "Fanatic!" There was no option but to keep buried every shred of anything that had to do with my sleazebag of a father. I congratulated myself on the fact that I'd been successful in keeping a particular incident buried fairly deep, the one from which the merest hint could send a cold claw walking up my spine.

I shuffled into the bathroom and leaned against the counter for a while, feeling like I might vomit as I smelled the hibiscus hand soap. When I caught a glimpse of a painting of a cow skull with flowers spilling out of it, a gift from Tonilynn, almost instantly I felt ashamed of myself for fussing about someone who only wanted my good.

I hobbled downstairs to the kitchen for a glass of water, and drank it standing at the kitchen sink. My eyes fell on back issues of *Music Row, Country Weekly,* and *Nashville Scene* on top of a pile of junk mail next to the telephone. On a whim I sat down at the breakfast table to leaf through them, pausing at a big splashy photo of blonde-haired, bright-eyed Taylor Swift laughing at something.

Taylor was from Pennsylvania and had moved to Nashville when she was thirteen. She was a household name like me, and I'd seen and heard plenty about her, including the story of her breakthrough in 2006 with the hit song "Tim McGraw." Her self-titled debut album had sold more than 3.5 million copies, and her album *Fearless* produced the hit singles "Love Story" and "You Belong With Me." Not to mention she'd won Top New Female Vocalist at the 2008 CMT Awards and had been nominated for a Grammy by the Academy of Country Music as best new female vocalist. Besides all the success, it struck me how peaceful Taylor seemed. Where I was all angst and heart-wrenching lyrics, Taylor had a freshness that was appealing. She was light and playful. I didn't know exactly what to call her, maybe not innocent, but she sure looked happy and carefree.

All of a sudden, it was like I'd switched on the lamp after a long bad dream. If I could be like Taylor and write upbeat country pop songs, I'd be happy! She was proof that writing lyrics spawned in a troubled past was not a prerequisite for doing well in the country music scene. A change of image was what I needed for my passion and my sanity to coexist.

When Tonilynn brought up that foolishness about digging up the past, about Jesus and Freud, I'd tell her that the horrors of a person's reality could actually do them in, that true happiness lay in burying ugly stuff really deep and keeping it there. It was just common sense that a person couldn't undo what was done to them. In fact, I'd been pondering this idea about self-fulfilling prophecy; simply put, a person will act like who she believes herself to be. I'd heard reimaging referred to as "getting your game on," and it was, in my opinion, a very sound and effective solution when dealing with terrible things.

Talk about a makeover! I was a big, blank canvas, and here in these magazines was the inspiration to paint the new Jenny Cloud. I'd model myself after Taylor Swift and Carrie Underwood, another fresh, young country music star. I'd also study up on Reba McEntire, Kellie Pickler, and Faith Hill. Their artistry would fuel my own. I'd pick and choose my attributes; upbeat, sassy, gutsy, chic, giggly, breathless. I'd dream up Jenny Cloud's happy-girl persona, and shut down, totally and completely, the file marked "ugly episodes in Jenny Cloud's past."

I felt like dancing, like my only limitation was within my own mind. My headache disappeared, and I got up to go take a bubble bath.

To be the new Jenny Cloud, I needed big blonde hair, cut into flirty layers. And dramatic makeup. No more scrubbed clean, dark silken-locked, angst-ridden, soul-wrenching persona. Good-bye to serious and somber. I'd aim for adjectives like "lighthearted" and "playful." Speaking of playful, I decided I'd go get some long, acrylic nails, but nixed that idea as soon as I thought about strumming my Washburn.

I was stepping out of the tub a few minutes later when Tonilynn called.

"Wow!" she said. "You sure sound better."

"I feel better. Hey, mind if I borrow your pink cowgirl boots? I want to see how they look with my denim mini-skirt." Despite being a good seven inches taller than five-foot Tonilynn, we both had wide, size-eight feet.

"'Course you can. You going out dancing?"

I laughed. "I'm just bored with my Minnie Pearl crossed with Maybelle Carter look. I want something flirty."

"You're hunting a man."

"I'm hunting outfits to wear during my performances. Remember that flouncy little green dress I bought in California, with the spaghetti straps? The one you made me buy in that boutique because you said it brought out my eyes?"

"The one you've never worn?"

"Yep. How do you think that would look with some really high-heeled black pumps?"

"I think all the men would be dropping like flies."

That helped ease the transition to my next question. "Will you do a more playful hairdo on me?"

Tonilynn got quiet. "What did you have in mind?" she asked finally.

"Swingy blonde layers."

"Whoa now, Jennifer. I love your long, black silky tresses. You look like an Indian princess."

"I don't want to look like an Indian princess anymore."

"Well, okay . . . I reckon we might could do some swingy layers if we get a real powerful styling product. However, your coloring definitely wouldn't do for blonde."

It wasn't easy to let go of that mental image of myself with a blonde mane, tousled, tumbling as I strummed my guitar wildly, but I knew how stubborn Tonilynn was. "Okay, fine," I said. "Playful dark layers, then. Listen, I've been studying country singers and a lot of them are aiming toward a more mainstream pop sound. I'm sure you've heard them talking about 'the new contemporary country sound that spans genres'? So, I'm thinking it's time for me to make a change all around and I'm trying to change my image so I'll look the part."

She didn't respond.

"I'm remaking my sound, Tonilynn. No more twang. No more of the so-called 'real country sound' or 'tear-in-my-beer' type music. And I really need your talent and experience in the beauty department. You know, a lighter look to go with my lighter sound?"

Still she was quiet.

"Aw, come on, Tonilynn. I want more dramatic makeup too. You know what I'm talking about. Think Miranda Lambert, Taylor Swift, pop-and-country culture. I've heard folks saying Taylor's music is really the rock 'n' roll of the sixties and seventies."

Finally Tonilynn spoke. "You're not actually serious, are you, hon?"

"Sure I am."

I heard her take a deep breath. "Mike's going to blow a gasket."

"He will not." I laughed.

"Bet he will."

Mike picked up on the second ring. "Where have you been, Jenny girl? Thought you fell off the earth."

My voice was strong as I requested a "business meeting to discuss some things." He was clearly surprised, but we set a time for the next morning at nine. I loved the feeling of being in charge of my own destiny, and I turned on The Big 98 WSIX so loud I felt the beat of Martina McBride's "I Just Call You Mine" pulsing up through my bare feet. At the end of the song, while Martina was showing off her vocal prowess, I was inspired to step out the back door to gaze at the sun, a warm gold light streaming through the trees at the distant edge of my property. I let out a long, deep breath, and I knew where I needed to be.

Driving through the night, I could feel a strong yet gentle tug from downtown Nashville, like some great aunt beckoning me to climb up on the back porch and visit a spell. I smiled as I pictured those sweet days of living in the Best Western, me so eager to immerse myself in this city, to know all about her.

When the Nashville skyline came into focus, with the stately towers of the sharply lit Batman Building so tall and impressive, I laughed out loud. At the intersection of Music Circle East and Division Street, I felt another familiar pull, this one a powerful magnet drawing me toward the Cumberland. It had been too long, and I couldn't wait to see her, feel her quiet strength, tell her everything was going to be all right.

I parked in a lot near the intersection of Broadway and Third Avenue North, and half walked, half jogged to Riverfront Park, then up and across the pedestrian bridge, through the parking lot near LP Field, then down the banks to the cement boat ramp that disappeared into the river. I was out of breath as I knelt and twirled my fingers in the warm water of the Cumberland, watching the reflection of a three-quarter moon glancing off her surface. "I'm good now," I said to her. "Things are going to be okay."

For the next fifteen minutes, I sat by the river, inhaling and exhaling her strength. Feeling whole and strong, I walked back to the Lexus, planning on heading home. But on a whim, I decided to cruise along Broadway, past the honky-tonks, smiling at the memory of my ignorance about cover charges. It wasn't long before I felt compelled to turn onto Fifth Avenue North.

I slowed to watch a stream of people filing into the historic Ryman—the Mother Church of Country Music. Somebody big had to be playing tonight. When at last I saw the sign clearly, I knew the reason for the crowd. It was George Jones. I thought of just continuing to cruise along, enjoying the scenic tour of my town from the comfort of my car, but something wouldn't let me. I wanted to be a member of the adoring masses, enjoying a concert by the legendary Possum.

I found a parking spot and jogged back to the box office. It was a good thing I was wearing my fool-proof disguise. When

I stepped into the Ryman, it was five minutes until showtime, and to me, still a bit dazed from long days and fitful nights spent sequestered and struggling with the emotional fallout from my career, the lights and the energy felt sort of unreal. I climbed up into the balcony and side-stepped along until I came to my row. My seat was three in, past an ancient man and woman, their hands clasped together in her lap. I slid past them carefully, murmuring, "I'm sorry, please excuse me, I'm sorry."

"You're not hurting a thing, dear," the old woman said, smiling up at me as the old man guffawed, looking down at his feet, saying, "Nope, not hurting a thing. I walk on 'em too." Which confused me until she began giggling, and I realized he was making a joke.

I sat, waiting in that hundred-plus-year-old sanctuary, aware of the tangible bond of honest, pure affection, the completeness between that couple beside me. From the corner of my eye, I saw she wore a diamond on her frail hand, and I imagined him on bended knee sixty-plus years ago. As a fiddle, a drum, an electric guitar, and a keyboard began making music, a number of people stood up, swaying and clapping, calling out, "We want George! We want George!"

My elderly couple remained in their seats. The old man turned to me and said, "Reckon they're worried he won't show up."

"Really?" I asked, although I knew the story.

"I remember him missing so many booked engagements, they started to calling him No-Show Jones. His drinking had a hold on him."

I'd heard about George's legendary alcohol consumption. The tabloids credited his current wife with rescuing him. At last he strutted out, grinning big, wearing his famous amber-lensed glasses and a brown suit with sparkly designs sewn on the shoulders. He had his guitar and without warning launched into, "Why, Baby, Why." Next he did "Wabash Cannonball," and then "Golden Ring," a song he used to sing with then wife Tammy Wynette. The audience knew every word to every song, and sang along raptly, especially when he got to one of the greatest country songs of all time: "He Stopped Loving Her Today."

That was when I felt the power of a certain presence in the crowd growing even stronger, a totally encompassing sensation bordering on worship. *They're adoring George Jones, idolizing him, and he enjoys being famous and entertaining them,* I thought. *And I do too. Guess that's part of our job description as country music stars. But look at this precious man and woman beside me. Isn't it better to be loved by just one person who really knows you, heart and soul, than by millions who don't even know your real name?*

Once upon a time, this notion of unconditional, committed love would have depressed me to no end because I was afraid I'd never have it. But now a particular face swam into my thoughts, making every single cell in my body fill up with hope: Bobby Lee.

<hr>

For the first time in months, I slept soundly. It felt good to be finally hungry, starving, in fact, holding a cinnamon crunch bagel and hot espresso at Panera Bread. I'd just settled into my chair when Mike breezed in with a pile of reviews. He plopped them on the table, thumped them with his pointer finger, looked at me, smiled, and said, "Girl, this new song of yours is some kind of hit!" Leaving only the faint woodsy trace of Herrera for Men, he headed to the counter.

I guzzled my espresso and moved my behind to the edge of the chair, ready. Mike returned and began adding packet after packet of raw sugar to his coffee. Finally he took a long swallow, patted his lips with a napkin, and said, "I've been talking to some folks about the next CMA Awards, and there's some talk about Brad Paisley being the host again, and another equally famous, well-known female country music diva being his cohost. Maybe someone we know?" He smiled with one eyebrow raised.

What a perfect lead-in! As the current Jenny Cloud, there was no way I could picture doing a three-hour show while exchanging funny banter with Brad. Billed as "Country Music's Biggest Night," the glittery network television spectacle of the annual CMA Awards was where dozens of country music's biggest stars would be performing and sharing what they called "backstage stories" and "memorable moments." It wouldn't do to carry all that baggage up there, parading it around while trying to perkily introduce singer after singer and answer questions about my own painful songs. An artist who popped into my mind right away was giggly Carrie Underwood. Carrie would be a perky hostess with the mostess—the most smiles and happy comments, unshackled by a dysfunctional past. Or perhaps bubbly Kellie Pickler, a bleached-blonde diva folks were calling a "modern-day Dolly Parton."

"So what do you think?" Mike prompted when I'd held my thoughts a little too long.

"I'm thinking the producers would rather go with one of the more contemporary artists," I said. "You know? The so-called new country sound?" I threw those terms out there quickly to judge his reaction. "Somebody like Carrie or Kellie or Taylor? Get more crossover fans that way. Bigger audience, and isn't that the goal?"

Mike swallowed his coffee down the wrong pipe. "What?" he sputtered. "You ought to be jumping up and *down* at the thought of being a cohost for the CMA Awards!"

My words obeyed my brain and rolled off my tongue like well-aimed BBs. "I called this meeting because I've been doing a lot of thinking, Mike, and I've decided to change my image. I want my songs to say, 'This is a gal who doesn't take life too seriously.' I want fun songs with silly lyrics, more of a mainstream-pop sound. From now on, I'm gonna be the happy-go-lucky country diva. Tonilynn said she'll do big hair and heavy makeup, and I'll wear flirty minidresses with cowgirl boots."

Mike laughed, a humorless little snort. "This is crazy. You're not the big hair, heavy makeup, and minidresses type."

"I can be," I shot back. "I don't want to pay the high price for 'lyrics that touch my audience's souls' anymore. I don't want 'the music to call me home' anymore. No more so-called 'reflections about her troubled past.'" I was on a roll. "I can't change the past, but I *can* choose what I sing about, and I'm going to focus on upbeat songs with catchy, fun choruses. I'm going to reinvent myself as pop-country. No more twangy tunes for this gal."

Mike took a deep breath. "Jenny, you *are* steel guitar-drenched, old-school country, tear-in-your-ear ballads. You *are* twang."

"I'm tired of tears, Mike. When I started out in this business, you decided who you wanted me to be. You pigeonholed me into this angst-ridden singer with the dysfunctional past."

"You had no part in it? Aren't all these songs carved from *your* experiences? I didn't make them up out of thin air."

"I'm saying I was ignorant about a lot of things. You can't sit there and tell me all you Music Row executives don't have your own agendas!"

"Jenny, Jenny, this is extremely serious. You've got intensely loyal fans who think they know you, who expect pain inflected, slice-of-life snapshots like "Honky-Tonk Tomcat," and "Daddy, Don't Come Home." You can't just go and decide to recreate yourself. Like it or not, those are the ramifications of life spent in the public eye."

Those words *life spent in the public eye* circled in my head like angry bees as I ripped a bite of bagel with my teeth.

"Please tell me you're joking," Mike pleaded. "Don't you listen to the television talk shows? Don't you read the magazines, the Internet? 'Jenny Cloud lives out her songs.'"

I didn't answer.

He stabbed a finger toward the stack of reviews. "'Jenny Cloud's lingering vocals and world-weary sound as she grapples with the memories of her Southern roots!'" His loud voice was causing a stout woman with a Liza Minnelli hairdo to stare open-mouthed at us. I pulled the bill of my hat even lower. She looked like a talker, maybe even a gossip columnist.

"Get a clue, Jenny! Don't you know we're hit-makers here?" Mike made a fist and pounded the table. "Three consecutive albums debuting at number one on both Billboard 200 and Billboard Country! You want to give all that up? Throw it away?" His face flared beet-red.

I lowered my voice, pleading with him. "Please, Mike, listen to me. I'm not talking about giving up singing. Music's who I am, and I couldn't run away from it even if I wanted to. But I don't want to live like this anymore. I *can't* live like this because my sanity's important to me. Those songs hurt me to write, are hurting me to sing. A person doesn't have to live out the pain in their songs to sing them." What could I say to explain my precarious mental state? Mike knew I didn't have a pleasant childhood, but he had no idea the extent of what I'd endured.

"People change," I said, after a long, uncertain pause. "It'll still be country, but it'll be modern country that crosses genres and has a wider audience!" There, that ought to do it.

Mike set his coffee cup down with a loud thunk. "Both from an artist's viewpoint and a management perspective, there's *nothing* worse than abandoning your sound. It would be the end of Jenny Cloud."

I stared at him, suddenly flustered. The Liza Minnelli woman was gone, but I noticed a couple at the nearest table hanging on our every word. "You don't know that," I said.

"Oh, yes I do. It'd be the death knell of your career if you started writing mainstream pop stuff. Your popularity with fans is phenomenal. And when country fans talk, artists have to listen. We're making a product here! A successful product, and if we change it, it's all over. I can promise you that."

I was a product?

All at once I felt very tired. I got to my feet while Mike stared at me with his mouth hanging open for a second before he pushed me back down with his words. "You're not throwing away all we've worked for. What's it going to take to convince you?"

I ran a hand through the straggly hair poking out from the side of my cap.

"Hey! I know how to convince you!" Mike slapped his thigh. "You know the song 'Murder on Music Row,' by Alan Jackson and George Strait, don't you?"

I nodded. Everybody in country music knew that song. Portions of the catchy lyrics floated through my mind, words about the death of country music as it had always been.

"Then I'm sure you also recall how that song sparked a debate in the country music community about whether or not the traditional country music like you do was dead, dying, or not." Mike's eyes were huge. "Went on forever. Do you recall that album of Alan's called *Like Red on a Rose* that came out back in 2006?"

It was funny to think of the twang king, Alan Jackson, teaming up with bluegrass superstar Alison Krauss for an album of love songs. The soft notes of their ballad "Anywhere on Earth You Are," gave me a wistful stab. Yes, it was definitely different than Alan's usual, but I admired how he'd broken out of his shell to try something else. "I liked it," I said.

There was a long pause, and I thought I'd made my point.

The expression on Mike's face was impossible to read. "There was a huge outcry from fans who thought he was abandoning his traditional past and aiming toward a mainstream pop sound." Mike rubbed his chin. "Alan's no dummy. He's been around long enough to know that when certain names are mentioned—names like Johnny Cash, Merle Haggard, Hank Williams—people think hard-core country. He knew he had an image to uphold, too, an image he absolutely had to go back to if he wanted to make his fans happy. And, for his next album, he went back to his previous producer, back to his real country roots." Mike drew in a deep breath through his nostrils. "You, my girl, are hard-core country when it comes to the females of country music. You *are* twang. And don't forget it."

My heart was pounding. "Why do you care? Worried you won't be able to make any more money off me?"

"Jenny, Jenny," he said in a disappointed voice, "your career could crash totally, and I'd still be sitting fat. Don't you remember last year when Dad left me everything?"

I nodded. I'd gone to the funeral of Mike Flint Sr. He'd been a widower and loaded, and Mike Flint Jr., his only heir. When Mike Sr.'s lawyers had everything settled, I recalled Mike taking his family on a big European vacation, then buying a $1.8-million beach home in Florida as well as a ski chalet in Vail. He redid the interior of Flint Recording and bought himself a flashy red Corvette. I was fairly sure he was set for life and beyond. I knew it wasn't for the money that he worked so tirelessly at Flint.

"I'm sorry, Mike. It's just . . . "

"Just what? What's going on, Jenny?"

"You asked me once, twice actually, about the pressure. From fame, stardom, I'm guessing you meant. At that point I remember I said to you, and I kept saying to anybody who asked because I wanted to believe it, 'I'm good. I'm coping. Things are A-OK.' But the truth was, *is*, Mike, there are times when I'm absolutely hanging on to my sanity by a very slim thread. I feel like I'm about to lose it if I don't change some things."

Mike stared at me.

"Remember that night I freaked out over 'Honky-Tonk Tomcat?' "

"That was a long time ago. I thought you were over that, Jenny. I thought you were okay."

"I know. It's not your fault. I've been keeping it all, mostly, inside. But I'm telling you now, Mike, I *despise* looking into my past. Digging all that stuff up to write songs hurts. I adore singing and I adore the stage, and I really, truly love my fans, but the other part, the so-called 'autobiographical heart-wrenching lyrics,' well, it makes me so . . . I don't have . . . it's killing me is what it is, and I DON'T WANT THE MUSIC TO CALL ME HOME ANYMORE. I DON'T WANT TO GO HOME!"

It seemed the coffee stopped percolating, that everyone in the restaurant stopped breathing. I felt my espresso and cinnamon crunch bagel trying to come up. Mike's face looked terrified. The next thing I knew, he was crouching beside me, his arms around me. "Jenny, Jenny, calm down now. I believe you need to talk to somebody. A professional, a shrink. We need to get you all fixed before your appearances at the CMA Festival."

My arms were shaking as I drove home. I'd totally pushed thoughts of the upcoming CMA Festival out of my mind. Held the second week of June each year in downtown Nashville, it's the music highlight of the year, and I was scheduled to perform at both Riverfront Park and LP Field.

When I walked inside Harmony Hill, I felt a bit unreal and planned to go make a cocoon out of the covers on my bed. But my phone rang and for some crazy reason I answered it.

Aunt Gomer's voice sped into my mind before I could register who it was. She said she'd been outside feeding chicken manure to her tomatoes when she got the strongest urge to march right into the house to call me and invite me to come eat supper, and, by-the-by, did I like fresh figs?

I couldn't get my thoughts together quick enough to come up with an excuse, and I hesitated, saying, "Well, I've got to um—," and she cut me off and told me she'd pick me up at four and I ought to come prepared to spend the night up on Cagle Mountain because she had something to show me.

"I want you to see them by dawn's early light, Jennifer. You would not believe how absolutely gorgeous my light purple Mary Franceses are. They just take your breath away, partickly in the morning light."

"What?" I was trying to wrap my mind around a woman named Mary Frances who was light purple.

"Irises are the Tennessee state flower."

"Oh, well, that's nice, Aunt Gomer. But now that I think about it, I've really got a lot of things to tend to and so I better not—"

"You be ready, honey. I need to run because Bobby Lee's helping me with my seeds and we need to get them out before it gets too late."

I stood there stunned, the dial tone buzzing in my ear.

———∞∞∞———

The more I thought about it, the idea that someone wanted to share her joy with me was profoundly touching. It made me happy to think of seeing Erastus and Bobby Lee. I could sure use a distraction, and finally, I decided I would go up to Cagle Mountain, but definitely I wouldn't spend the night.

I spent a couple of hours listening to some new CDs, then turned on daytime television without really connecting to what was on. I looked at the clock—two. I decided to hit Walmart before Aunt Gomer's arrival.

I slunk through the pet-food aisle in my ball cap, my shapeless top, and jeans and chose a box of Milk-Bones for large breeds. Wheeling my cart through the garden center, I hunted something for Aunt Gomer since she was the one who'd invited me. But as I paused to look at all the different plants, the bags of mulch, and spinner racks of seeds, my mind went blank. Seemed she already had everything in the world when it came to gardening. Finally I saw a floor pallet full of what the sign called "Knockout Roses." Their cherry red petals were so gorgeous I knew Aunt Gomer would love one even if she already had a few.

In the fishing section, I stood looking at rows and rows of tackle boxes and nets.

"Need some help, ma'am?" A gaunt teenage boy wearing a Walmart smock appeared at my elbow.

"Yes, please," I said, ducking down under the bill of my cap like a turtle. Something about this kid put me in mind of a country music fan. "Do you have catawba worms?" Bobby Lee had told me that the Indian name for catalpa was Catawba and that a lot of fishing experts referred to the caterpillars as Catawba worms

"Yes, ma'am!" he said with so much enthusiasm I knew he had to be a fisherman. "Insect larvae is choice bait!" His gigantic feet began leading me down an adjacent aisle where he paused to point at a peg holding a cellophane package of worms. "Now, we don't carry the live ones, you understand. But we got the artificial ones. I hear they're not as good as the real things," he said. "But what artificial's got going for them is they're a lot cleaner to use, and they'll last for years in a tackle box."

Bridge: Aunt Gomer

Today was one of those beautiful spring mornings that make a body feel the joy of living so strong she wishes she could somehow just stop time, press it in a scrapbook, and climb back into it when things aren't so pretty. I ate my oatmeal standing out in the garden and soaking up the sun. Then I fed my tomatoes and spent a fair amount of time weeding my cantaloupe patch before I went inside to get Bobby Lee to come out and help me hunt for iris borers.

"I can't hardly see those pesky little varmints," I told him after he'd mashed a good dozen between his thumb and forefinger.

"Maybe you need to go get you some new glasses, Aunt Gomer."

"Oh, pshaw. I don't need new glasses." I could feel my neck getting tense and so I changed the subject. "Be time to go fetch our sweet little Jennifer before too long."

"Jennifer's coming?" Bobby Lee perked up. Erastus was sitting at the edge of the flower patch, and I swan, when that dog heard Jennifer's name, he hopped to his feet, trotted over, and laid his chin on Bobby Lee's knee, smiling and wagging his tail to beat the band.

"Yessir. Called her after I heard this interview on the radio where Big D was talking to the artist of some album debuting at number one on Billboard Country. He asked this gal about what had inspired her to write one of the songs, and she said her sorry daddy had, and then Big D kept calling it a "childhood rocked by emotional ambushes." I thought I recognized the voice and come to find out it was our own Jennifer!

"So, what I'm figuring, Bobby Lee, is that the Louvin Brothers or maybe Bill Gaither might do the trick."

"Huh?"

"Our girl needs her some home cooking and gospel music to elevate her spirits. The other morning when I had one of my sinking spells, I turned on the Statler Brothers and listened to "Just a Little Talk with Jesus," and I declare if I didn't feel 100 percent better. Gospel music can lift a person right up. Some of those songs are so sweet they make me cry, but in a good way, you know?"

Bobby Lee didn't look convinced about my plan. He doesn't listen to gospel music. He doesn't even go to church. Seems like he blames God for being paralyzed, and if I've said it once, I've said it a thousand times, "Motorcycles don't crash themselves." Sometimes I remind him what those doctors said about how he's lucky to still be alive and still be able to use his mind and his hands.

"Let's go pick the figs that are ready," I said to him. I like us doing things together because when our hands and eyes are busy, it gives us a chance to talk from our hearts.

"It's too early for figs, Aunt Gomer," Bobby Lee said, but he wheeled along beside me to the fig tree at the back door. I examined the figs while he took a twig and poked at the little tiny cans I hang from the tree's branches with twine to keep the bugs and birds away.

"You get hold of Mr. Pintar about that job down at the recycling center?" I asked after a spell.

Bobby Lee didn't answer.

"You've got to decide you want to be independent, son. Don't you let your mama tell you you can't do nothing, because you're smart and capable. I know Tonilynn's stubborn, but you've got to stand up to her. There's plenty of people in wheelchairs who are independent."

He still didn't say a thing, and I got to feeling so mad I yanked a little green fig off the tree. "I'm going on in the house to cook."

"Aunt Gomer?"

"Yes?"

"You remember she's a vegetarian, don't you?"

I did not, but I changed thinking directions in my meal plans right quick. "'Course I do. But I don't know how a body can live without any meat. Even this fig tree loves its meat. It could no more thrive on a meat-free diet than a human could!" Every evening after we washed the supper dishes, I carried the dishpan full of greasy water and flung it out the backdoor onto the tree's roots.

"I'm fixing the macaroni and cheese casserole I do at Thanksgiving." It was comfort food to a T: elbow noodles, eggs, cheese, milk, and cream-of-mushroom soup, with a nice buttery top crust of breadcrumbs and more cheese.

Bobby Lee was sitting in the middle of the den when we got home. His hair was shiny clean, and he had on a fresh T-shirt. Every lamp was turned on, and there were flowers everywhere. Daffodils spilled out of a milk jug on the telephone table, and a bouquet of calla lilies and phlox was nestled in a bucket on the hearth. Irises in Mason jars lined the mantel and the windowsills and sat on the kitchen countertops.

"Ohhhh," sighed Jennifer. "This is *beautiful*." She was holding a Walmart bag, twirling around with her green eyes wide.

"Glad you like it," Bobby Lee said. I was shocked that he'd done all this, and for a moment I had the sensation of being inside a dream, one about a funeral home, but maybe that's because I was holding a pot of roses Jennifer had given me and they had that heavy, sweet scent of burying folks. I set them down on top of the tin box where we keep the kindling.

"It is mighty pretty," I said. "Every cloud has a silver lining, and this here's our reward for all that rain that kept us indoors."

Erastus scampered over to put his nose on Jennifer's knees. "There you are, sweetie pie!" she squealed, kneeling down. "I brought you something." And then she leaned over and actually *kissed* that dog on top of his head! It wasn't just a little air peck, either.

"Where's your mother?" I asked Bobby Lee, but he didn't answer so I went on in the kitchen to put my casserole in the oven and mix up the biscuits. I'd already put bacon drippings in the butterbeans, so all I had to do was heat them and the beets. The tea was made, and I'd bought a bag of Pecan Sandies for dessert. I could hardly wait until we were sitting around the table, eating my good casserole.

While I was kneading the dough, I made up my mind to conduct my own interview with Jennifer about her new song. Seemed like every time Bobby Lee put on The Big 98, there she was, singing about a father who'd crushed his little girl's heart. The song made out like the girl triumphed in the end by cutting him right out of her life, but every time I heard it, I remembered Jennifer's voice trembling and pitiful as she answered Big D's questions.

Once the biscuits were in the oven, I showed her the guest room at the end of the hall. "I put a washrag and a towel on your bed, hon, and soap and such is in the shower. Just help yourself to anything in the kitchen."

"Thanks. But I don't believe I'll—"

"I generally rise at six, but I had a mind that tomorrow we'd . . . " Now it seemed there was something I needed to tell the girl. Something to do with the morning, but all I could think of at the moment was making sure I kept a close eye on the biscuits. I tried to think of things to do with the morning to see if that wouldn't jar my memory—feed chickens, make coffee, let Erastus out the back door. *Coffee . . . Chickens . . . Erastus . . .* I was getting mighty frustrated. I clenched my jaw so hard my teeth hurt, and finally, as I was stirring the butterbeans, it came to me.

"I have a splendid idea!" I called to Jennifer. "In the morning we can get up early and sit outside to have our coffee and watch the sun coming up on the Mary Franceses. Irises are the state flower. Did you know?"

"Um, yes," she said, coming into the kitchen to wash her hands. "I believe I've heard that somewhere."

I began breathing a little easier now that matter was settled. I figured the odd expression on the girl's face came from the fact that she was just stunned at all the good things coming her way all at once. I peeled the tinfoil off the casserole to sprinkle on the last half cup of cheddar and a bowl of crushed Ritz crackers mixed with melted margarine. When it was back in the oven, the kitchen started smelling like hot buttery cheese.

Tonilynn had come home, and she stood in the den talking a mile a minute. It sounded like she was real surprised to see Jennifer. I poked my head in to tell Bobby Lee to go ahead and put on some gospel music. He was just as agreeable as he could be, scooting right over to the cabinet where my albums and the record player stay. "This one?" he asked, holding up my Louvin Brothers album called *Satan is Real*.

"Yessir." That one has such a pretty cover I wouldn't mind hanging it on the wall. Charles and Ira Louvin are wearing white suits and they're surrounded by big bright flames to look like hell, and behind them is a huge, cross-eyed statue of the devil. Every time I see it, I am struck by how sneaky the devil is.

I set out forks and knives to the beautiful harmonies of the Louvin brothers singing, "The River of Jordan." When they got to "The Angels Rejoiced Last Night," I had to run in the den and hush everybody. "This is one of my favorites," I told them. "And I want y'all to hear the words." The reason I said this is that the song is about a father who holds Satan's hand, gambling and treading down the path of sin. Finally, when the mother dies, she asks him to raise those children right, and he accepts Jesus as his savior.

"Wasn't that uplifting?" I said when it was over. I touched Jennifer's wrist and she jumped. "Did you know Charles and Ira Louvin write most of their own songs like you?" I encouraged. "I heard you talking to Big D about your new song."

"Oh."

Bobby Lee cleared his throat. "When's supper, Aunt Gomer?"

"Reckon we'll eat in fifteen minutes or so. Plenty of time to visit."

"Jennifer brought me a present." Bobby Lee held up a little plastic bag.

"That's real nice," I said. "Candy?"

"No. It's fishing lures—rubber catalpa worms."

"Fake worms? You don't need fake worms!"

"I do too!" Bobby Lee was practically shouting. "I've been itching to see how they compare! I told you the other day I wanted to get me some artificial catalpa worms and compare them to the real thing."

Well, I didn't remember that, but there were plenty of times I didn't remember where I put my handbag or what I'd eaten for supper the evening before. When I told it to Myrtice, my prayer partner at church, she said everybody did that, even young folks, and it was nothing to worry about. They were all looking at me, waiting. "Well," I said, "those folks in China can make just about anything they set their minds to."

Little Jennifer sat there biting her lip. Soon as the Louvin Brothers started singing "There's a Higher Power," I managed to get my thoughts back on track. "Whenever I'm feeling down, I get out my gospel albums, and I turn up the volume and close my eyes and listen until I'm lifted right up out of my troubles. 'Just a Little Talk,' and 'Fourth Man' by the Statler Brothers make me feel like I'm walking on clouds. It's powerful stuff. Do you listen to gospel music, hon?"

Jennifer blinked. "Sometimes."

"Well, that's good. Partickly if folks have trampled your dreams like you said on the radio."

"Aunt Gomer," Bobby Lee said in this dark tone. He shook his head.

"I'm just telling her what helps get me through *my* trials and tribulations. I knew when I heard Big D doing that exclusive interview about 'never-before-heard stories behind the songs' and Jennifer was telling about her inspiration for 'Daddy, Don't Come Home,' she needed something to elevate her spirits."

Bobby Lee grimaced, but I ignored him.

"You're more than welcome to borrow any of my albums, hon. It just broke my heart to hear you so sad on the radio. Just broke my heart."

"Thank you. I'll remember that." Jennifer twisted her hands together in her lap.

"You're more than welcome. I'm going to pray and ask the Lord to carry you through your hurts. He's helped me deal with a lot of hurt in my life, and as the Good Book says, he's no respecter of persons. Your Heavenly Father'll help you deal with the issues you have with your earthly father. Didn't you tell us one time you wanted him dead? Or did I just dream that?"

"She told Big D she's managed to cut her father out of her heart entirely." Bobby Lee said through his teeth.

"Her words may've said that, but her *voice* certainly did not."

"Look, Aunt Gomer, if you're so smart, you ought to know there are some things that don't make for pleasant conversation."

"Tonilynn," I said, "are you going to allow Bobby Lee to talk to me like this in front of our guest?"

"Far as I'm concerned, he's right, Aunt Gomer. You're meddling in stuff that isn't your business."

I was so embarrassed I couldn't think of a thing. The Louvin Brothers were singing the last song on the album, "I'm Ready to Go Home," and that's exactly how I felt.

"Please y'all," Jennifer said after a bit. "Stop fighting, and I'll tell you the real story about 'Daddy, Don't Come Home.'" She took a shaky breath and closed her eyes. "The lyrics, everything I said to Big D about the song, was the honest-to-goodness truth. At one point anyway. I thought I'd managed to cut my father out of my heart because I never let myself think of him. For a long time, I did pretty good.

"But then, and this is the awful part, when I started digging up memories to write the song, the hurts came flooding back fresh. And I got furious all over again.

"I try to tell myself that I'm my own woman now. That I'm strong and I ought to rise above it all. The way he did me ought just to be fuel on the fire of my ambition! I don't need his or my mother's approval in my life! I'm a million times richer than they are.

"I just don't understand," she continued with this trembly voice, "why my mother never saw the bad things about my father. Why she can't see them now! I guess she'll deny them to her dying day. She doesn't care about me." Jennifer's face crumpled, and Tonilynn tugged a tissue from her handbag on the floor and pressed it into her hand.

I could feel my heart clench up just like a muscle cramp. "Oh, child," I said. "That must've been awful."

"Yeah, it was. Is."

"I remember you telling us you didn't have nobody you could turn to. Well, you've got us now."

For a moment Jennifer said nothing. I think she was trying to decide if she should continue her story. Finally she said, "Thank you, Aunt Gomer. But I wasn't completely honest with you earlier, because I *did* have someone."

"Is that a fact?"

"When I got to high school I met a wonderful man. At first, I would shuffle into the music room, so anxious and awkward and pathetic I couldn't hardly swallow, and each day I'd leave a little stronger. My teacher, Mr. Anglin, said stuff that transformed my crazy self into something that made sense. I absolutely lived for chorus.

"In tenth grade, I still didn't have any friends my own age, but I didn't care anymore because Mr. Anglin was my teacher, my best friend, my parent, and my mentor, all rolled into one. But he didn't seem like a grown-up. He was slim like a teenage boy, and he had this head full of wild, curly hair with no gray, and he didn't grump around drinking coffee in the teacher's lounge like all the rest of the teachers did. Every day me and him talked after class because it was my last period.

"One day, we were sitting on the stage to one side of the chorus room, and we could hear feet moving fast on the gym floor next door because the boys' basketball team was practicing. There were tons of loud hoots and hollers. Boys just letting off steam after being in class all day, and Mr. Anglin said to me, 'If we could bottle some of that testosterone, we'd be rich.' I was sort of shocked, because besides when he was singing or playing the piano, Mr. Anglin was a pretty meek, mild kind of man. Then he shocked me even more. 'Speaking of getting rich, Jennifer, I'm on fire to help you get ten songs absolutely perfect. We'll make a demo, and we'll take them to the record labels in Nashville, Tennessee. I knew the first time I heard you that you were destined for something bigger than Blue Ridge. You're born for stardom.'

"This was my dream, you see, and I could hardly believe I had somebody dreaming it with me! I got brave and started carrying my song notebook to school, and Mr. Anglin helped me polish stanza after stanza, shine up choruses.

"Sometimes an idea for a new song or a tune would hit me during history or algebra, would make me want to literally jump out of my skin. My hand could hardly get the lyrics down fast enough. I'd be humming melodies during class."

She paused, and Bobby Lee said, "I'm curious. Do you get the words or the melody first?"

"Most times, I hear the words first, and then I get the music. Back then, it was like Mr. Anglin's faith in me was literally pulling songs out whole. Words and melodies were pouring out constantly. It was almost scary."

Jennifer stopped and I realized I'd forgotten to breathe. Tonilynn and Bobby Lee were sitting up on the edge of their seats too. "So, what happened?"

"Well, I focused on that spotlight shining on the stage of the Ryman where Mr. Anglin told me I'd be standing. Every school day, we'd work on my songs, on the demos, and I just knew my dreams were going to become reality.

"One day I came home from school feeling, well, the only word I can come up with that fits is ecstatic. Mr. Anglin and I had just finished recording my demo. He'd pronounced it absolutely perfect, and it felt like nothing could go wrong."

When Jennifer paused this time, I about couldn't stand it. She nestled her hands down into Erastus's neck fur, laid her head on his back and sighed from the depths of her soul, as they say. Thankfully, after a minute, she sat up and continued. "Mother warned me to keep my voice down soon as I came skipping through the front door with a song on my lips. 'Your father's home,' she whispered. 'He's out back.'

"I just shrugged. You've got to understand I had absolutely no urge to gallop out there to say 'Welcome home, Daddy.' We didn't have that kind of a relationship. But mother grabbed my arm and pulled me into a chair at the table. 'Jennifer, just stay inside and let him have a chance to calm down. He's not himself.'

"I didn't have to ask what she meant by 'not himself,' but it was still hard to sit there, feeling about to burst with my news. Usually when I got home from school I went outside to visit with my cat or walk along the creek. That particular day, it took a minute for reality to set in because my father'd been gone off for one of his longer stretches, over six months, and I guess I'd gotten forgetful about how he could be, you know, I was used to doing what I wanted?

"At any rate, I sat there while Mother peeled and sliced potatoes for supper, mixed up some cornbread, and swept the floor. I could tell she was tiptoeing on cornflakes. After a while, I couldn't stand it anymore. 'Got to use the bathroom,' I said, and she turned from the stove where she was stirring potatoes and whisper-yelled, 'Be careful!'

"Our toilet was in an outhouse behind the cabin, so I went skipping toward the back door, and literally stopped dead in my tracks when I heard something."

Jennifer sighed and looked down at her hands. The rest of us sat looking at each other for what seemed like forever.

"Tell us what you heard," Tonilynn patted the girl's wrist.

"Well, I thought when my mother said my father was not himself, he'd be knee-walking drunk, but he was sitting sort of upright. He'd dragged a kitchen chair out onto the cement off the back of the cabin, and he had a radio going near his feet. He didn't have a shirt on, and his hair was in this greasy hank over one shoulder, and he almost looked like a painting the way the afternoon sun was on him. His eyes were closed and he was singing along with Merle Haggard to 'Okie from Muskogee.' But here's the thing." Jennifer paused a bit and her eyes got big. "His voice was absolutely *magnificent,* this really gorgeous baritone singing 'We still wave Old Glory down at the courthouse.' I'm not kidding when I say I could literally picture *him* up on the stage at the Ryman, the audience totally lost in his voice.

"I'm not lying when I say I could hardly get a breath down in my lungs. I just stood there, absolutely paralyzed. I'd never heard my father sing before, and I had no earthly idea he was so phenomenal! People who write reviews about singing would call it 'lush, pained notes of a rich timbre' or something like that.

"I realized we had this beautiful connection. I was thinking *I got my singing from him, along with the Indian looks!*"

Jennifer paused again. I felt my heart hammering, and it looked like Bobby Lee was in a trance. "So, what happened?" I poked her a little bit in her side. She jumped but then she took right off with the story.

"Well, apparently I made some kind of noise because my father flinched a little, turned his head, opened his eyes, and I could see this sort of slightly unfocused look in them. He held up a floppy arm, and I saw an empty liquor bottle lying on its side at the edge of the cement. If I hadn't had this urge to connect with the man, I probably would've listened to my mother and beat it. I mean, I knew what alcohol did to him, but it was like some magnet pulling me out onto that warm cement.

" 'You're an awesome singer,' I told him. 'You sound exactly like Merle Haggard. No, you sound *better* than Merle Haggard.'

"He just said 'Whoop-tee-do' and twirled his finger in the air.

" 'Seriously, you're really good. I don't think I've ever heard you sing before. I'm good at it too. I love to sing. I sing all the time. It's my most favorite thing in the entire world, and I'm going to be a country music star. Mr. Anglin said so.'

" 'Country music star?'

"I stepped closer to him because I not only thought I'd finally found a connection between us but also thought it could help him make money. We never had enough money. 'Yeah. You could be a star too. We could be a father-daughter group. You know, like The Crist Family, or The Nelons, or Jeff & Sheri Easter? We could call ourselves The Singing Clodfelters.'

"He didn't say anything, and his cigarette burned down to near nothing so I thought it must be scorching his fingers. Finally he flicked it away into the grass. Then he coughed and spat in the yard. 'Who's this Mr. Anglin?'

" 'My teacher. He says he's never heard anybody who has such a natural ability to write the words, hear the melody, and sing like I do.'

219

"For a spell I thought he wasn't going to respond, then he cursed and spat. 'That's stupid, Jen. He's probably just a horny old coot trying everything to get in your pants.'

"I'd forgotten how he called me Jen, and I absolutely hated that, because in my mind's eye, I saw it spelled out like g-i-n. I'd asked him a million times to please call me Jennifer, and every time he just laughed. But then I realized what he was saying about dear Mr. Anglin, and his words made me sick to my stomach. 'Liar!' I screamed at him. 'Mr. Anglin's never laid a hand on me!' It was true. He'd never made me feel what we had together was anything more than two souls who shared a love of music.

"My father threw back his head and laughed. That was when I knew this definitely wasn't going to be like I'd imagined. My heart was pounding, so I tried to calm myself by taking deep breaths. 'Mr. Anglin is a good man,' I said. 'A nice *Christian* man, and I'm not going to waste my life. I'm going to do like he says and go to Nashville and *be* somebody!'

"For a drunk, my father was on his feet quick. 'A kid like you don't know nothin' about wasting life. Don't know nothin' about nothin' and I'm gonna tell you something, there ain't a thing wrong with fixing cars, or hauling logs, or toting scrap metal for a living! Who do you s'pose it is that feeds your ungrateful mouth? Tell me that, *Jen.*'

"I thought I could slide past him and run to the woods. I didn't think he could say anything worse than what he already had."

Jennifer turned so pale I thought she might pass out.

"Take yourself a nice, deep breath, hon," I said to her real soft. "Everything's all right. You're with people who love you now."

"Yes, we love you," said Tonilynn and Bobby Lee at the same time.

At last Jennifer cleared her throat. "He stepped toward me with this crazy sort of smile and said, 'I'm gonna give you some real wisdom, some fatherly advice. You don't need to be singing or worrying about making money. You don't need to worry about working on nothing but a big chest and pleasing the men. *Then* you'll get everything else in life you want. Females got it easy, 'cause when I see me a fine piece with a rack like Dolly's, I ain't got no problem whatsoever emptying my pockets out for her, buying her anything her little heart desires.'

"I started shaking. Felt like bending over and vomiting my guts out. 'You make me sick,' I said. It was only a whisper, but he heard me.

"'What'd you say?' My father's eyes were wide and scary as he moved toward me, trying to unbuckle his belt. 'You need to learn some respect for your elders! Ain't a thing wrong with a man enjoying the finer things in this life! Girl wants jewelry, a big house, fancy clothes, vacations, in exchange for what she can give me, why not? You ain't gonna turn into a killjoy like your saintly mother, are you?'

"He was too drunk to unfasten his belt, but it didn't matter. The things he'd said were a million times worse than a whipping. The air went out of me and I couldn't run. But I kept my head down so he wouldn't see me crying."

I have to say you really could have heard a pin drop for a spell up there on Cagle Mountain. I'd never heard such a story in my life, and I didn't feel too much Christian love in my heart for that man.

"What happened then?" This was Bobby Lee, with his face like he'd seen a ghost.

"That night I lay down in my pallet on the screen porch, and I put my radio up next to my ear, and I tried and tried to return to living high on my dream. I even pretended I was

Mr. Anglin's daughter, but I could not conjure up a single picture of me in Nashville. The sun was coming up before I finally fell asleep, and when I did crawl out of bed, I knew one thing. I wasn't going back to high school."

Jennifer squeezed Erastus so tight, his eyes bulged, but he didn't complain. "And that," she said, "unfortunately, was the real inspiration for 'Daddy, Don't Come Home.'"

"Heavens," I said after a long quiet moment. "Sometimes I wonder how the Good Lord lets certain folks live the way they do. Did Mr. Angel drive you to Nashville with your music demos?"

"No. Actually, um . . . what happened is . . . I . . . um . . . I . . ." That poor child's words got all clotted in her throat like spoiled buttermilk. I hopped to my feet to pat her back and help them out, but it was to no avail.

"Eat your heart out, Big D," I said in a bright voice. "You're always crowing about your 'exclusive, never-before-heard stories behind the songs,' but us folks up here on Cagle Mountain, we've got *the story behind* the story behind the song. And now, I believe it's time to celebrate with some good home cooking."

We gathered at the table, I asked the Lord's blessing and passed around my perfectly browned biscuits. Jennifer helped herself to a biscuit and some butterbeans and said, "Thank you for fixing such a nice supper and inviting me, Aunt Gomer."

"It's my pleasure," I said. "Won't be long until we get our first ripe tomato out of the garden, and *that's* the day I'm waiting for. You'll have to come eat tomatoes fresh off the vine with us. I've made many a meal on tomatoes and biscuits. I believe I could eat tomatoes every single day of my life and never get tired of them. What's your favorite food?"

"Depends on if I'm at home or on tour. Usually I have cereal or a PowerBar if I'm at home."

Tonilynn started talking about some restaurant they liked to eat at that made soup bowls out of bread, and I got to wondering how in heaven's name it could hold soup without leaking.

"I don't know what I'd do without my fried bologna sandwiches," Bobby Lee said. "That and a Pepsi to wash it down."

Jennifer smiled. "I've got to have black coffee the instant I get out of bed."

"Well, I'm *addicted* to Diet Cokes." Tonilynn laughed and hefted up the big Pyrex casserole dish and helped herself to the first corner. "Mercy me, this is heavy," she said, grunting as she passed it to Bobby Lee.

I ate my beets and recalled a time when I was a little girl, no older than ten, when Mama fixed beets for supper and I was so hungry I must've eaten a gallon of them. That next morning when I went out to the outhouse to do my business, I thought I was bleeding internally, and I just knew for sure and certain I was fixing to meet my Maker. I decided there were some sins on my heavenly account I needed to confess, and I went running back to the house. I told my sister about cutting up her paper dolls, and my cousin, Delphine, about stealing an orange from her Christmas stocking, and my great-grandmother about switching out her vanilla ice cream with mashed potatoes, and finally I felt like my soul was clean, and I lay down to die. Mama knew something was up, and when I told her I'd made out a list of who was to get what of my earthly possessions, she put two and two together and explained to me about how beets can color your movement like nothing else. Well, I just about never lived that down, and after I got older, it was funny to me too. However, I decided it wasn't a good story to tell at the supper table.

Nobody said anything for a while. Forks and knives were clinking on the plates, and it was real satisfying. I looked across the table at Jennifer, and I thought she looked fairly happy and that made me happy. I was trying to think up something interesting to say, as the hostess, when Tonilynn hopped up like she'd seen a snake. She was jumping on her tiptoes, and she grabbed Jennifer's wrist and started shouting, "Don't! Stop! Put that down!"

I followed Tonilynn's line of vision to the end of Jennifer's fork, where inches from her mouth was hovering a bite of my delicious casserole. I was what you call dumbstruck as Tonilynn continued, saying, "I swear it's got tiny little faces! It's got tiny little faces!" Bobby Lee and Jennifer sat there like statues, and I'll be honest, it flashed through my mind that Tonilynn was crazy, or maybe possessed. I'd never allowed swearing at my table.

"Tell me that's not the body of a *worm* curled around those fork tines!" she said. "Tell me those aren't eyes!"

My heart was racing a mile a minute as I peered down into my casserole. I bent over closer. "That's not eyes! That's parsley on the end of a macaroni noodle! The recipe calls for parsley."

"Is too eyes," Tonilynn said, and then her chest started heaving and she was holding her stomach like she was fixing to vomit. Then so help me, Bobby Lee and Jennifer started heaving, too, and it wasn't long until Tonilynn was bent over the kitchen sink spilling her supper and Bobby Lee had upchucked onto his plate and little Jennifer onto the floor by her feet. Then everybody was up, swishing out their mouths with tea and spitting into the sink.

I could tell everyone believed Tonilynn's story. She was rifling like a madwoman through the trashcan underneath the sink and then through a pile of empty Glad containers in the sink, waving a fairly big rectangular one, saying to Bobby Lee,

"Ain't this what you put your worms in to freeze them?" and he was bug-eyed, nodding. It was like a scene from a horror show. Several minutes passed with no one talking, and the only creature that seemed happy was Erastus as he was enjoying licking the floor clean.

I sat there feeling pretty mad. Thinking if someone had fixed me supper out of the goodness of their heart, and I'd seen a hair or something in the food, or I just didn't like the way something tasted, I definitely wouldn't mention it. I would just quietly spit it into a napkin or slide it to the edge of my plate. That's just good manners, and I thought I'd instilled good manners into Tonilynn. I don't have no use for rudeness. Finally, Jennifer sat down, never said a word, and Bobby Lee kept saying, "Wow, man. Wow," and shaking his head. I knew I had to say something. I didn't care if she was forty-eight years old.

"First off, Tonilynn, even if it is worms in there, and I said *if*, which I do not believe it is, it's been blessed, and blessed food is food that's good for the body. Says so in the Bible. Furthermore, I saw on PBS, or maybe it was a National Geographic show, there are some societies what eat rats and grubs, and if rats and grubs are good enough for them, and let me tell you, they sure looked healthy to me, then I don't see what the fuss is. Thirdly, it is rude to complain about something somebody has fixed for you. It's bad manners to point out anybody's shortcomings."

Tonilynn was sitting there twisting her gold bracelet around on her wrist. Jennifer's eyes were cast down and Bobby Lee was texting away on his cell phone. When no apology was forthcoming, I looked directly into Tonilynn's eyes and said, "Don't you think there's something you need to say to me?"

She reached across the table to pat my hand. "Please forgive me, Aunt Gomer. I didn't go to insult your cooking or hurt your feelings. Jennifer's a vegetarian, as you know, and I didn't want her to offend her own conscience."

Well, I must say I felt right good about that explanation, though I cannot for the life of me understand why a person would want to be a vegetarian. And then, what about Tonilynn and Bobby Lee's excuse? But the Bible says to forgive and forget, so I said, "Bobby Lee, put that casserole dish down for Erastus, and I'll go perk us a pot of coffee."

While I was waiting on the coffee, I shook the Pecan Sandies out onto a nice plate and carried them to the table. Then I felt like a waitress at the Waffle House, serving mugs of coffee and cream and sugar on my silver tray. I was worried that the mood was broken, but we all sat around the table laughing and visiting until after eight and polished off that whole bag of cookies.

11

I awoke from a heavy sleep to find myself lying on a lumpy mattress in a fetal position. A full moon was shining through the window at my feet. For a while I lay motionless, trying to remember where I was and how I'd come to be there. Gradually, I realized I was on Cagle Mountain. It wasn't so bad until I recalled what had happened the night before, and just the fleeting thought of that flung me into a state of shock. Eating the worms (I'd consumed half my serving of casserole before Tonilynn alerted us) was a picnic compared to purposefully revisiting the genesis of "Daddy, Don't Come Home."

I thought I'd been a mess after my conversation with Mike at Panera. But this was like jumping from the frying pan into the fire. How in the world had I let my guard down far enough for the fullness of *that* memory to get out? What was it about these people that made me spill stuff? Did I really know them? Could I trust them with my baggage? When it came down to it, could I trust *anyone* with my baggage?

I blinked in the murky dark and rubbed the crust of drool off my cheek with that awful memory dancing around in my head, particularly nauseating when I considered what an idiot I'd been that next day—the years of anguish my foolhardy reaction had spawned. My heart hammered so I could hardly get a breath.

I wrapped my arms around myself until I was calm enough to swallow. Thank goodness the music had not called me home to other events lurking in my past. I would sooner die first. I lay there awhile, until I could ignore my full bladder no more, so I wrenched myself out of bed and crept down the cool plank floor of the dark hallway. I shut the door to the bathroom as quietly as possible, tugged the string to turn on the lightbulb overhead, used the toilet, then closed the lid before flushing and stood at the lavatory until it had finished making noise. I decided I'd tiptoe back down the hallway and crawl into bed, wrap myself in the quilt and wait until the sun was up to go find Tonilynn. I'd ask her to take me home. I knew already what I needed for my peace, my sanity. I needed the Cumberland River.

I jumped when I stepped out of the bathroom, and Aunt Gomer grabbed my arm. "Morning, honey child," she said. "I heard you up, and I figured you were chomping at the bit. I'll perk us some coffee to carry outside."

Dazed, I followed her to the kitchen. In the sink, I saw the big glass Pyrex casserole dish from last night's supper, upside down and sparkling clean.

"Reckon you're excited about watching God's morning show." Aunt Gomer ladeled coffee into a percolator.

"Oh, well, sure." I'd forgotten about seeing irises in the sunrise. I stood there a while, listening to the coffee gurgle and belch, a rooster crowing right outside the house. It was five forty-five by the oven clock.

"Nobody up but us chickens." Aunt Gomer teehee'd as she poured two cups of dark steaming brew. "Come on," she said, putting one into my hand, "let's make sure we get front-row seats."

I followed her out onto the gray porch, where she sat down in a rocker and patted the one beside her. "I'm so tickled we can share this together." She took a noisy slurp of her coffee and began to rock gently, back and forth, her chin lifted as she looked out expectantly toward the horizon. "I sure do enjoy experiencing the world before it wakes up, don't you?" she asked. "Everything all fresh and clean and new. It just makes a person feel like so much is possible."

"Yes ma'am," I said, but all I really felt was impatient. I could hardly wait for the sunrise to be over and done with so I could get home.

"On that rise yonder is my iris bed." Aunt Gomer pointed somewhere in the pearly half-light of the moon. "They love full sun. My grandmother grew all kinds of what she use to call 'bearded irises.' When I was up at her house, I would go stand over them just looking for their beards. Only thing I ever saw that resembled a beard was this little dark patch of bristly stuff in the middle of the bloom." She laughed. "Granny loved the white irises called Immortality the best. Said they reminded her of spring and new life. She used to make the loveliest arrangements for her church with the Immortality.

"My favorites are the Mary Franceses and the Savannah Sunsets. Savannah Sunsets are bright orange and the Mary Franceses are lilac, and they are absolutely beautiful when you plant them beside each other."

I just sipped my coffee and rocked, listening to the excited chatter of birds in some nearby trees.

"Sleep all right?" Aunt Gomer looked over. "You're mighty quiet. You must not be used to sleeping on a feather bed."

"It was fine. Guess I'm just not used to being up this early."

"Well, hon, you'll be glad you gave up a little shut-eye for this. I've seen thousands of sunrises in my life, and I never get tired of 'em. Every one is different. Words can't hardly do them justice. I lose myself in the whole production."

"Really?" I said after a bit because it seemed as if she were waiting for my response.

"Mm-hm." She took a deep, satisfied breath. "My Mama used to say it's darkest right before the dawn, and I do believe she was right."

I feigned a smile. How much longer would it be until the sun did its thing and I could excuse myself?

Aunt Gomer's old voice took on a dreamlike quality. "One summer I put some foxglove in the back of my hardy border, and Canterbury Bells right in front of them. That following June, they bloomed, and it was the loveliest combination you ever saw. Bloomed two whole weeks. I'd lose track of time just sitting out here looking at them. I ever tell you about how one year I planted blue larkspurs next to orange zinnias? Every soul who came up here was beside themselves at the beauty."

We rocked in tandem a while, and just as I was entertaining thoughts about how maybe this was some crazy-old-woman thing to do, the sun peeked over the horizon. Golden rays broke through misty clouds and splashed onto the earth. I was so surprised at the heartbreaking wash of pinks and yellows spilling over the swell of Cagle Mountain, I stopped breathing. A glorious blur of pomegranate and lemon against robin's egg blue and cottony white, the light on the yard radiant, throwing long velvety shadows.

Aunt Gomer rocked back, an "ohhhhh" cascading out of her mouth, tears spilling down her wrinkled cheeks as the tender, rosy light of new day began to spread.

Then we were witnessing the glorious colors of the Mary Franceses and the Savannah Sunsets as the sun moved up to shine behind them. I gazed out, lost in reverie, biting back my own tears. I knew what Aunt Gomer meant by losing herself.

All of a sudden, the front door swung open and out bounded Erastus, making a huge racket. He bounced down the steps and scurried through the yard, smelling here and there, racing around and around the clumps of flowers, stopping to lift his leg on a stump for what seemed like forever. I didn't even hear Bobby Lee roll up beside me.

"Morning, Jennifer," he said, and I jumped, turning to look at him. His hair was wild, and he was wearing a Led Zeppelin T-shirt, gray sweat pants, and no shoes.

"Good morning." I couldn't help smiling. Wasn't long ago that being so near this man in a wheelchair made me feel shy, uncomfortable. But now I hardly noticed Bobby Lee was without the use of his legs.

"Mercy!" Aunt Gomer almost fell out of her rocker. "Boy, you scared the daylights out of me! What in heaven's name are you doing up so early?"

Bobby Lee laughed. "Figured I'd eat breakfast, then go see about that job before I get to fishing." He was looking at me the whole time.

Aunt Gomer yelled, "Hallelujah!" and threw her hands up in the air.

He raised his eyebrows. "Mama doesn't seem too excited about it."

"Tonilynn's up?" I hopped to my feet.

"Yep. But I'd let her finish her Diet Coke if I was you. She's kind of grumpy."

"I don't mind. I need to talk to her about something. Y'all excuse me, please."

Tonilynn sat at the kitchen table where a lone iris drooped over the side of a jar. Her head was thrown back, her eyes closed as she drank straight from a two-liter bottle. The space where Bobby Lee generally sat had some playing cards laid out in a half-finished game of Solitaire.

"Morning, Tonilynn. Mind if I talk to you about something?"

Tonilynn looked at me. "Have a seat," she said in a clipped voice, nodding at the chair across from her.

"I mean somewhere private."

She shook her head.

I was shocked. Never had I found Tonilynn to be anything but agreeable and accommodating when it came to lending a listening ear. "Please? I need to go somewhere we can be private. Hey! How about while you're driving me home?" I lowered my voice to a whisper. "Would you please drive me home? I'm scared to death to ride with Aunt Gomer. On the way here she kept switching lanes without looking, and people were honking at us like crazy."

"Oh, good grief. Guess it's time to take her license away." Tonilynn sighed. "Listen, I'll drive you home. We'll talk, but it'll have to be later. There's something I need to hang close for."

I knew what that was, but if I was going to survive, I had to stand my ground. "Please. I really need to talk to you in private. Now."

Tonilynn got to her feet, hugging her two liter, and using a nod motioned for me to follow. We stepped out the back door onto a footpath winding past a tin roof on four poles that was Aunt Gomer's car shelter, then a small shed with no door where I saw garden tools lining the walls, then a leaning chicken coop where it looked like they stored firewood, and finally to this old barn I'd noticed before but never really *seen*. It was half-hidden behind a row of azalea bushes on one side and a massive oak on the other. There was no door, and we stepped over a threshold into a large musty-smelling place. The walls were ancient logs laid one atop the other with cracks big enough to slide a flattened palm through, and the roof sagged here and there, and a few patches of sky were visible.

Several mule collars hung from pegs, and in one corner sat a dilapidated sawhorse.

Tonilynn sat down on the wide-planked floor, settling the two-liter between her knees.

"How old *is* this place?" I whispered.

"Aunt Gomer claims it's over a century. Her great uncle put it together without nails. You don't have to whisper. Nobody ever comes out here."

I sat Indian-style, facing Tonilynn, and before I could figure out my opening statement, she said, "I know, hon. You're upset about the worms."

"No. Honestly. I just need to—"

"Well, me too," Tonilynn cut me off, something else that shocked me. "Last night was *proof* she doesn't need to be alone. The woman's losing her grip and doesn't need to be by herself, and here she is pushing my boy to go out and hunt for a job! I could just about wring her neck! If I hear her saying, 'Tonilynn, you've got to stop babying Bobby Lee,' one more time, I'm liable to snap!" She made a fist and pounded the floor.

I sat there looking at Tonilynn's face, wishing I knew what to say. Bobby Lee seemed excited about finding a job.

"You'd think she'd understand that having Bobby Lee here will mean she doesn't have to go to an old folks' home. Aunt Gomer's a proud, stubborn woman."

Tonilynn was pretty stubborn herself. She liked to claim she'd laid her past out there for all the world to see, but she hadn't exactly been Miss Honesty when it came to revealing Bobby Lee's father to Aunt Gomer. She raised the two liter to her lips, threw back her head, and guzzled it down. I'd never seen her like this. I could literally feel the fury spilling out of her. She didn't say anything for quite a while and this gave me time to decide on my opening line.

"You know how we were discussing my new image a few days ago?"

"Yeah, right," she answered in a distracted voice.

"How I was going to talk with Mike about it, and you were going to make me over to be flirty and fun?"

"Yeah, yeah."

"Well, Mike said I needed to see a shrink."

"What?" Tonilynn banged the empty two-liter down beside her.

"Basically, he trashed my idea, just like you said he would, and then he said I needed to talk to a professional. He thinks a shrink can help me deal with my traumatic memories."

Tonilynn nodded. "Listen," she said, "I knew he'd pooh-pooh all that career makeover stuff. Man knows his business. And I don't think he's off the mark wanting you to talk to a shrink either."

It flashed through my mind that the two of them were in cahoots, but that notion died with Tonilynn's next sentence.

"I know I've told you this already, but I've had lots of clients say I'm even better than their so-called shrink that they pay hundreds of dollars to for every visit." She raised her eyebrows. "Shrink. Isn't that a funny word? Reckon why they call them that?"

"Because they're supposed to shrink your problems?"

"Well, I swan!" She slapped her thigh, shook her head. "I'd never have thought of that in a kazillion years, but I believe you're right. They shrink your problems! Well, you don't need to go find one, because I can help you shrink your problems. With God's help, I mean."

My heart fell. "No. Please don't go there again."

"Oh, hon. You know you can tell Tonilynn what's hurting you. I promise, what's said in the Hair Chair stays in the Hair

Chair." She laughed. "Even though we're not *actually* in the Hair Chair."

"No," I said, surprised at the sound of my firm voice spilling out into the quiet barn. "Revisiting that memory I shared before we ate supper last night was bad enough. That was unacceptable."

"Bless your heart." Tonilynn leaned forward to pat my hand. "That really was something. It makes me sick your father treated you that way!"

"That's nothing compared to some other things he did. If I could get away with it, I swear I'd kill the man."

Tonilynn shot to her feet. I was frozen at the sound of her venomous hiss as she yelled, "By the blood of the Lamb, I command you to get behind us, Satan!"

I felt all the hairs on my arms standing straight up as she closed her eyes, raised her face, and began moving her lips silently. After a long, charged silence, she opened her eyes, reached down to take my hand and looked hard into me. "I know you're hurting, Jennifer. Believe me, I know. Sometimes I look at these tattoos of mine, and I remember things that hurt like you wouldn't believe."

I'd gotten so used to Tonilynn's tattoos, I really didn't see them anymore, but in the barn's half-light I focused on the intricate designs stenciled on her wrists and up her forearms, disappearing into the cap sleeves of her blouse.

"What I do try to do," Tonilynn said, "is look at them from a different perspective. They're my very own monument, testifying to how far I've come—what God's brought me through. Like I've said, I'm actually *glad* I went through all that stuff because if I hadn't I wouldn't be who I am today. In God's timing, he used them for my good.

"And he wants to do the same for you, Jennifer. He's no respector of persons, and he wants to shrink your problems.

But you've got a part in it too. You've got to allow him to help you dig them up."

More light was filling the barn. Tonilynn lifted the empty two-liter and tried to shake a few more drops into her mouth. She never ceased to amaze me with her inexhaustible effort to push her religious views on me. She wasn't dense, she couldn't have failed to notice it made me uncomfortable when she talked to the devil around me, when she gushed about God's redeeming love.

I narrowed my eyes. "My Nashville dream wasn't the only thing that died because of the event that inspired 'Daddy, Don't Come Home.'"

Tonilynn gave me a curious look.

Some part of me had known all along the exact moment a certain silence had fallen on my spirit, the instant my childlike faith had turned up its toes and died. Roy Durden had only confirmed what I'd learned that awful night. "After my father imparted his so-called wisdom, I was thinking I just wanted to die. So, that night I got into my pallet and turned on my radio that had always been my gateway to joy in life's darkest moments. They were having a gospel show, and it used to be that every hurt and care fell away when I'd listen to hymns by Elvis and Mother Maybelle Carter, or "Amazing Grace" coming from a giant pipe organ. I closed my eyes and prayed that I could find peace, and then I listened hard, expecting the sound to lift me up above all the ugly hurts. I thought it would be like usual and I'd feel the presence of God, and he'd fill me with peace so I could fall asleep. You know, the way it usually happened? But that night it was like . . . nothing. I was all alone. Inside of me was dark and empty. I knew then that God couldn't care less about me."

Tonilynn reached for my hand and said in the softest voice, "But look at you now, Jennifer. Your father didn't *keep* you down. You've built an impressive career."

"He did keep me down! I don't even want to tell you another thing that happened as a result of that night, but it's haunted me for years! And I cried rivers while writing 'Daddy, Don't Come Home!' and IT RIPS MY HEART TO SHREDS EVERY SINGLE TIME I SING IT!" I yanked my hand from Tonilynn.

She flinched but quickly regained composure. "Oh, hon. You can't undo what your father did to you, but please, ask God to help you forgive him. Forgiveness is so liberating, and then, God will use what you went through for his glory. He can heal you up from all those ugly memories so you'll have peace."

Forgive my father?! Was she serious?! My brain was screaming as I stumbled over the threshold sprinting from the barn and back to the house. I slammed the door to my bedroom, shoved the back of a wooden chair underneath the doorknob, and dove onto my featherbed, breathing so hard I thought I'd hyperventilate.

Close to noon, there was a knock at the door. Groggily I moved the chair, opened the door, and saw Tonilynn standing there, her makeup flawlessly applied, her generous thighs in extra-tight blue jeans.

"Ready for me to carry you home, hon?"

"I guess." I smoothed the wrinkles out of my blouse. I had nothing to pack since I hadn't planned to spend the night.

Aunt Gomer stood on the porch, wearing a purple blouse, red polyester slacks and blindingly white sneakers. "I'm so proud you came to visit, hon."

"Thanks," I said. "Thank you for inviting me."

"Can't you stay a spell longer?" She grabbed my elbow. "Be proud to have you for supper again tonight."

I shook my head. All I could think about was getting myself to the soothing waters of the Cumberland.

"Jennifer's got things to tend to in Nashville," Tonilynn said, tugging me down the steps before Aunt Gomer could respond.

As I opened the passenger door of the Pontiac, I heard tires on the gravel. Bobby Lee smiled big beneath a camouflage bill cap. Dressed in a mud-splattered T-shirt and black waders, he had a tackle box nestled in beside him, and two fishing rods stuck up like antennae behind his back. Erastus was standing beside him, panting.

"I heard the screen door slamming, and I figured you might be fixing to leave, and then I figured you might rather go see if the fish are biting today. Check out the artificial catalpa worms?" He said all this in a rushed, hopeful tone. A hoot owl called from the trees beyond the house as a bittersweet longing washed over me. I pictured fishing from a pond on a spring day, frogs kerplopping into the water, bugs scuttling along in weeds at the water's edge, the quiet anticipation of a bite.

"Might be the inspiration for that perfect country song," Bobby Lee urged.

I ran a hand through my hair. It was a Friday afternoon, no appointments, no . . . Quickly I remembered why I felt the urgent need to get back to Nashville. "Sorry. Can I have a rain check?"

He nodded and Tonilynn ducked down from the driver's seat to look right into Bobby Lee's face. "Keep an eye on Aunt Gomer, hear?"

We rode a long ways without talking, lulled by the whine of the Pontiac's tires speeding along the main road once we'd descended Cagle Mountain, and it came as a sort of shock when Tonilynn said, "To everything there is a season, and a time to every purpose under heaven."

"What?" I looked over at her.

"That's a Bible verse."

"I thought it was a song by the Byrds."

"It was a Bible verse first. Anyway, Jennifer, after you ran out of the barn, it just sort of popped into my head like a neon sign while I was helping Aunt Gomer hang out the wash, and I knew it was God talking to me about your father."

Did she ever give up? "I said I don't—"

"Didn't you say those demos Mr. Anglin helped you make were burning a hole in your pocket until you could get to Nashville?"

I couldn't stop my nod.

"You were way too young at sixteen to hit Nashville," she said. "See what I'm saying?"

"No."

"I believe God is telling me that it was a *good* thing, a blessing in disguise, when your father said all those ugly things to you and crushed your dream."

"That's stupid! Nothing good came of that awful day!"

"Don't you see?" Tonilynn was pleading. "Sixteen-year-olds get chewed up and spit out in Music City every day! They're way too vulnerable and immature. You'd never have made it, hon, especially without anyone to take care of you." Tonilynn paused dramatically. "Sure doesn't sound like your mother was supportive."

I knew where they got the expression "seeing red" when a person was angry.

"You were how old when you got to Nashville? Let's see, you're twenty-eight now, and you've been singing for close to six years, so you were twenty-two when you arrived in Nashville, and twenty-two minus sixteen equals six. Six years! You didn't leave for six years, and six years makes a *humongous* difference. It's night and day between a little sixteen-year-old girl and a twenty-two-year-old woman. I'm living proof of that!"

I wanted to think of something sarcastic, but I had no words, and anyway, it seemed Tonilynn was impossible to offend. I didn't know if it was because she was so emotionally stable or simply clueless.

"Don't you see, Jennifer? It just wasn't *time* for you to hit Nashville when you were sixteen. You needed those extra years to mature. So your father actually did you a favor. In God's economy, even things we think are hurting us can be used for our good."

I could not believe the words coming out of Tonilynn's mouth. *God's economy?* If Roy Durden were here, he'd laugh his head off! If we hadn't been going seventy-five miles an hour, I would have wrenched my door open and jumped out into the ditch. We sped past the sign saying Davidson County and Tonilynn was still talking a mile a minute about God's providence, how his hand is orchestrating all this stuff, good and bad, to get us to our destinies at just the right moment, and we needed to live by faith that it's all going to work out for our good in the end. She was still going as we pulled through the iron gates of Harmony Hill.

She turned to me when the ignition was off and said with this incredulous voice, "You know what? I still haven't heard the story of how you finally *did* get to Nashville."

I looked her right in the eye. "Well, it sure wasn't *the Lord's doing.*"

"Please tell Tonilynn," she said, ignoring the snide tone in my voice. "Was it dear Mr. Anglin?"

"No," I said, feeling the sides of my throat beginning to ache. "Mr. Anglin died in a car wreck."

"Oh, nooooo. Hon, I am so, so sorry. I know he was very special to you."

"Yeah, he was," I said, "and what's worse is that his death was my fault."

Tonilynn's eyes were wide. "Were you in the car with him?"

"No."

"You were in the other car?"

"There was no other car. Mr. Anglin lost control of his car and skidded into a wall."

"Then why was it was your fault?" Tonilynn whispered.

My voice was a whisper too. "Because you'd have to understand what a sensitive soul Mr. Anglin was. He felt things very deeply, and I could tell it really hurt him the day after my father crushed my dream, and I went to the school's office to tell Mrs. Vestal I was dropping out. Of course I didn't tell her the ugly story about my father. I lied and told her I had to get a job to help support my family. Anyway, Mr. Anglin overheard us, and he ran in there. He had this pink face and he was saying in a real loud, shaking voice, 'No! You can't drop out and go to work! You'll never get out of Blue Ridge! You'll never get to Nashville! I'm not going to stand for this!' You should have seen him, all wrought up and waving his arms. Mrs. Vestal got up from her desk, patting on Mr. Anglin and saying, 'Now, calm down, Ron. Just calm down. Take deep breaths and come sit down.'

"I couldn't tell anybody why I was really dropping out, about my father. I said, 'Mr. Anglin, I have changed my mind. I don't want to sing anymore, so chill out.'

"He flew into an even bigger fit, said I was squandering my talent. Then, that very night, I heard he'd crashed into the brick wall at Sayer's Corner on his way home from work."

"So?"

"Everybody knew not to go fast on that curve. We were always getting warnings to take it easy at Sayer's Corner, and Mr. Anglin drove like a granny anyway. The minute I heard he'd crashed, I knew it was my fault." I could feel myself shaking as I finished.

Tonilynn squeezed my hand. "Jennifer, look at me."

My pain was mirrored in her big brown eyes. "I know that was hard."

"Yeah. It was."

"But you don't really know. You shouldn't blame yourself."

"Trust me on this one, Tonilynn. There is absolutely no doubt in my mind."

"So you dropped out of high school?"

"Yeah. I started working at McNair Orchards to help Mother with household expenses."

"For six years?"

"Yeah. Picking apples, peaches, and blueberries was a good job for somebody who likes the sky above them."

"I guess so. But did you really quit singing?"

I shook my head. "I sang to the trees."

Tonilynn laughed. We sat there in the garage, and I told her stories about picking jonagold and honeycrisp apples, about keeping the windows down in the little pickup truck parked nearby, the radio in the dash blaring so I could sing along as I worked, so I could be in another world. I told her about Mac, the owner of the orchard, who walked around wearing only jean cut-offs. Tonilynn got a kick hearing how he was such a hairy man—legs, arms, face, back, chest, except for right on top of his head where there was this bald, shiny circle like the part of him from the top of his ears up just popped through the carpet.

"One day, it was September, and I was picking apples and belting out 'Delta Dawn' with Tanya Tucker. I was totally lost in the song, and I about jumped out of my skin when Mac tapped me on the shoulder. I started to apologize, but he said, 'You've got one heck of a voice, Jennifer Clodfelter,' and then he said the same thing Mr. Anglin used to say, that I had a responsibility to use it, and had I ever thought of heading to Nashville, and trying that scene."

"Did you tell him about Mr. Anglin?" Tonilynn had her palms pressed against her cheeks.

"No. I told him I had a notebook with seventy-two original songs, though, and a demo with ten really polished ones, and he said he'd miss me at McNair Orchards, but in the grand scheme of things, he couldn't live with himself if this gift of mine wasn't shared with the world, and he was ready to make me an offer on the spot and wouldn't take any answer but a yes. The memory of those words coming from that hairy hole between Mac's mustache and beard made me smile.

Tonilynn clapped her hands. "Did he give you money?"

"He gave me an early paycheck, and he matched it so it came to almost a thousand dollars. Then he said his cousin could give me a lift to Nashville."

All of a sudden Tonilynn's eyes filled up. "Oh," she said, her voice breaking as one tear slid down her cheek. "That is an awesome story. I love how the Lord put this Mac fellow into your life, and when the time was right, or ripe, I should say," she teehee'd softly. "Then he practically forced you to go to Nashville. That's the Lord for you, proof about what he can do in his time, his sovereign plan, hm?"

I tried to wrap my mind around the ridiculous spin Tonilynn was putting on my life. After a minute, after failing, I slowly exhaled the words, "Haven't you been listening? Haven't you heard what I keep saying about all the pain? Sometimes I feel like I'm losing my mind."

Tonilynn's voice was full of compassion. "I know. The past eats at you like an ulcer. Like a little taste of hell. But I'm telling you, hon, the Lord can give you peace. He'll give you the strength to forgive. He'll change the way the past has shaped you."

I slammed the door of the Pontiac behind me.

"Bye, hon!" Tonilynn trilled her fingers out the window. The last thing I saw was the double strands of barbed-wire tattooed around her wrist.

———— ∞ ————

Monday came, and Tonilynn didn't show up to get me ready for my afternoon photo shoot. That wasn't like her at all. She was generally fifteen minutes early to everything. Then it dawned on me I hadn't seen her or talked to her for close to three days, which was very odd. I began to feel like a boat with no anchor, wandering from room to room inside Harmony Hill, finally stationing myself at the window overlooking the drive. I dialed her cell phone and the house phone up on Cagle Mountain half a dozen times with no answer.

At two o'clock I headed for the garage, planning to drive to Cagle Mountain. I'd backed out and was at the gate when I saw Tonilynn's bicolored Pontiac. I felt a huge surge of relief as I let her through, backed into the grass to turn myself around and followed her to the house.

Tonilynn looked like death warmed over, smeared lipstick, her hair so flat and lifeless it put me in mind of a damp mop sitting on top of her head. Her eyes literally disappeared without their black liner and contouring shadows. She didn't have her usual wheeled suitcase spilling over with beauty products and tools. I stood there, debating if I should say "Hi!" like nothing was out of the ordinary, or ask how she was doing. "Hi, Tonilynn," I said finally, in the most level tone I could manage. "Sure is good to see you."

"Hi, hon." Her voice was weary. "Can we sit down somewhere?"

My heart was beating like mad as I led the way to the kitchen where we sat at the table, looking at each other for a long, oddly silent moment.

"Aunt Gomer had a stroke," Tonilynn said finally.

"What?!" My skin tightened. "Is she okay?"

Tonilynn shook her head.

"Oh, no!" My eyes flooded with tears. "She's gone?"

"No. She's still kicking. Believe you me."

I breathed out a sigh of relief. "What happened?"

"Well, it was Friday, not long after I got back home and we were sitting on the porch. I went in to get a drink, and I asked Aunt Gomer did she want me to bring her more tea, and she didn't answer. Then I saw she'd fallen over and her eyes looked weird and her mouth was hanging open and she couldn't speak.

"I yelled for Bobby Lee to call 9-1-1, and they sent an ambulance to carry her to the hospital and me and Bobby Lee followed. The doctor said she'd had a stroke. They admitted her to see how bad it was and could they do anything."

I could barely swallow. "Is she still there?"

Tonilynn shook her head with a weary sigh. "It was a minor stroke. They sent her home, told her to take it easy, and she does not like that one bit. I haven't had a wink of sleep in days." She rubbed her temples.

"I'm sorry." I reached over and patted Tonilynn's wrist.

"You should have seen us at the hospital. Aunt Gomer hollering, 'Tell it to me straight, Tonilynn! Am I in an old folks' home?' and 'Jesus, come fetch me and carry me on to Glory right now, 'cause ain't nothing worse than being in an old folks' home!'

"I kept saying, 'Calm down, Aunt Gomer, you're in the hospital.' Well, she kept trying to climb out of her bed, telling me she had to tend to her garden. It took two nurses, big women, to get her back into bed.

"Yesterday the doctor said she could leave, so we carried her home and put her in the front room on that recliner to where she could see out the window, and we could keep an eye on her. She's been going on and on about needing to get to the grocery so she can buy some corn meal to make muffins. We had a fight because I told her she couldn't drive anymore. I told her she needed a little R&R after a stroke, and she ought to let me and Bobby Lee serve *her* for a change. She is fit to be tied!"

"Wow."

"Yeah. She's wearing me out. And it breaks my heart when she gets confused. She'll put her shoes on the opposite feet, and she keeps saying she needs to go out back and feed Ebenezer."

"Ebenezer?"

"Her donkey that died thirty years ago."

12

That next Sunday when Mike called for a "quick little meeting" to discuss details regarding the 2010 CMA Festival, I felt like a two-by-four had smacked me upside the head. The festival was six weeks away, and all I wanted was to put it completely out of my mind—from my fan club party on Thursday, to my performances at Riverfront Park and LP Field on Saturday. I swore under my breath at him for his excited tone.

It was late, a little after seven p.m., and I was still in my playclothes: shapeless khaki shorts, a ratty old blouse, and flip-flops worn so thin they were like paper beneath my soles. I'd already had my Sunday morning ritual at Panera Bread, but Mike wanted me to meet him there at eight.

I went upstairs, washed my face, brushed my hair, and changed only my footwear, sliding my feet into an ancient pair of Nikes. I applied face powder to my shiny nose and a smidgen of Vaseline to my lips.

The sky I could see out the windshield seemed darker than usual, and I wondered if maybe a storm was moving in. It was beautifully quiet inside the Lexus. I needed to think and was very thankful for radio dials you could turn on and off at your pleasure. I wished I could turn Tonilynn's voice in my head off. It was like a scratched record album, stuck on one song.

Even more than usual, she'd been picking and prodding at the foundational bricks of my shaky adult self.

In fact, she'd called Saturday morning, as I was on my way to the river, with something she referred to as "A distinct word from the Lord I got for you, Jennifer." I could hear her lilting voice saying, "Listen up, here's what he said: 'Be brave, my child. You've repressed those memories because you're afraid. But you don't have to be afraid. Put your hand in my Son Jesus' hand, and we'll bring them to the light together. It will be cathartic.'" Tonilynn paused, and I could hear pages rustling. "I had to look up that word *cathartic* in the dictionary and here's what Webster's says, 'A purifying release of the emotions or of tension, especially through art' and also, 'A technique used to relieve tension and anxiety by bringing repressed material to consciousness.' See? You gotta look stuff in the eye to be healed."

When I didn't respond, she continued. "I ask you, Jennifer, how could Freud, and Webster, and *the Lord* be wrong? Please ask Jesus to help you dig everything up. Then, commit it to him, and he'll help you write it into one of your brilliant songs to help other folks. Be healing for you and for them! I've known since I heard you the very first time that you have a message and a mission with your music!"

She paused, and when I didn't respond, she plowed on.

"You can let him pour out his love on hurting, vulnerable folks through your music. Isn't that awesome, hon?"

Still, not a word would come out of my mouth.

"Jennifer, I promise you, it's your calling. You already transform folks with your music. I see 'em with tears in their eyes when they listen to you."

I held the phone away from my ear, wondering if anybody could ever be so totally unselfish as it seemed Tonilynn thought I could be. There were two very important components missing from her fantasy. Number one, my willingness to go back and sacrifice myself. I'd made it too much of my mission to stay one step ahead of my past to ever consider it as some way to minister. Second, I still saw Tonilynn as kind of out of her mind. Not totally connecting with reality. For a moment I latched onto that phrase the sound technician had used: "One of those wack-job born-agains who acts like Jesus is her best friend." But I cast it out quickly because no matter how put out I was with Tonilynn, I loved my friend.

A bit later, while sitting on the bridge watching the Cumberland, I found myself intrigued in an odd kind of way by this fictitious Jenny Cloud that Tonilynn had come up with. I smiled, picturing myself sort of like Mother Teresa, humble and resigned, pouring my life out for the good of many. But right on the heels of that image came the terrible knowledge that before this could happen, I'd have to allow a certain time in my past to surface.

Sweat beads popped out on my forehead as I toyed with the thought of *that* memory coming to life. I forced my thoughts to return to the beautiful, peaceful Cumberland. Maybe I couldn't change my past, but I sure could choose to keep certain stuff stamped down and speechless. I'd never give it, nor Tonilynn, the satisfaction!

I took a deep breath and tried to focus less on Tonilynn and more on what Mike might have in mind. It felt odd to be visiting Panera in the evening. I walked along the shopping center's sidewalk beneath street lights blinking to life in the cloudy dusk, marveling at what a change it was from my usual. The Great Room felt strange too. Loud and bright, with smells of onions and hot cheeses mixed in with the coffee aromas.

There was a different crowd as well, which discombobulated me even more. I was standing there, staring at the menu board, when my thoughts were interrupted by my cell phone.

"Hi, Jenny girl!" Mike said. "Wanted to let you know I'm gonna be running a few minutes late. I'm talking with the management team, then going to run by and see Scott briefly. How 'bout ordering me a ham and swiss—extra pickles. Large ice tea. Be there shortly, and hey, I think I'll be bringing you some real exciting news. That sound good?"

"Sure," I said. I ordered Mike's food and a regular coffee and carried it to the dining room. It was fairly crowded; a single businessman who took up a whole booth with his laptop and newspaper, an older couple sitting across from each other but working separate crossword puzzles, a young couple in running attire sipping smoothies and leaning toward each other intimately. I sat nursing my coffee, thinking how this had once been my safe retreat, and now I had to work to feel relaxed in here, to keep my thoughts and eyes away from the various stacks of tabloids. Not only did it hurt to see the carefree faces of Taylor and Carrie, but the incident with Holt had given me a lasting horror of those things.

Outside the window, I could see storm clouds gathering, and I wondered what would happen if it stormed during the CMA Festival since a good portion of it was held outdoors. There were shows for free during the day at Riverfront Park, but you had to buy a four-day ticket to get a seat in LP Field for the nightly shows where the big stars performed in front of seventy thousand fans. A lot of artists celebrated with their fans who purchased tickets to fan club parties, which often included a private performance, a meet and greet, and food. Mike took great delight in planning the menu for my fan club parties. Last year, it had been shrimp and grits, along with cheddar biscuits, fried Moon Pies, and icy RC colas in bottles.

I thought about how I used to urge the days to pass more quickly so I could climb into that four-day weekend, with music playing downtown from early in the morning until after midnight. Now I was dreading the festival with every fiber of my being. Getting up on stage at LP Field to sing "Honky-Tonk Tomcat" and "Daddy, Don't Come Home" was unthinkable.

Something else weighing on my mind was how perky I would need to be for my fans, for those long lines of autograph seekers and people who wanted to pose for a picture with me.

I sat there gritting my teeth and thinking: *How many times can I sign "Best, Jenny Cloud" and not lose my mind? Absolutely no way I can get up there on the stage at LP Field and not fall apart. This is not how I want to use my gift of music—dreading what I used to love. So what if my life would be purposeless without music? Purposeless is better than miserable. I'll never be happy living like this. Never be able to make peace with my past. The only way to keep that shameful incident buried is to bow out now.*

As this realization swept through my mind, it was like something came into Panera Bread and possessed me. From the soles of my feet to the crown of my head, I knew it was time to drop out of the Nashville scene. I'd always had the knowing of it in the back of my mind, that this day would come, and here it was. I sat very still, waiting.

At 8:49 Mike stepped into the restaurant, flashing a smile beneath a cowboy hat dripping with rain. I couldn't help marveling at him as I always did, at the way his tall, solid body wore khakis and a button-down shirt in what I thought of as "casually rumpled elegance."

"Hey, beautiful. Sorry to be so late, but you won't care when you hear what I've got to tell you." Mike sat down, removed his hat and set it on the table between us. "How's life treating my favorite star today?"

"Okay," I said, "How are you?"

"I am wonderful, absolutely wonderful." Mike took a bite of his sandwich, and spoke with his mouth full. "Aren't you chomping at the bit to know what the exciting news is?"

"Sure." I lifted my coffee and almost gagged on the cold, bitter slug.

"I was talking with Scott, and he and I both agree your number's about up for being invited into the Country Music Association's Hall of Fame."

A little laugh flew out of me of its own accord. Images of my idols—Patsy Cline, Loretta Lynn, Barbara Mandrell, Emmylou Harris, Dolly Parton, and Tammy Wynette—formed in my mind. Then came Minnie Pearl, Johnny Cash, Glen Campbell, The Statler Brothers, Roy Clark, and Tom T. Hall. Wasn't Elvis a member?

Surely Mike was teasing! How would *Jennifer Anne Clodfelter* be among those legends in that hallowed institution? I could almost see myself being invited into the Grand Ole Opry, *almost*, a hope birthed in me when Carrie Underwood had been inducted into the Grand Ole Opry by Garth Brooks in 2008. But to be in the Country Music Association's Hall of Fame seemed unreal.

"Who is this Scott person?" I felt my heart beating fast.

"That would be Scott Borchetta," Mike said, his eyes twinkling like a kid's on Christmas morning. "Scott is CEO and President of his own label too. Big Machine Records. That ring a bell?"

I had to nod. Everyone knew Big Machine Records was Taylor Swift's label. "Is Taylor's number up too?" The competitive spirit of my question stunned me.

Mike shook his head. "Neither Taylor Swift nor Carrie Underwood are up for being invited into the Hall of Fame." He took a long drink of tea. "I'm suspecting their work isn't twangy enough. Not pure country enough."

A million emotions started zigzagging around inside me. I had a mighty impulse to rise up on my feet, thrust a fist into the air and shout, "Yes! I made it! I'm one of them now!" But of course, I didn't. Some cold, analytical part of me reached back into my brain for my recent decision and forced myself to remember the pain, that overwhelming fear whenever the memories came. I drew in a long breath. "Well, I'll tell you something, Mike. It doesn't really matter to me about that possibility, because I don't give a fig about the Hall of Fame."

He stared at me.

"What I mean is, I'm done with the whole entire country music scene. I'm getting out."

"Getting OUT?" Mike's eyes bulged, and a little vein throbbed in his temple. "Didn't you hear me? We're talking the Country Music Association's *Hall of Fame*! Are you insane?!"

If I hadn't been sitting there thinking about this for an hour, preparing my thoughts, I might've crumpled under Mike's fury. "Mike, Mike," I said wearily. "We've discussed it all before. Several times. I just can't take the pain anymore."

He stared at me for a long, silent moment. "We discussed you seeing a professional, Jenny," he said in a barely restrained voice.

I flinched. I wrapped both hands around my mug, but one escaped and found a silky strand of hair at the base of my neck to twirl so hard it hurt.

"'Daddy, Don't Come Home' is still number one on the country charts, Jenny. That's huge! Flint Recording is leaving Big Machine Records in the dust! In the dust! Everyone thinks Taylor Swift is so high and mighty, but now it's us! It's Jenny Cloud. *We* are the ones headed to the Country Music Association's Hall of Fame! Aren't you excited?"

Mike's pleading tone hit me in the gut. My goal wasn't to leave anyone in the dust, was it? His mouth was a grim line when he spoke again. "Haven't I given you what you wanted? I seem to remember meeting this little girl at the Bluebird, this green-around-the-gills bumpkin who assured me all she wanted was a chance to make it big in Nashville and she'd be happy."

My neck tensed. It hurt where I was twisting the hair. I could see that me being inducted into the Country Music Association's Hall of Fame would be *Mike's* moment of fame. I pictured myself standing onstage to receive the award, saying, "I owe it all to Mike Flint and Flint Recording," And rightly so. The man was absolutely tireless when it came to positioning, publicizing, and promoting. My album sales continued to rise, my singles zoomed up the playlists on radio, and Mike had gained phenomenal support and visibility from the digital retailers. He had visibility for us in places where country music normally didn't even have a presence.

"You can't jump ship, Jenny!" Mike shook his head. "Especially not now. Your staff's been talking up your fan club party for months through Twitter, through your website, and I've gotten more response than ever for this year's fan club party. This year we're offering bonus perks—an exclusive Jenny Cloud T-shirt and an autographed CD if they buy a one-year fan-club membership. I'm even thinking about doing a guitar drop like they did at First and Broadway on New Year's Eve." He blew out a gust of air to illustrate his exasperation. "I've already ordered pulled pork barbecue from Rippy's. Got thousands of loaves of gummy white bread scheduled to arrive."

I just stared at Mike's intense face.

He pulled out his best weapon. "You wouldn't disappoint your fans, would you? All those folks who've paid their good money to see Jenny Cloud?"

I managed to squeak out "Of course not," just as a deafening boom of thunder rattled the Panera.

Mike gave his head a quick shake like a dog after a dip in the lake. "Good. Let's talk about rehearsals."

———&oeao;———

Bobby Lee rolled down a narrow footpath to the water's edge, then a good ways around the perimeter of the lake as I followed behind with Erastus. Strapped to the handles of his wheelchair with crisscrossed bungee cords was a small Coleman cooler that bounced in rhythm to the ruts. Bobby Lee began telling me how Aunt Gomer had woken him up yesterday morning at four, talking about fallen fruit.

"Really?"

"Yeah, she wanted me to get up and help her with the June drop."

"The what?"

"June drop. When the fruit trees—the apples, pears, peaches, plums, sweet cherries, whatever—drop a lot of fruit. You know, just this natural way trees thin themselves out to a manageable crop size?" Bobby Lee shrugged. "She took a notion it was time to gather, and she started quoting Scripture about a 'good tree bringeth forth good fruit; but a corrupt tree bringeth forth evil fruit,' and 'Ye shall know them by their fruits.'"

I couldn't help smiling. "But it's not even May yet."

"Well, I couldn't convince her of that or to get back in bed. Couldn't make her get dressed either, so she went outside in her nightgown, her stringy white hair wild. I went along so I could keep an eye on her."

I swallowed a laugh. "That was sweet of you."

"Yeah," Bobby Lee said in an uncertain voice. "Then, when we got outside, she decided she needed to feed Ebenezer."

"The donkey that died thirty years ago?"

"Yep. She dragged me to the barn, ordering me to put clean, fresh hay in Ebenezer's stall."

"What did you do?"

"Well, I made out like I did it." He turned to look at me. "Know how they say 'Old age ain't for sissies'?"

"Mm-hm."

"Well, *dealing* with old-timer's ain't for prissies. I've decided that to survive I'm just going to have to hang loose and go with the flow. Makes it easier to deal with all the fallen fruit and the asses."

We looked at each other and busted out laughing. We laughed so hard my knees gave way, and I sank down into the grass. Just when I thought we were past it, we'd look at each other and start up all over again. That was the best I'd felt in years, it seemed.

"Know what?" Bobby Lee said with a glint in his eye when we'd finally calmed ourselves.

"What?"

"I'm going to have to get me a job so I can get some rest!"

We cracked up all over again.

When we were moving forward, I walked along admiring the sculpted muscles of Bobby Lee's arms and shoulders, glad he was wearing a tank top. I was jolted from my admiration by Erastus's sharp bark.

"What ya see, boy?" Bobby Lee came to a stop.

Erastus was rigid, unblinking, staring at the water's edge. "Woof!"

A bloated armadillo corpse floated on its back, all four legs pointing stiffly toward the sky. By instinct, I stepped back, mouth hanging open ungracefully, looking at this exquisite creature. *Gothic beast*, I thought, my imagination running away with me as I admired the platelets of armor. When I looked over at Bobby Lee, he smiled and said, "Pretty magnificent, huh?" then quickly admonished Erastus, "Leave it be, boy."

We moved on down the trail, Bobby Lee maneuvering his way through brambles and roots and wild blackberry bushes, quick and spry as any two-footed man, amazing me with his chivalry, holding branches until I'd passed by. He wasn't even breathing hard.

We reached a little clearing of sorts, and it was littered with spent bottle rockets, cherry bombs and beer bottles. "Somebody had themselves a little party, hm?" Bobby Lee said, bending to pick up a lapful of debris, then stuffing it all into a small satchel hanging off one side of his chair. "I don't mind the partying, but I hate it when they litter."

What a good-hearted man! I couldn't help admiring someone who cared about the earth the way he did, who was so respectful of animals. I looked at him and thought, *I really like this man. Wonder what he thinks about me? Does he think of me as family like Aunt Gomer says I am? Like a sister to have fun and play outside with?*

"Here we are," he said, coming to a stop on a hard-packed dirt surface I knew had seen lots of fishing. He put his tackle box down beside a stump, reached around and unfastened the fishing rods, and with hardly a pause rolled out into the lake midwheel deep. "C'mon," he turned to me, smiling. "The water's perfect."

"Okay." I slipped out of my flip-flops and stepped into the warm, murky edge, feeling slimy mud oozing up between my toes when I was out a little ways. I kept my eyes fastened on Bobby Lee's face and went on until I reached his side.

"Fish oughta be biting real good today." Bobby Lee's line sliced through the air. I heard the plop of the artificial catalpa worm as it broke the water's surface. "Other one's yours." He nodded at a blue rod lying across his lap.

I reached for the rod and just held it. "I don't know how to cast. Only thing I've ever used is a piece of bamboo with some fishing line tied on."

"Watch me," he said, his muscles flexing beautifully as he drew his right arm back, then forward with a little snap. As his line zipped out again, I focused on his well-defined torso, tight and lean, like art. Much more alluring than Holt Cantrell's soft, doughy paunch and flabby arms.

I worked at casting for a good fifteen minutes, fantasizing about catching a big one and Bobby Lee admiring me. But this did not happen. It didn't happen for Bobby Lee either. He cast over and over again, his jaw tightening more each time. Finally I could tell he was throwing in the towel.

"Ain't nothing like the real thing, baby," Bobby Lee's soulful voice rang out across the water, sounding for all the world like Marvin Gaye. He moved close to me, put his hand on my wrist and raised his eyebrows to say, "Is it now?" in a throaty voice that sent electric pulses through me.

I looked into Bobby Lee's eyes, and my mind supplied another line of the famous love song, and lake water lapped at my knees as I imagined us wrapped in the shelter of one another's arms, just like in the song. I would've paid a million dollars to linger in that moment, a pastel sky above and a breeze rustling the delicate fronds of a nearby willow tree.

"So," Bobby Lee said, "got a cold six-pack on the bank yonder. What do ya say we have our own private little party?"

My dream evaporated instantly. I knew nothing, really, about this man. Could he hold his liquor? Was he a mean drunk? A womanizer when he got loaded? I watched him wheel out of the lake, slinging water as he made his way toward the cooler.

"No, thank you!" I called in a shrill, tight voice.

Bobby Lee raised his eyebrows, smiled that nice, wide smile of his, and while watching me, lifted the lid off the Coleman, pulling out a half-dozen unmistakable red, white, and blue cans of Pepsi-Cola. "Oh, no. Looks like I'm gonna have to party all by myself."

I was speechless for a bit, then broke down laughing. "Save one for me, Bobby Lee!"

We drank our Pepsis sitting in the shade, birds singing in the background, bugs buzzing nearby. Somewhere across the lake a bullfrog sang a series of bass notes that sounded like "jug-o-rum."

"Looking for a babe, huh, Jeremiah?" Bobby Lee called. He turned to me, "That's my buddy. He's jealous. Wants himself a beautiful lady frog to hang with."

I didn't know what to say, so I just nodded and stared out across the water while Bobby Lee launched into a long discourse on the benefits of live bait. "What's new in your world?" he asked finally, popping the top on another Pepsi.

I didn't want to ruin the mood by mentioning the CMA Festival in five weeks. "Well, let's see, it's Saturday, and usually I spend some of the day at Riverfront Park."

"Ah, yes. That's right. Mom says you've got this thing for the Cumberland."

"Gotta get my fix. Same as you with fishing."

"Birds of a feather." Bobby Lee stretched his arms above his head. "I love it out here, at the water's edge. Just something about it."

It pleased me that he compared us. I knew he understood my need, and I didn't feel self-conscious when I said, "It's like the river pulls all the bad stuff from me and carries it away. I feel so new, so peaceful when I leave there. It's my sanctuary."

"Yeah, sanctuary," Bobby Lee said, the word lingering between us. And before I knew it he was leaning in to hold my cheeks with his fingertips, in a tentative way like he might kiss me. It surprised me so that I laughed a little bit. Then I looked at Bobby Lee's eyes in that beautiful face, and all I could think about was kissing him. I swallowed and moved closer, my lips softening. But then, this tug-of-war began in my head. I felt like maybe I could trust this man with my soul. He knew some things about me, some places where I was wounded, but not all. I imagined sharing my innermost heart, my hurts, for that is what I knew it would take to have a real relationship. And it was then I realized I just wasn't capable of that.

I pulled away from Bobby Lee using the pretense of swiping at a bug. Then we just sat there on the bank, drinking our Pepsis and watching Erastus play.

13

It was the last day of April, a Friday, almost a week since I'd fished with Bobby Lee. I hadn't seen him since, but we'd talked on the phone several times, and he was a wonderful conversationalist. I was tons more open with him than I'd been with Holt, but still very careful not to mention the dilemma with my career. The CMA Festival was almost upon us, and I kept telling myself that once that long weekend had come and gone, I would do as I darn well pleased. I had enough to live a very comfortable existence if I never sang for money again. What good was being in the Country Music Association's Hall of Fame if you were miserable?

Looking out the window, I could see the day was beautiful, but I felt nauseated, dreading the interview/photo shoot Mike had scheduled for the afternoon. I didn't want to paste on another smile, or answer one more question about "Daddy, Don't Come Home."

At a quarter 'til nine I heard the beep and hit the button to let Tonilynn's Pontiac through the gate. She breezed in the door pulling her big beauty suitcase and holding what I thought was a bowling ball. She leaned in to give me a hug. "Morning, hon!"

"Morning." I sniffed what I thought to be her new musky perfume. "You smell good."

"That's not me." She sounded exasperated. "It's this cantaloupe Aunt Gomer insisted on sending. Pitched a fit to get out in the garden this morning while it was still dark as Egypt and pick the very first one of the year for you. I don't even think they're all-the-way ripe yet."

"That was sweet."

Tonilynn sighed and sat down heavily on a stool at the counter, beckoning me to sit in my usual chair for her to work her makeup magic. "Yeah, sweet, I reckon, but she's driving *me* crazy with all her craziness. The hard thing is how unpredictable she can be. She'll be just fine for days, I mean, like you'd never know she had the old-timer's, but then all of a sudden she'll take a notion about a certain thing and there's no way you can tell her any different."

"Oh, that's not good," I said, but my mind was on the fragrant cantaloupe, and my mouth was watering. I loved cantaloupe. It was my favorite of all the melons, delicious sprinkled with black pepper. I smiled over at that netted golden globe on the table, one side with this bleached-out looking oval patch on it like the sun had kissed it with hot lips. *I have people who love me,* I thought, *I have people who care about me and send me things.*

"Hey, what was Mike going on about so much last week when we were in the studio?" Tonilynn steadied the heel of one hand with the fingers of her other hand to stroke on my eyeliner.

"Ah, nothing," I said, hoping she'd let the subject go.

"Come on. Tell Tonilynn."

I knew she wouldn't hush until I told her. "He said I might, *might* be getting an invitation to be inducted into the Country Music Association's Hall of Fame."

"Get out!" Tonilynn's jaw dropped. She started bouncing around on her tiptoes, laughing and waving the mascara wand like a sparkler. Then she hugged me. "That's awesome, girl! What more could you want?"

That question went around and around in my head as I stared at the cantaloupe and listened to myself breathing.

Tonilynn looked into my face. "You all right?"

I shook my head. "What I want. What I want is something a lot of people get for no reason at all. Just by luck. I want it more than anything in this world! But I can't get it by being in the Hall of Fame, Tonilynn. I can't get it by singing, by making tons of money. It's not something you can buy or earn. And people who have it don't know how priceless it is."

Tonilynn laughed, high and breathless. "You're full of riddles. What is it?"

"Why? I can't ever have it."

"Yes, you can! I'll help you get it."

"I'D GLADLY TRADE BEING IN THE HALL OF FAME FOR A HAPPY CHILDHOOD!"

Tonilynn flinched, then closed her eyes, lifted her face, her mouth moving silently for several long minutes as I sat waiting. Finally she looked at me. "It's never too late to have a happy childhood, Jennifer. However . . . " she paused dramatically, "the second one is up to you. I just did what you call an intercessory prayer, and again, the Lord told me you just need to grab his hand and go with him back there to your childhood to pull all that painful stuff up and deal with it."

"You've got to be kidding."

"Nope. Just ask Jesus to give you the strength."

I sat there in shock, and then I surprised myself. "Stop cramming all this Jesus-is-going-to-fix-everything crap down my throat! If he's so all-fired up to make me happy, maybe he should've thought about it earlier and given me a different father!"

When Tonilynn had been quiet too long, I swallowed hard and said, "I'm sorry. I just can't stand to hear you talking about letting God do this or that anymore. About how good God is."

She didn't respond right away. She clamped her top teeth on her bottom lip, worked on my eyebrows a bit until suddenly, she jerked bolt upright, put her hands on her hips and shouted, "I rebuke you, Satan, in the name of Jesus Christ, by the power of his blood! I command you to get behind us. Leave us alone! You know you've been overcome by the blood of the Lamb, so git! Go to hell, where you belong!"

Tonilynn's wide-open brown eyes below sparkly blue brow bones would be branded in my memory for years. I didn't realize I'd been holding my breath until I felt her warm hand on my shoulder. "Listen, hon, I know it isn't easy for you to trust a Heavenly Father. But you need to realize, he's not like your earthly one. Speaking of your earthly one, staying mad with him will only eat you alive. It's poison." Tonilynn plugged in a straightening iron. "You've got to make peace with your past so it won't screw up your present. And you can't do it alone. God'll give you supernatural strength to forgive your father if you just ask."

I wasn't sure Tonilynn and I were occupying the same realm. "Even if I did ever manage to let certain stuff surface, Tonilynn, to say I *forgave* him would be like saying it didn't matter! But it did matter! Does matter! He hurt me, and I'll never forgive him for how he ruined my life!"

"Oh, Jennifer, Jennifer. Forgiveness is such a powerful weapon. Inside and out." Tonilynn took a sip of her Diet Coke. "You need to get shed of your bitterness. Start by opening up to Tonilynn and spilling your baggage. Always does me a world of good to talk things out with another human I trust, as well as the Lord. You're safe with me, hon. Start with something small. I'm all ears." She laced her fingers together and waited.

I closed my eyes to block her out. If I opened up to Tonilynn about even something small, that other memory, that insidious thing I felt nipping at my heels might surface. And I definitely could not risk *that*, even though I knew somehow that that piece of my baggage was the very reason I couldn't break through to intimacy that would let me love Bobby Lee.

Tonilynn spritzed a sweet-smelling mist onto my hair and began running a straightener from crown to ends. "So," she said, "remember me talking about that word *cathartic* a while back? How music has the power to heal? Remember that?"

I concentrated on not answering.

"Anyhow," she continued, "I was listening to this show on the radio a few days ago about Carly Simon, and I still can't get over how much power music has in it. It is simply miraculous when it comes to healing."

I sighed.

"I did not use the G word, now, did I?"

"No."

"So anyway, Carly developed this awful stammer when she was just a little bitty girl. She had the hardest time saying anything. It was painful. Hurt her so bad when the teacher at school would ask questions and she knew the answer but couldn't say a word because she was afraid of her face squinching up and her words sounding funny. Imagine being a six-year-old who stutters, and how mean kids can be at that age. Anyway, finally Carly's brilliant mother told her to tap out a beat on her leg and sing what she wanted to say to the beat. Her mama taught her to speak-sing with rhythm, and the only time Carly's stammer went away was when she was singing.

"The entire family started singing everything around the house. You know, stuff like 'Come eat supper,' or 'See you this afternoon.'" Tonilynn put a hand on my shoulder. "Isn't that amazing? Don't you just love Carly's songs? 'You're So Vain' and 'Anticipation'? She's recorded over thirty albums, won two Grammies, influenced a whole generation of women."

Tonilynn waited. But I had no words.

"Well, it just proves that life may have been really traumatic for Carly when she was little, but it turned out to be a blessing in disguise. Turned out music was cathartic. I just love that word!" Tonilynn pointed at me with her straightener. "You know what? Music therapy is Carly Simon's special cause now because of the powerful way singing helped her work through her disability. She's helping others by being a spokesperson for stuttering awareness."

I shrugged. Certainly it was painful, and I wasn't downplaying Carly's affliction, but I would give anything had my cross to bear been something physical like stuttering.

I knew what I needed for my hurts, and I was counting down the minutes until my weekly trip to the riverbank in the morning.

After the photo shoot, Tonilynn asked if I wanted to grab a cheeseburger and a Coke at McDonald's. We ordered at the drive-through, then sat in the Pontiac to eat and talk. The sky was overcast and gloomy, but I was feeling a huge sense of relief to be done with the interview and photo shoot. We laughed about all the young couples hanging out in the parking lot, hands in the back pockets of each other's jeans, their faces turned toward each other with rapturous expressions.

"Love is blind." Tonilynn's eyes lingered on one happy couple.

"Yeah." I knew just what she meant. I didn't associate Bobby Lee with a disability, even when I was standing right beside him. His wheelchair was invisible to me. I loved his sense of humor, his kindness, his compassionate brown eyes. I hadn't accepted any of his continual requests for dinner and a movie, nor had I mentioned to Tonilynn that he and I talked on the phone so often. I looked sideways at Tonilynn, her confection of hair and spidery lashes, wondering how it would be to have a mother-in-law who was also my beautician and best friend. I loved her like a mother. It could work. I felt giddy inside for one brief instant, before acknowledging I wasn't capable of intimacy with any man.

I ended up asking Tonilynn if she wanted to take a ride to downtown Nashville, to Division Street. Something in me craved to see the Best Western, reminisce about those days when I'd just arrived in Music City, maybe talk about dear Roy Durden some.

"You want to go cruising, girl?" Tonilynn turned to me with a mischievous grin.

I nodded, smiled, thinking, *Isn't forty-eight a little old for cruising?* Then, just as quickly, *It's not like twenty-eight is that young either, particularly for a girl's first time.*

All of a sudden, we were pulling out onto Old Hickory, and before I could hardly think, merging onto I-65 North, zipping along with the radio blaring as Tonilynn wove in and out of traffic while singing to Dwight Yoakam's "Guitars, Cadillacs" in a very loud, off-key voice. Seemed lots of other folks had the very same idea for their Friday night, headlights and taillights glowed in a cheery line all along the interstate. "Man, I sure hope we wake up tomorrow to clear skies," Tonilynn said, taking a swallow of her Diet Coke.

"Me too." I was hoping with all my might against the weather forecaster's words. I knew April was all about rain, but tomorrow was May first, and I needed my infusion of peace at the Cumberland. It wasn't fair for it to rain on a Saturday!

We took the exit for Demonbreun, turned left, then circled the Musica statue in the roundabout at the top of the hill. "Here we are, hon," Tonilynn said in an excited voice as we turned onto Division Street. I saw the familiar gold letters and the red crown that formed the Best Western logo, and I got that warm glow inside when something's deeply familiar in a good way. We slowed to 'cruise speed' and I soaked it in, picturing Roy behind the counter, dancing in his seersucker suit, the joyous anticipation of a gourmet feast on its way to him.

"Little bit smaller than Harmony Hill, hm?" Tonilynn teased.

"Yeah." I laughed, and feeling a rush of boldness, I said, "One day you ought to bring Aunt Gomer and Bobby Lee to Harmony Hill for a visit."

"It'd be like the Beverly Hillbillies!" Tonilynn laughed. "That reminds me, Bobby Lee said the fishing trip he took with you was wonderful."

"We didn't catch anything."

"Don't gotta catch nothing to have fun, now do you?" she said in a singsong way, and I wondered if Bobby Lee had revealed any intentions to her. But I didn't want to ask, for fear he hadn't, and I didn't want to ruin the mood.

We made a U-turn and drove over to Broadway, watching people streaming by in happy groups on the sidewalks, admiring the lights of nightclubs and restaurants. Being in the thick of the glittering city after sunset made excitement bubble in my bones like ginger ale. I thought how nice it was to be in the heart of Music City, where the beautiful Cumberland wove her way through the earth like a thread. I smiled, thinking of my trip to see her tomorrow.

I was in a truly blissful place mentally, until all of a sudden something sucked the breath right out of me. I hadn't been paying close attention, and Tonilynn had wound her way back over to Demonbreun where some neon words on the storefront of the Déjà Vu branded themselves on my retinas. *Showgirls! Full nude dancers!*

I'd been by the club a hundred times, walking from the Best Western to the Cumberland or getting off the interstate to head for Music Row, but generally, I averted my eyes quickly, keeping old memories locked up safe. Occasionally, I'd feel sorry for the girls inside, nothing more. Now . . . maybe I'd been away too long . . . maybe I'd been too open, thinking about possibilities with Bobby Lee, or maybe, as Tonilynn so often said, "It's all in the timing."

I'll never know why, but in that moment, the neon glare hit me as it never had in all my years in Nashville. Chills raced up my spine, shame radiated out from my center, a nerve-racking clench of fear prevented me from swallowing, and my heart pounded like a jackhammer as a skeleton from my closet began clawing it's way up out of that red Georgia clay, its bony finger twanging a string I never wanted played.

I didn't even have to close my eyes and I saw that scene—a little story playing out all those years ago in that falling-down house in Blue Ridge. What startled me most, as I am generally an auditory rememberer, was that it was so *colorful*. Everything was hypervibrant with color. I was sitting cross-legged on the green Naugahyde sofa that mother had bought at a yard sale for ten dollars, a slit in the middle cushion had cream-colored stuffing oozing out. I saw Mother's feet in dingy pink slippers on the warped kitchen floor, and the yellow counters with a set of copper-colored canisters reading Flour, Sugar, Tea, and Coffee. My father was home on one of his rare Friday evenings. It was early yet, eightish, and he was pacing around in his navy sock feet, his brown arms sticking out of a light blue short-sleeve shirt with Foster's Garage and *Omer* embroidered on the pocket in red. A vanilla-colored dial phone that hung on the wall above the breadbox rang.

I broke out in a cold sweat at what I knew was coming. "No!" I slumped down in the Pontiac's front seat and held myself stone still, staring at the latch on the glove box, trying to will it away.

Tonilynn hit the brake so hard I slung forward. "You okay?"

My teeth chattered. I shook my head.

"What's wrong?"

I couldn't speak.

"Talk to Tonilynn, Jennifer. Please." She pulled into a parking lot and cut the engine.

I sat frozen, the scene in living color playing inside my head. "I was just . . . I swear I didn't invite it."

Tonilynn's eyes bathed me in love, her hand gave mine a squeeze. "Tell me."

I swallowed the knot in my throat. "It was a Friday night, stormy out, and we'd just finished supper. Mother was in the kitchen cleaning up; I was sitting in the den, and the phone rang. It was O'dell, one of my father's poker buddies, calling to say they were all coming over around nine. I knew Mother wasn't happy, but she didn't say anything. They always got really drunk and loud, you know, tore stuff up. I didn't like it because I could never get in my pallet when they played poker at our house because they dragged a card table out on the screen porch."

"That was hard, hm?" Tonilynn raised her eyebrows.

"Yeah. I wanted to run outside and hide in the woods, but like I said, it was storming, and plus, they usually stayed until the wee hours. That night my father got into the whiskey before the rest got there. Mother said to him to take it easy and he said for her to keep her trap shut.

"I went in the front room, out of sight, to read a book, well, not really reading but just looking at the words and trying to act casual even though I was shaking, and . . ." I felt tears, warm on my cheeks.

"And?" Tonilynn blotted my face tenderly with a McDonald's napkin.

"Later, after they'd been there awhile I was still curled up in the chair underneath an afghan, listening to them getting drunk, laughing, and playing cards. I guess I fell in and out of sleep, because I heard my name, and I was groggy, and then my father said, 'Jennifer can be our dancing girl.'"

I closed my eyes, felt Tonilynn's hands grasping mine.

"He walked into the front room, yanked the afghan away and said, 'Get your top off and come dance for us, girl.' My brain wouldn't work, my legs wouldn't go. I thought I must be dreaming. Then he said it again, and I guess it sunk in that this was real. I was so scared, so embarrassed. I was only fifteen, and I thought I better do what he said because he was so drunk and full of himself. He was a mean, violent drunk, and I didn't know all that much about men or sex or any of that stuff."

My neck felt hot, but I looked straight into Tonilynn's eyes. "Next thing I knew I was standing there on the screen porch, bare from the waist up. So I guess I did get up and undress even though I don't remember it. I moved, but it felt awkward, just kind of letting my hips swing. I figured out pretty quick I had to close my eyes and imagine I was alone, dancing for the trees. The men really liked it, they were all whooping and grunting and saying stuff like, 'Yeah baby, dance!' and 'Shake them thangs!'"

"You were just a child," Tonilynn whispered.

"I was fully developed."

"Did anybody *touch* you?" Tonilynn cupped my face in her warm palms, her question reverberating in my shocked brain. "Did any of them touch you? Tell me they didn't touch you."

She sounded angry, and I liked that. I shook my head. This was something I'd marveled at all these many years, that none of them had "taken advantage" of me that night. It was one of those things in life that makes a person incredulous—them grabbing their crotches, out of their minds and me in my vulnerability—that no sexual intercourse had happened.

Tonilynn stroked my cheek. "But your innocence was shattered. He robbed you of your dignity."

I nodded, feeling my face crumple.

"He made you feel dirty." Tonilynn squeezed my hand. "And you bottled it up all these years."

My finger was twirling my hair so fast and furious, I felt it ripping out strands, but I liked the pain. I needed the pain. After a bit, Tonilynn reached up and stilled my hand. She pulled the hairs from between my fingers and let them drift to the floorboard. "Where was your mother? She didn't stop them?"

"No." The word gagged me. After a spell, I was able to speak again. "She never would say one word to me about it. I remember she came out of her bedroom when the men started getting rowdy because they liked my dancing, and she looked out on the porch while I was dancing, but she just put her hand over her mouth and ran back into her room. But the next day, when I finally gathered up the nerve to confront her about it, she denied it had even happened." I slid off the seat, onto the floorboard, my hands over my face.

Tonilynn draped herself over me. "That's right," she murmured. "Cry it out. It's good for you. You've done a brave thing, Jennifer. That's been bottled up inside you all these years, and this is the first step on your way to healing."

Hours later, up on Cagle Mountain, I lay on the featherbed, my heart raw from the memory I'd dreaded with every cell in my body for the past thirteen years. That memory I'd spent my energy running from like a mouse aware of a hungry cat. Tonilynn had said to cry it all out and I did. I cried about how Tonilynn and I had been in one of those gilded moments of life, cruising along in perfect harmony, our spirits soaring, until a dark cloud from the past moved in and destroyed it. I cried about how she said my father had stolen my innocence. I cried about how my mother had sided with denial instead of her daughter. How she might never know the real me or celebrate my success, or hold me close and say "I'm sorry. I know that hurt, and I should've done a better job of protecting you. Please forgive me." I cried about Tonilynn's concern, how when she got me back up into my seat, she'd fastened the seatbelt and kept her right hand on my shoulder the whole time she sped home to Cagle Mountain, saying, "You don't need to be alone right now. You need to be with people who love you," continuing her sympathetic words as she half-carried me into the guestroom, removed my shoes and oh-so-gently helped me into bed.

I cried over the fact that it was Saturday, and I might miss my trip to the Cumberland, miss her calm waters, that dose of peace, and then I cried because longing for that made me feel selfish when I had people here who loved me. Speaking of feeling selfish, I also cried over the lifeblood that Mike Flint spent on me, the very fact that he'd believed in me from the start and had no idea what I was hiding. I cried for those young dancers behind the walls of Déjà Vu.

Finally and most of all, I cried about the years I'd spent running, so messed up and pathetic, and the fact that life had dealt me a pathetic hand, had cursed me with such a depraved and filthy-minded father who was the root cause of *all* my travail.

That was when the hatred rose up within me like a tidal wave. The fury dried my tears, and I rolled over, my swollen face cool in the dark room. What amazed me was that despite bawling for hours and no sleep (by the glowing digital clock on the bedside table, it was three a.m.) I felt like I could run a marathon. I wanted to go to Déjà Vu and hit somebody, fight for all those young girls with dreams of being a country music diva like me who were having to pay the bills by dancing at that so-called gentlemen's club. None of those places downtown or along the highway were for *real* gentlemen! Mr. Anglin was a true gentleman, and I had sent him to an early grave. Because of my father!

I sat up, swung my legs off the bed and marched to the kitchen where I found Tonilynn at the table, working a jigsaw puzzle and drinking a Diet Coke. I sat down opposite her. "Flowers?" I pointed at some pieces with red shapes like petals.

"Eiffel Tower in springtime." She fitted the piece in her hand along the bottom, leaned back in her chair and considered me. "Feeling better, hon?"

"Feeling mad."

"I hear the Hair Chair calling our names big time."

I shook my head, but smiled at Tonilynn, thankful for her attempt to lighten the mood. Behind her, out the window, I noticed it was raining hard.

"'Bout time to build an ark, hm?" Tonilynn pressed another piece into place. "Speaking of the ark, Old Noah was a man of great faith."

One thing I did not need was a conversation about faith. We sat quietly for a while, Tonilynn sorting puzzle pieces by color and me waiting for the right moment to ask her to drive me back to Harmony Hill. Riverfront Park opened daily at six, and I'd never been that early, but something in me thrilled to think about visiting the Cumberland in darkness. Surely the rain would let up shortly. Thinking about Riverfront Park led to thoughts about the upcoming CMA Festival. My chest tightened at the thought of singing, though I reminded myself that having the river beside me would help me get through it, and that I'd quit the music scene totally after my festival performances were done.

"People of faith can change this world." Tonilynn reached for her Diet Coke. "Jesus said faith is strong enough to move mountains." Her eyebrows were raised up high over eyes soft with concern. "Faith can change the way we see our world now, Jennifer. Also the way we look at things tomorrow, and also, maybe most important for *you*, the way the past has shaped us."

I frowned.

She paused to sneeze, and for a moment I relaxed, thinking she was going to hush about it. But in the next breath, she asked, "You hear what I'm saying? Praying, mixed with faith, is a mighty force."

Tonilynn was getting a little too close for comfort, and I stood up to go back to my room. She grabbed my hand. "Doesn't it feel good to have gotten that memory out, hon? That there's no more hiding from the past? No more running from the pain? Now it's time to go to the One who can totally set you free. Who'll help you forgive your father."

I wouldn't even try to play along. Nothing, no one was powerful enough to help me forgive that man! Like she could read my mind, Tonilynn said, "Jennifer, to forgive him doesn't mean you're excusing what he did, or saying it didn't matter. Because it did! He victimized you, and your anger is understandable! I promise you, God's mad about it too. Your forgiving your father won't exempt him from the just judgment of God, doesn't mean he won't be held accountable for what he did to you.

"But if you keep living with such bitterness, you're chaining yourself to your father *and* the hurt! I know some people who are so obsessed with revenge that their whole life revolves around it. They're captive!

"Forgiveness is so liberating. Remember when we were talking earlier and I said that when you fantasize evil toward your father, you're giving the enemy ground? Satan loves that! On the other hand, Satan trembles when we pray. So, please, hon, listen to Tonilynn—pray and ask God to help you get rid of the hate and the bitterness. If you don't, it'll destroy *you*!"

I focused on the rain pelting the window.

"Jennifer, look at me. If you really wanted to get even, you could do it easy enough. You could run his name through the mud. Everyone would hear what Jenny Cloud had to say! But would that erase what happened? What purpose would it serve? Knowing you, you'd probably feel even worse. You've got to think of forgiveness as *a powerful weapon*."

Tonilynn reached for my hands, held them in hers, running her thumbs over the calluses on my fingers from years of playing guitar. A little thought snuck in. What if my heart had become calloused too? But just as quick I cast it out. It wasn't that I didn't think what Tonilynn had, her faith, was real. I believed that, for her, it was a very powerful solution, a healing to her wounded past. But I knew for me, someone whose innocence had been stolen, my anger was my soul's way to reassert its worth. I had a lot invested in my bitterness. Without my fury, who would I be? a doormat like my mother? some weird, wacko religious nut? I didn't see the benefit of all this self-denial, this "letting God redeem your past and use it for the glory of his kingdom."

A wave of mental exhaustion hit me, and I almost said, "Okay, I forgive him, now will you drive me back to Harmony Hill?" But Tonilynn would know it was a lie. I picked up a corner piece of puzzle and turned it this way and that, pretending to consider where it fit. "Please drive me back to Harmony Hill?"

"Oh, Jennifer." Tonilynn took the piece from me and fit it in its place precisely. "It's not an experience that will bring us down or shatter us. It's our *response* to that experience. You know who Fanny Crosby is?"

Reluctantly, I nodded.

"When she was six weeks old, the doctor seeing to her didn't do right, he fouled up certain procedures, which caused her to be blind! Being blind was no picnic, but Fanny didn't get bitter and all eaten up with mad. She forgave that doctor, and she wrote more than eight thousand hymns! She *used* her adversity."

"What happened to her is totally different, Tonilynn."

"Not really. You and Fanny were both given a gift—the gift of music. Gifts are easy—they're given, after all. But forgiveness is a *choice*, a choice that can be very difficult. And she forgave, Jennifer.

"See? You can fill your heart with revenge or release, hate or hope, fear or faith. Bad stuff can have eternal value if you view it from God's perspective. The things that hurt you can have a purpose. He'll use them for your good, make you stronger, and you can use them to minister to others.

"Hey, I know!" Tonilynn slapped the table and the puzzle jumped. "Jennifer, you need to write a song about this topless dancing incident!"

"What?!" I felt like running outside in the pouring rain. "That'd be the *worst* thing to do! Believe me, I know!"

"Jennifer, Jennifer. First, forgive your father, and then you can use the energy of your anger in a positive way. I'm convinced your own healing is through your music. It'll be cathartic to write a song about it. You know how powerful music is. Think of the words on that poster at Flint Recording! 'Music can transport, transcend, and transform.'"

I didn't answer.

"Your song can be somebody's therapy." Tonilynn was standing now. "There's a lot of hurting, vulnerable people out there. What if you knew there was some young girl experiencing the same kind of thing you did, but she's afraid to speak up? You could speak up for girls who have no voice, or don't know how to use it. You could help some young girl find her own strength. Wouldn't that be reason enough to brave the heartbreak?"

Tonilynn hit a nerve. I recalled the heart-stopping terror of opening my mouth about what my father had done—to anybody except my mother that one time. I was scared people would be disgusted with *me,* or judge *me* if they knew what had happened. Afraid they'd think I'd somehow invited it. It really was some heavy baggage to lug around. Guilt and shame are powerful emotions, even if they're unwarranted. But did they excuse me from caring about all the young girls out there being abused, victimized by men in their families? Girls who were scared to speak up?

Wasn't that just like Tonilynn to pack my bags for a big guilt trip! Saying a star like me could speak out and do wonders! I turned away from her, mad. There was only so much one singer could do. In a way I was outraged that Tonilynn wanted me to throw myself on the altar! Into my mind's eye came Roy Durden, saying, *If you need that kind of stuff, a crutch to lean on.* Did I not realize on the day I first sat in the proverbial Hair Chair that Tonilynn was simple? That Tonilynn wasn't dealing with reality?

I was ready to lash out at her, though that very next instant I also felt an enormous compassion expanding inside me. I remembered how Tonilynn had drawn me under her wing from the start, showering me with her friendship, restoring my dignity when it came to Holt Cantrell. She'd made me laugh with her Aunt Gomer stories, accepted me into her family, held me in her arms, and cried right along with me, saying, "I know it hurts, hon." All this shot through me like a current, shorting out my superior airs. If I had anything good, any friend on this earth, it was Tonilynn. She knew the entire me, and she loved me. And here I was acting like an ungrateful snot! A snob.

The rain came down in sheets, and I swallowed my argumentative words. Later, there would be a time to tell her just the way it was going to be. First I needed to get myself to the Cumberland and organize my thoughts. I reached across the table, took Tonilynn's hand in mine, and said, "Let's get this puzzle finished."

⟨∞⟩

Tonilynn shook me. "Huh?" I said, in a fog of confusion.

"Wake up, hon. I need to tell you something."

The serious note in Tonilynn's voice made pin pricks on my skin. I opened my eyes. I was in the guest room at Cagle Mountain. The room was murky, and I heard the steady drum of rain on the tin roof. Tonilynn looked bad: deep circles of exhaustion beneath eyes wide with fear. I was scared to ask what, but I didn't have to.

"Aunt Gomer's had another stroke. She can't move a muscle, can't say a word. I called and an ambulance is coming to fetch her. Bobby Lee's going to ride with me to the hospital. Help yourself to anything in the kitchen. I'll call you."

I heard her talking to Bobby Lee in the hall, her voice panicky, a far cry from the sure and sassy Tonilynn I was used to. When they were gone, I lay still. The clock said it was a little past two p.m.

Perhaps it was from sleeping odd hours in an unfamiliar place, the shock of being wakened with bad news, or fear of what might happen to Aunt Gomer, but I was feeling unreal. It was all too much on this first day of May, after everything I'd been through. Plus, my feelings were hurt at the way Tonilynn had rushed around without even inviting me to go with them to the hospital. Did she truly think I was family?

I knew my imagination was going wild, and I got mad at myself because I also knew in my gut that this was not about me. It was only concern for Aunt Gomer that was in Tonilynn's mind now. And the idea of what Aunt Gomer was going through was horrific. What if she had to go in an old folks' home? What if she died? Feeling panicky, I wrapped myself up tight in the quilt and concentrated on the drumming rain. When I heard Erastus's muffled sigh as he poked his head into my room, I was overjoyed. "C'mere, sweetie!" I called, hugging his ribs when he sidled up next to the bed. When he decided to head out, I swung my bare feet to the pine floor and followed him to the kitchen.

The Eiffel Tower in springtime covered half the table. I got one of Bobby Lee's Pepsis out of the refrigerator and turned to Erastus. "You need some water?" I filled his bowl at the kitchen sink and slumped down in a chair at the table. After lots of lapping, Erastus plopped down at my feet. A quarter 'til four and the afternoon sky was so overcast it seemed like night.

"How about let's see what's on television," I said after a good quarter hour of watching my cell phone.

". . . record-breaking torrential downpours are causing flooding in parts of Nashville . . . thus far, the southeast side of town has been hit the worst . . . many streams and creeks, normally slow trickles are now raging torrents, and there are reports of trucks submerged on the highway, residents chased from their homes by rapidly rising waters . . ." The weatherman's face had a look of seriousness like it was carved from granite as flood advisory warnings scrolled across the bottom of the television screen in bold letters.

I stood stock-still, my head spinning and my heart pounding as the cameras panned the dark brown waters of many swollen creeks and tiny streams now turned to raging torrents. There was the Cumberland, big drops of rain hitting the surface hard enough to splash up and bounce before they melded in with the rest of their kind. Overhead the clouds gathered and roiled, like froth on cappuccino, so thick you couldn't even see the city skyline.

I couldn't watch anymore. I turned the television off and dialed Tonilynn's cell phone. No answer. I stepped over to the window at the kitchen sink and looked at my reflection in the window glass. Could things get any worse? It made me feel dizzy, like I needed something to grab hold of and hang onto for dear life. Erastus pressed his nose to my hand and I sat down on the floor and hugged him. For a while, we stayed like that, staring wide-eyed at nothing.

A half hour later, there was still no word from Tonilynn. I stepped outside and Erastus watched me from the porch. Rain hit my hair and trickled down to my scalp, ran down my forehead, my neck, and soaked my chest. Hard drops hit the dirt yard, making a giant puddle, flattening Aunt Gomer's irises. I kept seeing the Cumberland in my mind's eye, the television images of those people evacuating their homes.

It was around five o'clock when I went back in, dried myself on a kitchen towel, and hesitantly turned the television back on. It seemed the water had stopped rising. I wept in relief and released a breath I hadn't known I was holding. "Oh, thank

God! I cried out, and in the next instant wondered where in the world *that* had come from. I sure wasn't in the habit of communicating with *him*.

"Well, buddy," I said to Erastus, "looks like we can breathe easier now. About the flood anyway."

I dug around in the refrigerator and made a bologna and mustard sandwich on white bread, then poured some dog chow into Erastus's bowl, and we ate supper together. At last, a little after seven, my phone rang.

"Aunt Gomer's suffered a major stroke," Tonilynn said wearily. "She's in ICU."

I swallowed. "She's a tough old bird. I'm sure she'll be fine."

The line was quiet for a moment, then Tonilynn said, "Doctor says to prepare for the worst."

Seized by fear, I stammered, "She made it through the last one."

"She still can't move a muscle, can't utter a word. I can just tell she's not in there."

"What do you mean she's not in there?" I clutched my phone.

"She's gone on to wherever saints go when the spirit leaves the body."

I didn't know what to say. "Well . . . you never know. Miracles happen. Hey, did you hear about the flooding?"

"Some."

"Well, thank goodness that's over. Looks like dear Nashville's safe now."

It seemed Tonilynn was too distracted to pay attention to what I'd said. "We're staying here at the hospital tonight."

My heart sank.

"Would you mind staying there to keep an eye on the place? Look after Erastus?"

"Sure. You can count on me. Will you be home tomorrow?"

"Guess I better get back to Aunt Gomer. I don't want her to . . ." Tonilynn's voice faded and the line went dead.

I sat down at the table, resting my head in the crook of my arm for a long time, thinking about how disposable, perishable, temporary, the human body is. What struck me hard was how much I'd miss Aunt Gomer if she died. I had some things I really wanted to tell her, like how beautiful her flowers were and how seeing the sunrise with her had been priceless. Things on Cagle Mountain would sure be different without her around.

I didn't want to be alone, and I didn't know if Erastus was allowed in the featherbed, so close to nine, I made a pallet on the floor of the front room from an old army-green sleeping bag I found in the coat closet. I lay down and invited Erastus to join me. "Lie down, boy," I told him. "Let's go to sleep." But I stayed awake for a long time, waiting for what I did not know.

I awakened around six the next morning to a loud clap of thunder. Erastus buried his head underneath the sleeping bag and his hindquarters trembled. "It's okay, buddy," I crooned, and lay for a while on my pallet, wondering what was going on with Aunt Gomer and how early was too early to call Tonilynn. Then I started thinking about getting back to Nashville, to Riverfront Park for my missed time at the river. Whenever I missed a visit—and that was rare—it felt like an important piece of me was missing, and I was not myself. I was lost somehow.

Finally, I let Erastus outside, went to the bathroom to cup my hands and splash water on my face and made my way back to the kitchen. As I was scooping coffee into the percolator and pouring food into Erastus's bowl, he came barking at the back door. When I opened the door to let him in, his fur was slick from the drizzle, and the land beyond him stretched out dreary and wet.

I can't say I was surprised when I turned on the television to see more warnings about flooding in Nashville. The rains continued. Roads were submerged and houses were surrounded by water where people were climbing out of windows into boats. The sight of a house trailer tipped on its side as it floated by made me draw in a breath and hold my hand to my mouth. The deluge was incredible! It seemed almost like a movie: concerned officials warning, citizens stunned and stuttering, their hands slicing the air as they described what was happening. The camera panned to a woman sitting in a rescue boat. Her voice was shaky, her red hair falling crazily into her distraught face. "It's all I have," she said, nodding toward the floating mobile home. "We never dreamed . . ."

Moved to tears, I pulled my eyes away, and just as I did there came a long rumble of thunder laughing at me. "It'll be okay, boy," I sang to Erastus as he quivered beneath the kitchen table.

That entire May weekend record-breaking amounts of rain fell in Music City. If I turned on the television, there were muddy rescue people, reports of power outages, gloomy skies, and gloomy forecasts. Erastus and I paced the farmhouse, listening for word from Tonilynn. Through lunch it rained, and all that early afternoon, steady, soaking, and surreal.

At three my phone rang, and I hit the Talk button while looking out the window at trees slumped dark and dreary in the downpour.

"She's gone, Jennifer."

I held the phone, Tonilynn's words like a punch in my stomach.

"Jennifer?"

"*What?* What do you mean?"

"Aunt Gomer crossed the Jordan at 12:14 p.m. She's with Jesus now."

"No!" Tears bloomed in my eyes.

"Yes, and I'm glad," Tonilynn said in a faltering voice that belied her words. "Aunt Gomer didn't want to suffer the indignity of growing feeble and losing her faculties. Anyhow, I wanted to warn you that when the news hits the church's grapevine, there'll be ladies by the dozens bringing food to the house. If I'm not back yet, could you please let them in and keep up with who brought what?"

"Sure. When are you and Bobby Lee coming home?"

"There's a few things to handle here, so I'd say not until late. I talked to the preacher, and it'll be a few days until we can get things together for her funeral. I can carry you back to Brentwood tonight after you help me pick out something for Aunt Gomer to be buried in. Will you help me with that, hon?"

"Of course." I was pretty sure Tonilynn was unaware of the severity of the flooding, and I didn't want to tell her because a big part of me wanted to deny it was actually happening. Earlier I'd caught snippets of television footage of Brentwood. The Little Harpeth River was almost white water rapids at the Brentwood Country Club, and the golf course was a lake. Also, it looked like Manley Lane was flooded and the road surface of Holly Tree Gap Road was buckled from floodwaters. I heard a reporter say Granny White Pike was literally under water.

"Tonilynn? I'd like to stay up here on Cagle Mountain tonight."

"You sure? What about that cat of yours?"

I heard the teasing mixed with the gratitude in Tonilynn's voice. "I'm sure."

"Thanks, hon. You'll be a big comfort. I better go see about Bobby Lee. Now, watch out, I imagine they'll start showing up any minute with food. Help yourself to whatever your heart desires."

Erastus went berserk at the sound of Bobby Lee's wheelchair on the ramp. Zigzagging around the den, he went straight to Bobby Lee's knees to whimper with delight the instant the door opened. For a while I watched their reunion, then Tonilynn putting her handbag away in the pantry, peeking up underneath tinfoil and Tupperware lids, wedging some dishes into the already overflowing refrigerator. She looked decidedly unglamorous—flat lifeless hair, dark smudges of mascara underneath her eyes, clothes wrinkled and weary. I stood wordlessly in front of the pantry, feeling useless in the face of such grief. What could I do to make things better?

"Hey, Jennifer." Bobby Lee wheeled over to me in his wrinkled Allman Brothers T-shirt, his hair in a tangled ponytail, one of Aunt Gomer's pale blue bedroom slippers perched on his thighs. "How are you?"

"Okay," I said, feeling tears starting in my eyes. "I'm sorry about Aunt Gomer."

"Yeah. I still can't hardly believe it. I'm gonna put on one of her albums."

I understood. Without Aunt Gomer, the house seemed empty, too quiet.

I went into the guest room, lay down on the featherbed, and listened to the Louvin Brothers singing. I must've fallen asleep because the next time I was aware of anything, the quilt was spread over me and it was pitch dark. The luminous numerals on the digital clock read 4:22 a.m. A faint aroma of coffee drifted to my nostrils.

Tonilynn was in the kitchen hunched over a shoebox full of photographs. I saw she'd laid several out on the table: a feathery-edged sepia-toned portrait of a baby in an old-fashion buggy, one from a 1960s Christmas if you went by the clothes, what looked to be a young Tonilynn, ten or so, holding a basket full of kittens with Aunt Gomer standing behind her, four women with matching bee-hive hairdos posing behind a banner that read "Bake Sale," one of Aunt Gomer in 1980 with her brand-new Ford. Tonilynn looked up at me, her face haggard. "The funeral director asked me to gather up some pictures of Aunt Gomer. He wants to put them up on a screen at the front of her funeral, rolling like a movie! Ain't that crazy?"

"Well . . . maybe it's so people can remember when she was in a younger, happier time of her life."

Tonilynn shrugged. "He asked me to bring them with the clothes we want her buried in. I'm thinking she'll look best in her magenta pantsuit and that cream-colored polyester blouse with the bow at the neck."

I poured myself a cup of coffee and sat down across from Tonilynn. "I think she'd rather be in her gardening getup—the straw hat and that threadbare chambray shirt and those ancient men's khaki's she held up with a rope."

A laugh flew out of Tonilynn. "Let's do that! Oh, Jennifer, wouldn't she be proud of all this food in her honor?"

"She would."

Tonilynn looked thoughtfully at the counter. "Whenever Aunt Gomer heard somebody'd died, she was the first one there with a fresh-from-the-oven cake. I'm amazed when I think of all the cooking, serving, cleaning, gardening, and putting-by she used to do." She paused, and got a faraway look. "Aunt Gomer stayed right by Bobby Lee's side for months after his wreck. Fixed him breakfast, lunch, and a big supper every day. Refilled his tea, fetched the remote for him. She *lived* to serve folks!

"Remember after her first stroke, when I had to feed her? I thought she was just ornery and stubborn and didn't want to accept help? But now I think it was that she couldn't get up and do for folks! She wanted nothing more than to hop up out of that bed, get home, and take care of me and Bobby Lee!"

Tears ran down Tonilynn's cheeks. "She spent her lifeblood caring for others. For me! And I wasn't easy. I don't deserve all that woman's done for me. Know what, Jennifer?"

"What?"

"I had issues with certain stories in the Bible, some stuff that bothered me? Well, Aunt Gomer's stroke gave me a whole new perspective."

There were a lot of things I had issues with, but at last I asked, "What?"

"Remember that woman Jesus healed in the gospel? She had a fever, and Jesus touched her? Well, she hardly got herself a breath before jumping right up from her sickbed and serving. I always thought that was awful, sexist. I mean, here the poor woman's been at death's door, and then she hops right up and starts serving the menfolk! I thought she deserved a little R&R. Let the men serve themselves for a change!

"But I bet she was like Aunt Gomer. She was absolutely thrilled to death to serve, to be able to fix a nice plate of loaves and fishes." Tonilynn's jaw shook with her fervency. "See?"

"Um . . . sure."

Tonilynn smiled. "Oh, hon, I appreciate you saying that, but you don't really." I started to argue, but she held up her hand. "It's okay. We all have things that are difficult to wrap our minds around."

I was thinking, *Yeah, like letting Bobby Lee go to live his own life?*

Tonilynn looked at me hard. "Before she passed, I told Aunt Gomer who Bobby Lee's father is."

I knew what a huge thing that was for Tonilynn, but immediately I discounted it by telling myself that Aunt Gomer had been mentally out of it.

Leave it to Tonilynn. "It was before her first stroke, when she was still mostly in her right mind. It computed with her, Jennifer. It really did. I know because we had several conversations about it."

"Okay."

"I showed her the tattoo. For once, she didn't give me her sermon about desecrating the temple of the Holy Spirit. She just started bawling about a memorial garden her friend Viola got her to plant at the church in Robert's honor."

"What?"

"Might help if I told you Robert was the son of her best friend, Viola Gooch, the pastor's wife. Robert died in a motorcycle wreck when Bobby Lee was an infant. He never told nobody he was a father."

"Is that why you didn't tell her who Bobby Lee's father was?"

"Well, partly. A baby out of wedlock was a huge scandal, and I didn't want to crush Reverend and Mrs. Gooch any more on top of burying their son. Just didn't seem necessary. But there were other reasons. I realized I still loved Robert, and Bobby Lee was like my secret, a way to hold Robert to my heart."

I was quiet a while, pondering the odd thought that it had been a motorcycle wreck that claimed Robert's life and another that had disabled his son. I stood unsteadily, squinted at my watch, which said five a.m., glanced toward the window. No moon, no stars were visible. Only low, dark clouds. "Mind if I turn on the news?"

"Go ahead, hon."

It was like a slap in the face to hear the National Weather Service meteorologist saying, "Weekend storms dumped more than thirteen inches of rain in two days. Dark brown waters are pouring over the banks of Nashville's swollen Cumberland River, spilling into historic downtown where businesses are being shut down and authorities have closed off streets. In residential areas, the catastrophic flooding has ruined homes, and families are being evacuated. Four bodies have been discovered dead in their homes, two in cars on the standstill lane of the interstate and four outdoors. Stay tuned for—"

Tonilynn pressed her hand to her mouth. From behind it came a piercing wail like someone had stabbed her. I stopped breathing, felt like I was spinning away in weightless space. I ran out the back door and down the steps, not caring about the sloppy mud sucking at my feet or the bushes slapping my arms.

Sinking onto the floor inside the ancient barn, rainwater ran off my face, trickled down my body. I patted myself stem to stern. My heart was still going, air still moving in and out of my lungs, blood coursing through veins, flesh and bone connected.

But my soul was crushed. I could not stir a single hopeful thought. Everything I'd had, thought I'd had, was changed. I tried to picture my Cumberland, but all I could see were the muddy, raging torrents from the television screen. Massive, sweeping devastation.

It wasn't cold, but it was damp and I wrapped my arms around my knees and let the tears flow down my face and neck. I cried so hard and long it just sucked the starch right out of me. I fell over and lay like a dry husk, barely breathing.

After a spell, lying there in my weakened state, snippets of Tonilynn's sermons began. *Jennifer, where do you run in times of trouble? In your hour of need, who or what is your refuge? Jesus Christ is the fountain of living waters*, and *I'm telling you, for us believers, Jesus is the hope that anchors our souls. What's amazing is we can cling to him through whatever trials we're facing. As long as there's a God like him, no situation's hopeless. He understands our hurts, and he'll bring us through them, make us stronger. Before I was born again, I used to—*

I made a fist and beat the floor. Lifting my face to the rafters, I shouted "You think you're so great, and look, you can't even keep one measly river between its banks! Some Holy Force you are! And while we're at it, you let my father steal my innocence! He trampled my tender little heart, so shame on you! Now you've ruined my whole entire life, and I hope you're happy!"

I collapsed again and lay there in the damp—for hours it seemed, until I heard someone approaching. I opened my eyes to see Bobby Lee inside the barn. "You okay, Jennifer?" he asked, squinting. He was wearing Aunt Gomer's straw gardening hat. At first I thought he'd done it to make me laugh, but then I heard the grief in his voice, and I knew how hard all this was for him.

I sat up. "I'm okay."

"Do you need anything?"

"No. How'd you know where I was?"

"Mama said she thought you'd be out here. She said to ask you to come back inside to dry off and get some food."

I shook my head.

He peered into my swollen face with his beautiful eyes, and gently asked, "Want to talk?"

"No." Though I'd thought it impossible for my body to produce any more tears, I began to cry.

"Hey, hey. What's all this?" Bobby Lee reached for my hands.

"I . . . I never thought something like . . . like a flood could happen in Nashville! Feels like there are no safe places anymore." A tear fell off my chin onto his forearm. He kissed it away and tingles ran up and down my spine. It was odd to feel grief mixed with such tender longing.

"I know. They're calling it 'the single largest disaster to hit Tennessee since the Civil War.' This is one of those times I really miss my legs."

"Oh."

"Downtown's so bad President Obama declared it a disaster area. Aid organizations are rushing in, and all these different local groups are stepping up too. Nashvillians are joining work crews all over Davidson County, using boats and jet skis to pluck stranded residents from their flooded homes. There's still a bunch needs to be done—mucking out rooms, tearing down ruined drywall, cleaning up debris. What's worrying me is a lot of folks are ignorant about electrical lines. They'll go sloshing through murky water without a thought."

While I was nursing my own hurts, this man was thinking about how he could help other people! I promised myself that when I got home I'd do something big for flood relief. It had to be better than focusing on myself. I was growing so tired of myself. Tired of listening to my own thoughts, of eating and drinking and walking through this world with just myself. "You're an inspiration," I told Bobby Lee.

"Talk about an inspiration." He pulled my hands to his mouth, kissed each fingertip. "I've loved you from the first moment I saw you." I looked into Bobby Lee's soulful eyes, eyes he got from his mother, and I felt the strength of his love like a soft blanket draped over me. My heart started galloping a mile a minute and I so wanted to wrap my arms around him. But something inside me wouldn't let me. I was unable to find any words either.

Bobby Lee felt my fear because he pulled me up onto his lap, cradling me in those strong arms until the world faded away. It was the most natural thing in this world, and I had no reflex to pull away when he whispered, "It's okay. You don't have to answer. But it breaks my heart to see you crying like this, and I'm gonna hold you long as you need me to."

The minutes passed, and I had this thought about how I wouldn't mind staying right there forever. Then, just when I was realizing the strange sensation of aching lips, Bobby Lee bent forward and kissed me so hard on them that every single thing inside of me melted.

14

Two days later Tonilynn drove me home to Brentwood; we watched the sun shining down on the slick roadsides of Williamson County the way you watch a dog that's bitten you in the past. Luckily, Harmony Hill was untouched by the flood, but it felt emptier than ever, like there was something critical missing, the way it feels when you wake from a dream and only pieces of it are still floating in your mind.

A long day passed and at dusk I wandered outside like a stunned sleepwalker through the sticky heat. I thought about Bobby Lee as I strolled by the fountain, as I sat on the bench at the fishpond, and as I dragged myself back into the house close to midnight. In my mind's eye he was a firm island, safety in the midst of choppy seas. I liked how he was so calm, so sure of who he was.

His whispered words of love were my soundtrack, my background music of hope for a future filled with fishing trips, long talks in the moonlight, nights of peace and security strung together over the years like pearls on a necklace. I craved those tingles that the gentle-firm feel of Bobby Lee's lips on mine sent through me. I'd never felt anything like that before, had once thought it was just a figure-of-speech when people said kisses sent electrical currents through them.

Didn't Bobby Lee make me come alive? Yet I still hadn't uttered words of love to him in return. I still wasn't quite sure how to have the intimacy I was pining for—this thing that made my soul ache I wanted it so!

Sleep would not come, and I turned on the bedside lamp to play around with some song ideas, but nothing would flow the way it used to, needed to. No melodies, no lyrics begged for expression. It seemed my gift had totally dried up. But, I didn't feel unhappy. I kept telling myself it was better this way, and that I would pour my whole self into learning how to be a regular person.

Right in the midst of this realization, a beautiful, evil hope charged through me: perhaps the CMA Festival wouldn't happen! From news coverage I'd seen of Riverfront Park and LP Field, the two main venues for shows during the festival, there was no way in this world they would be operational in time for June tenth. The park was a wasteland and the stadium looked like a swimming pool.

If anything good could come out of this flood, would it not be the cancellation of the CMA Festival? If I could contemplate anything redeeming at all, it was to be released from my final commitment to perform! I could feel this vision of the new me burning its way into my soul, crowding out the wounded diva wearing her heart on her sleeve, and it seemed the flood was like this natural delineation, this liquid line cutting between what was and what would be.

The new Jennifer Clodfelter would not have to dredge up torment and sadness for songwriting. She would never bolt awake at night, alone and shaking at the arrival of a memory.

I'd missed a couple of Sundays at Panera, and two days later when Mike called to say, "How about Panera at ten?" I smiled and said that sounded downright heavenly because not only was I feeling withdrawal pangs from my cinnamon crunch bagels I was also ready to get out of that cavernous, too-quiet house.

The next thing I knew, we were in the Great Room, sunk down in chairs across from each other beneath the lofty ceiling, enshrouded with the familiar scent of coffee brewing and fresh bread baking. A little chitchat and half a cup of coffee later, Mike leaned back in his chair, laced his fingers across his belly, and said, "Guess what? The CMA is saying they're going to donate *all* the proceeds from this year's festival to charity. Half to music education in the Metro public schools, and the other half to help victims of the flood. I mean, we're talking 100 percent here! This is even *more* of a lure, can't fail in getting folks to come out to the festival and help our great city rebuild."

I didn't know what to say. One hand began twisting a strand of hair at the base of my neck around and around the index finger, and the other reached up to pull my faded ball cap down past my eyebrows.

"Something to celebrate, huh?" Mike raised his cup in a toast. "Kind of bittersweet, I got to admit, but hey, it's incredible to see the CMA's outpouring of love and generosity. I'm not surprised, though, because I believe country music stars, and country music fans, have got the biggest hearts in this world." He looked directly into my eyes for a long moment, and when I still didn't respond, he prompted, "Isn't that great, Jenny? The way we're leading the efforts to help rebuild our beautiful city? That we're helping hurting folks recover from this disaster?"

My thoughts were spinning so fast, all I could manage was to nod my head up and down.

"The Cumberland sure did a number on us, huh?" Mike said finally, his sandy Keith Urban hair moving as he shook his head.

Still I didn't utter a word. From a Brentwood homeowner's perspective, the flood had hardly affected me. There'd been some power outage, but no real water damage in my upscale suburb. I'd been lucky because the news for Nashville and Middle Tennessee was heartbreaking.

"Well?" he said.

"I . . . I don't know what to say."

"How about 'That's great, Mike. I sure want to do my part to help.'"

"I do! But to tell you the truth, I don't see how the festival's going to happen."

"Oh, it's going to happen. Believe me, because now it's even more vitally important to the Nashville business community." Mike put his mug on the table with a thud. "The festival's estimated to bring in almost thirty million dollars in revenue, money this city desperately needs. I know you know that the flood was a major hit to the economy of downtown, and officials are talking about 'budget shortfalls' with every breath. Say they're looking to the festival to help. So you better believe they're gonna make sure the cleanup is far enough along by June tenth."

I tried to keep breathing as Mike continued. "Know what's really hurting? The Opryland Hotel got hit so hard it's gonna be closed indefinitely, and it brings in a fifth of Nashville's hotel tax revenue. The other downtown hotels are already booked to near capacity for the festival, and they're gonna have to pick up as many of those tourists as possible. Could be some bad traffic jams downtown."

"Hm."

"Hurt the Grand Ole Opry too. They'd booked Charley Pride for two shows during the festival, and now they're going to have to move him. I'm thinking they'll move him to the Ryman since it wasn't affected by the floods, thank God."

"That's good," I mumbled.

"Yeah, s'pose that's something to be grateful for. Speaking of major hits, the Convention Center and Opry Mills Mall are hurt pretty bad. And our friends at Soundcheck are reeling like you wouldn't believe!"

"Really?" My heart went out to the good folks I knew at Soundcheck, those who helped with my tour preproduction on such a grand scale.

"Yep. Hey, speaking of money, heard from our friend Scott Borchetta that Taylor Swift has made a significant donation to relief efforts, and she's asking others to do the same. Now that's a smart career move."

I thought about Taylor Swift and her honest, uncynical face. Sure, it couldn't hurt her image. But she really was a caring soul. I looked directly into Mike's eyes for a long accusatory moment. "Smart career move?"

"Well, it's sweet, too. Really sweet."

I smiled a little. He was trying hard now.

"Hey, I've got the perfect idea for you, Jenny Cloud!" Mike's eyes got huge. "What we need to do is have you rip another page out of your life and put it to music. A brand-new song expressly for the festival, something that really tugs the heartstrings the way you're so good at. Dedicate it and *every cent* of the proceeds from it to flood relief! Isn't that brilliant?"

Given the choice, I'd rather be shot. I sat there and listened to my heartbeat booming in my ears like background music that accompanied the familiar, anxious-ridden twist in my gut. What I really wanted was to jump up from my seat, push through the doors of Panera, and run and run and run. Couldn't

Mike see how hard that would be? How much it would hurt? But I didn't want him thinking I was selfish. I tried to think of some explanation that might satisfy him.

"I hate to say it," I said finally, "but here lately it seems I've contracted a terrible case of songwriter's block. Nothing but a vast wasteland these days. I'll just do like Taylor and give a humongous donation."

"Aw, I bet you could do it, Jenny girl. Bet you'd be surprised if you just closed your eyes and drifted back to another one of those tough times in your childhood."

I hated Mike's offhanded tone, like what he suggested was not some dangerous trek through a place littered with emotional land mines. "No. It's like I'm totally barren. I've never, ever been like this."

Mike frowned. He had creases between his eyebrows from worrying over bottom lines and business strategies. Over my career. For a while the only sound was the muted conversation of several patrons a distance from us. I thought Mike was finally accepting my news, that he realized I was a big enough star that I could refuse things.

I stood up after another bit, smiled. "Thanks for the coffee, but my head hurts and I need to get home."

"Wait a second." Mike reached into his pocket and handed me two envelopes. "Your fan mail."

I glanced at a plain white business envelope, my name typed in black capital letters, and a fancy pink envelope, my name in blue cursive. "Thanks." I slipped them into my purse, breaking out in an instant sweat. Many fans wrote, most asking for an autographed picture, or to be included in my fan club, and some sent along song ideas. But occasionally there was that letter from a tortured soul who needed a friend and decided I should be the one she poured her feelings out to.

I'd stopped reading my fan mail not long after "Daddy, Don't Come Home" debuted.

—⁂—

On Thursday, the Cumberland River finally crested and started to recede. Parts of the city were still without power, others without water since one of the treatment plants was flooded. Every night, I watched the updates on recovery attempts, my heart still breaking from the way the Cumberland had mauled the city I loved.

One evening early that next week I sat very still on my leather couch at Harmony Hill, watching a special report. I gritted my teeth, clenched the remote, and cringed at the newscaster's forehead creased with concern. "Torrential downpours on Saturday, May 1st, and Sunday, May 2nd, flooded the Tennessee capital of Nashville," he began in a grave voice. "While the record rains in Nashville and Middle Tennessee have abated, life is far from back to normal for many, especially for those who've lost loved ones in the flooding. Or for those who've lost their businesses, their homes, and their possessions. It is especially hard for those without flood insurance, which accounts for the vast majority of homeowners whose homes were damaged."

I stared at the screen as the camera panned a water-filled area full of floating trees, some two feet in diameter, ripped up whole and bobbing around like giant broccoli stalks. I was trying to wrap my mind around this image when the camera zoomed in on a portable school building that had torn loose and was floating down I-24 in the floodwaters, breaking up as it hit cars, trucks, and bridges. Next the newscast showed stretches of buckled asphalt, road surfaces with huge cracks, and a subdivision where folks were fleeing their homes because of water overflowing the banks of one of Nashville's many creeks. Recycling bins, trash cans, and doghouses swirled in angry torrents.

There came a voiceover saying the southeast side of town had been hit the worst, and proof came as camera footage of water in all its raging power ripped pieces of buildings away like Lego blocks. Electrical lines were tossed into the water where they snapped and snarled like high-voltage whips. Fences, signs, and outbuildings floated by in the murky waters like it was the end of civilization.

For the longest time I sat there gape-mouthed because what I saw on that screen seemed merely two-dimensional, incomprehensible, until finally I absorbed the fact that these were *real* scenes, *real* lives, and not some horror movie of death and destruction. I never dreamed it could rain so much! The sad drama became even more painful as it showed rescuers guiding boats and Jet Skis over frothing waters to pluck stranded residents from homes and cars. My heart nearly stopped as the voiceover listed the names of the ten Nashvillians who'd lost their lives in the flood.

The grave report continued, "Floods caused by the record-breaking rain caught many more than the folks in Davidson County off-guard, claiming more than thirty lives in fifty counties, and shattering countless more. There is an estimated one billion dollars in damage. While waters subsided in many places after the rain relented on Sunday evening, still more flooding occurred the following Monday due to the Cumberland River rising thirteen feet above flood stage. Muddy waters poured over the Cumberland's banks, spilling into Music City's historic downtown streets. Let's go to the east bank of the Cumberland and take a look at our Tennessee Titans' stadium."

My eyes were riveted to a clip of LP Field on the television screen. It was full of dark brown river water, bits of debris floating around the mostly submerged goalposts. Was this really LP Field, that sacred venue for the CMA Festival that held almost seventy thousand country music fans? My earlier hopefulness for the cancellation of the festival seesawed with hot prickling shame.

The camera shifted to another area hit savagely by the waters. "On Sunday night, flooding forced an evacuation of the Gaylord Opryland Resort and Convention Center, an area about five miles east of downtown," said the voiceover. "One thousand five hundred guests were moved to a local high school." The picture switched to an interior shot of the hotel where restaurant chairs and crates of wine glasses floated by.

I was still staring incredulously at the television screen when the camera zoomed in on a final image: a life-sized statue of Elvis, missing his guitar, lying on its back in the parking lot of the Wax Museum of the Stars.

I turned off the television. Tears ran freely down my face for the way the deadly water had filled the lungs of its victims, for their bereaved families, for the way it had laid waste my beautiful city.

I had something I needed to do.

⸙

I marched across the Pedestrian Bridge, through the parking lots of LP Field, to reach the bank of the Cumberland in late afternoon light. There were none of the usual joggers with their determined faces, none of the loving couples sitting and staring moony-eyed at the water, no dog-walkers or bicyclists. The Cumberland was practically deserted in her disgraceful state. The receding water had left behind a wild stretch of mud and debris. Hands in my pockets, the folded letters clenched in my sweaty fist, I walked, listening to the mud sucking at my feet with each step. Thick coats of goo began to cling to my boots like pancake batter, growing heavier with each footfall as I picked my way downstream past trash and plant debris.

What had been a pleasant stretch was transformed into a dirty wasteland the grayish brown of a rat's hide. I stumbled on a smooth stone the size of a muffin, threw it back into the river where it hit with a small glugging sound. It was going to require a ton of money and a lot of work to be ready for a music festival by June tenth.

All of a sudden I felt compelled to touch the river. I went sideways like a crab down the slick slope of the bank, squatted and trilled my fingertips in the water. As I did, my mind went zipping backward to my pilgrimages, those days I'd come here looking for renewal. I tried with all my might to recapture just one moment, desperate to feel that sense of sanctuary.

But it was like looking for a toothpick in a haystack where everything comes up a limp piece of straw. What was the Cumberland that I'd looked up to her so? Worshiped her in a sense? I'd once thought there couldn't be any more serene, restorative place in the world.

Who was I kidding to think she could save me? She sure wasn't the mother she'd claimed to be. Water that looked relatively safe on the surface moved quickly and dangerously below. I thought about her deception. How she rose up, abandoning her banks, exchanging her broad slow curves for a raging brown torrent that gouged paths of destruction, drowning everything for miles.

"You ain't no saint!" I yelled, feeling like a protester for a worthy cause as I raised up tall, planted my boots firmly, stretched my neck, and aimed a mouthful of saliva into the Cumberland. I stood awhile, watching the foamy patch of spit on the surface of the water move slowly downstream, wondering, *Did that make me feel any better?*

Walking downstream again, I heard a bullfrog's bass notes of "jug-o-rum," which brought to mind fishing with Bobby Lee, and then I recalled how frustrated he'd been when he couldn't join the groups stepping in to help after the flood. *Not everyone is the center of her own universe, Jennifer.* With a pang of guilt I reached into my pocket and pulled the letters out.

Tucking a trembling finger into the edge of the pink envelope's flap, I unsealed it and pulled out a piece of stationery printed with a butterfly border, and jam-packed with the handwriting of someone who put little curls on their capital letters and dotted their i's with hearts.

Dear Jenny Cloud,

I want to thank you for your song "Daddy, Don't Come Home." I'm indebted to you, and I thank God for giving you the gift to sing. I'm going to try to put into words how much your song means to me, how God used it to help me feel like I could finally express myself. I, too, had, well, have actually, a father who is troubled and needs help. But I couldn't find the strength to tell anybody what he was doing to me. I think part of my problem was I didn't feel like I really mattered. One time I even tried to kill myself. Most of the time I was just scared to death. But I got strong through listening to your hit song! I looked at you, and I said, 'If Jenny Cloud can be bold, I can too!'

So, I told my counselor at school about my father, and she stepped in and got me professional help. My life is much better now! For the first time, I'm happy and sleep through the night. Thank you from the bottom of my heart!

Love, Victoria

This was a victory song if I'd ever heard one! Something in me toyed with writing her back so we could exult together. I searched the envelope—no return address. I slit open the other letter before I lost my nerve. It was formal black lines of type, several words smeared.

Dear Jenny,

I don't go around telling this because I'm afraid if people found out about it they'd think I caused it, asked for it, you know? But I didn't, and I know you'll understand and won't be disgusted because it sounds like your father wasn't the hottest on the planet either. I'm glad you had the guts to call him on his meanness and drunkenness!

My mother passed away when I was six, and my father is a perverted type of person who started messing around with me when I was eight. I'm fifteen now and it makes me absolutely sick that I endured it so long, but I was so scared and it wasn't until I heard you singing about being brave, and then your interview on the radio, which happened to be on this night last year when I was at the end of my rope, and it felt like this voice was saying to me, 'Haley, there's your answer.' I decided right then that it was time to do something about it. I went to my preacher.

Well, my father had to go get help somewhere far away, and I went to live with my aunt on my mother's side who's really sweet. She even looks like my mother! Well, it sure feels good to tell you how much you've helped me! Thank you for listening, and keep on singing your beautiful songs!

Your # 1 Fan, Haley

My hands were shaking as I stuffed both letters back into my pocket. Another flash of that night appeared on the screen of my mind. I heard my father's drunken laughter, the cat-calls of his friends, felt the hot flush on my chest as I gyrated topless, praying that any minute my mother would come out and save me from the shame. I saw myself later that night, the realization that my mother was incapable of standing up to my father, that we were utterly dependent on a man who was not only a drunk but also a depraved man in a multitude of ways.

It was not unlike turning on the television and finding that the place you ran to for security had no resistance beneath a couple days of hard rain.

A blanket of deep, black despair wrapped around me, growing heavier with each heartbeat as I trudged along toward the boat ramp, wondering, *Where would I go for my sanctuary now? My peace?*

I passed a huge tree branch, like driftwood on the banks, and I heard Tonilynn's words circling in my consciousness: "Speak up for those who're afraid to, or don't know how. Your autobiographical songs can be somebody else's therapy. Wouldn't helping some young girl be reason enough to keep braving the heartbreak?"

For an instant, I decided Tonilynn had written the letters, as some sneaky tactic, but just as quickly knew that was ridiculous. She wasn't that type. I was relieved when she picked up her phone after the second ring. "Tonilynn?"

"Hi, hon! How are you?"

"Fine."

"You don't *sound* fine."

"It's just the reception out here."

"Where are you?"

"At the river."

After a weighted pause, I heard Tonilynn say, "Seriously?" and the tone of her voice told me she was concerned. I felt bad for adding this on top of Aunt Gomer's passing, but I didn't need to be alone. I told Tonilynn about watching the flood report, how I'd spit in the Cumberland, and that I was standing on the LP Field side, on the boat ramp, feeling panicky. "Don't move a muscle," she said. "I'm on my way!"

I didn't say a word of protest about having to wait two hours, and it's odd, but it sure didn't seem like that long until here she came slipping and sliding in her pink boots. Out of breath, Tonilynn reached out and pulled me to my feet, wrapped her arms around me, and held me close, one hand patting my muddy backside in a little flurry. "How's my girl?"

"Um . . . hurting," I answered, because something in my chest region was pulsing so bad I thought I might be having a heart attack. But the pressure of Tonilynn's hug made it go away enough so I could get a good breath. "Better now," I added, and Tonilynn drew back, holding my shoulders. There were bags beneath her eyes, her lipstick was smudged in one corner, but her blonde hair was teased up tall and firm, perfect as ever, and her smile was glorious.

"Tell Tonilynn what you're thinking."

I shrugged.

"C'mon now, *try* to put it into words. What do you need?" she asked, her been-there-done-that-and-survived-it aura really strong.

I didn't know what I needed. I needed her to keep holding me, to worry about me, to promise me I wouldn't ever be alone again.

"You watched a show on the flood?" she encouraged.

"Mm-hm."

"Awful, isn't it? Pure heartbreaking." With a final squeeze, Tonilynn released me, and I stood there, feeling like a small child, inhaling her honeysuckle perfume. "Jennifer," she continued in a firmer voice, "you know it's best to talk about things. Can you tell Tonilynn what you're feeling right now?"

I looked across at downtown's skyline, scene of the crime. Well, part of the scene. I swallowed the lump in my throat as I thought about the unimaginable destruction. People who'd drowned, the devastated faces of their loved ones, folks fleeing their homes while their possessions were swept away. "Tonilynn?" My voice sounded shaky even to my own ears. "Some people are calling the flood an 'act of God,' and some are calling it a 'natural disaster.' What do you think?"

From the corner of my eye I saw Tonilynn flinch, then shut her eyes to murmur something. Finally she drew herself up tall and said, "I believe it was both."

I made a sound like 'Hmph!' in my throat. She'd never be able to vindicate God after the devastation I'd seen.

"Look, Jennifer, God *allowed* the flood, but he's sad about all the hurting folks and the homes that got ruined. He's sad about our broken-down city."

"Oh, really?"

"Really."

I must've been frowning because Tonilynn bent her head sideways to have a good look at me. "I know, I know." She laughed. "Sometimes I could literally wring Eve's neck for eating that apple. Ruined our perfect existence! Just think of our life on earth as this sort of in-between time, like when you put something on layaway, and you know it's gonna be yours eventually, and so you dream of it, and it makes your heart happy to do that, but you don't actually have it in your possession yet.

"We're in an in-between time down here, an imperfect time that isn't going to go on forever. Our perfect eternity is on layaway in Heaven."

I frowned.

"It's hard; you don't have to tell me!" Tonilynn shook her head. "First, the Fall, or whatever you want to call it when Lucifer decided he wouldn't serve, and now us having to *live* in the fallen world, the so-called Human Condition! I just take comfort in the fact that God's still sitting on his throne, and it ain't gonna be like this forever! I know there's a life for us yet unseen, which is gonna be so wonderful we can't even imagine it."

I felt a smirk come on my face, an expression of unbelief I didn't manage to cover quick enough.

"He hasn't abandoned us, hon! If you're his, you're on layaway, and eventually he's coming back for you, and everything's gonna be perfect."

"That's so comforting."

"I didn't mean to sound flippant, hon. I'm not downplaying the hard stuff in this world. Life's crazy sometimes! Even for believers. Especially for believers! But the thing is, we don't have to travel the path of life alone. I have good days and bad ones, but none of my days are ever *alone*. Jennifer, I want you to learn to let the Lord be your strength too! I promise he'll help when you take refuge in him. When the devil lets loose his evilness and the going gets rough, God Almighty will hold your hand! Sometimes he'll even carry you over the rough, scary places! It's not easy. I'm not saying that. But it helps if you keep the perspective that even in the dark times, he's there, and nothing can separate you from his love."

"Not even a flood that sweeps a bunch of folks into an early grave?" This burst out of me like a sneeze.

"It's hard for me to wrap my mind around some stuff too." Tonilynn lowered her voice. "Satan wanted the flood because he loves showing off 'the hand of death.' He loves to see people weeping, loves chaos and distress. And God, in his sovereignty, *allowed* it. We just have to remember God came down here once already, when he sent Jesus, and he's coming back to claim his own. Meantime, we're caught in that in-between *layaway* time of what is and what's gonna be. In this life there's gonna be pain and suffering, but we're not abandoned! God permits those things, Jennifer. Some he even *uses* to draw us to him, or to mold us into his image better. But I can guarantee you, he's got his eye on his own, and he's coming back for us. In the end, for all time, everything's gonna be all right."

Tonilynn touched my arm gently. "Let me baptize you, Jennifer. You need the Holy Ghost inside. Then you'll be able to look forward to the time when all our tears'll be wiped away forever!"

I shook my head.

"Oh, hon, can't you feel it?" she pled, holding her hands upward and pulling them apart in an expansive gesture. "Can't you feel God Almighty calling you to be his?"

I wasn't sure if I could. I wasn't sure I could buy all that about us living in this layaway time, about God permitting the evil, knowing our hurts, and still caring. But, that said, part of me couldn't help loving Tonilynn's explanation of the eventual happily ever after. Plus, I often felt alone, and I liked thinking that might become a thing of the past. She touched my cheek when I didn't answer, and I squinched my eyes shut tight and tried to feel it the way she did, and somewhere inside me, I thought she might be right.

Maybe.

Not so long ago I'd taken a lot of dark things personally—the evil seemed directed straight at poor Jennifer Anne Clodfelter. But it came to me now that I no longer thought that way with the intensity I once had. Now I toyed with an idea I thought of as the "Big Picture." We humans weren't necessarily the stars of our own biographical movies but bit players in the larger story.

I wondered when it was I'd changed. Was it just getting older? The other morning I'd looked at my face in the mirror and it definitely had more lines and wrinkles. What shocked me, though, was that my eyes were carbon copies of my mother's, and instead of contempt, I'd felt compassion. Part of me realized all too well why my mother stuck her head in the sand about things she felt she had no control over. Hadn't I done that exact thing?

After all, we were both poor, pitiful, limited humans. We couldn't make sense of everything. We could hardly keep up with our own life, much less other people's. This life could get crazy sometimes, like water running through our fingers, everything dripping and splashing and moving away so fast. And that was only here on Earth! I gazed upward. There were whole other galaxies beyond our puny planet, places we might never know, and certainly over which a human had no control. I was a drop of water in a vast ocean.

Just contemplating all this made me feel very small and tired and scared. I decided it might be a relief to just place it all in some huge sovereign hands. It wasn't hard to imagine that the Cumberland was a created thing, sprung from the mind of a mighty being. Someone who, in my finite state and limited understanding, I couldn't fathom, who had us all—

rivers and people and land and sky—in his great big hand. Ready to yield, I plunged my own hands into my pockets and turned to Tonilynn.

Then my fingers felt those letters and a searing pain ripped through my heart, fresh blood spurted from where the scab had been recently ripped away. "I can't forgive my father for . . ." I don't know why I thought I could *say* the words when I couldn't even get a breath.

Tonilynn tilted her head, narrowed her eyes. "Hold on. I've got something, well, some*body* I need to tend to." I knew what was going to happen before she turned her back to me, put her hands on her hips and lifted her chin. Her blonde confection of hair caught the last rays of dying sun, looking for all the world like the tip of a giant lit match. "Get behind us, Satan! I command you, in Jesus' name to pack up your bag of lies and go! You want to keep Jennifer down, you snake. You just want her ineffective for the kingdom of God." Her fiery head bobbed with every syllable. "Well, I'm telling your sorry self right now that she's gonna use it for good. Anyway, you know you've already been defeated when the Lord kicked you out of heaven. So, go back to hell!"

Tonilynn stamped one pink boot and turned back to me, her face with this well-that's-all-taken-care-of expression. She fanned away a bug that was exploring her hair. "Okay, hon, just close your eyes and mentally lay that anger toward your father at the feet of Jesus, and tell him you need some supernatural help to forgive the man, and then be ready to receive an incredible sense of release and peace."

I could hardly look Tonilynn in the eye as I said what came into my heart then. "If I forgive my father, then God'll forgive me for killing Mr. Anglin. Right?"

"You really need some peace about that, don't you?" Tonilynn asked softly.

"Yeah."

"Well, Jesus paid it All with a capital A. He crossed out the debt for every single sin. If you think you killed Mr. Anglin, then confess it to the Lord, and he'll forgive you, and set you free."

My hands were trembling as I placed the palms together beneath my chin and murmured, "Forgive me Lord, for ending Mr. Anglin's life too early." Then I stood, picturing Jesus dying as he gazed out upon humanity, his heart literally breaking as he bore all the ugliness, the agony of every person's sin on his tender flesh. It was beautiful to think that maybe all the dark things in my life weren't a waste, weren't just meaningless suffering. That they could be recycled into good for helping other souls.

"As far as fathers go, hon," Tonilynn said, putting her arm around my shoulder after I opened my eyes, "the Lord's the best. He won't ever let you down."

Was there anything I craved more than a father with great big, strong arms? I ike those pictures of Atlas holding the ball of earth on his shoulders. Something in me knew trust was the key, the key that would open the iron doors that had held me captive in a cell of fear and anger and bitterness, that would open the doors to peace and freedom. I just had to trust there was a sovereign God, that all that came to creation, from man or nature, was permitted by him, and that if I looked beyond my circumstances, beyond my pain, I'd see there was a purpose to it all.

Was I ready to take that step, to trust and let it all go? I stared at my mud-caked boots sunk in the riverbank.

Tonilynn called my name, and I looked up. She was inching toward the river, beckoning dramatically for me to follow, like John the Baptist. I reached for her hand, and we eased down the boat ramp into the Cumberland. The water was cold, and we stopped when it was to our hipbones. My feet felt the fierce current at the bottom. Tonilynn stood to my side. She put one hand on my shoulder and one across my lower back. "Jennifer Anne Clodfelter," she said, "I baptize you in the name of the Father, the Son, and the Holy Ghost," and dipped me backward and under so quick I barely had time to close my mouth.

I emerged from the water to a cheer from Tonilynn. "You're a whole new creature now! The old things have been washed away!"

I stood blinking fat drops of water from my lashes, my past floating away downstream behind me and leaving a girl who'd never despised her spineless mother or wished death on her depraved father or thoughtlessly caused the death of someone she loved, who'd never shut her ears to souls crying out for help. I felt a shift inside, something like an earthquake of my body's cells, this tremendous sense of release, and I knew, without question, a dark veil had lifted.

I was free, my life stretching out indescribably sweet and hopeful before me.

***

By force of habit, I searched the front desk for Roy. How many times we'd sat back there, the two of us holding each other up in a world where we were both running from our past. We'd been like wounded orphans, scrabbling to make sense of our losses, to numb them; him with food and me with dreams of fame.

"Can I help you, ma'am?" An Alan Jackson look-alike glanced up from the computer.

"Is room 316 available for the night?"

"Hmmm . . . room 316," he said, running his finger down the screen. "Looks like . . . you're in luck! How'd you like to pay for this?"

I swallowed. It was hard to believe that, looking the way I did, I could convince the man I had any money at all, much less enough to buy and sell the hotel ten times over. But I could not for the life of me remember where I'd put my purse. It wasn't in the Lexus. I raked my wet hair off my face and said, "Listen, I'm Jenny Cloud, and if you'll let me take the room on my word, I promise I'll come back with cash tomorrow."

He looked at me wide-eyed and slack-jawed, then nodded. "Well I'll be! You *are* her! We need to put you in a luxury suite, get you a private hot tub! Some flowers and chocolate! You deserve—"

"No, no. Please. Thank you, though. Really, all I want is room 316. It's got special meaning."

"Well, okay. Wow, man. I cannot believe this, but yeah, you go right ahead, Miss Cloud. It's on the house. But first, can I please get an autograph? My girlfriend's a huge fan of yours. You can't possibly know what your music means to her. Her name's Polly Finley."

"Of course," I said, ripping a sheet of Best Western paper from a pad, grabbing a ballpoint pen, and scribbling, 'For Polly, God Bless, Jenny Cloud.' I gave it to him and held out my hand for the key card, turning quickly to the elevator.

When I got the door to my room open, I literally fell inside and flung myself face-down across the bed. "Oh, God," I breathed, half-prayer, half-astonishment. When my heart slowed, I raised my head and looked around. Nothing had changed. The two queen beds, the long chest of drawers, the television set like a big charcoal eye, and through the door, my own private bathroom. I knew if I went inside, I'd find tiny bottles of shampoo and lotion smelling of flowers and stacks of plush towels. I saw myself, frenziedly inhaling all the luxury, dreaming of making it in Music City. A few years ago. A lifetime ago. I remembered how naive that girl was, thinking she could dance across the ground where those things that had formed her were buried like land mines.

I lay for a while on my bed, imagining all the bones I'd buried resurrected and doing a line dance, exulting in their new life. There would be an even greater depth to my music now.

My heart was knocking around like tennis shoes in a dryer as I sat up, leaned against the headboard and reached my hand into the drawer of the nightstand. Just where I knew it would be, I found a pen and paper to let the music call me home. "You've really gotta help me write this one, Father," I prayed, feeling those words shoot like an arrow up to God's sanctuary.

I never heard the Creator of the Universe talking directly to me, but I felt the skin on the back of my neck rising and unexplained chill bumps on my arms in affirmation that this was a supernatural conversation as I heard not an audible voice, but words in my spirit saying, *Okay, daughter. I know it was hard, because even though you couldn't see me, I was right there, permitting that even as it broke my heart. Now I want you to open your heart, and let it all out into a song. Remember, you've made it through the storm, you're safely on the shore, where you can help those souls still struggling in the eye of their own storm. Help them find strength and hope and peace.*

I finished at four a.m., the verses of "When the Music Calls Me Home" spread across the bed. It was one of those songs that sprang to life pretty much from the time I got the title. The chorus especially just sort of wrote itself. I did work a bit on the verses, moving them around to get them in the right order. Though I didn't have my Washburn, the melody for the chorus was like taking dictation from a master composer, and once

I'd written that down, I began humming a couple of different rhythms for the verses. I decided on the key of D major, the vocals spanning one octave, with a sort of twangful sound. I thought it might be nice to have a violin solo at the completion of the break.

When at last I turned out the lamp, I held the song to my heart, almost weeping from relief. At the start of my intensive night of songwriting, my heart ached for that young girl I was, writing about the shame she'd endured. But, as I continued, all the hurt and rage and bitterness dissolved into the lyrics, and I was flooded with a sweet and comforting sense of peace.

Tonilynn was right. Freud was right. Webster was right. God was right.

It was cathartic.

Chorus

That morning of Thursday, June 10, 2010, the first day of the festival, was hot and humid. The Judds were giving the kick-off performance at Riverfront Park and I didn't have to be up on the stage until two p.m., so I decided to walk around downtown awhile, trying to look like a regular person until my noon appointment with Tonilynn in the Hair Chair at Flint Recording. I figured I was pretty safe from getting mobbed since I had on my ball cap pulled low and my bag-lady clothes. I felt sweat beads trickling down my spine as I walked along Commerce Street past the Chamber of Commerce then the huge exhibit hall of the Nashville Convention Center.

I turned and walked down Fifth Avenue South toward the Country Music Hall of Fame, thinking of greats like Reba McEntire, Dolly Parton, Tammy Wynette, Loretta Lynn, and Patsy Cline, how much I used to dream of my portrait hanging with theirs. I recalled how desperate I was for that particular stamp of approval as I stopped and stood in that sweltering sun, looking at the quote from Conway Twitty etched into a foundation stone: "A good country song takes a page out of somebody's life and puts it to music." I thought of all the pages of my past that had sculpted me, and I knew those were gifts bestowed on me right along with my voice and my songwriting ability.

I walked on in the gathering heat of that June day, marveling at the resilient spirit of club owners, shopkeepers, and restaurateurs, businesspeople who despite the losses and the traumas from the recent devastation—though there was still a great amount of work to be done, some recovery yet to happen—were filled with graciousness and expectation. The great American city of Nashville was indeed rising again, and no matter how much she'd been damaged, she would unquestioningly offer her song of survival.

I felt a little nervous about singing my new song in public for the first time, so I whispered a prayer of thanks that I'd survived, too, that I didn't have to live like I was just plopped down onto some crummy path I had to walk the rest of my life. Maybe I couldn't predict what life would hand me, but now I knew how to respond, and I was free to dance!

That's what was circling in my brain as I climbed up on the Riverfront Park stage after Neal McCoy's show. I began my performance with a calm and happy spirit, strumming my Washburn, singing and occasionally strutting across the stage. Tonilynn had made me beautiful and put-together on the outside, and I was feeling beautiful inside, tossing my hair, enjoying the applause of my fans. The spirit of survival and freedom hit me even stronger as I began my encore song. From the minute I strummed the first chord, belted out the first verse of "When the Music Calls Me Home," I could see the crowd connecting.

> I went down to the waterside,
> climbed into my little boat of memories.
> The music called me home,
> And I was rowing happily.

But then the storms began,
the water surged up high,
The skies above turned gray,
and I lay down to cry.

That's when I faced the music,
of my innocence torn away.
Fifteen, not yet a woman,
Bad memories made big waves.

Dirty words that tore my heart.
Teardrops fell like rain,
All alone in the eye of the storm,
Bad memories made big waves.

I rowed my little boat through the dark,
Saying, "I want some sunny days."
Nobody seemed to hear me,
Bad memories made big waves.

Then I saw Jesus, walking on the water.
I saw Jesus and I rowed harder.
"Don't be afraid," he said, stepping into my
boat.
"There's a rainbow up ahead, and you're not
alone.
You got the three men you will need the most."

CHORUS

There may be thunderclouds above me,
I may be drifting in the pouring rain,
But there's a rainbow up ahead,
And my Father holds my hand.

My guitar pick was firm in my fingers as I twanged away, pouring my heart right up and out of my open throat, watching people's eyes well with tears, many in the audience pulling tissues from pockets and purses, me so gripped by the intensity of my own story that as I finished I flung the microphone stand down to the stage and yelled, "Yeah! My Father holds my hand!" Whistles and whoops erupted, and I stood there bathed in a long, loud ovation.

Beyond the crowd I could see the sun streaming down through clouds like cotton stretched thin, and below those, I knew sunlight shimmered on the surface of the Cumberland as it wound serenely alongside downtown. Picking up the microphone, waiting until the applause at last died, I said, "Thank you very much. I've been blessed with a career I adore, and over my years in Nashville, I've found country music fans to be some of the most generous and caring folks on this planet. That said, I'm not surprised to see the CMA joining the efforts to help Music City rebuild after the flood.

"I was walking around our city this morning, and I saw proof that Nashville is rising again, and I believe we'll fully recover from this disaster. In fact, I believe we'll emerge even stronger! Tennessee is the Volunteer state, and if there's ever a time you could see people actually living out that name, it's now, in the aftermath of the flood! I've heard tons of stories of people caring for each other during the flood, about the compassion of our great city and how we came together as a community.

"This afternoon, my dream is to spread the word about ongoing relief efforts. There are still people who need our support, and we can all help by making a donation to flood relief. Personally, I've decided that every single cent of profit from 'When the Music Calls Me Home' will go to flood relief efforts."

⊸∞⊷

A few days later, Mike told me someone in the audience caught "When the Music Calls Me Home" on video, and it did one of those Internet phenomenons they call "going viral." Mike said it had spread worldwide to more than a hundred million people. "It'll go platinum," he said, "believe you me."

He was right, and I'm proud of the proceeds that have gone to flood relief. It's two years later and my career keeps me so busy I hardly have time to think about the fact that induction into the Hall of Fame hasn't happened yet. I'm in no rush, because I know being invited into the Hall of Fame is usually what you call 'a lifetime achievement acknowledgment,' and most inductees are past their performing years, or the main part of them anyway. They didn't even induct Elvis until 1998!

However, I was added to the Walk of Fame. When I think back to that day I walked along Music Row, knocking on doors with my demos, I never could've imagined standing on the sidewalk in front of the Country Music Hall of Fame while Mayor Karl Dean kicked off a ceremony where I got my name in a big red star on the concrete.

This year I've got forty shows on my touring calendar, traveling with an entourage that includes my beautician and mother-in-law, Tonilynn Pardue, and a really sexy driver for the Eagle who goes by B. L., which is short for Bobby Lee. B. L. also runs my merchandising operation, and we're the proud parents of Erastus, a dog who travels with us and has his very own Murphy bed on the bus, but prefers to crawl into bed with his people.

In the linen closet on board the Eagle is a stack of patchwork quilts from the hand of Aunt Gomer, a woman who seemed to have saved every scrap of clothing she ever owned, and who cut them up over the years to sew together into wacky patterns, revealing this sort of practical and organic beauty in each interlocking piece of fabric, leaving in them a part of herself for us.

The night Bobby Lee worked up the nerve to ask me to marry him, he said, "More than anything, I want to spend my life with you, Jennifer. But sometimes I feel like I ought not ask you, because what if you say yes but later wish you'd married an able-bodied man? What if you get sad, thinking you've gone and squandered all your youth on somebody like me?"

I didn't have to think a second. I said, "Bobby Lee, in my opinion, no other man on this earth is half the man you are! And anyway, it's too late now to think about all that because I already love you." I honestly didn't see his disability and hoped he would not see my disabilities and love me less for them.

Neither one of us saw the point in a long engagement and we decided to get married that very next day. Bobby Lee thought we ought to aim for something a little more special than going to the courthouse. I told him, "Hey, I know just the place! It's on Music Row, near Bobby's Idle Hour Tavern." And so we went to the Vegas-style Rhinestone Wedding Chapel on Sixteenth Avenue. Tonilynn did my hair and makeup and dressed me in a pretty white tea-length gown. Bobby Lee looked gorgeous in a gray tux. You could choose to have your ceremony done by the house wedding official or, for no extra charge, an Elvis impersonator. "Elvis," Bobby Lee insisted with one of his smiles I simply cannot resist, and I figured we'd be just as married, so I said okay.

After we said our vows, we toasted with the sparkling nonalcoholic bubbly that the Rhinestone Wedding Chapel provided. There was also a four-layer wedding cake, and a marriage certificate created by the famous Hatch Show Prints.

The staff rang bells and tossed birdseed as Bobby Lee and I left hand-in-hand, and I heard Tonilynn's voice crack as she hollered, "Congratulations!" and "I sure wish Aunt Gomer was here to see y'all."

Although you choose the person you marry, you don't choose your parents, and I remain cautious when it comes to interacting with mine. My mother is still with my father. We talk occasionally on the telephone, and it sounds as if she still carries the torch for him, hanging on to the faith that he'll change. And though I have forgiven my father, I don't seek a close relationship with him nor visit the old homestead.

It's said that music is the only true barometer of a person's soul, and I know my decision to forgive my father has changed me to my very core. Being in a happier place has certainly changed my artistic direction. The heart I bared in those earliest songs bears little resemblance to the one that has been pouring stuff out of my throat lately. There's one place I can witness that clearly. My most recent album, *Beautiful Journey,* is proof of a significant turning point for this woman who built her career on the fallout from childhood ghosts.

I used my pain over Mr. Anglin's passing to write a song called "Watching Me Down Here," and whenever I sing it, I feel him smiling on me. I know faith's the substance of things hoped for, the evidence of things not seen, but I have to say there are these little random moments—holding Bobby Lee's hand as we stroll around the grounds of Harmony Hill, driving up to Cagle Mountain and seeing Erastus dart off through the kudzu after something, composing a new melody in my head while sitting in the Brentwood Panera, hearing Tonilynn yelling at the devil—when I feel a distinct presence, a crescendo of almost painful happiness, this glimpse into the eternal.

Think of the way a song sometimes lifts you up to a better place mentally, or illuminates your heart and mind about a certain person or emotion. It's like that, the movie soundtrack for my life, playing along beneath the ordinary and extraordinary moments, sometimes apparent, sometimes not, but always what holds everything together in perfect harmony.

Dear Reader:

I love country music, and I read a comment from Merle Haggard about his music that struck me as exactly how I feel about my writing. Merle said, "Music is a positive vibration that we all need. It comes through me, and I believe it comes from God. The Lord is just using me as an instrument, and I'm just doing the best I can to respond to what He wants."

I know certain songs have pulled me up out of many a dark hole, and I believe people's stories are positive vibrations we need as well, for escape, entertainment, and enlightenment. Sometimes when I'm in the midst of my own story, however, I don't see a speck of redeeming beauty in it. It's not until later that I can look back and see how an experience, an event, or an encounter with a certain person affected me. Sometimes I realize it gave me deeper insight, polished my rough edge, or birthed a certain compassion. As the Apostle Paul said, "Now we see a reflection in a mirror; then we will see face-to-face. Now I know partially, but then I will know completely in the same way that I have been completely known" (1 Corinthians 13:12 CEB).

Every single one of us has something we struggle with, hard moments, dark valleys, or challenging relationships. We may think, *How could that possibily be good?* Like Paul said, our vision here on earth is dim. The stories of our lives are like songs. When we turn them over to the great Composer, He can make something beautiful and good from our hurts and mistakes. They can become beautiful melodies that lift others up.

It's my heartfelt hope and prayer that *Twang* will be a source of entertainment, illumination, and encouragement for folks on this terrestrial ball.

Truly,
Julie

Discussion Questions

1. Jennifer believes it's her destiny to be a country music diva. How much of a person's life is determined either by their individual talents/gifts or by their belief about what they're "meant to do"?

2. Though Jennifer gets that thing she wants so badly—fame as a country music superstar—the consequences of this create yet another problem. Has there ever been anything you wanted very much but that turned out to have a hard side?

3. Jennifer believes she can repress her troubled past and it won't affect her. Do you think people can bury their pasts with no repercussions? Why or why not?

4. Tonilynn assures Jennifer that instead of emotionally crippling her, she can pour her painful memories into art. Do you believe that expressing feelings through art can promote healing? How?

5. Tonilynn has strong spiritual beliefs and is very vocal about them. Do you believe people have supernatural "gifts of the spirit" such as the word of knowledge Tonilynn claims to have? What do you think about how Tonilynn talks back to the devil?

6. Roy Durden says some people use religion as a crutch. Do you think people use religion in harmful ways?

7. Do you think people have to come to their own decision, in their own time, when it comes to faith in God? Can faith in God be forced? Explain.

8. Does having an earthly father like Jennifer's make it harder to relate to a loving heavenly Father? How?

9. When does Jennifer's faith in the Cumberland River evaporate? Do you believe that natural disasters/acts of God force people to realize that they don't control life?

10. Aunt Gomer's two biggest fears are Satan and going into a nursing home. What are your greatest fears?

11. Jennifer feels the young girls inside Déjà Vu are victims as she was. She believes men are using them and that real gentlemen don't visit these "gentlemen's clubs." How do you feel about the so-called gentlemen's clubs and the girls who work there?

12. Jennifer blames her father for her screwed-up life. She doesn't want to offer him forgiveness because she feels that would be like saying what he did to her didn't matter. Do you agree or disagree? Why?

13. If a person doesn't get rid of hate and bitterness, can it destroy them? Do you agree with the statement: "Forgiveness is such a powerful weapon for any survivor or victim of crime?" Why?

14. Forgiveness is a choice that can be very difficult. When you forgive people, you don't get an instant case of amnesia. Jennifer says she has decided to forgive her father, but then states in the epilogue that she does not have a close relationship with him. Do you think she'll ever be able to have a good relationship with her earthly father? Why or why not?

15. For lots of girls/women, even if their relationship with their father was a flawed one, they're drawn to men who remind them of him. Do you think this might be why Jennifer fell for Holt Cantrell? Why did it take her so long to lose her feelings for him?

16. Jennifer despises her mother's weakness in denying her father's drinking problem and for turning a blind eye to the way he treats women. How does Jennifer display this contempt toward her mother?

17. Were you surprised toward the end of the book when Jennifer feels some empathy for her mother? Why do you think Jennifer changed?

18. Do you think God cares about every detail of your life? Why?

19. Can God redeem a person's past and use the bad stuff for the glory of His kingdom? How?

20. We're told that in Heaven we'll understand everything clearly, that God will take his children by the hand and show them how all their heartaches and losses down here on earth were of value, that beautiful and good things came of the most difficult circumstances. Do you think this hope is enough to help you make it through the dark valleys? Why?

Want to learn more about author
Julie L. Cannon and check out other great
fiction from Abingdon Press?

Sign up for our fiction newsletter at
www.AbingdonPress.com
to read interviews with your favorite authors, find tips
for starting a reading group, and stay posted on what
new titles are on the horizon. It's a place to connect
with other fiction readers or post a
comment about this book.

Be sure to visit Julie online!

www.juliecannon.info

Abingdon Press fiction
a novel approach to faith

Plan your escape.

For more information and for more
fiction titles, please visit
AbingdonPress.com/fiction.

BKM122220002 PACP01110786-01

A good book means a great adventure.
history • intrigue • romance • mystery
love • laughter • faith • truth

BKM112220004 PACP01034644-01

a novel approach to faith

Learn more at AbingdonFiction.com

What They're Saying About...

The Glory of Green, by Judy Christie
"Once again, Christie draws her readers into the town, the life, the humor, and the drama in Green. *The Glory of Green* is a wonderful narrative of small-town America, pulling together in tragedy. A great read!"
—Ane Mulligan, editor of *Novel Journey*

Always the Baker, Never the Bride, by Sandra Bricker
"[It] had just the right touch of humor, and I loved the characters. Emma Rae is a character who will stay with me. Highly recommended!"
—Colleen Coble, author of *The Lightkeeper's Daughter* and the *Rock Harbor* series

Diagnosis Death, by Richard Mabry
"Realistic medical flavor graces a story rich with characters I loved and with enough twists and turns to keep the sleuth in me off-center. Keep 'em coming!"—Dr. Harry Krauss, author of *Salty Like Blood* and *The Six-Liter Club*

Sweet Baklava, by Debby Mayne
"A sweet romance, a feel-good ending, and a surprise cache of yummy Greek recipes at the book's end? I'm sold!"—Trish Perry, author of *Unforgettable* and *Tea for Two*

The Dead Saint, by Marilyn Brown Oden
"An intriguing story of international espionage with just the right amount of inspirational seasoning."—*Fresh Fiction*

Shrouded in Silence, by Robert L. Wise
"It's a story fraught with death, danger, and deception—of never knowing whom to trust, and with a twist of an ending I didn't see coming. Great read!"—Sharon Sala, author of *The Searcher's Trilogy: Blood Stains, Blood Ties,* and *Blood Trails.*

Delivered with Love, by Sherry Kyle
"Sherry Kyle has created an engaging story of forgiveness, sweet romance, and faith reawakened—and I looked forward to every page. A fun and charming debut!"—Julie Carobini, author of *A Shore Thing* and *Fade to Blue.*

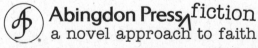

Abingdon Press fiction
a novel approach to faith

AbingdonPress.com | 800.251.3320

BKM112220003 PACP010344642-01

Discover Fiction from Abingdon Press

BOOKLIST 2010

Top 10 Inspirational Fiction award

ROMANTIC TIMES 2010

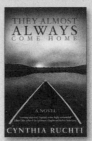

Reviewers Choice Awards
Book of the Year nominee

BLACK CHRISTIAN BOOK LIST

#1 for two consecutive months,
2010 Black Christian Book
national bestseller list;
ACFW Book of the Month, Nov/Dec 2010

CAROL AWARDS 2010

(ACFW) Contemporary
Fiction nominee

INSPY AWARD NOMINEES

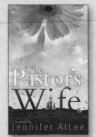

Suspense   General Fiction   Contemporary Fiction

Abingdon Press fiction
a novel approach to faith
AbingdonPress.com | 800.251.3320

FBM11222220001 PACP01002597-01

2 1982 02729 5686